Yesterday's Soldiers

HANNAH HARLESS

Copyright © 2024 by Hannah Harless

All rights reserved.

No part of this publication may be reproduced, distributed, or transmitted in any form or by any means, including photocopying, recording, or other electronic or mechanical methods, without the prior written permission of the publisher, except as permitted by U.S. copyright law. For permission requests, contact contact@hannahharless.com.

The story, all names, characters, and incidents portrayed in this production are fictitious. No identification with actual persons (living or deceased), places, buildings, and products is intended or should be inferred.

Book Cover by George Miroshnichenko

1st edition 2024

To my mother, who has always been my best editor.

Chapter One

"There are only two ways to live in this city. You can take the smart road, stay a civilian, follow all the rules, do what you're told. Every day will be the same, from the day you're born until the day you die. By the time Death comes for you, you'll greet him with a heartier handshake than you accord your neighbors. Or you can join us. You'll still follow all the rules and do what you're told. You will die young, make no mistake about it. But you will truly live before you die."

The military bark filled the yard and lit up the faces of the kids standing at attention. That monologue never changed; only the audience differed. The sergeant delivered his speech with practiced ease, and the prospective recruits eagerly observed the bustling veterans beyond him, little imagining that each hardened face had belonged to another hopeful youngster only a couple years past.

Most veterans ignored the new recruits, but Kit paused to look them over. She smirked as some of them turned red and looked away, then she went about her business. She had somewhere to be, and it wasn't here watching the new kids stumble over their own feet. It was unprofessional to be late for a briefing.

She left the mugginess of the yard for the coolness of a metal-paneled hallway, so long and straight and smooth that it felt like walking down the barrel of a gun. On either side, polished, unmarked doors—all tightly closed—led off into the sprawling grid of the complex. You could get lost here if you didn't follow directions exactly. It discouraged wandering—and dawdling. She picked up her pace, turning right, then left, then right again, passing nearly a dozen doors in starkly identical corridors before coming to the correct entryway. Her distorted, pale reflection reached toward her as she leaned forward to punch her code into the keypad.

When the door slid open, making only the slightest hiss, she saw that the rest of the team was already inside, sitting around a semicircular table on hard plastic stools. No one acknowledged her arrival, but as soon as she took her seat, a low hum signaled that the briefing was in session. A thin panel rose from the flat edge of the semicircle, and the flashing red light at its base turned green.

Their unit lead stood up and puffed out his chest. Stev rattled off their unit codes from memory, giving a brief status report on each member: STV1622, fit; AVN1424, wrist healed, fit; MRC1827, new member acclimating well, fit. She sat up a little straighter as she heard her name. KIT1642, fit. It figured. Stev was good to have at your back in a fight, but he wasn't heavy on praise for his subordinates. Then again, they were all still breathing after their last mission, even short-handed as they'd been, so that was reward enough for her. Kit was glad a fourth member had been assigned and she could stop worrying about pulling double duty. The new girl fidgeted nervously on her stool. Hopefully the kid was tougher than she looked, because Kit really didn't want to lose another teammate so soon. A wave of melancholy threatened, and she firmly turned her attention to the proceedings. Stev had finished his recitation and resumed his seat, folding his large, muscular frame onto the small stool with the ease of long practice.

As soon as he'd seated himself, the console light turned red again, and the panel retracted. Another door slid open to admit the Monitor. This one was tall and thin with a pinched, unpleasant look around his mouth. She grimaced slightly; you could often judge how bad a run was going to be by the Monitor they sent. One time after getting a gangly insect of a fellow with terrifyingly long legs and a hooked nose, they had been stuck chasing Swamprunner rebels on the city outskirts for three weeks. She'd had so many mosquito bites that they'd nearly fused into one giant, red welt by the time she'd returned to civilization. Luckily, they never had to deal with a particular Monitor more than once—or if they did, she never recognized them. As this Monitor sniffled and rubbed at his red, upturned nose, she caught a slight frown lurking on Stev's face.

"I hereby present you with your duty, by the will of the Congress." His voice was a nasal whine. He paused, and they all murmured, "By the will of the Congress."

"Block 8342, level 16, stack 9-3—arrest anyone on the premises. Neutralize resistance. Charges are classified." The Monitor turned around and left. Kit was glad. As unpleasant as he'd looked, she appreciated the terse ones. Of course, with the classified cases, there really wasn't much more to say.

Stev stood up and turned to the rest of the group. "Since it's all classified, assume armed, assume trained. Gear up and head out." As one, the unit stood and filed from the room.

Fifteen minutes later, they were double checking their gear in the yard. Stev and Avin performed the chore with the disinterest of those who'd done it a hundred times, but poor Mercy worked with feverish intensity. Stev looked up from his own preparations and grinned. Walking over to Mercy, he put a large, calloused hand on her shoulder and leaned over to whisper something in her ear. Mercy's face flushed bright red. Kit's eyes narrowed. Whatever he had said, it certainly didn't seem to be calming down the new recruit. With a last twitch of her shoulders to settle her pack, she went over to join Avin at the weapons charging station. Her pistol was at eighty-six percent and she wanted to top it off before the mission.

"What do you figure this time? Wish they'd give us more to go on with the classified ones," Kit commented as she plugged in her gun. Avin shrugged.

"It'll probably be the usual," she mused. "The same old idiots stockpiling guns that were obsolete fifteen years ago, just a bunch of big men who think waving old pistols in the air makes them worthy of testosterone."

"Probably," Avin replied, eyes fixed on his gun, the charge indicator slowly climbing its way toward full. Kit sighed and retrieved her weapon as Stev signaled it was time to move out.

The target address was in the Stacks, mid- to low-income housing for the frugal, struggling, desperate, and downright criminal. Each utilitarian building filled an entire block of the city, creating a grid of square towers that soared into the sky but still managed to give off the impression of being squat and brooding. At one point, they had been the pinnacle of modern efficiency, each living space logically identified within the massive building by its X and Y coordinates on each level. They were marketed as the middle class solution to urban living—don't get a house in the suburbs, move into a city apartment for less! Help solve the traffic crisis, be close to work, and keep the world green! Only once the Stacks in the city filled up, the suburbs started building them too, and eventually it all merged into one bigger city. The original Stacks became slums, and with so many people in such a small area, they became nearly impossible to police.

In a way, Kit was grateful to the Stacks. As hellish as they were, if they hadn't engendered an unprecedented wave of crime and corruption in the city, the ORG would never have been created, and she wouldn't have this job. The original incarnation of the Official Residential Guard had been much more in line with an expanded police force for the newly increased urban population, but now it had become another beast entirely. In some ways, Kit could say she owed her life as she knew it to the Stacks. In other ways, however, she could really do without them—especially when sitting in the back of a dimly lit transport scuttling along the city streets towards who knew what. One of the hydraulic legs stumbled into a pothole, and the whole vehicle tipped and bounced. She gritted her teeth. Weren't they supposed to have hovercraft by now? To pass the time, she started a system check on her MDU. Numbers and symbols flickered in front of her left eye as it tested its visual output and her ear filled with a series of dings and alarms.

The Military Diagnostic Unit was a sleek little piece of equipment. With both an external and an internal component, each one was custom fitted to its wearer. The external component was all matte black plastic, reaching from the bridge of the nose to the ear, covering the non-dominant eye. It clipped to the top of the ear firmly but comfortably, and then plugged into tiny flesh-colored ports in the side of the nose and ear. The ports interfaced with the internal component, surgically installed directly into the brain of the user. Thus, things could be seen without actually seeing, heard without actually hearing. The series of appallingly loud beeps now echoing in Kit's head were entirely inaudible to anyone around her, and though she could see the scene around her quite clearly with both eyes, her left was actually covered with a thin sheet of metal and cushioning synthetic. The MDU could do all sorts of great things—prevent friendly fire mishaps, warn of approaching hostiles, provide silent communication between teammates, and predict enemy maneuvers—though Kit rarely used that capability. It felt like cheating. She was grateful, though, for the aural filters and implants that kept her from being deafened by gunfire and protected her ears from damage without the need for cumbersome or unreliable external ear protection.

The pre-fight diagnostic wound down and finished with a subdued ping, transmitted to all her team members to let them know she was online and ready. Stev nodded his approval, and Mercy and Avin began running their own diagnostics.

When they reached Block 8342, the transport inserted itself into the elevator dock, and its long metal legs telescoped jerkily upward until the door was even with level 16. With a whir, a short walkway extended to the level 16 portal. If they had been there on a more routine matter, they could have boarded a motorized platform, punched in the 9-3 coordinates, and been ferried right to the door, but the ferries were useless for ORG purposes. When this structure had been built, the neighborhood had been a nice, middle class sort of place, so these ferries politely buzzed each unit to announce that someone was coming to visit—the perfect early warning system for those who were up to no good. Instead, the unit carefully stepped onto the narrow suspended walkway which hugged the side of the platform tracks. Once intended only for maintenance workers and emergencies, these open-air pathways were now the primary means of travel within the Stacks.

Their rusted, grime-laden surfaces buckled where the occasional support had given out under the stress of too many tramping feet.

This was one of the reasons that conventional law enforcement had been useless in patrolling the Stacks. The ferries themselves were more than wide enough for regulation law enforcement exo-armor, but they were thoroughly impractical for sneaking up on anyone—and there was no way that police exo-armor was ever going to fit onto these walkways. And frankly, if you took a police officer out of his exo-armor, he became pretty useless. Thus she and her teammates, more operatives than officers, were outfitted in much sleeker and more maneuverable armor, with smaller but deadlier weaponry. The entire ORG had been designed for close-quarters urban warfare.

They reached the housing unit in good time and formed up, Mercy in front with a riot shield, Avin and Stev backing her up. Mercy's nerves had her tied in knots, but Kit hoped she'd be solid when it came down to it. Despite her fragile good looks and slender build, there was enough muscle on her to show she'd taken her training very seriously.

Kit moved to take her own position. Hers was a more solitary task—and she preferred it that way. Treading softly, she turned onto the bridge that connected this walkway to the next column of ferry tracks. These bridges turned the Stacks into a giant grid, each square containing four units. A tight smile sprang onto Kit's lips when she realized that they had been assigned to the northwest unit on this square. It was by far the easiest to infiltrate due to an annoying but otherwise harmless structural defect—one of the digital architects had gotten lazy, and these units developed whistling drafts in one of the would-be bedrooms. That room was generally shut up tight to stop the noise and the rancid city air from penetrating into the rest of the apartment.

A ping from her MDU told her that the others were prepared. She sent her own ping in return, and with the flick of a mental switch, her MDU activated the specialized equipment in her gloves and boots. It came online with only the faintest crackle and hum, triggering the extra power source she carried in a pocket just over her breastbone, sending an intense electrical current flowing down her arms and legs through specially designed conduits in her uniform. Kit wasn't quite sure how it worked, but she knew that if it shorted out just once, the massive backlash would fry her before she even knew something had gone wrong. When everything was going right, though, it let her clamber over the vertical brick facade of the Stacks with the ease of a fly scuttling up a wall. She didn't see the point in worrying; nothing had gone wrong yet.

Kit gripped the cracked and crusty railing with her gloves and swung herself up. The soft, flexible soles of her boots let her cling to its uneven surface with her toes. Carefully, she stood upright upon the railing; then, with the confidence of long practice, she let herself fall forward, palms outstretched. Hands and forearms both locked onto the facade as her gloves took over. She released her tenuous hold on the railing, swung to grab the wall with her toes, then anchored herself with her knees. She had heard that the first designs for climbing gear had only allowed traction on the palms and soles of the feet; thankfully, it had come a long way since then. The entire surface of the gloves and boots, which covered past her elbows and knees, could sprout tiny electrical tendrils that held fast to even the smallest of faults in any surface, responsive to her slightest thought.

Kit flowed up the wall, as comfortable here with sixteen floors of open air beneath her as she was on the ground. She reached the window and tried to peer inside, but was unsurprised when she found the opacity setting of the window pane had been turned to frosted—just transparent enough to let in a little light, but still blocking all view of the interior. The infiltration abilities of the ORG were no secret, even though the technology itself was highly classified. Very few people left their windows clear, even when they had nothing to hide. A quick shove showed the window to be tightly secured with an electrolock—the most basic of security systems. With her thumb, she pushed a flat button on the second pad of her middle finger, and an electronic lock pick sprang from the glove like a retractable claw. Clinging to the building with her feet and one hand, she deftly manipulated the electrolock until the circuit was broken. The window pane retracted behind the facade, and she slipped inside.

Piles of boxes and stacks of plastic data sheets loomed, covering the floor. She edged around, clinging to the walls rather than chance climbing atop the boxes, and finally touched down in a narrow alley between the teetering heaps. She quickly scanned the room with her MDU for any evidence of weaponry or contraband and found—nothing. Rescanned. Nothing.

The smart ones would post guards on the other side of the defective room's door. A heat scan showed an empty hallway. No weapons, no guard. She walked soundlessly to the interior door and tested the handle—unlocked. A nagging unease crept over her, but there was little she could do about it. She had her orders.

Kit moved through the unit in ghostly silence, disturbing nothing, until a low hum of voices led her to the kitchen at the rear. A shrill shrieking momentarily overshadowed the chatter. Her disquiet increased; was someone being tortured? The last time she had heard a human make a sound like that was when they had raided a re-facer's den. The "patient" on the table had been the stuff of nightmares, and she considered it a kindness that he had died during the scuffle. If that was the cost of a fresh face and a new identity—well, she would prefer to just stay out of trouble.

With swift steps, she made her way to the front of the unit, quickly disabling the electrolock. It was a much more sophisticated model, but that made no difference when it was being unlocked from the inside. The rest of the team quietly moved in, Mercy taking point, as Kit indicated the location of the targets with a gesture. Kit moved to the tail of the formation, hanging back to warn the others of any reinforcements or ambush. She switched off her auxiliary power and drew her pistol.

The shrieking from beyond the door continued as they positioned themselves for the strike. Almost before the signal ping had reverberated through her MDU, Stev and Avin had breached the door. Nearly flung off its rickety hinges, the door swung back only to bounce off of Mercy's riot shield as she bounded forward to cover the men. While Kit applauded Mercy's reflexes, the action proved unnecessary. Two women and a man were sitting at an old table, one corner propped up with a haphazard stack of concrete blocks, and the top spread with coffee cups and data chips. The tabletop collapsed off to one side, the cups skidding down to shatter on the floor as the man leaped to his feet, looking desperately for something to defend himself with. The shrieks were cut off in the throats of six or seven children, now huddled together at the back of the room.

Oh—they were laughing—I didn't recognize the sound...

Without missing a beat, Stev moved a half step forward, gun still trained on the adults, as if they might suddenly pull weapons out of thin air. Avin was pointing his gun towards the children, his expression implacable. Kit froze, her arms leaden, the pistol—so light and sleek just moments before—now a dead weight in her hand.

"By the will of the Congress, everyone on the premises is to be arrested and held, awaiting their justice." Stev's voice was expressionless, practically careless, as he spoke the oft-repeated phrase.

One of the women, a mere stick of a thing, clearly starving and sick, made a sound of such anguish that it barely sounded human, a twisted mewling in the back of her throat. That was all the warning they had before she threw herself towards them, screaming, her fingers crooked into claws as if she could take them out barehanded. Kit's weapon swung up out of pure reflex, but she never got a chance to pull the trigger. Both Avin and Stev reacted more quickly; one blast caught the woman in the head and one in the neck, spraying her blood across the room. The children began to shriek again, a terrified, high-pitched sound that cut at the ears, as the man instinctively reached to catch the crumpling body. Stev stepped forward, ramming him with the butt of his weapon and knocking the breath out of him. As the man folded to his knees, Stev smoothly tagged him with a tranquilizer stamp, and he collapsed the rest of the way to the ground. The other woman, still in shock and wavering on her feet, let Avin tag her with a tranq without a fight. Stev slung his weapon out of the way, and heaved the unconscious man over his shoulder. Kit quickly followed suit and grabbed the live woman. When they returned to the transport, Stev would call for a corpse cleanup for the other. The place would be all neat and scrubbed within hours, waiting for its next occupant.

Avin and Mercy got the children quieted and lined them up one behind the other. There were seven in total, three girls and four boys, all appearing between the ages of seven and twelve. Street children, most likely—their clothes were ragged and worn, but looked freshly laundered despite old stains, and the children's faces had the half-sunken look of starvation scarcely beginning to abate. Old but well-loved toys were scattered across the floor, many of them now damp with blood. On their way out, Stev made a cursory check for "backup," but it wasn't likely that an illegal orphanage would have many street thugs on call. As Stev signaled the all clear, Kit stepped out onto the ferry, making room for Avin and Mercy to load the children. She hefted the woman to settle the weight more securely on her shoulder. Her burden was older, careworn but sturdy—not unlike the caretakers Kit remembered from her own childhood. Kit tried to shift so that the bone of her shoulder didn't dig into the woman's side quite so much.

Mercy came out of the building, leading a wavering line of children. She knelt outside the unit's door, counting them as they passed and murmuring comfortingly to them. Mercy had a surprisingly gentle manner for someone who had chosen the life of an operative, but it came in handy now. The sobs quieted into sniffles and hiccups, and the ride back to the transport was, for the most part, spent in silence. Kit gazed off toward the end of the tracks and tried to ignore the crowded state of the ferry.

When the ferry stuttered to a halt at the end of its track, they squeezed all seven of the children into the holding cell in the rear of the military transport along with their two unconscious caretakers. Whatever comfort Mercy had given those kids was only temporary. The low-pitched hum of the vehicle and the occasional clunk of machinery weren't loud enough to drown out the renewed sobs and whimpers of the frightened children on the way back to the compound.

A bubble of light and conversation surrounded her, but Kit felt apart from it all. She usually enjoyed their trips to this hole-in-the-wall booze joint after a successful job. Sure, it was illegal, but it was a nice, familiar little place, and most of the people in here were part of the ORG anyway. There was an unspoken agreement with the owners—they wouldn't report the behavior of the teams and the teams wouldn't report the establishment. It worked well most of the time.

Kit sipped her beer and tried to relax in the casual atmosphere; it was an escape from the sterility and starkness of the ORG headquarters, even if it was a bit dirty. She'd been going on missions in the city for two years now, so she'd seen worse. Tonight though, the dingy lighting and raucous patrons seemed to create long, grotesque shadows between the battered old plastic tables. Every so often, a thrown bottle or piece of food would jostle the lanterns hanging from the low ceiling, causing the lighting to flicker wildly. Each lantern hung on a rusty chain that creaked ominously as it swayed, like the pendulum of a great clock slowly winding to a halt. Everything familiar seemed like it had been replaced by a more sinister version of itself. Kit twitched irritably, trying to shake off the mood.

Avin was sitting with several other operatives at the far end of her table, drinking and lounging, silent but seeming no more perturbed than usual. One of his companions was cracking jokes about the other patrons, who jeered back and tossed bits of food at him. They all seemed to be having a good time. She even saw Avin flash a derisive smile at one point. It was odd, though, that Stev wasn't at the center of such a group.

In a dark corner, her sharp eyes found Mercy, her back to a wall. Stev was standing in front of her, leaning down, looming over her. His face was close to hers—very close. From here, she couldn't see Mercy's face, couldn't see if she welcomed the attention or not. Kit didn't really care. Mercy was only a kid, fresh from her first mission with the team, flushed with success and drink. Kit stood, slamming her mug down on the table, and strode across the room, her stomach tight with anger, fists clenched.

"Mind if I join the party, Boss?" Her voice was quiet, but close enough to startle Stev into retreating a step or two away from Mercy. At this range, Kit could see that Mercy was blushing and befuddled, not sure whether to be upset or relieved by Kit's arrival.

"I was just getting to know our newest member...a little more personally." He turned a carefully charming smile on Mercy, who smiled tremulously in return, and began to turn his back on Kit. Rage boiled up into her throat. Before she'd realized what she was about to do, she'd grabbed his shoulder, spun him around, and slammed him against the wall next to Mercy. The younger girl let out a startled yip and jumped away. Stev's face was slack-jawed with shock, quickly converting to fury.

"Have you already forgotten why we *needed* a new member?" Kit growled. "You keep your hands the hell off her." She shoved him away and wiped her hand on her jacket as if she'd touched something foul. With one last disgusted look, she turned and slipped away into the crowd, all of whom pretended they hadn't seen anything. She left her drink unfinished on the table and ducked out into the twilight alone.

Chapter Two

The city became eerily silent during the night hours. After the curfew, not a creature stirred in the streets except the little robotic monitors, whirring and clicking around their designated areas. Despite their small size, they were remarkably effective at keeping all but the most desperate in their beds, boasting an array of tranq and poison darts that varied in lethality depending upon the offense. Wandering around outside the ORG wasn't the worst crime, but it would still get you a low-grade hallucinogenic dart that made it impossible to walk straight, let alone infiltrate a closely guarded military complex. It left barely enough coherence to allow the sufferer to wander home. On the other side of the complex near the detention center, a trespasser wouldn't be so lucky. A heavy-duty tranq would leave its victim slumped in the street until one of the prison guards noticed and arrested the unconscious offender. That usually didn't happen until morning, though the guards did have passes which allowed them to walk among the bots with impunity at night. They just didn't care to stir themselves.

Kit lay in her bunk and listened to the mechanical whispers outside. Sleep eluded her. Heavy breathing emanated from the other three corners of the room. She had feigned sleep when each of her teammates had stumbled in, wafting beer fumes about the room, but they had all found their way to unconsciousness before her. She was both embarrassed by her outburst and satisfied by it. She shouldn't have—but it had been deserved. Now she would have to ride out the unpleasantness and keep reminding herself that it had been worthwhile. Her teammates would forgive—or at least forget—soon. Still, her mind wandered here and there, like a monitor on patrol, refusing to settle.

The mission had been a full success, so there was no reason to be concerned about that. It had been strange to see children though. It had been years since she'd seen kids. The occasional group of teenagers would tour the complex, like the one this morning, or she'd come across a class of new recruits or trainees, but they were always fifteen or older.

She had been raised with other children, of course. All offspring of law-abiding citizens were removed immediately after birth and placed in a communal nursery. Kit's earliest memory was a dormitory in that nursery with rows and rows of little white beds in neat ranks. During the day, she had gone to school to learn her duty to city and Congress, and at night, she had made it her mission to sneak out of that dormitory—not because there was anything she wanted outside of it, but to prove that she could.

Now that she considered it, she had never seen any adults but her teachers and caretakers before she graduated to the ORG. She had always been with others her own age, isolated from the adult world. Perhaps it was because of precisely what she had seen today—adults getting too attached. Kit couldn't imagine anyone wanting the bother of raising a child alone, though historically that had once been normal. The modern way was much more efficient. Children got the care and education they needed to be contributing members of society, and their parents got to continue contributing to society without losing their minds.

Like the woman who had died today. Definitely kid-crazy, charging them with empty hands. One of those children must have been hers. Something happened to adults who weren't separated from their children soon enough, especially women. They got irrationally attached, sometimes to the point where they would sacrifice health, money, well-being—everything, just to stay with their child. That wasn't good for the child either; it was much healthier to be raised in a stable environment like the nurseries. If these people really cared about their kids so much, they would give them up and let them live good, normal lives in the nurseries. Instead, they ended up in places like that orphanage—cramped and run down, where they were deprived of a good education and often hungry to boot.

Some of those kids were merely unlucky. Conceived through illegal intercourse, unregistered kids were seen as commodities in certain parts of the criminal community. They were abandoned by terrified parents who didn't want to face the consequences or sold for money or drugs, becoming prized possessions within gangs who wanted to circumvent the curfew and the night monitors. A small, agile child had a much better chance of avoiding detection and was able to take advantage of the people who felt safe in their homes after curfew. The gangs who managed to keep a steady supply of child thieves and assassins were among the most powerful.

Kit would like to think that was the fate she had helped rescue those children from. But that unit they had lived in—bright and open, careworn yet clean, filled with toys, not weapons. No, it was more likely that they had raided a refuge, a place that took in illegal children who were abandoned by their parents or rescued from gangs. She wished that she could believe that returning them to the system at that age would help them, but she'd seen some of the special needs classes where such children would be placed. The discipline was harsh and unforgiving, and they were all fitted with specially modified versions of the MDU—no military capabilities, just constant, all-day surveillance and monitoring. They had been kept strictly separated from the normal children, and Kit had been glad of it. Their uniformly blank expressions had given her the creeps.

Still—that treatment was designed to make them into functioning adults rather than criminals. It had to be better than gang life and the streets. It was a shame that they had to suffer for their parents' mistakes, but it wasn't her choice to make. She had only been doing her job.

Just as her thoughts finally began to sink into the drowsiness that presages sleep, a low but insistent tone sounded in her left ear. Her eyes snapped open. With a reluctant groan, she rolled out of her bunk. She had nearly forgotten her night watch assignment.

Atop the compound wall, the night air was tepid and heavy with moisture. Irritably, she shuffled her feet against the wet concrete, stamped a couple times, and then settled into an attitude of motionless attention. Human guards hardly seemed necessary with the monitors whirring around outside the walls, but if her superiors wanted her on the wall, she wasn't one to argue. Of course, now that she was honor-bound to stay alert, the sleepiness came on full force. She concentrated with all her might on staying awake—to the point where she almost missed the flicker of movement to her right.

The wall upon which Kit stood was tall and featureless, illuminated by bright spotlights set a short distance away from its imposing height. The lights shone inward, obviously placed to illuminate the towering wall and its guards, rather than to give the guards a better view of their surroundings. Beyond this pool of light, the streets seemed unnaturally dark, with only the blinking lights of the sentry bots to confirm that the world did indeed continue. The dark-on-dark blur that moved out beyond the perimeter tonight, however, had no blinking lights, no mechanical whirr, no slight metallic reflection. With rising disbelief, Kit realized that the mysterious shadow was roughly the size of a human. She reached for her station's alarm button, but hesitated. Could it be a guard from the detention center? The bots were ignoring it as if it had every right to be there.

Kit squinted against the lights, cursing the ORG's need to make a spectacle of its security. Despite the bots' attitude, the shadow didn't move like someone who had a right to be there. It slunk, it bent over, it...motioned a whole line of smaller shadows past it and away into the blackness of the night.

Children...being ushered away from the detention center by someone who had a guard's pass, but clearly wasn't a guard. Could they be the same children from the mission, or was she jumping to conclusions?

The blank little faces she remembered from school flashed into her mind and superimposed themselves over the tear-streaked ones from this afternoon. Duty warred with reluctance. Her hand hovered over the button. And then the shadows were gone.

Breakfast the next morning had a mixed air of gloom and awkwardness. Kit didn't really feel like chatting, her mind still occupied by the shadows of the previous night, but her lack of conversation was nothing compared to the determined silence being projected by the rest of the table. Stev pointedly ignored Kit, his jaw tight. He couldn't formally reprimand her; he was at least as much in the wrong, as far as the rules went. Fraternization without legal approval was strictly forbidden, especially within the ORG and even moreso within teams. Not that it ever stopped anyone. Every operative was here because they had a certain disregard for the rules—but they didn't snitch on each other. Stev knew that Kit wouldn't turn him in, and she knew she wouldn't be punished for her disregard for authority. She would just have to ride out this period of sulking.

Mercy was unmistakably embarrassed by the whole thing. She wouldn't meet anyone's eyes, though Kit tried to catch her gaze more than once. She didn't want Mercy to think that Kit blamed her for Stev's behavior. Eventually Kit gave up and decided to emulate Avin, who was mechanically shoveling food into his mouth, seemingly unconcerned by the tension all around him.

Turning her attention to her food wasn't all that fun either. Kit poked unenthusiastically at her porridge. It was a gloppy mishmash, made from the same dehydrated meat and grain bars as the rest of their meals. Lunch would be the bars themselves, with a salted jerky bar and a sweetened grain bar. For dinner, another meat bar would be rehydrated, chopped up, and fried, then served with a side of rehydrated vegetables. Every once in a while they would get a treat of dried, diced fruit for dessert, but that was extremely rare. She had heard stories of what fresh food tasted like, but she never expected to taste it herself. Once, when she was accepted into the ORG, she'd gotten to enjoy a special celebration dinner with the other graduates where they'd been given some sort of frozen, highly-processed mixed meat patties with canned tomatoes. That was—and probably would remain—the best meal she'd ever eaten. She was lucky to have what she did—but that didn't make it taste any better. She scooped a spoonful of gluey porridge into her mouth and chewed unenthusiastically as her mind turned once again to the meaning of those little shadows fading into the darkness.

They had a couple days of downtime before their next mission was assigned. Kit was thankful for it, since it gave Stev's temper time to cool. It wasn't the first time she'd gotten on his bad side, but he was nearly as quick to forget as to anger. She wasn't sure if he ever forgave, since he had never mentioned any of his outbursts to her after he'd calmed down.

Their new job was going to be a multi-day mission that would take them to the outskirts of the city. That explained the break they had gotten beforehand. Roughing it at the city limits was wearing, so it was best to go in fully rested. The Stacks might be the hub of all the petty gangs in the city, but the serious criminals and revolutionists congregated in the Limits. The Congress couldn't even enforce curfew out there; bots patrolling the area had a tendency to simply disappear, despite an increasingly deadly arsenal.

It was a two-day trip through the city to get into the Limits. Kit hated traveling. The transports were cramped and dark and confining. They spent their days playing inane card games, and their nights sleeping uneasily while the transport tramped on. There was barely room to move in the tiny lavatory that served the transport, and they subsisted entirely on dry nutrient bars and lukewarm water. Underneath the veil of grumpiness and discomfort ran a strong current of unease. Operatives wouldn't be sent into the Limits for anything trivial—the entire ORG would have to commit to policing the Limits to even create a pretense of order.

The transport didn't have windows, but Kit knew what was out there from a hundred other missions. After they emerged from the sprawling shadow of the Stacks, they would pass through one of several government zones. She knew this area held administration buildings, courts, the huge schools and nurseries, and even factories, but she couldn't have said which zone held which. The ORG wasn't needed in these areas, which were closely monitored by the regular police and their bot sidekicks. Here, the monitors were active night and day, every entrance and exit checked and registered. This protected both the gov zones and those who lived in the Stacks from the criminal element in the Limits. You couldn't pass through on a whim; you had to have a legitimate reason to get from one side of the gov zones to the other, no matter which way you were going.

Past the exterior checkpoints, smaller apartment houses huddled up against the gov zone walls, as if trying to leech some security from their proximity. These people were usually government workers who hadn't been able to secure lodging in the inner Stacks—generally law-abiding but un-lucky. From there, the houses became smaller and smaller, lower and low-er—not because they had been built like that, but because the upper levels had often collapsed in on themselves due to neglect. People still lived in the lower levels, just hoping that the roof wouldn't collapse any further. A lot of excavation had taken place around these unstable hulks, and those who could afford it lived underground, protected from falling rubble by old, unused infrastructure. Past that point, people had actually begun to steal rubble from the collapses to build their own shacks and shanties. It looked like a giant had picked up one of the concrete buildings, crumbled it up like a cracker, and scattered the chunks. And beyond that...well, that was where the city truly ended and the Swampies' domain began. Kit hoped she would never have to venture into that dank, muggy wilderness again, and she couldn't imagine how anyone survived out there—or why they wanted to.

As time wore on, Kit became restless. She had a strong urge to pace the length of the transport, but that would drive her fellow passengers crazy. For the moment, Stev was dozing, and she didn't want to provoke another rancorous glare by waking him. Mercy was jumpy enough without feeding off of Kit's nerves, and Avin—well, he was staring at the opposite wall so calmly and patiently that it resembled meditation.

Just when Kit thought she was going to start grinding her teeth from tension and boredom, the transport grated to a halt. They had reached the outer border of the gov zone. It was too dangerous to take a transport any farther into the Limits; it brought the wrong sort of attention.

After two days in the transport, the damp air hit Kit's face like a wet blanket. It wasn't cold, but she broke out in goosebumps from the shock of moving air against her skin. It was late afternoon according to her MDU, so they still had plenty of time to make some progress toward their goal.

Soon the boredom of the transport was nothing but a fond memory. As they slunk along the littered streets, tension and wariness became the new norm. In the distance, they could hear the sounds of normal life—yelling, occasional bangs, the grinding of wheels against the gravelly road—but in their immediate vicinity, all was silent. It was clear they had been noticed. Thus far, no one had seen fit to bother them, but that didn't mean no one would. Their supplies alone would be extremely valuable out here, and their weapons even more so.

As the shadows grew longer and the skyline began to smolder, Kit checked the pre-programmed route on her MDU. There was no way they were going to make it to their goal before the sun set, and she hoped Stev had the good sense to call a halt soon. They would need time to fortify a campsite before full dark. Not that they couldn't use night vision if they had to, but it was easy to miss things when everything looked green. Camps weren't something they had to deal with often, either. It was better to be careful.

Stev pushed them on longer than Kit would have liked, but she seemed to be the only one bothered by it. Mercy had left her nerves in the transport. Now she skulked along the streets as if she belonged there, making as little noise in her combat boots as Kit did in her lightweight climbers. Avin also seemed tranquil, following Stev's orders with the unconcern of one who knew the decisions were out of his hands. Kit wished she could share his calm. That was how an operative was supposed to behave, she reminded herself severely.

Finally, when the last vestiges of light were fleeing down the rubble-laden streets, Stev pinged a halt outside a dilapidated building. Its second and third stories had toppled to one side, their wreckage slumped drunkenly to the ground. Half of the first floor was also collapsed, but the rest of the buildings in the area were in significantly better condition. That made it the most likely to be genuinely abandoned. Kit ran a quick heat scan over it, though she was sure that Stev had already checked. It came back cold; a couple spots of warmth showed in the neighboring buildings. Stev waved them inside without any fanfare. Kit frowned; if it had been her choice, she would have continued down the street a ways, ducked into an alley, and doubled back less openly. Maybe Stev had determined that no one was currently watching them, but she couldn't imagine how.

The choice of building also made her nervous. Once she was inside, the sheer number of possible entrances—doors hanging off their hinges, windows with no panes, even cracks in the concrete walls large enough to crawl through—was astonishing. Most of the interior walls were at least partially demolished, leaving the first floor as essentially one room. Even if they all stayed awake, it would be hard to watch everywhere at once.

Out of the corner of her eye, Kit saw Avin murmur something to Stev. She couldn't hear the exact conversation, but in a moment Avin began to move around the exterior wall, removing things from his many pockets and fiddling with them as he went. Of course. Avin, with his numerous toys and gadgets, was going to booby trap every entrance. He carried all sorts of things—trip wires, flashers, noisemakers—and she even saw him take out two miniature versions of the robotic monitors. Heaving a sigh of relief, she commenced unpacking her bedroll. As Mercy and Stev did the same, Kit moved her bedding between them as casually as possible, not meeting anyone's eyes. Three dings sounded in her MDU; third watch for her. She set an internal alarm, then clambered into her sleeping bag, hoping Avin's traps would keep them all safe.

⸺◆O◆⸺

Their sleep was mostly uninterrupted, despite Kit's nerves. The only incident occurred on Mercy's watch, and she seemed to think the intruder hadn't even known there was anyone inside. A blinding flash of light had sent him scuttling for the shadows, never to reemerge. Even though it had all worked out, Kit couldn't help thinking that they'd gotten lucky as she gnawed on a nutrient bar in the thin morning sunlight.

She checked the map on her MDU as she packed up her gear. They should have no problem making it to their goal today, probably around noon. If things went smoothly, they might even make it back to the transport by this evening, avoiding another night in the Limits. When she finished her own gear, she kept moving and packed up Avin's too, since he was busy reclaiming his toys from the perimeter. He nodded curtly to her when he saw what she had done. He was unsmiling as always, but she assumed he was appreciative beneath the cool exterior. If nothing else, Avin liked efficiency.

The Limits seemed less threatening in the full light of the morning sun. The buildings became more and more ramshackle as they progressed, and a few of their less careful denizens became visible. Kit was sure the able-bodied were still getting out of their way, but now they began to see junkies sprawled here and there, delirious smiles plastered on their faces, completely tuned out from the squalor around them. Once, a man hobbled past them with a crutch, averting his face in terror. Kit assumed that people with the use of both legs were clearing the roads and scrambling through the rubble filled alleys, but this poor bastard didn't have that option. A couple boys, looking barely old enough to be out of school, strolled past with carefully cultivated nonchalance. Kit grinned at them wolfishly; their nerve broke, and they ran.

The sun was still slightly below its zenith when they reached the pile of rubble that was their goal. None of the building was actually standing—just propped up, really. Some of the largest bits had been piled into an arch to create a makeshift doorway. It did a fairly good job of being inconspicuous, too, except for the well-worn dirt path that ran through the weeds straight to it.

They crept around the exterior of the building looking for other exits or guards, but found nothing. Kit would have preferred to sweep the surrounding buildings as well, but she knew from past experience that her suggestion would be brushed off. She grumpily played rearguard as the rest of the team entered the archway. She hated being superfluous, but it was obvious this was going to be an underground operation, and that left her nearly useless unless they found an alternate entrance. This place didn't seem to have one—or if it did, it was in one of the neighboring buildings that *someone* didn't consider important enough to sweep.

Whoever was hiding here hadn't bothered to conceal their trap door. They could see a section of the flooring had been cut out, and it had been in use long enough to wear down the corners a bit. The rest of the room was bare and featureless. Perhaps this carelessness came from being left alone for too long, lapsing into false security. Kit hoped so, because the other option was that they were walking into an ambush. Before Stev opened the door, Kit sent out a warning ping with the code for Danger, Possible. Stev raised his head to look at her irritably. Too obvious, she mouthed to him. He rolled his eyes and motioned Mercy over with her shield. A countdown beeped through her MDU - 3 - 2 - 1...

Stev yanked open the door and Mercy hopped down without any hesitation. Kit gritted her teeth until she heard Mercy's feet hit the ground a moment later. Following orders was one thing, but jumping without even looking first was simply stupid. She was lucky it hadn't been that deep—and, Kit mentally added after a momentary silence, that there hadn't been anyone waiting for her down there. Stev and Avin quickly jumped down after her, leaving Kit to bring up the rear again. Her eyes flickered around the entryway once more, then she swung down into the pit.

It was relatively dark down below, and Kit got that disorienting lopsided feeling she always did when lighting changed quickly. Her MDU adjusted automatically and instantly for changes in lighting, but her right eye took a moment to acclimate. The trap door had dumped them into a tunnel, obviously built by hand rather than fabricated. Bits of rubble were being used to shore it up, and Kit felt increasingly uneasy as she looked around. The whole thing could come down at any minute. Then again—there were indications that this tunnel had been here for a while. A deeply scuffed path, some minor graffiti on the supports, a few bits of litter half buried in the dirt floor, nutrient bar wrappers and the like—this place looked well traveled. She relaxed, but only slightly.

The tunnel was very short, but a sharp turn halfway through made it look longer than it was. Stev shouldered past Mercy to peek around the corner first, then pinged the all clear. As they followed him forward, Kit saw that the tunnel let out into a space that had probably once been the basement for the wreckage above. Now, it looked like it housed a fairly large number of people. Pallets were laid out on the floor in rows, shelves lined the walls, and more bits of rubble had been piled into partitions to form several rooms. None of the inhabitants were visible, and the whole place was utterly silent. Even more tellingly, a heat scan returned nothing. Kit wasn't reassured. A gang this big had to have something of value in their hideout. Why wouldn't they leave at least one guard? But then she looked more closely. The shelves were empty of everything but trash, the pallets were askew and stripped of whatever bedding they might once have had—there was nothing useful left here.

"They knew we were coming," Avin commented. Stev looked like he wanted to argue, but finding no logical alternative, angrily shoved his gun into its holster.

"It's not like we really hid our approach very much," Mercy offered tentatively.

"We could have been going anywhere," Kit disagreed. "Unless these people evacuate every time they see someone suspicious moving in their general direction, they must have had forewarning."

"They could just move periodically and we got unlucky?" Mercy seemed bent on finding an explanation, and Kit could see fear on her face.

"They can't blame us for this," Kit assured her, though she was by no means certain herself. "We followed orders."

"Stop chitchatting and do a sweep," Stev growled. "We're less likely to get burned for this if we can provide some intel on who was here and where they went."

Privately, Kit wasn't sure she agreed. This was another classified job, and that meant Congress didn't want them to know anything about the people they were hunting down. While learning certain things in the course of an op couldn't be avoided, actively seeking out information was liable to get them in trouble. Then again, arguing with Stev in this mood was more immediate trouble, so she moved off to poke around.

There wasn't much to find. Unless Stev wanted a truckload of nutrient bar wrappers to prove that these people had eaten, Kit didn't see what good picking through trash was going to be. As she nudged a pile of garbage half-heartedly with her toe, she noticed something underneath it. Something... furry?

She brushed off the crumpled papers and plastic wrappers with her foot and found a small stuffed bear. It looked like it had been inexpertly made out of old carpeting, and the crinkling noise it made when she picked it up indicated that it was stuffed with more refuse. Its eyes and nose were uneven chunks of black plastic, probably gouged off of one of the shelving units, and glued messily onto the carpeting. There was no possible purpose it could serve except as a child's toy.

Kit took up the hunt with more determination. A tiny sock, made either for a small child or a large doll, a discarded diaper, even the unusually short length of the pallets—it all began to add up. They had been sent after kids again. Possibly even the same kids. Kit's stomach roiled. Was this the

Congress's way of saying that they knew what she had done, what she had allowed to happen? She left her discoveries where she had found them. If someone else came across these clues and made the jump, then so be it. She couldn't bring herself to say anything.

Soon they were on their way back to the transport, Stev quietly fuming in the lead. If anyone else had discovered anything, it seemed they had their own reasons for keeping quiet.

By the time they arrived back at the ORG complex after five days in the field, Kit was exhausted. She wasn't surprised when they were given several days to rest and recover. More days passed though, and then a week. As the second week ticked by without any new assignment, she began to feel unsettled. There was no shortage of work; other teams came and went as usual. Did they know that she had failed to sound the alarm? Had they captured the mysterious shadow, and had that person betrayed the neglectful guard who had stared down at them? The questions made her jumpy, but she worked her hardest to appear unconcerned. The quickest way to convince them she was guilty of something was to act guilty.

Stev started to complain of boredom and wonder aloud why they weren't receiving any missions. Kit kept her mouth shut.

Nearly three weeks passed, and they received no orders for anything besides guard duty. They spent most of their time training—a little too much time, actually. The extra nerves and energy came out in practice, and other units started to avoid them. Avin had blackened several eyes while sparring, and Mercy managed to break a much larger man's nose. Stev had even started a brawl at the bar. Kit wasn't sure whether it had been intentional or not.

Judging by her puffy, dark eyes, Mercy hadn't gotten an uninterrupted night of sleep since they'd been back. She snapped at anyone who spoke to her and was so easily startled that the rest of the team had begun deliberately making extra noise when coming up behind her. Kit assumed that she was worried about her position as the newest team member, but Mercy kept to herself. Avin, on the other hand, had grown bizarrely talkative. He was constantly in the company of one or more of the unit, asking questions about their activities in the weeks before. Luckily, he hadn't asked Kit anything relevant; she had an unsettling impression he would be able to tell if she lied. She was usually able to brush him off before he pried too deeply, but she'd seen Mercy nearly come to blows with him. The combination of those two was turning into a ticking bomb.

Meals remained a strained affair at their table. When Kit entered the mess hall, the most she hoped for was that Avin's attention would be directed elsewhere, but it seemed she was especially lucky today. He had apparently decided to take the day off from his incessant questioning and was eating his meal quietly. Stev was trying to draw Mercy into some banter about a practice session they'd shared earlier, but wasn't getting much beyond single syllable answers. He had been wrapped in a suffocatingly thick aura of false cheerfulness lately, trying desperately to boost morale. It wasn't working. He tried to engage Kit in conversation as she sat down, but she grunted noncommittally and began to gnaw a jerky bar. He returned his attention to Mercy.

As they choked down their meals, a subdued chime interrupted them. Everyone froze—everyone in their unit, at least. The rest of the cafeteria went on with their business. It was only their unit that had been summoned. Mercy had frozen with a bar halfway to her mouth; now she put it down uneaten. Stev swallowed the food in his mouth with an audible gulp, and they all looked at each other. Without speaking, they stood up and left the cafeteria.

The chime summoned them to their immediate superior, a grim-faced old officer who had more wrinkles on his face than anyone else Kit had ever seen. He grunted when they walked in together, Stev in the lead, and shoved a data sheet across the table at them. Stev picked it up, read it, glanced at the officer, then read it again more carefully. Finally, he straightened and said,

"Yes, sir," to the officer, who didn't look as if he cared to reply. He simply returned to his work. Stev turned to leave, and they all followed. Once the door was closed, he faced them with a baffled look.

"We've...been called before the Congress." He tried to keep his voice firm, but it shook a little anyway. Kit didn't blame him.

"Did it say why?" Avin murmured, his voice so quiet the question could barely be heard. Stev wordlessly shook his head.

"Everybody go get ready. The last thing we want to do is keep them waiting."

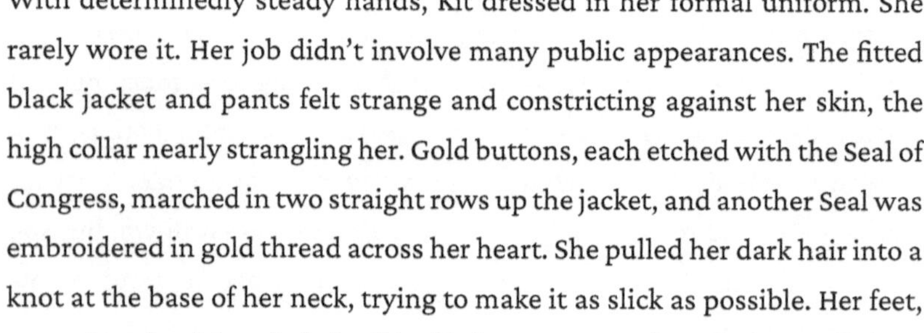

With determinedly steady hands, Kit dressed in her formal uniform. She rarely wore it. Her job didn't involve many public appearances. The fitted black jacket and pants felt strange and constricting against her skin, the high collar nearly strangling her. Gold buttons, each etched with the Seal of Congress, marched in two straight rows up the jacket, and another Seal was embroidered in gold thread across her heart. She pulled her dark hair into a knot at the base of her neck, trying to make it as slick as possible. Her feet, so used to the thin-soled, flexible climbers, protested as she jammed them into stiff, polished boots.

Kit couldn't help wondering if they were being called there for her own trial and punishment. Laxness on guard duty would usually be punished by psychosomatic inducement or summary execution. Kit shuddered at either option. Execution was bad enough, but she'd seen operatives who had undergone the inducement and continued their duties. It wasn't pretty. No one knew exactly how inducement was performed, and it left no physical scars to provide a clue. The mental scars, however, left a person utterly incapable of making the same mistake again. With some, the conditioning was so extreme that they'd chosen to kill themselves rather than repeat their offense. You could always tell when someone had gone through heavy inducement; they walked around blank-faced and emotionless, like a permanent trauma victim. The ORG often used them for the most undesirable or dangerous missions because they didn't seem to much care whether they lived or died. Kit shuddered and tried not to imagine herself in that zombie-like state.

The rest of the unit met her in the yard. They fell into a diamond formation behind Stev and moved toward the front gate. They were met by a pair of expressionless guards wearing the gold uniforms of the Faithful. Kit hid a shiver. The Faithful were the guards in charge of the security of both the Congress and the Congressional Seat, and they were put through inducement as a standard part of their initiation. They were incapable of betraying their masters or disobeying their superiors. The guards fell in behind the team as they passed, and Kit felt as if they were being herded along. A sleek, black vehicle was waiting for them, as different as possible from the dull, spider-like mission transports. The Faithful shut the doors behind them and moved to the front enclosure to input their destination. The team seated themselves on two long, padded benches, avoiding each other's eyes across the aisle. The quiet creaks and mechanical groans of the transport echoed loudly within the silent compartment.

The ride to the Congressional Seat felt even longer than the one to the Limits. When the transport's doors finally opened, the Congress's grandest political structure loomed over them, and Kit realized for the first time how unusual it was. Its strange, stately style of architecture looked older than anything else in the city, even the ruined buildings in the Limits. There were no sleek metal sheets, concrete bricks, or jutting corners on this building. The entire thing was constructed of massive stone blocks—something Kit knew a fabricator couldn't handle. That meant that this whole ridiculous place had been built by hand, even the towering, intricately carved stone columns and the ponderous wooden doors, bound in heavy strips of blackened metal. Both wood and stone were rare and precious materials these days, though that had been different in the distant past. The gray whorls of the stone enclosed hundreds of tall windows filled with numerous panes of glass rather than the featureless sheets of sturdy plastic that filled modern window frames. The exterior was hung with black and gold banners featuring the Seal of Congress.

Rumor had it that the Congress had been instated in the formerly hallowed halls of a fallen government during the Great Establishment, which would explain the apparent age of the building. No one could guess who had comprised that long dead government or what they had governed, and it was best not to try. History began at the Great Establishment.

There was the faintest of groans as the wooden portal swung open. Four sets of gleaming boots clicked on floors tiled with the same swirling gray stone as the outside of the building, here polished to a mirror sheen. The walls were hung with ancient portraits, perfectly preserved in airtight enclosures. None of the paintings gave any indication who their subjects had been. For all anyone knew, they could be the original masters of this ancient hulk of a building, left to hang forever and watch as their conquerors ruled in their place. Between the paintings, firmly closed doors lined the long hallway. The Faithful led them past many of these inscrutable doors, finally opening one on their left. With a commendable lack of hesitation, Stev led them through the doorway and into a sparsely furnished chamber. At the far end, a slightly raised dais held a long black table with four chairs behind it, all upholstered in black velvet. A black drape with gold trim was laid over the table. Stev led them to the center of the room, facing the table, and they all stood at attention to wait.

After what seemed like hours, four personages clad in black and gold robes with close-fitting black masks pushed aside the curtain hanging behind the table and entered one at a time. With solemn formality, they filed around the table and arrayed themselves in a line, facing down the operatives. The stately, androgynous figures stared at the increasingly nervous operatives for an endless moment. Then one of them spoke.

"Congratulations," said the one on the far left in a dry, expressionless voice. A nearly imperceptible wave of relief washed over the whole team. They weren't here to be reprimanded. They were safe. But the next words replaced their relief with shock.

"You have been chosen as the Elite." All four robed figures descended from the dais as one, each producing a tiny gold emblem studded with onyx. Each pinned an emblem to the breast of one of the operatives. Then, wordlessly, they filed out the same way they had entered.

Kit and her team were escorted to an entirely new suite of rooms within the residential wing of the Congressional Seat. Of course, Kit realized, the Elite wouldn't room in the barracks like common soldiers. The Congress's pet team would live in luxury where they could be called upon at a moment's notice. The Faithful respectfully waved them into their new rooms and the door closed behind them with an audible click.

They stood in a central living area that, to Kit's eyes, was filled with far too many things. Massive, deeply cushioned sofas formed a circle in the middle of the room. Sleek, black datacells lined the walls, which, upon closer inspection, proved to be filled with government propaganda publications and volumes on military tactics. Off to one side stood a gaming table with four chairs, complete with cards and chips. An arch in one wall led to a formal dining room, and four other closed doors led to private bedrooms. Black velvet and gold leaf covered every available surface. Some would call the effect sumptuous, but Kit only found it garish. She immediately longed for her simple, functional quarters back in the ORG.

Stev looked around and whistled loudly. A wide grin split his face.

"Well, we've done it now, guys," he said proudly. "Our hard work has finally paid off!" He puffed out his chest a bit and began to strut around, examining the rich fabrics and valuable ornaments that were sprinkled everywhere like confetti.

Kit supposed he was right. The Elite squad was the top of the food chain, the very best the ORG had to offer. To be chosen was the height of accomplishment—and yet, she didn't feel very accomplished. They had all but failed their last mission, and the few before that had been nothing special. The orphanage, for all it had troubled her, had been a breeze, logistically speaking. Before that had been the capture of a few low level drug dealers, and then taking out that gang who thought they could fool the night monitors with EMPs...she tried to recall as many missions as she could and found nothing exceptional, nothing that distinguished them from every other team. Not to mention losing a team member in an avoidable conflict—that should be points against them. Mercy seemed pretty good, but she was barely broken in yet. Kit frowned, and glanced at their newest member.

Mercy looked as if her thoughts were in line with Kit's. Her brows were creased with worry, her eyes flickering around the room nervously. When she saw Kit's gaze on her, she immediately smoothed her expression and plastered a cheerful smile on her face. Probably smart. Kit relaxed her own face and tried to forget her confusion for the moment.

"What do we do now, Boss?" Avin said. He still stood near the door uncertainly.

"Enjoy yourself until the next mission!" Stev said expansively, throwing his arms wide. Avin looked skeptical, as if he wasn't quite sure how to do that. For that matter, Kit wasn't sure where to begin in this place either. Mercy was, though. She had found a glass-doored cabinet among the data-cells, and she turned back from examining its interior with a large bottle in her hand, a lopsided smile on her face.

"Who wants a drink?" she asked.

Chapter Three

The room was too quiet. Tonight, no heavy breathing, no soft rustlings of bedding, no mechanical whirring from outside reached Kit's ears. For the first time in her life, she was sleeping in a room all by herself. She felt exposed. Even with the relaxing hum of alcohol in her veins, it took her a long time to sleep.

Morning greeted her with a dry mouth, a throbbing head, and a sluggishly churning stomach. Whatever that stuff in the glass bottle had been, it was certainly stronger than she was used to. She stumbled out of bed and dragged herself into her own private washroom. Now there was a privilege she could get used to. She splashed some water on her face and gulped a few swallows directly from the tap. It was possible she might survive the day.

After dawdling longer than she usually would have in the shower, Kit found that her normal uniforms had been neatly folded in a set of drawers in the bedroom. A relief—she really didn't want to put on her formal uniform again. She didn't see her climbers anywhere though, and had to settle for wearing regular boots.

Stev and Avin were already in the common room but also looking a bit rough around the edges. She wasn't surprised that she had beat Mercy out; if her blurry memories were correct, the small, slender girl had done her best to out-drink all of them, then treated the whole team to a rather slurred dissertation on the finer points of MDU programming—a particularly strange subject for a drunken rant, since she'd had no idea Mercy was interested in such things. It was a difficult and uncommon area of study, since most people regarded the MDUs as a pinnacle of human achievement, not to be tampered with by mere mortals.

When Mercy had gotten too unsteady on her feet and started repeating the bit about correct application installation techniques, Kit had half carried, half dragged her to her bed, shooting a warning glare at Stev. That had probably been unjustified; Stev had many flaws, but she didn't really think he would take advantage of a drunk woman. At least, she hoped not.

"Breakfast's in there," Stev grunted, motioning with his head towards the dining area. Kit nodded and went to investigate. Maybe here in the Congressional Seat there would be something interesting to eat.

She was out of luck on that score. It was the same gloppy porridge that they were served in the mess hall. She shrugged and set out to tame her unruly stomach by weighing it down with food. Her success was minimal, but better than nothing.

As she finished her meal, Mercy wandered in. She looked much the worse for wear, eyes sunken and cheeks slack. She hadn't even bothered to tie back her hair, which hung around her face in limp black strands. Kit smirked a little.

"You brought this on all of us by finding that evil brew," Kit accused.

"I didn't hear you saying no," Mercy retorted. She slumped into a chair and put her head in her hands. As an apology, Kit got up and filled a bowl with porridge for her.

"Thanks," muttered Mercy. She poked at it with a spoon but seemed in no hurry to actually put it in her mouth.

"I'll leave you two alone," Kit chuckled and returned to the common room.

What should she do now? Her days were usually filled with training, duties around the barracks, standing guard...none of which could be done in this suite. She wandered over to the datacells and took a look at the selection: *Counter-terrorism: An Operative's Guide; Congress Victorious: A Brief History of the Great Establishment; Style and Decorum for the Modern Military; The Science of War and the Madness of Rebellion...*

Nothing really caught her eye, but she pressed the tab for *Congress Victorious* and received a tiny data chip in return. She slumped down on the sofa and plugged the chip into her MDU. The semi-transparent title page of the book sprang up in front of her left eye. She could leave it there if she chose, but if this wasn't a safe environment, then nowhere was. She closed her eyes and let the MDU take control of the neural pathways controlling vision. The MDU smoothly transitioned into fullscreen mode. Now it seemed as though she was looking at a wider, more solid version of the book. If she chose, she could also play an audio file off of this same chip, but she enjoyed the aesthetics of the written word. Back in school, she'd heard people grouse about the inconsistencies of the language, especially after spelling tests, and claim that it was a waste to learn to read at all. Kit liked all the double meanings, the silent letters, the bizarre spellings. It was a nice break from the purely practical concerns that seemed to dominate all other aspects of life.

Unfortunately, her choice of literature proved to be a biography of the First Congress members. It was extraordinarily dry and full of insincere flattery. She kept getting distracted by Stev and Avin, who had set up some sort of strategy game across the room. Kit couldn't really decipher the rules; both players took turns, and they had only a set amount of time to make them, but further than that, she had no idea. All she knew was that the longer they played, the more frustrated Stev became. That entertained her greatly.

"Dammit, Avin, couldn't you let me win just one round?" Stev finally snapped. Kit opened her eyes to see Avin smiling slightly. He hadn't quite tipped over into smugness, but he was teetering on the edge. Mercy, who had gone over to spectate after finishing her breakfast, reached out and patted Stev's arm comfortingly. Stev laid a hand over hers possessively and she flushed an uncomfortable red. Kit's expression darkened, and she determinedly returned to her book. It was none of her business.

Their schedule stayed the same for most of a week, which meant that they were basically free to do anything they liked within the suite. Meals were delivered to them three times a day, and otherwise they saw no one. Someone popped in to clean the common areas during the night. None of them were brave enough to venture outside the suite without permission, and no one showed up for them to ask. The suite, which had originally seemed so spacious, began to feel as cramped as a mission transport with the full unit bottled up inside.

All four of them were used to strenuous physical activity, and they got restless very quickly. The suite had no gym, no training facilities, and very little space that wasn't taken up by a multitude of things. Why, Kit wondered grumpily, did a small, decorative lamp and a couple nicknacks need their own table? She started doing a routine of pushups, crunches, and squats in her bedroom every morning.

Mercy happened on the brilliant idea to move the circular sofas from the center of the room to the edges and use the space for sparring. It certainly tested their control, since the outside of the room beyond the sofas was still lined with datacells and other breakable objects, all of which probably cost more than their lives were worth. Every morning, the sofas had been restored to their original placement in silent admonishment of their activities. Kit got a bit of a thrill from it.

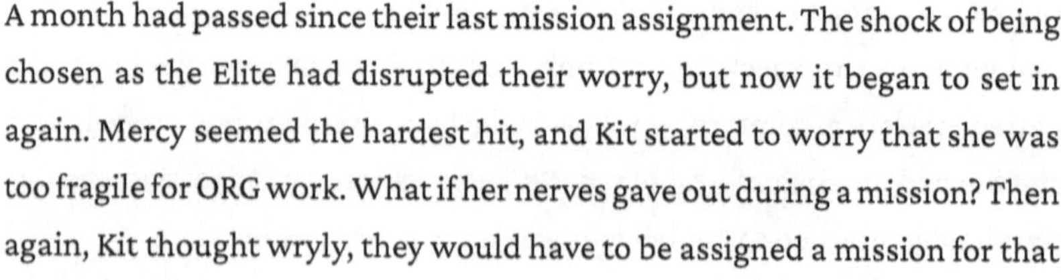

A month had passed since their last mission assignment. The shock of being chosen as the Elite had disrupted their worry, but now it began to set in again. Mercy seemed the hardest hit, and Kit started to worry that she was too fragile for ORG work. What if her nerves gave out during a mission? Then again, Kit thought wryly, they would have to be assigned a mission for that to be a concern.

Boredom nagged at Kit. Her muscles were sore and weary from all the exercises she was doing. She still hadn't dragged herself all the way through that biography, but it held absolutely no appeal right now. What could possibly be the hold up with a mission? They were the Elite, weren't they? There had to be plenty of things they could tackle!

Listlessly, she wandered around the common room, poking at the baubles and curios scattered about. She picked up one of the nicknacks that adorned the tops of the datacells and snorted. It was a ridiculous chubby creature that her old biology teacher had said was called a "cat." They had been extinct for a long time now, and if this was an accurate rendering, Kit could see why. It looked particularly stupid with the tip of its pink tongue protruding from its mouth. She turned it idly in her hands, noticing the metallic gold leaf that coated the tip of its black tail. She scoffed a little at the overwhelming predominance of the Congress's chosen colors and was about to set it down when she noticed a small indentation on the bottom. Within it was something which didn't look like it had any relation to the chubby cat figurine. A couple metal bits, some wire, a red light…Kit scanned it with her MDU, and it quickly responded with an answer: this was your standard issue ESB-400 audio-visual transmitter. She tugged at it gingerly and it came away, showing that several wires ran up into the statuette. Now that she knew its purpose, she could tell that the bit on the bottom was a tiny microphone. She flipped the cat over and looked at its round, glassy eyes. She couldn't see anything, but she was willing to bet that the camera component of the bug was looking back at her.

Hastily, she returned the cat to the datacell, questions dancing through her brain. Why were they being spied on? What did the Congress hope to learn?

Her breath caught in her throat. Had they discovered her lapse? Did they suspect she was part of something bigger? What should she do now? She couldn't tell the others about her guilt, but how could she not tell them that they were being watched? How could she do even that much without being observed? She wasn't naive enough to think that there was only a single bug in the whole suite.

She hadn't come close to a decision when a sound made everyone in the room raise their heads alertly—the sound of the door handle turning. Two of the Faithful entered their suite without any announcement. Nerves tingling, Kit felt the lack of her own weapons acutely; the guards were very obviously armed. They must have observed her discovery of the bug. They were coming to take her away.

To her surprise and horror, the Faithful's imperious gesture was directed towards everyone. They all rose from their various pursuits, and fell in behind one of the guards. The other guard brought up the rear of the formation. Neither bothered to tell them where they were going.

They were escorted through interminable hallways and finally deposited in a room that looked much like their usual briefing room at the compound, but for the inclusion of the Congress Seal on nearly every available surface. The guards made sure that all of them were safely inside, then exited, closing the door behind them. Slowly, they all took seats around the sleek black table, trying to imagine that this was merely a normal briefing. It looked like they were about to be given their first mission as the Elite. Kit's muscles were still tensed for flight. The timing was far too coincidental.

A long silent moment passed, and then the door at the other end of the room opened to admit their Monitor. Instead of the normal government uniform, the featureless figure wore an amorphous robe and veil obscuring its entire face. There was no identifying detail visible.

"I hereby present you with your duty, by the will of the Congress." Out of habit, they all murmured, "By the will of the Congress."

"Research Laboratory #24. Contact has been lost. You will enter the lab, ascertain their status, and destroy any hostile forces. If you do not report within 24 hours, the facility will be deemed lost and the entire structure leveled." With that, the Monitor turned and left.

Immediately after the door shut behind the Monitor, the Faithful filed in from the hallway. Instead of a simple escort of two, there was now a full squad of six. This squad surrounded them as they left the room. The reason became apparent when they arrived at the armory. All of their own equipment was there, including Kit's climbers. Kit breathed a sigh of relief when she traded out her normal boots and drew the long gloves up over her elbows, plugging both into tiny ports built into her uniform.

A double capacity assault transport was waiting for them outside. The guards apparently meant to escort them all the way to their destination. She glanced at Stev, and saw his lips thin with anger. She knew exactly how he was going to take this: as an insult to his authority and his ability to keep his team in line. Don't do anything stupid, she thought desperately.

They approached the transport, and Kit would have boarded it immediately, but Stev raised his hand to signal a stop. The guards stopped with them, and while they weren't openly aggressive, Kit saw a few too many hands on weapons for comfort. Stev turned to the lead guard and said, "Final gear check. Protocol." After a long moment, the guard nodded slightly.

They all went over their gear one more time; Kit made very sure that nothing had been tampered with in its absence. She didn't know if there was any way to bug weaponry, but she did her best to check anyway. Stev strutted around to each one of them, approving their checks. When he'd made his rounds, he gave the signal to move out, his pride assuaged, and they all piled into the transport. The entire squad of guards made sure to sit between them and the exit.

The transport scuttled along the gray streets, overshadowed by gray buildings and crowned by an overcast sky. They passed through the Congressional zone and entered another one of the gov zones. Judging by their assignment, it was probably where all Congress-authorized scientific research took place. The buildings were squat and heavy, with high walls or electrified fences. There was the usual guard checkpoint at the entrance, but their transport passed through with barely a pause, raising itself up to second story height on telescoping metal limbs and simply striding over the line of vehicles waiting beneath it. Kit had wished many times in the past for that very privilege, but it now awoke nothing but apprehension.

When the transport ground to a halt in front of Laboratory #24, the Faithful filed out and formed a column on either side of the gate, funneling the team into the laboratory yard with unnecessary fanfare. The yard itself was surrounded by a high concrete wall, the solid metal gate firmly bolted on the outside. A regular guard, wearing a standard black uniform rather than the Faithful gold, stepped out of a little shed near the gate as the team exited the transport. With an indifferent glance, the guard turned his back on them, punched a code into the keypad on the gate, then yanked open the bolt. The push of a button caused the gate to slowly groan open of its own accord. Beyond it was yet another squat, ugly complex of buildings, at least three within sight, and a barren dirt yard. The main building was connected to each of the others by raised and covered walkways. Not a single sign of life was visible.

They moved forward cautiously, keeping an equal eye on the yard ahead and the Faithful behind. As soon as they had passed inside, the gate guard punched the button again. The gate squealed as it closed.

Stev spun angrily. "Hey, what are you doing? You'll cut off our line of retreat!" he shouted.

The guard smirked. "You're the Elite, aren't you? You shouldn't need to retreat." The gate ground shut on his words.

"Fine!" Stev yelled at the closed gate, determined to get the last word. "It doesn't matter anyway," he continued in a more normal tone. "Kit can scurry up and let us out when we're done. We don't need anyone else to open our doors for us."

Even if ordered, Kit wasn't about to scale the wall to the outside right now and face all the Faithful by herself. If the Faithful didn't want to open that gate for them, she doubted they would allow her to do so, but she kept her thoughts to herself.

They crossed the yard cautiously, weapons ready. Kit's MDU scanned the ground ahead for mines and traps as they progressed, but found only bare earth. Not even weeds grew here. The front entrance loomed ahead, and the team fell into defensive positions, covering both the closed door and the bleak yard behind them while Mercy went to work on the keypad. No entrance codes had been provided for them, but it took Mercy less than a minute to hack into the security and gain them entrance. This was her true specialty, but Kit hadn't yet gotten a chance to see her in action.

When the thick metal doors slid open to admit them, what greeted them was not the actual interior of the building, but only a bare antechamber. The walls and floor were nothing but unadorned metal, and there were no openings except the second security door in the far wall. As they moved forward cautiously, the door slid shut behind them with a thunk. Mercy jumped. Ever wary, Avin slipped to the back and tried the interior door controls. The door whooshed open again at his touch, and an air of embarrassed relief filled the room. After a brief moment, the door shut again, and they turned their attention forward. Mercy again moved to the keypad. Tension radiated from each of them as the interior door opened smoothly and silently. The scene that greeted them defied all expectations.

Kit's brow furrowed. She was looking at...an office. The walls were a purposefully soothing and businesslike shade of light blue-gray. The floor was an indistinct stretch of flat carpeting a shade or two darker than the walls. There were desks and cubicles and scattered papers, but not scattered as if in a struggle. Scattered as if everyone had been working and just decided to step away for a break. And yet there was not a living soul in sight. In fact, there was nothing more threatening in the tableau than a stapler. There were no weapons, no experiments, no guards—in short, nothing that made sense.

By the thinning of his lips, it was obvious that Stev was coming to a similar conclusion. He signaled to them all: *Spread out. Search the area.*

They dispersed among the cubicles, checking under desks and around corners. The computer equipment in the cubicles seemed oddly antiquated and bulky for a cutting-edge research facility. Kit wondered what they could have been working on here. She even tried to read some of the papers on the desks, touching the precious sheets with delicate fingers, but they turned out to be nothing but gibberish to her. If the writing was in code, neither she nor her MDU could decipher it.

When she rejoined the group, it was clear that everyone shared her unease. The place felt wrong, too quiet, with a strange, dead quality to the air.

"Any signs of life?" Stev asked quietly. The question was greeted with head shakes all around.

"Not even a roach," Mercy muttered.

"And no sign of a struggle," added Avin.

"Maybe the scientists were evacuated to a safe room?" Mercy said, brow furrowed. Kit privately thought it unlikely. Why move the scientists farther into the facility when the exit was right there?

"No clues and no contact means we have to move farther in," Stev said. "Everyone, biofilters on. We don't know what they were working on here; there could be a disease or drug in the air."

Kit quickly pulled her biofilter out of her pack and shoved it over her mouth and nose, simultaneously running a quick bioscan on herself. She kicked herself for not thinking of the possibility before entering the building. She'd been too focused on actual attack to think of the more sinister reasons the place could have been compromised. But the scan came back with nothing more toxic than elevated adrenaline levels.

The only exit from this room was an elevator set in the far wall—again unexceptional, with no additional locks or security codes. It was flanked by decorative urns and looked like it probably led to nothing more exciting than another ten levels of offices exactly like this one. The whole place reeked of bureaucracy and boredom—exactly what Kit had joined the ORG to get away from.

The elevator fit all of them snugly. Even now, Stev managed to end up next to Mercy, reaching around her to hit the button for the floor below them. Kit grimaced and glared at him, but then the elevator gave a bizarre lurch and emitted a grinding noise. It was so unlike the smooth, silent elevators Kit was used to that it dissolved her anger, replacing it with fear for her life.

Stev had chosen the next lowest floor, probably intending to pronounce each floor clear as they descended, but judging by the buttons, there were ten levels of basement in this lab. It had looked like the building was at least two stories high from the outside, but if that was true, there didn't seem to be a way to access higher floors from this particular elevator.

When the elevator ground to a halt and dinged loudly, they all tensed. However, the scene revealed by the opening door was once again quiet. The office itself looked identical, down to the decorative urns, but the equipment looked even more dated. Bulky boxes of electronic components sat on the floor, attached to cumbersome cube-like screens. Cords ran everywhere. And here were the first signs of something wrong—papers scattered on the floor, chairs overturned, objects dangling by their cords. The lights flickered erratically. There wasn't a single person in sight. Kit had dealt with a hundred dangerous situations, but this eerily quiet office sent cold fingers up her spine. She wasn't alone either; as the team exited the elevator, Stev signaled: *Stay together*. But there was no need, in the end. This level was as barren of life as the other. Thoroughly unnerved, Kit filed back into the elevator with the others, squirming her way behind Mercy so that they could greet the next floor with her riot shield.

She almost expected the same scene again when the elevator dinged to a halt. Against her own better judgment, she was beginning to relax. This place was weird, but so far nothing had been threatening. Maybe there had been a malfunction somewhere, and all they would need to do was find the safe room and escort everyone out. Just as she finished that thought, the doors creaked open on Sub-Level 2.

The first thing that she saw was blood...blood everywhere. She was used to blood—blood spray, blood splatter, blood in the pattern of a one-hit kill. That was how the ORG operated. Kill in one hit, clean it up, move on. This place looked like some mad artist had indulged in an orgy of finger-painting. Blood was smeared everywhere. Gruesome hand prints adorned the walls and cubicles. Great streaks covered the floor and walls like the rays of a macabre sunrise. The rusty red was so overpowering that it even momentarily overwhelmed the realization that the room contained bodies—bodies that were horribly mutilated. It was no longer possible to tell what these people had looked like, or even whether they had been male or female, with their faces ripped off and their torsos swathed in entrails. Most of the bodies had been tumbled together in heaps, and the soothing blue-gray of the carpeting had turned a strange, murky purple-brown in a wide pool around them.

They exited the elevator swiftly, smoothly falling into defensive positions behind Mercy's shield. There was a flurry of MDU activity as they all scanned for life signs or electric impulses indicative of robotic enemies. A single soft ping indicated a negative. They moved forward and surveyed the area, but they were too distracted by the morbid contents of the room to notice the most important detail until they were nearly in its center. Mercy signaled a halt and gestured toward the far wall. This room, unlike the floors above, had another door. It was made of thick, clear plastic, set in a wide window of the same material. More smears and handprints of blood partially obscured the view of the hallway beyond, but what they could see looked empty. The door was currently wedged open by the shoulders of a corpse, and the red light over its keypad promised that it would lock, given the chance. Stev nodded curtly to Mercy, who picked her way across the room to the keypad. The corpse wasn't going anywhere, but why take chances? The rest of them continued to sweep the room, looking for anything that could explain what was going on.

The power flickered, dimming the lights momentarily, as Kit advanced into the web of cubicles filling the room. She once again tried to decipher the writing on the stack of documents there. She turned the full force of her MDU's decryption capabilities on it, to no avail. The symbols didn't even look like any letters that she knew of. She shuffled through the stack, but found nothing that she could understand. The further she went, however, the more she noticed a pattern in the symbols. She turned her MDU loose on the very last page—and it pinged a successful translation. With a mental cheer, she pulled up a visual.

And then everything went black for a moment. When her vision returned, she was still holding the piece of paper, but the translation file was gone. When she tried rescanning the page, her MDU stubbornly refused to believe that it could translate it. Shaken, she put the page down on the desk and carefully covered it with the rest of the incomprehensible stack. True, the MDU was inextricably integrated with her brain, but it was never, ever supposed to be able to override the functioning of her own senses. She felt otherwise fine; why had she blacked out? She quickly reassessed her surroundings, locating her team members, who all seemed to be peering under desks and checking the walls for hidden compartments and passages. She gritted her teeth and went to examine the pile of bodies.

As she approached, the reek of death overwhelmed her, and she had to use her MDU to dull her sense of smell, even through the biofilter. The corpses looked as if they were relatively fresh, stiff and bloated. The flesh had been stripped down to the bones in many places, but not through natural decay. Most bodies were missing parts, often an arm or a leg. She forced herself to examine the wounds closely to try to figure out what could have created them, but she was no expert. Her line of work was more in the business of creating wounds, generally a simple gunshot or stab. She leaned in closer...were those teeth marks? Had there been an animal, perhaps? A lab experiment gone wrong?

Her concentration shattered as a scream stabbed through the silence, high-pitched and terrified. Mercy? Kit sprinted for the far door, dodged around a cubicle, and came in sight of Mercy just in time to see her unload her gun into—the corpse?

The body which had been blocking the door was awkwardly trying to pull itself free of its confinement, its bloated fingers wrapped like a vise around Mercy's leg. Its blackened lips gaped obscenely. Mercy fired shot after shot, but the thing still kept squirming after her. Avin stepped forward calmly and fired two shots into the eye. Finally, its grip slackened, and Mercy wrenched free. Kit realized, to her shame, that she had frozen in place, merely watching as the scene played out.

Stev was still staring at the corpse in disbelief. Determined to act sensibly from here on out, Kit spun around, weapon at the ready, to scan the rest of the room. Not a second too soon either, as the corpse pile she had recently been so carefully scrutinizing began to stir. The gutless, limbless bodies on top tumbled to the ground as relatively intact bodies stood up from underneath and began to shuffle in her direction. She sent a warning ping to the rest of the team, who reoriented themselves to face the threat. As she aimed for the eyes, her MDU stubbornly continued to tell her that there were no life signs in the room besides herself and her team.

With this immediate threat, training took over. A rain of well-aimed bullets dropped the shambling forms one by one. Kit took aim at the last one and, attempting to incapacitate it for examination rather than kill it, took a leg shot. It stumbled, and its shamble became even more awkward and grotesque—but there was otherwise no indication that it had been shot, no indication of pain or that it had even noticed. She tried pelvis, chest, and gut—nothing fazed it. Its continued shuffling had brought it too close now; a shot to the eye dropped it like a stone. She and her team stood in the blood-soaked silence of the room, momentarily speechless.

"What kind of monsters are these things?" Mercy's voice was practically a squeak.

"This is insane!" Kit said, turning on Stev. "We have to withdraw."

"No!" Avin barked with uncharacteristic intensity. "We have to complete our mission."

"We can't just walk out there and admit that we couldn't complete our first mission as the Elite," Stev growled reluctantly. Kit turned to Mercy for support, but she shrugged helplessly.

"We finish the mission," Stev proclaimed. Kit knew what an order sounded like. There was no use arguing any further.

Chapter Four

Stev gathered the team together in front of the door, his expression grim. "Okay, now we know what we're up against. Aim for the head exclusively. No close combat if we can avoid it. Biofilters on at all times. We're going to have to clear each floor until we can be sure that there are no survivors. If we don't find any within our time limit, we head for the exit, declare the place a lost cause, and watch it get leveled. Understood?" There were nods all around. "Then let's go."

On the other side of the door, they found what Kit had originally expected in a lab: a long, white hallway stretching off into the distance, lined with doors. Some of the doors stood ajar, and more bloodstains marred the sterility of the hall. They advanced cautiously to the first set of doors, inset with blank windows that stared across the hall at each other. Both doors were closed. While the others covered him in all directions, Stev peered through the small window, shrugged his inability to see anything, then carefully tried to turn the handle. It was locked. Since there was no keypad, Kit moved forward before Stev could even turn to her. Hacking was Mercy's specialty, but Kit hadn't yet come across a lock that she couldn't pick. She flipped out her lock pick and went to work—or would have, if the electronic pick had made the least bit of difference. She looked closer and hissed in disbelief. The lock was mechanical. Some of the oldest buildings in the city still had mechanical locks, but she'd never come across one. She vaguely remembered instructions from her training, but she'd never bothered carrying that sort of lock pick with her.

"Kit?" Stev whispered. "What's the hold up?"

"I can't do it, Boss," she replied through gritted teeth. "It's not an electrolock. It's mechanical."

"How old is this place?" Stev asked in amazement.

"And why didn't they warn us?" Mercy put in with a frown.

Avin leaned closer to examine the door. "I think this may be more my job than yours. We must find the weakest point...and break it." He pulled a tiny tool out of one of the many pockets in his uniform with a gloved hand. With a deft twist and a flick of a tiny switch, a thin stream of white-hot flames ignited at one end. He applied this not to the lock, but to the door's hinges. Slowly and steadily, the metal melted and warped away from the plasma torch, leaving the door balancing in its frame. Avin stepped back, and Stev took his place, weapon at the ready. With a grin, Stev leveled a savage kick at the door. It slammed inward, twisting askew as the wall around the lock gave way, and fell half atop another heap of human remains. The buried shamblers squirmed sluggishly, but they were slow and awkward and easy to pick off. Now that the initial shock had abated, it was obvious that they wouldn't pose too much of a threat to the well-armed, well-trained team. The four of them quickly cleared the room, ascertained that there were no survivors, and regrouped in the hall.

They slowly worked their way down the hall, cutting locked doors off their hinges and checking inside any unlocked doors, killing the shambling creatures behind them. Some rooms were empty even of enemies. When they'd gotten through about a quarter of them, Stev paused.

"This is taking too long. We'll check the unlocked doors and leave the rest. We're on a deadline here."

"But survivors are more likely to be hiding behind locked doors," Mercy protested. Stev frowned at her, but Kit agreed, at least tactically.

"I have an idea." Avin stepped forward and banged his fist sharply on the door three times. He paused for a moment, then knocked again.

"I don't think they're going to let us in," Mercy commented dryly. No one laughed. Avin knocked one more time, and this time he was answered by a wet smack from inside. A blackened face with a gaping frozen grin slapped against the window, and bony, desiccated claws scrabbled at the other side of the door. Everyone but Avin reflexively aimed their guns at the door.

"Now we know there's no need to slow ourselves by cutting that door open. Survivors in that room are highly unlikely." Stev stared at Avin for a moment with a look somewhere between horror and respect, then nodded curtly.

They spread out, knocking on each door in turn, regrouping whenever they found an unlocked door. It took only a brief moment to dispatch any bloodthirsty occupants. In this way, they progressed down the hall at twice the speed they had before, leaving behind them a row of gruesome prisoners awkwardly throwing themselves at the unyielding doors.

Kit fell into a pattern: knock, pause, knock, pause, knock, smack, move on. When she'd gotten about three quarters of the way down the long hallway, she raised her hand, knocked, waited, knocked, and about jumped out of her skin when her second knock was immediately answered by a wild pounding from inside the room. She peered through the window as she pinged an alert to the rest of the team. She heard muffled yelling now, though she couldn't discern any words. All she could see of the person on the other side was a vague shadow through the dirty window. She couldn't even tell whether it was a man or a woman, but they were clearly panicked beyond sense, and for some reason unable to unlock the door from the inside.

Avin came running with his plasma torch at the ready, closely followed by Stev and Mercy. Kit made way for him, keeping her weapon trained on the door. What waited inside was different from the previous rooms, but that didn't mean it wasn't dangerous. The top set of hinges was almost severed when the pounding from inside stopped abruptly. The tone of the yelling changed; it was no longer demanding or pleading, but full of terrified hysteria. Then the telltale awkward thunk of one of the shamblers reverberated through the door.

"Can't you get it open any faster?" Mercy urged, standing on her toes to peer through the high window of the door. Avin shook his head and continued to gnaw away at the hinges with the torch. Everyone was fidgeting with impatience. No one was pounding on the door itself now, but they could still hear muffled yelling and crashes from inside the room.

Finally, the last bit of metal parted and Stev shouldered Avin aside, kicking in the door with a crash that pulled the shambler's attention away from its victim. Stev's momentum carried him down to one knee, removing the bulk of his frame from the doorway. Quick as a blink, Kit took aim at her target and dropped it with one well-aimed shot to the brain. The shambler dropped, rot-colored fluid oozing from its eye, and Stev leaped to his feet, moving swiftly towards the shambler's victim. The woman was wild-eyed, covered in bruises, and splattered with gore. Her hair was so dark with blood that it was hard to tell what its color had originally been. She huddled in a corner, an upturned table standing between her and the twice-dead corpse like a barricade. Her eyes were locked on the crumpled form of her attacker, her limbs frozen, as if any movement on her part might awaken it yet again. When it became obvious that she was not going to move on her own, Stev scooped her up and carried her outside. She looked like a small child in his arms, pale and unresponsive. As she passed through the door, however, she came alive and began to sob and babble incoherently, holding onto Stev with a vise-like grip. Now it was Stev's turn to freeze. A sobbing woman was not something they were trained to handle.

Mercy beckoned Stev farther down the hall, away from the thudding of the roused shamblers. When he lowered the woman's feet to the ground, her knees buckled, fingers clenching his shoulder with surprising strength. Kit could see her knuckles turning white. Stev detached her grasp firmly, but lowered her to the ground with surprising gentleness.

Mercy acted as if he had dropped the woman off a bridge. With a venomous glare, she knelt by the woman, now crumpled into a heap on the floor. and pulled a tiny square of folded fabric from her pocket. Once removed from its case, it shook out into a full-sized blanket, quite warm, waterproof, and even fireproof, suitable for use as a tarp in the rain or a lining for a fire pit. Now, Mercy carefully wrapped it around the woman, then took out a small antiseptic cloth and began cleaning the blood off of the woman's face with slow, soothing motions. The woman's sobs quieted, though tears still trickled down her face. Avin and Kit stood back awkwardly, alternating between watching the hallway for enemies and watching the events unfolding on the floor.

"You've been very brave," Mercy said softly to the woman, who only stared at her in response. "Can you tell us your name?" Kit thought that seemed like a pointless question under the circumstances, but it appeared to have been the right thing to say. The woman focused her eyes on Mercy with some difficulty.

"Caroline," she said. Her voice cracked on the last syllable. Her brow furrowed in concentration. "But...everyone calls me Carrie."

"And you work here, Carrie? What do you do?" Mercy asked.

"I – I'm just a junior lab tech. I don't do anything important." She started shaking slightly again. "I was cataloging samples when...the screaming..." She buried her face in the blanket.

"What was the experiment you were working on?"

"I don't even really know," Carrie whispered. "Something with tissue regeneration. They didn't let me near any of the important labs."

"Where are the important labs?" Suddenly she had everyone's attention.

"Sub-Level 11," Carrie replied, her voice muffled by the blanket.

"Eleven?" Stev cut in. "There were only ten levels listed in the elevator."

Carrie raised her head, her eyes wandering vacantly up to his face. "Yes. You have to enter a code, and only the top scientists had access."

"If there were other survivors, where would they have gone? Is there a safe room or something?" Mercy regained control of the questioning.

"Anyone else..." Carrie's brow furrowed in concentration. "Sub-Level 6. It'll be sealed off...but..."

"But what?" Mercy's voice stayed soft and even, projecting a sense of calm.

"But..." Carrie's shaking increased. "These aren't things that just escaped, you know? They're people who worked here. These were...my friends..." She started quietly sobbing again, and any further attempts to question her proved fruitless.

Stev gathered them all together a few steps away from their new companion, who had pulled her knees up to her chest and was huddled within the blanket like a scared child. She seemed barely aware of anything going on around her.

"Okay, speed is now our top priority," said Stev tersely. "We can't assume that whatever happened to these people won't spread to us. We can't even assume that the biofilters will protect us; they only filter air. So we make straight for the safe room; the rest of the facility will be considered lost."

Kit and the others nodded. It made sense to get out as soon as possible, minimize all contact with the infected, and then advise that the whole place be leveled. Lots of explosives seemed just the thing.

"What about her?" Mercy said with a jerk of her head towards the sole survivor. "She's injured and in shock. We need to get her out of the building first."

"No chance," Stev said sharply. "We can't spare the time to get her out. She'll have to keep up with us or be left behind." Mercy opened her mouth as if she was about to argue, but then closed it again with a snap. A wise decision, Kit thought. You didn't argue with the unit lead on a mission—even if you occasionally yelled at him while off duty, she amended her thought guiltily.

"What about the Sub-Level 11 labs? They could provide us with valuable information to report," Avin put in quietly.

Stev appeared skeptical. "If we do find those with access codes on Six, then we'll have enough information to make a call on that. If not, then we book it out of here as planned." Avin acquiesced silently.

Stev led the team back to the survivor—Carrie, Kit reminded herself. Carrie's eyes were closed now, chin pressing against her chest, and her breathing was slow and regular. She had fallen asleep during the time they had been talking.

"It may be hard to get her on her feet," Avin commented. "She's exhibiting signs of exhaustion." It was said so blandly that it was impossible to tell whether it was an expression of sympathy or a statement of fact. Kit glanced at him sidelong, but his face revealed nothing.

"If she doesn't walk, she doesn't come with us," Stev replied sharply and stepped forward, reaching for the woman's shoulder to shake her awake, but Mercy shouldered him aside with a glare. Stev was so surprised that he forgot to be angry. Mercy had only been with the team a short time, but nothing she had said or done thus far had indicated that she would so blatantly and casually disregard his authority. Now she proceeded to ignore him utterly as she carefully woke the sleeping woman with a combination of quiet words and gentle hands. Stev stood by with a darkening countenance, but didn't interfere. After her short nap, Carrie seemed a bit more coherent, and Mercy was able to coax her into standing up. She was still gripping the blanket in a fist beneath her chin, wearing it like a cape. The blood in her hair was drying up and flaking off in a shower of red-brown dust.

Soon they were making their way towards the elevator, though at a slower pace than Stev would have liked. He kept glancing with frustration at Carrie's unsteady steps. While many of the shamblers had returned to a state of torpor, a few still doggedly banged on their doors, making Carrie jump and stumble. As they walked, Kit watched her curiously. Carrie matched this building in a strange way; she felt vaguely antique, from her bloodstained knee length skirt and lab coat to her antiquated name. Kit tried to think how long it had been since the Congress phased out three syllable names. It had to be three or four generations, and nicknames had been frowned upon even before that.

They reached the elevator without incident and crowded inside. With Carrie along, the space became uncomfortably tight, and the ride down to Sub-Level 6 seemed interminable. Kit seriously considered shoving her way out through the ceiling and climbing down the shaft under her own power. As the elevator ground to a halt, she gripped her weapon more tightly. She was acutely aware that there was no room for any of them to maneuver or aim in this tightly packed space. She peered over Avin's shoulder, watching the door intently. A pulse of adrenaline thrilled along her nerves.

As the elevator doors grated apart, a hand thrust itself between them, groping wildly. The nail beds were blackened with rot, the fingers blue and swollen. The smallest finger had been severed completely, while the ring finger's second joint was attached only by a thread. For a moment, Kit was hypnotized by it, swaying back and forth like a grotesque pendulum. Then the moment was past, and she was swinging her weapon up as Avin ducked under the grasping hand and rolled forward, neatly dodging past the hand's owner. As he came up onto one knee, the shambler that had been groping so wildly into the elevator staggered and fell, Kit's bullet lodged in its brain. With quick, sure steps, they all exited the elevator and formed up behind Avin. In that time, he'd already dropped another two of the shamblers heading for them, but each shot only attracted more attention.

They stood in a small vestibule. Concrete blocks showed through cracks in the white plaster walls like bones behind slashed skin. Opposite them, a heavy metal door fit seamlessly into the wall; judging by the scuffs on the floor, it retracted into the wall itself, eliminating the need for hinges. No keypads or locks of any kind were visible, but that was the least of their worries. Shamblers were pushing up against that wall in ranks three deep, pounding and scrabbling against wall and door alike, leaving trails of blood and rot behind their hands. The sound of the bullets had caught their attention though, and now they slowly turned away from their fruitless assault to focus on the small group outside the elevator.

Mercy reacted first—by reaching into the elevator and punching the button to close the door before quickly dancing back outside. Kit caught a glance of Carrie's frightened face before the door sealed.

"What the hell do you think you're doing?" Stev bellowed at Mercy.

"Protecting an unarmed civilian!" Mercy shouted back angrily. Kit mentally winced; Mercy was going to be in much more trouble for disrespecting authority after this mission than Kit had been over the bar incident, even though tactically it was the right move. A scared, untrained woman would just muck things up in a fight.

Kit aimed carefully for the heads, but shot as quickly as she could, thankful that she had never relied too heavily on the capabilities of the MDU. That piece of hardware, cornerstone of the ORG's strategic effectiveness, still insisted that they faced a room full of dead bodies. Threat assessment: 0%.

Mercy and Avin joined her in trying to stem the tide one shot at a time. Stev, on the other hand, decided to take the overkill approach and pulled his SMG off his back. Bullets sprayed wildly into the horde as a manic grin spread across his face. While he rarely got a direct hit to the brain, the punishing force slowed the shamblers even more, sometimes shredding limbs and occasionally pulping a skull. Anything to slow the shamblers. The room was small, and the hideous things were gaining ground much faster than Kit liked.

No matter how many bullets they poured into the creatures, the shamblers kept pressing forward. Much too soon, Kit could make out the detail of their faces, the eyes red with burst blood vessels, and the blackened, swollen tongues protruding from their gaping mouths. One got close enough to make a grab for Mercy, who stumbled backward, awkwardly avoiding its grasp. She recovered with a solid kick to its chest, shoving it back into its fellows, and a quick shot to the head. It toppled to the ground, but still more filled its place. They were about to be overwhelmed.

Something had to be done. There was no time to think, no time for a plan. It was suicidal. She didn't care.

She holstered her gun and lunged for Avin. She could see the item she wanted—a circular bulge in the pocket on the side of his pack. She pulled open the pocket and grabbed it without bothering to ask permission, shoving it into a pocket on her own uniform. Avin shot her a surprised glance, and their eyes met for a brief moment. Something like fear flashed into his expression. She paused for one more split second, terror and adrenaline piercing her like a needle, and then she jumped.

At the apex of her leap, her climbers activated, grabbing onto the ceiling with spread palms, and she swung herself up until the suit latched on at knees and toes as well. She clambered across the ceiling as quickly as she dared; the suit wasn't meant for this sort of thing. Despite how well it allowed her to climb vertical surfaces, it had limitations, and having her entire body weight suspended beneath it was risky. Climbing was always risky though. Vaguely, she heard shouting from the rest of her team; she didn't dare look behind her to see whether they were shouting at her or at the shamblers.

Past the horde, there was an empty space. Everything in the room was throwing itself at the elevator doors. She dropped to the floor, dangling for a moment from her fingertips before slipping lightly into a crouch. None of the shamblers had followed her. Yet.

With steady fingers, she drew the odd-looking little item from her pocket. The tiny robot looked like a matte silver globe on wheels. Usually used for subduing crowds, concussion bots made a sound loud enough to stun even the most riotous citizens without actually hurting them. She placed the bot on the floor, turned the noise dampening settings on her MDU up to full, steeled herself, and pulled the pin on top.

The bot whizzed off towards the far corner of the room, putting as much distance as possible between it and her team. As a single use weapon, it was designed to only go off when it reached a target, detected through a combination of pressure and motion sensors. If she'd tried to send it off while on the other side of the mob, it would have detonated almost immediately, stunning her team far more than the shamblers. As it was, it zipped away unhindered until it crashed into a bloody mound of flesh just short of the far wall. The muffled boom vibrated in her teeth, and she was glad that everyone else was farther from the concussion. She held her breath and waited to see if her plan would work.

At first, nothing happened as the horde's momentum continued to push inward towards their prey, but then there was the slightest pause, a ripple of confusion. The ripple grew into a wave, and the horde was turning, milling, looking for the source of the sound. Some of them turned to shuffle off towards the far corner, investigating the burned out remains of the bot. They bumped into each other, several of them falling over on their unsteady, mutilated legs; instead of standing back up, they crawled along the floor on their bellies. This only succeeded in tripping up more of their fellows. Kit would have found all this hilarious if part of the group of shamblers hadn't begun to close in on her corner, having noticed fresh meat behind them.

The team had very correctly stopped their fire when the grenade went off. There was no point in turning the shamblers back towards them with the noise of new gunfire. They would let the horde stumble as far away as possible before renewing the attack.

This left Kit in a bit of a bind. If she fired to defend herself, the whole group would zero in on her. The ceiling was low enough that, without the distraction of the rest of the team, she doubted she would be able to crawl back over the shamblers without them grabbing at her, and if they got a hold of her, she'd be helpless to defend herself, her hands latched to the ceiling. Remove even one point of contact at that precarious angle and she'd fall right in the middle of them.

The group closing in on her was made up of six shamblers, all clad in the ragged remains of lab coats. One had a gnawed-on stub where her arm should have been. Another had an eyeball hanging from its socket, waggling back and forth on his desiccated cheek as he shuffled forward. They moved with agonizing slowness. Behind them, she caught a glimpse of the team by the elevator, edging slowly around the room in her direction. She knew they'd never get to her in time, and if they did, they'd still be too close to the horde to open fire again. With every second she hesitated, the shamblers came closer. She gritted her teeth and drew her knife, pushing the power switch to activate a thin, keen blade made of solid electrical force. She dove forward.

She'd chosen her path carefully; she dodged around the side of the sham-bler with the missing left arm. It was a good plan in theory. There was enough of a gap between that shambler and the next one that she thought she might be able to slip by. And she was technically right—the one-armed shambler certainly didn't make a grab for her. As she passed by, it turned its head, much more quickly than she would have thought possible, and snapped at her, teeth clicking in the air far too close to her ear. Startled, she jerked back without thinking, hesitated for one second too long—and the shambler on her other side latched onto her arm. Its stiff fingers dug in with shocking strength. Reflexively, Kit swung it around and smashed it into the one-armed shambler, using its poor balance against it. The one-armed shambler went down in a mess of flailing limbs, but the other one stayed locked onto her arm. Its momentum carried it all the way around until it staggered to a halt facing her. She flicked the switch on her knife to the strongest setting, wire thin and diamond hard. It went through the shambler's neck without resistance, slicing through vertebrae, muscle, and sinew. The head popped off and rolled away. A spasm passed through the fingers, and they locked even tighter around her forearm. Before she could free herself, another shambler attached itself to her from behind. Weighed down as she was, she couldn't dodge or escape. For the first time, panic gripped her as tightly as the shambler's bony fingers. She struggled hopelessly, and the hold on her shoulders tightened. The jagged nails drew blood, digging gouges in her flesh, and the entire weight of the shambler seemed to be hanging from her shoulders, bearing her down.

Then the hands spasmed and released her. Another head bounced away across the blood-splattered floor. More splatter ran down the back of her neck, oozing behind her collar.

Avin held the headless body of the shambler he'd pulled off of her. With startling speed, he turned and tossed the body into the face of the shambler coming up behind him. As both creature and body went down, tangled together, he leaped in, severing another head. Swift as a thought, he danced among the shamblers, making them look even more clumsy in comparison. His knife was a blur, separating heads from necks, limbs from bodies. As he held off the surrounding enemies, Kit hurriedly used her own knife to sever the arm of the headless shambler that had encumbered her. Freed from its dead weight, she joined the fight. The hand was still clamped to her arm, but she used the protruding stump to batter back the snapping jaws of the next shambler, beheading it while its teeth were buried in the arm of its deceased comrade. The added weight of the head pulled the now-loosening fingers from her arm, and she continued the fight unfettered.

Mercy and Stev still hadn't reached them; Avin had left them to hold off the bulk of the attackers and used his superior speed and agility to come to Kit's aid. Now the two of them fought their way back to the group. Reunited, battered and bruised but all in one piece, they sheathed their knives and once again brought out their best firepower.

The tide of battle had turned. The closest shamblers were quickly picked off. The farthest milled uncertainly for a moment before turning and beginning the laborious journey back across the room towards their prey. Nearly a third fell before they'd made up their minds which direction to go. By the time the last of the shamblers reached the group of fighters, the numbers on both sides were nearly equal. With only a few shamblers to deal with, the team was able to use their mobility to better advantage, spreading out around the room and neatly lobotomizing the last remnants of the horde.

As they picked their way through the remains that now littered the floor of the antechamber, bits and pieces continued to twitch spasmodically, as if they were trying to reunite with their other parts. Kit shuddered and placed her feet carefully; she could feel much more texture than she'd like through the thin soles of her climbers. When they'd all completed a survey of the room without incident, Kit breathed a sigh of relief. The dead seemed to be staying dead this time.

Chapter Five

Without waiting for orders, Mercy stalked to the elevator and pushed the call button. The doors slid open; Carrie was right where they'd left her, cowering in the corner of the elevator and clutching a rail that she'd pried off the wall. Kit's estimation of her rose slightly. At least she'd been prepared to fight, even with a woefully inadequate weapon. However, Mercy had to coax her into exiting the elevator, and she stepped very gingerly, trying to avoid the blood and guts despite the fact that her shoes were already ruined and the rest of her wasn't much cleaner than the floor. Stev stiffly ignored both Mercy and Carrie, but Mercy ignored him in turn, her expression defiant even as she spoke softly and comfortingly to Carrie. Stev huffed and muttered to himself as he carefully examined the sealed door to the safe room. No opening mechanism was apparent.

"Over here." Avin shoved a body that had been pinned up against the wall. As it toppled to the floor like a freakish rag doll, a panel with a speaker and a single large button was revealed. Stev strode over to examine it, peering closely, but it gave no intimation of its purpose. After a moment of rumination, he motioned them into defensive positions around the door, braced himself, and hit the button. As soon as his finger left it, he jumped backward, whipping his gun around to aim at the door. The door stayed stubbornly locked. Cautiously, he pushed the button again, with similar non-results. Finally, in frustration, he pushed the button and held it, but still nothing happened. He turned to face them, finger still holding down the button.

"Maybe it's broken," he said, frustrated, and released the button.

"Hello?" squawked a distorted voice. "Hello, is someone out there?"

Stev jumped at the unexpected voice; the rest of them clutched their weapons a little tighter.

"Who's there?" Stev yelled, trying to cover his discomfiture.

"Hello?" the voice came again. "Can you hear me?"

"I think you have to hold the button, Boss," Avin advised quietly. Stev frowned, shot Avin something that bordered on a dirty look, and pressed the button down.

"Congress Elite, reporting for rescue and salvage operation. How many survivors do you have in there?"

"Thank goodness! We have about fifty people in here." There was a pause, and they could hear some voices muttering in the background. "Are any of you injured?"

"No injuries," Stev barked back. "We need to start the evacuation process immediately."

There was a long pause, then the heavy metal door slid open grudgingly, stuttering as it caught on the bodies that had fallen against it. They moved through it cautiously, Mercy gripping Carrie's arm to keep her from either bolting or fainting; it was unclear which. A large, circular room of stark metal surfaces opened out around them. Doors radiated in all directions, and the central space looked like it would hold upwards of five hundred people. Only a fraction of that number huddled at the far side of the room.

A small group broke away and approached the unit. Two of them were security guards, judging by their stained and rumpled uniforms and the weapons they carried. Kit sized them up and determined that they were no threat. Standing around all day wearing a gun couldn't provide the same level of skill as constant combat. Their eyes were frightened and their grips uncertain on their weapons. Between them was a man in an immaculate lab coat. His hair and close-cropped beard, dark brown flecked with gray, were clean and neat. Evidently he had missed the worst of it, whether through foresight or forewarning. He carried no weapons that Kit could see, but she strongly suspected that he had taken charge of the situation as quickly as possible. That guess was borne out when he immediately began yelling.

"You idiots! What are you doing bringing her in here?" The man extended a dramatic finger towards Carrie. "Get her out of here!"

"What?!" Mercy exclaimed before Stev could formulate a response. "No!"

Stev's face reddened, though whether he was angry with the officious man or with Mercy for preempting him was unclear. When he responded, his voice sounded like it was coming from between gritted teeth.

"This woman is a civilian in need of treatment. She does not present a current danger."

"You had no right to jeopardize everyone by bringing her in here!" the man in the lab coat ranted on, gesticulating wildly. "Do you know how hard we've worked, what we've sacrificed, to make sure this area stays clean?"

"No, and I don't care," Stev bellowed, losing his tenuous grip on his temper. "We're here to get you ungrateful morons out, and we don't have time for this!"

The two men glared at each other for a long moment, both red-faced with anger. Then the man in the lab coat deflated.

"If you insist on bringing her along, at least put her in quarantine until we can be sure she's not infected. She could spread this to the entire population if she's brought outside the lab."

Stev glanced at the battered woman, who was now staring glassy-eyed into the distance, seemingly unaware that she was being discussed. Mercy had put an arm around her shoulders to steady her, or she probably would have fallen over. Stev nodded sharply at the man in the lab coat.

The stranger heaved a sigh of relief. "My name is Dustin Knowles. I am—was the assistant to Charles Greyridge, the scientific lead and visionary of this project." He turned to one of his guards. "Take that woman to quarantine immediately."

"I'll go with her," Mercy said, shooting a suspicious glance at Dustin, who shrugged.

"I don't care who enters quarantine as long as you don't come out again until we're sure you're clean," he replied.

Mercy jerked her head in a nod, according the man the barest civility. Avin cleared his throat quietly and nudged Mercy in the ribs with his elbow. She jumped, and then blushed.

"Requesting permission to accompany the civilian to quarantine, Boss," she said formally to Stev, who had been glaring daggers at her, but hadn't wanted to reprimand her in front of unknowns and erode their appearance of solidarity. Mercy's bizarre attachment to this woman was making her clumsy. Stev sounded mollified, however, as he granted permission.

"Stay outside the room, though. You can guard her from there, and we might need your skills at some point," he cautioned. She nodded and left with Carrie and her guard. Stev turned to Dustin. "How long does she have to stay in quarantine before you're satisfied?"

"It would be safest to give her a full twenty-four hours—" Dustin began. Stev cut him off with a sharp gesture.

"Impossible. If we don't report within twenty hours, this place will be leveled, with or without our recommendation. We need to get you and the rest of these people out well before then. Especially since once we're out, I'm still going to recommend leveling it."

Dustin frowned. "Well then I recommend leaving her here to get leveled with it. But since you're clearly not going to take my advice, 18 hours, absolute minimum."

Stev nodded. "We won't take any chances. What are the signs of infection?"

"Nausea, vomiting, and swelling around the joints are the most visible early symptoms. She won't be able to keep anything down. Merely walking will become excruciatingly painful, and about the time she's unable to walk anymore, her organs will begin shutting down. They usually beg for food right until the end, even though they vomit immediately upon eating." Dustin shuddered. "It only takes about an hour for them to get up and start walking again, and they'll eat anything with a pulse."

"What about everyone else here?" Stev asked. "They've all been through the quarantine process?"

"They didn't need it. The condition only spreads through direct contact of bodily fluids. Saliva to blood, mostly, but blood to blood can work as well. When we realized that, we put everyone with any wounds out into the antechamber. We couldn't risk having them turn in here."

Kit's memory flashed to the scene when they'd first reached the safe room. All the shamblers, lined up and beating on the door, as if they were begging to get in...

Some of those people could have been perfectly healthy—until they were thrown into a room with someone who wasn't. Her jaw clenched, but she swallowed her words. She couldn't help any of them at this point.

Stev seemed oblivious to the implications; he just wanted to plan and complete the mission. He and Dustin launched into a discussion on the logistics of moving fifty people up to the exit in one small elevator, fencing over the details like two children squabbling over the last fruit bar. As the two walked off towards the survivors huddling at the end of the room, Avin started a thorough gear and injury check, and Kit followed suit. The gouges on her shoulders stung a bit; her uniform had stuck to them as the blood dried. Her breath hissed through her teeth as she pulled the fabric away gently. Stripping down to her undershirt, she coated the wounds with antiseptic gel and experimentally flexed her shoulders. The pain was minimal and shouldn't impair her in any way in the next fight. An in-depth bioscan revealed nothing unusual; she was a bit bruised, but not, as far as her technology could tell, infected with anything.

Relief washed over her, leaving sudden hunger in its wake. She sat down to look through her pack for a nutrient bar. Avin folded bonelessly into a cross-legged seat on the floor beside her to do an inventory of his remaining supplies.

Kit gnawed on the tough bar for a while as the semicircle of gadgets surrounding Avin grew. Silence floated around them in a bubble, mirroring their relative isolation in the middle of the huge circular room. Kit's eyes wandered around the perimeter, picking up Mercy's small figure near one of the doors, patiently standing guard.

"I wonder if that woman—Carrie—if she'll be okay," Kit mused, not really expecting a reply.

"She's tough." Avin didn't look up from his inspection, but there was a reserved respect in his tone.

Kit raised her eyebrows in surprise. "She's a civilian."

He lifted his head for a brief moment and captured her with his intense silvery eyes. "She's a survivor." Then he firmly turned his attention to his work.

A little shaken, Kit gnawed on her bar a bit more. There must be some aspect of the woman's personality that Avin, with his eye for detail, had caught. She searched her memory for clues.

Then it came to her. Before she had knocked on the door of the room where they had found Carrie, it had been dead silent. The shambler had been unaware of the living woman locked in with it, so she must have been hiding. A quick mental review of that particular lab showed no closets, no cabinets—everything had been on free-standing, backless shelves. And despite her own relatively light injuries, Carrie had been absolutely covered in gore...

Horror swept over Kit. It made a gruesome sort of sense. When anything that moved, anything that lived, was being hunted—you played dead. How better to play dead than by burying yourself in a pile of the newly deceased? But to lie there, surrounded and covered by the decomposing, partially eaten corpses of friends and coworkers, probably unable to see your adversary, aware that it it if it heard you, you were dead; if it saw you, you were dead; if it even got a bit hungry and accidentally grabbed your leg to gnaw out of everyone in the pile, you were dead...

It was no wonder Carrie seemed nearly comatose.

Kit carefully wrapped up the remains of her nutrient bar. She'd lost her appetite.

Stev and Dustin soon returned, with Mercy stalking unhappily behind them, forcibly relieved of guard duty.

"There's no need to wait for the quarantine period to end before we start shuttling people out. We'll send people up in groups of four with one guard, either us or the building's security people. I don't expect we'll have any trouble; the first floor was clean when we entered, and I doubt these things know how to use the elevator. Mercy, you'll stay up top to supervise people as they exit and make sure the doors stay open. Avin, Kit, escort duty. I'll stay down here to organize and make sure these people don't mob the elevator."

As they scattered to their assignments, Kit saw Mercy grip Stev's arm and whisper something to him. While she couldn't actually hear what was said, she could guess. *Don't leave her behind.* Stev's face turned into a thundercloud, and Kit worried that he might abandon Carrie just to teach Mercy a lesson in authority.

The evacuation began. Kit would bring up a group of four, then Mercy would usher them out of the building while the elevator returned Kit to Sub-Level 6. When the elevator opened again, Avin or one of the security guards would be waiting there with another group of four, ready to be shuttled up. The hardest part was avoiding the stampede to get into the elevator. People apparently found waiting in a room full of dead and still twitching shamblers to be unnerving.

The last group to go included Dustin and his security guards. Though they hardly needed it, Kit escorted them to the first floor, leaving Stev and Avin to perform a final inspection of the safe rooms. They rode the elevator up in silence, and then walked through the still strangely untouched first level. Mercy stood to one side of the exit, waiting. She scowled at Dustin and shifted her weight impatiently. As Dustin passed through the security door into the vestibule, he turned around to address his rescuers from the other side of the threshold.

"Thank you for what you've done here. We never would have gotten out of that room without you."

Kit nodded in acknowledgment and shifted her weight uncomfortably. She wasn't used to being thanked for her work. To cover her discomfiture, she fell back on protocol.

"When you report to the Faithful, tell them the situation is under control and we'll be out in—" she checked her MDU, "—about sixteen hours to provide our final report."

"I wish I could tell them that," Dustin said, assuming a tragic expression.

"I see no reason you can't," Mercy snapped.

"It would be a lie." He retreated a step, and both guards drew their weapons, training them on Kit and Mercy before they realized what was going on. Both women froze, caught entirely off-balance. It was the first time since training that Kit had been taken so completely by surprise, and she cursed herself roundly for it. She should never have trusted these civilians.

"I can't let you take that woman out into the world and start this nightmare all over again. If you won't leave her, then you'll have to stay with her. There can be no compromise." As Dustin spoke, he was walking backwards, taking careful steps towards freedom. "Lock the door behind us," he told the guards as he reached the outer portal. One of them continued to cover the women with his weapon. The other turned to hit the door controls.

As the door slid shut, Mercy sprang towards the keypad. The guard who had been covering them jumped back in fright, but the door still closed before she could reach it. A shot reverberated from the other side, and all the keypad's lights blinked out. Mercy pushed buttons in vain, but it was entirely dead. Kit joined her in trying to pry the now defunct door open by hand, but the only result was strained arms and aching fingers. They were well and truly trapped.

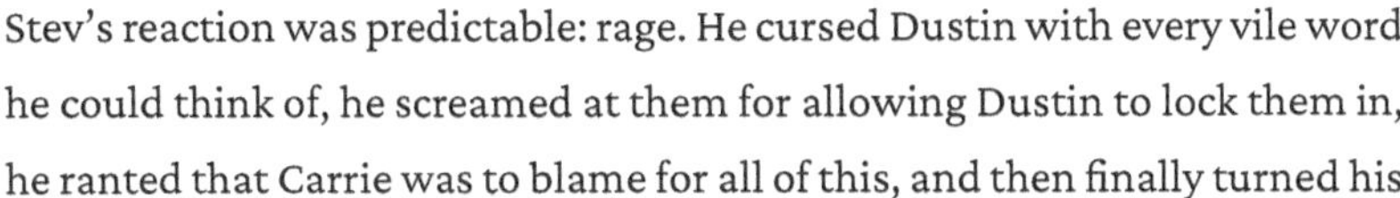

Stev's reaction was predictable: rage. He cursed Dustin with every vile word he could think of, he screamed at them for allowing Dustin to lock them in, he ranted that Carrie was to blame for all of this, and then finally turned his back on them, breathing heavily, to try to regain some semblance of calm. When he faced them again, his voice was rigidly controlled.

"Since our exit is now blocked, through circumstances which I'm sure were entirely unavoidable, there's only a few things we can do now. We either find a new way out, or we try to make one." Stev looked around at each of them as they considered their options carefully.

Avin was the first to speak up. "I don't have any explosives powerful enough to break through the walls. Maybe if we found an outward-facing window."

Mercy frowned. "There must be an emergency exit. There can't be a huge underground complex with only one exit. That would be a horrible design—especially with the lab's most important people on the lowest floor."

Stev scoffed, "Why would they put another exit from the lowest floor? More likely, they'd make a direct route from the bottom floor to the main exit. Then we'd be right where we started, but with less time."

"Why wouldn't they? Only one exit makes sense when you're trying to keep people from getting in, but not so much if you're making sure people can get out," Mercy countered.

"Why don't we ask Carrie?" Kit suggested quickly, before they could start an all-out fight. The last thing they needed right now was Stev and Mercy at each others' throats. "She may never have been to the lowest floor, but she'd certainly have more idea of the layout than we would."

"She's in quarantine," Stev snapped, turning his ill temper on her.

"From who?" Mercy snapped back, reclaiming his ire. "We're the only ones left, and we've already been exposed to her."

Stev's glare was becoming a permanent fixture on his face, but there was no arguing with the logic. Mercy spun on her heel and marched towards Carrie's quarantine without waiting for permission. When they returned, Carrie was moving better than before. She'd gotten a chance to wash up and change her clothes; Kit could now tell that her hair was a pretty honey blonde. Her wounds had been carefully cleaned and bandaged—by Mercy's first aid kit, probably—and it looked as though she was managing the pain well. She still seemed very nervous, understandably so, but she didn't look as if she was about to topple over at any given moment.

Stev didn't bother with any formalities. As soon as she was close enough to converse, he barked, "Well?"

Mercy had obviously filled her in on the content of the discussion she was being called upon to resolve. She didn't miss a beat in answering.

"There is an emergency exit for the senior staff down on Sub-Level 11. I remember there were complaints for a while that it wasn't properly sealed. Bugs were getting in and contaminating the experiments."

Stev glanced at Avin, who nodded his agreement, then at Kit—but immediately looked away again, dismissing her opinion. He was still mad at her over the whole Dustin debacle. She nodded her agreement anyway.

"You," Stev pointed at Carrie, "Feel like eating anyone yet?" She mutely shook her head. "Then let's go."

The elevator seemed to take forever to get to Sub-Level 10. It groaned and grated, as if its reluctance grew with each floor it descended. When they finally ground to a stop, the elevator door tried to open automatically. Stev jammed his thumb onto the close button with unnecessary force, keeping that barrier between them and whatever horrors lurked outside. The doors squealed, but didn't open more than a crack before closing again.

Kit didn't need any orders; it was her turn again. She slipped out of her pack and handed it to Mercy. The ceiling tiles in the elevator popped out easily, and she was able to boost herself up into the darkened shaft. Already, the light from inside the elevator seemed weak and distant, and her teammates might as well have been in another world. This place was hers alone, this darkened vertical highway full of cables and metal. She activated her climbers, reveling in the familiar thrill of power along her skin, and moved to the wall of the shaft. Carefully, she wedged herself into the small gap between the elevator and the shaft wall, squeezing herself down. Despite her slender frame, her ribs scraped against the wall. The back of her belt caught on something protruding, but she freed herself with a squirm and a tug. The abruptness of her release made her lose her footing for a second, but she was squeezed so tightly against the wall that she only slipped a couple inches downward before she caught herself. Taking a deep breath, she continued downward at a careful, controlled pace.

In a mercifully short time, there was nothing but empty space at her back. She was free to scamper down the walls, making use of all the available handholds and footholds with as much ease as another person would walk down a hallway. In less than a minute, the doors of Sub-Level Eleven loomed beneath her. She swung herself around, hanging upside down above the doors, and reached for one of the tools she kept tucked in the pouch on her belt. A small stub of metal telescoped out into a thin, strong lever. She carefully inserted it between the elevator doors; it didn't take long for them to give in and slide open with a reluctant chime. Kit winced at the volume of the sound and chanced a look through the doors, lowering her head into the doorway. What she saw made her retract her head again very quickly, heart pounding.

This level was designed much like the safe room, with an extra door for security once outside the elevator. There were only two or three shamblers in the antechamber, making their slow way to investigate the opening of the door. However, instead of a concrete wall, the antechamber was divided from the main lab by more of that thick, transparent plastic. Through its murky, blood-stained surface she could see a vast, shuffling crowd, completely filling the next room from wall to wall.

She took a deep breath and narrowed her focus. Her goal was to get the rest of the team down here safely. The horde behind the wall couldn't get to them in the antechamber, so she would work on emptying that first.

The lever she had used to pry open the doors was about the length of her forearm. She jammed it between the doors as they tried to close again, leaving barely enough room for her to slip through. Before she tried to enter the room, however, she had a couple more details to take care of. She drew her pistol. As she readied herself, the first shambler squeezed itself into the space between the doors, groping blindly into the shaft. The shot went straight through the top of its skull, and it fell as limp as a puppet with cut strings, still wedged in the door. The two shamblers following it pushed the body through with their mindless advance, and it fell to the bottom of the shaft with a wet thunk. These two had oriented on the sound of the gunshot and had a better idea of where she was. They groped upwards at her with awkward menace, but their efforts were futile. She quickly sent them plummeting down the shaft with their compatriot. When no more followed, she swung her head down for a quick check. The room was empty. The antechamber's door was firmly closed. She swung herself around, landing lightly between the elevator doors, which were still struggling vainly to close, and hit the call button.

She watched the floor of the elevator descend through the crack in the door. When it was level with the floor, the elevator doors opened all the way, and she deftly caught her lever before it fell, compressed it again, and stashed it away in her belt. The faces of her teammates went from triumphant to dismayed as they looked past her to the room beyond.

"Well," said Stev slowly, "even we aren't going to be able to fight our way through that. Maybe we should have tried another route." His tone was neutral, but Mercy shot him a sour look anyway, and she tossed Kit's pack back to her with just a little too much force. Kit frowned at her; no matter the outcome, Kit had done her job and gotten them down here. It wasn't her fault if it had been the wrong choice.

They stood in an oasis of relative calm. The room was bare; the only occupants had been the shamblers Kit had sent into the elevator shaft. No corpses littered the ground here, and thick concrete walls surrounded them on three sides. On the fourth side, the shamblers banged and crashed against the plastic panels with terrifying force. There was no way the team was getting through that door without somehow eliminating the shamblers first, and it looked as though there were tens, dozens, maybe even a hundred on the other side of that scratched and muddled plastic pane. Kit looked at the door helplessly. If they opened it, they'd be mobbed in seconds. She just didn't see a way around that, and she couldn't escape a sinking feeling that they were running out of both time and options.

It was Avin who saw what she'd missed: a ventilation grate set high into the walls. He'd pulled Stev aside and was whispering urgently to him, gesturing at the grate. Kit hadn't even noticed it was there until she followed the motion of his hands. Stev seemed to be raising some objection. She pressed her lips together in frustration and determination both; she was pretty sure she knew what was causing the argument. She moved towards them swiftly, and before either could address her, she interrupted them.

"I'll do it." She shook her head when Stev tried to speak. "It could be our only chance at getting out of here."

"It's too risky," Stev said stubbornly. "I refuse to jeopardize anyone on this team." Kit caught his eye, and a flush crept up his face under her unwavering gaze. *This time*, she thought, so fiercely she almost believed he could hear her. *This time you care. After we've already paid a price in blood for your carelessness.*

"It's a risk, but a calculated one," Avin said softly, recapturing Stev's attention. "We already decided on this course of action. Backtracking now would only waste time we don't have."

"I understand the risk, Boss," Kit said stiffly.

"You can get in, but what are you going to do once you're there? You can't fight all those things by yourself!" Stev responded angrily.

"And I don't plan to. I'll scout out the situation, see if we can use the vents to get past that horde, and then come back to report." There was no point in antagonizing Stev further, since she was going whether he gave the order or not. Stev stared at her for a long moment, brow furrowed.

"Fine," he finally said. "But don't take any risks!"

"*I* don't take unnecessary risks." Kit responded tightly. As if he was justified in questioning her judgment.

Stev raised his eyebrow skeptically. "You expect me to buy that after the stunt you pulled with the concussion bot earlier?" He walked away, shaking his head and grumbling.

"Nice catch," Kit said to Avin with a small smile, indicating the vent. Avin hesitated as though he wanted to say something. Instead, he nodded jerkily and walked away.

She made her way over to the vents to examine them more closely. It was going to take some real work to get into those vents. The construction was old, antiquated even. The grate cover was made of heavy, thick metal, secured by big, bulky screws. It was set near the ceiling, which was quite high, so she had to climb up the wall to get a closer look. A couple experimental tugs showed that tools were going to be necessary. She gave her lever a try, to no avail. This was a job for Avin and his box of tricks.

In the end, after his specialized tools proved too modern for the job, Avin found a clever way of jamming the flat end of her lever into the screw heads and twisting. It was surprising how easily they came out when pressed in just the right way.

It was also easier to get into the shaft than she'd expected. The interior was smooth, flat, and not as small as it looked; she was able to slither along on her stomach with very little trouble. Excitement coursed through her as she approached a corner. This wasn't like their usual missions in the Stacks—same layout, same procedure, same outcome, over and over. Anything at all could be around that corner.

She squirmed around the sharp turn with a little difficulty. Now she was heading in the right direction, if going towards a room full of monstrous creatures that wanted to eat her could really be called the right direction. Soon, she came to another offshoot of the shaft, a second grate visible at its end. She knew she hadn't gone far enough yet to bypass the milling mass in the next room, but she couldn't resist taking a look. She pushed herself around the corner and up to the grate, peering cautiously out.

The horde had focused on her teammates beyond the plastic wall, shoving and banging and grasping in their direction. She watched them for a moment, perplexed. They weren't just feral, they were absolutely mindless. Even a wild animal could be scared away from its prey by a superior predator, but these things showed no sign of fear, anger, or any other emotion. They sought their goal with complete single-mindedness. What scientific research could have gone so horribly wrong? She withdrew and resumed her progress down the main shaft.

Several more vent openings led back to the shambler-filled hall, and she passed them by. Finally, she came to a crossroads. The vent went off in two different directions with no sign of a grate either way. She used her lever to scratch a rough mark in the wall of the vent. The last thing she wanted was to get lost in a cramped labyrinth. She chose a direction at random and crawled onward.

She passed three more grate openings that showed her nothing but clusters of shamblers too large to fight unaided. The fourth, however, showed a relatively unoccupied and intact lab. Only one shambler was actually inside the room; all the others were milling in the hallway outside. The door looked like sturdy metal. If she could only get it closed before any more of them came in, she could investigate some of what had been going on here. Maybe here, on the most secure and secret level, there would be answers for her raging curiosity. On the other hand, slamming the door would attract the attention of all the shamblers in the hall. This would become a dead end—useless from a practical point of view. Was her curiosity worth the risk? She fought a brief but impassioned war within herself. Curiosity won.

She pulled out her lever, still in its compact form, and began to carefully remove the screws from the grating. She paused. Why were the screws on the inside of this grate, when they had been on the outside of the other? But there was no sense in questioning good luck. She started in on the second screw.

When the grate was safely removed and shoved into the shaft behind her, she poked her head out of the frame, planning her assault. The shambler inside the room seemed to be fully engrossed in something on the ground, giving her as good an opening as she was going to get. She climbed out of the shaft with tiny, measured movements, clinging high on the wall. She circled the room in a scuttling, sideways motion, staying up and out of sight. When she reached the door, stealth was no longer possible. It needed to be shut and locked quickly to leave her free to deal with the room's tenant. She glanced over her shoulder to check that it was still in the same spot, and saw that the object on the floor that had it so totally enthralled was another corpse. It was pulling entrails out of the belly and eating them greedily. The corpse's face was still intact, her eyes open and staring blankly. Kit's stomach turned as she averted her gaze.

The door opened inwards, which was a stroke of luck. If it had swung out into the hallway, this maneuver would have been far riskier. Stev's warnings wandered through her mind, but she shrugged them off. She positioned herself on the wall behind the open door, near its hinges, took a deep breath, and sprang into motion. She released her grip on the wall with one hand and both feet; with only one hand anchored, she skidded down the wall, swinging her legs as she fell. Her feet connected solidly with the door, sending it slamming into its frame.

The shambler's head snapped up from its meal, its bloodstained mouth gaping at her in a mindless approximation of shock. It stood up heavily and shuffled its feet, reaching in her direction as bits of intestine tumbled from its lips, forgotten in its quest for a fresh food source. It took no more than three steps before its eye exploded from the force of her shot.

That single opponent had been the least of her worries. Already there was banging on the outside, and she didn't trust the very simple lock to hold against the combined determination of the crowd in the hallway, though she turned it anyway. She found several old-fashioned and very heavy file cabinets and shoved them in front of the door, then piled odds and ends on top of them until the entire window was blocked off as well. If they couldn't hear or see her, maybe they'd lose interest.

Safe for the moment, she turned to the room's other contents. It was full of scientific apparatus, test tubes, dishes, and other miscellaneous equipment that she didn't even try to figure out. Instead, she went straight for the computer. It was another bulky antique, but she figured it was still her best chance at getting any relevant information. After some fiddling, she got the thing booted up. It was strange to use a machine that couldn't interface with her MDU and needed all physical commands. Security was minimal, only a couple of easily circumvented passwords. Navigating to the most recently viewed documents was also simple; problems arose, however, when she tried to understand the contents. She was no scientist; she didn't know what all those little dots and interconnecting lines meant. She used her MDU to take snapshots, then moved on. After browsing a few more incomprehensible files, she found her prize: the personal journal of the scientist who had run this particular lab. Kit pulled an overturned chair upright and sat down to read.

Day 1: Today we embark on possibly the most ambitious project in medical history. If we succeed, mankind will never need to fear injury or illness again. Perhaps even old age will be conquered! We could live forever! Lofty and grandiose it may sound, but in the future, they will look back on this day as historic. I may be just a tiny cog in this great machine, but I'm proud to be so.

Day 2: We dove into our work today with so much enthusiasm. I never dreamed infected tissue samples could be so exciting. The nano-machines will be the perfect symbiote for the human race. We should start getting results soon.

Nano-machines? That could certainly explain a lot. The rapturous tone of the journal entries was disturbing, though, considering how it had all turned out. Kit skimmed ahead to see if she could figure out the purpose of it all. As it progressed, the entries became less frequent and more informative.

Week 4: The experiments are progressing well. The nanos are now perfectly mimicking the surrounding skin cells. They blend in almost too well; it can be problematic to differentiate them for study. We are nearly ready to expand the study to muscle and organ tissue, and from there to bone, nerves, everything!

Week 7: The mimic nanos are working almost flawlessly. In skin samples with damaged or abnormal cells, they attack the abnormalities and replace them, replicating perfectly healthy cells. We're still having some trouble with other types of cells, however—mostly the nervous system, and especially the brain. Nerve damage is always the hardest to heal, though, so I'm not discouraged.

Week 12: The study is progressing fast. Too fast, according to some. Dustin is constantly badgering Charles and me about consequences and caution. Thankfully, Charles has enough vision to disregard him. He understands as well as I what we have to gain, and the sooner we accomplish our goals, the sooner we can heal the world. Imagine a world with no more cancer, no more heart or liver or kidney disease, a world where broken bones mend themselves in a matter of hours and scars are unheard of. We'll be progressing to animal testing soon. Lucky mice!

Things were starting to make more sense. Kit grimaced. She was pretty sure she knew where this was going, but she skipped to the end anyway.

Week 64: Some of the staff have started falling ill. The symptoms are odd, as if all their organs are shutting down. We're doing our best to maintain them in the infirmary, and have called in additional medical staff. We're keeping them on life support for now, and Charles and I are stepping up the final stages of the mimic nanos. Once it's complete, it won't matter what's wrong with them. The mimics will fix it. The mimics will fix everything. Everyone will live.

The last entry wasn't dated at all. It looked more like a letter than a journal entry, and Kit suspected that it was the last thing the mysterious scientist had ever written.

To whomever may find this:

I'm sorry. I'm so sorry. You have to know, you must believe that we were only trying to do good here. We were supposed to save the world. But we were so hasty, so sure of ourselves, and it all went wrong. There were so many clues that the mimics weren't working quite the way we expected, but it was working!

Charles wanted so badly to be the first human test subject, for science and for humanity. This was his project and his lab and his whole life. I just wanted him to live. I wanted the cancer that was gnawing him from the inside to disappear, and then we would have all the time in the world. He was going to die anyway, he said, so what was the point in putting the experiment off? The worst that would happen is that we would fail and he would die a little bit sooner.

If I'd had any idea how bad the worst could be, I never would have let him do it. I would have killed him myself rather than let him infect himself with the mimics. But I had no idea, and neither did he.

It wasn't long before Charles started showing the same symptoms as the poor, sick people in the infirmary, and we realized that it wasn't a mysterious disease that the mimics could cure. The mimics were causing the illness. They weren't only replacing healthy cells anymore; they were replacing all of them. By prolonging the life and suffering of those poor souls in the infirmary, we let the nanos spread to every cell in their bodies until they weren't even really human anymore, just shells in the shape of a human. The replication took a massive amount of energy, leaving them continually starving to death, but unable to actually digest anything. Every cell in the stomach was in the midst of being consumed at the same time.

When we realized what had happened, we knew we had to let them die. It was a kindness at this point. The mimicked nerve cells were only minimally functional. In the midst of a normal, healthy brain, they could fill in the gaps, but a brain made only of mimic cells was almost entirely vegetative. We let them go and focused on saving Charles.

It was not the worst mistake we made, but it was the most catastrophic. The poor souls died, but the mimics lived. They weren't dependent upon the whole system of the body to function, and once any remaining human cells withered away, it took up its primary purpose again: multiply. To multiply, it needed energy. For energy, it needed food. The bodies of the dead rose up to feed on anything that could possibly provide the mimics with the energy to multiply themselves, including plants, animals...and humans.

It spread like wildfire, and we were powerless to contain it. Any mimic nano that managed to get inside a person's body would immediately begin the process of replication. The mimic couldn't get through healthy skin, but any wounds, any at all, and you were susceptible. We tried to contain them, we really did. But when anyone in your midst could suddenly turn, how do you prevent it from spreading?

It's all over for us. The building has been locked down, and I pray no one tries to come in after us. I pray that this ends with us, that the mimics eventually starve and die. If someone does come in and find this...please believe that I never meant for any of this to happen. I'm sorry...so very very sorry. Forgive me! Forgive me, my poor Charles, for not stopping you, for not realizing the danger, for leaving you to die alone...

You cannot judge me more harshly than I judge myself, but have pity on me, and let the memory of my life end here. I prefer to die forgotten than be remembered as a villain by history and science. If there is life after death, I hope to find redemption there, for I will not find it in this world.

Forgive me.

Rose Greyridge

Kit sat for a moment, staring at the screen. It was no longer possible to view the situation here as one more military operation. She shouldn't get emotionally involved, she knew that, but Rose's testimony had now inescapably colored this tragedy in her mind. She stood, moved towards the dead woman on the floor, and looked at her more closely.

The face was strongly boned, probably upwards of forty, handsome rather than pretty. Her chestnut brown hair had a few strands of early gray. Her dead features were frozen in an expression of despair.

The lack of damage anywhere but her abdomen seemed unusual to Kit, until she noticed that there was something clenched tightly in one of her hands. She knelt down to get a better look, trying to ignore the mass of entrails glistening on the floor beside her. The corpse gripped a syringe tightly in her hand. That would explain her condition; she had likely killed herself before the shamblers had found her, so there had been no struggle, no noise or movement to draw their attention. Just the one had stumbled upon her and considered her a free meal. Kit reached out and carefully pried the syringe from the stiff fingers. She examined it carefully, but there was no way to tell what had been in it. There was, however, a gold ring that had been placed around the base of the syringe, nestled in the palm of Rose's hand. An engraving on the inside of the band read: *For my summer Rose. Love, C.* Kit's stomach contracted painfully and she swallowed around a lump in her throat. Without quite knowing why, she slipped the ring into a pocket. Carefully, she closed Rose's glassy eyes. Now Rose wouldn't have to stare endlessly at all the ruin she'd helped to create. Then Kit moved to the computer, closed Rose's letter, and shut the machine down.

Chapter Six

Back in the vent, Kit lay still for a moment and rested her head on her forearms, the metal of the vent cool against her stomach. Taking deep breaths and monitoring her own vitals through her MDU, she tried to process the whole story she had just learned—Rose, Charles, the nanos...

Her head jerked up so quickly that it banged against the top of the vent. She'd been using the MDU to scan for infection. Would it have picked up machines? She quickly broadened the scope of the scan to find anything even vaguely abnormal. All she received were notifications of small injuries of which she was already well aware. Feeling a little shaky (her MDU helpfully informed her that this was due to elevated stress hormones before she mentally swatted her vitals into background processes), she decided the best course of action was to get on with her mission.

The vent soon came to a dead end at another shambler-filled room. She was forced to squirm backwards until she reached a turnoff. There, she was able to turn around and return to the first crossroads, past Rose's lab. Taking the other path, she dutifully checked each grate along the way for any hint of the exit. Finally another dead end loomed before her. She was about to return in defeat—until she noticed that this shaft dead-ended at a grate. When she scooted up to it, she saw that unlike all the others along this path, it let out into a hallway rather than a lab or storeroom. And there, across from her in big red letters, was a sign that read "EMERGENCY EXIT" with a helpful arrow beneath it.

She would have liked to investigate further on her own, but there were too many shamblers roaming the hall for individual exploration. She wiggled in reverse, turned, and made her way back to the others.

When she emerged from the grate in the antechamber, she found Avin sitting directly beneath it—so much so that she had to move to one side to avoid him as she descended to the floor. He had scavenged some metal chairs from another floor and was busy sawing off the legs and welding them together to make a ladder—a smart move if the rest of the team, with their heavy packs and less flexible uniforms, needed to get into the vent. He jumped up when he saw her, though she wasn't sure whether he was relieved or merely startled. She shot him a smile and a thumbs up on her way to report to Stev. She almost thought she saw the corners of his mouth twitch upward in reply, but he turned back to his work so quickly that she couldn't be sure.

Stev greeted her return with a scowl; it was quickly becoming his sole expression down here. She told him all that she had found out regarding the mimic nano-machines and the path to the emergency exit, leaving out only the particulars relating to Rose. Sentimentality didn't have any bearing on their mission.

By the time she was done, Stev's brow had furrowed. "Are you sure that's the best way through?" There was a plaintive note in his voice. Mercy, who had left Carrie's side to listen to Kit's report, gave a sharp laugh.

"Afraid you won't fit, Boss?" she snickered. Kit gave Stev's wide, muscular frame an appraising look, then glanced at the relatively small vent opening.

"I'll fit if I have to," Stev growled. "But only if I have to."

"The alternative is to fight through that," Kit replied, jerking her chin at the crowd of shamblers still banging on the window.

Stev sighed. "Vent it is. Do we have anything that could be used to grease it? Just in case?" Mercy burst out laughing, and Stev looked hurt.

In the end, Stev's worries proved unfounded. Even his broad shoulders were able to squeeze through the opening to the ventilation highways, though he still wasn't happy about it. The entire trip was punctuated by Stev alternately insisting that he was fine and grumbling that his shoulders were getting rubbed raw. Avin followed behind Stev, keeping a lubricant handy in case it was needed. Mercy brought up the rear, following Carrie. There had been a brief hiccup when Carrie panicked at the thought of entering the shaft, but Mercy had managed to soothe her. It took twice as long to get to the final grate with the rest of the team along, everyone shoving their packs in front of them, but at least no one actually got stuck. When they finally got close, she shushed Stev's mutterings. The last thing they needed was a group of shamblers waiting outside while they tried to maneuver him out of the vent.

It didn't look like the scuffing and shuffling noises of their approach had been noticed. There were a few shamblers in sight, and it would still be tricky getting out, but at least they weren't going to be dropping directly into waiting maws. She went to work with the lever, noting with a vague unease that these screws were also on the inside. She caught the grate deftly before it fell, and passed the rectangle of heavy metal to Stev.

Moving carefully, Kit lowered herself out of the grate, a watchful eye on the shamblers. They hadn't noticed her yet. Stev dropped his pack down to her, and she slung it onto her back to keep it out of the way in the tricky operation to come. Stev eased himself forward to the grate opening while Kit clung to the well beneath it, but he couldn't get his broad shoulders to fit through the opening. He squirmed backwards a few inches, then extended his hands to Kit, raising an eyebrow. She grimaced and grasped his wrists in both hands. Then she braced herself against the wall and pushed off with her legs, using all her weight and strength to pull him out of the vent like a cork from a bottle. Kit quickly released her foothold on the wall, and slid down, cushioning and slowing Stev's ungraceful exit. This was effective, but not particularly quiet or stealthy. The shamblers' heads began to turn, and Kit and Stev quickly scrambled to their feet. Kit glanced behind her and saw

Avin sliding gracefully out of the aperture. Though he was taller than the women, his slender, wiry frame was much better suited for this than Stev's bulky muscles. He turned in time to catch Kit's pack, which had been given to Carrie so that Kit could lead the way more effectively, then helped the less agile scientist down from the grate.

Since Avin was manning the vent's exit, Kit returned her focus to the shamblers. Stev had already started a careful advance, making sure that none of them got too close to the vent before everyone had vacated it. Close quarters combat with these things was risky, but the noise of gunfire had its own special dangers. She looked to Stev for guidance, but before she could begin to ask the question, he opened fire. That answered that. Moving down the hallway in the opposite direction from Stev, she began to pick off the nearest shamblers. They cleared the hallway in both directions as far as they could, then regrouped.

"Let's move out," Stev said, glancing at the red arrow on the exit sign. Kit moved to reclaim her pack from Carrie, but the scientist shook her head and shrugged the straps onto her own shoulders, struggling a little when they got caught up on her lab coat's wider sleeves. It occurred to Kit how useless, how defenseless she must feel. Remembering how Carrie had grasped at the railing in the elevator as a weapon, Kit reached into her belt pouch and snatched up the telescoping lever. Extending it with a flick of her wrist, she handed it to Carrie and saw her eyes light up as she took it. Even though her grip was white-knuckled with nerves, her shoulders were a bit more square, her step a little more confident as they set out towards the promised escape.

They soon realized that the sign wasn't there because the exit was right around the corner; these signs lined the walls at regular intervals to guide panicked scientists in an emergency. Barring the occasional shambler surprising them by popping out of an open doorway, they followed the signs to their end with relative ease. They were able to clean out the shamblers ahead of them without too much trouble, and the ones behind them never caught up. The trail of signage led to a set of red doors. When Kit looked up, she saw another big red sign above the swinging doors that read "INFIRMARY."

Stev cursed under his breath. This was the point of origin for the infection, where the first shamblers had risen. It was bound to be crawling with the monsters. Kit steeled herself. Stev sent out a query ping to all of them, and Kit responded in the affirmative. She didn't know if she was actually ready, but they couldn't stay where they were. A crowd of shamblers had slowly followed them as they traversed the hallways, and it was only a matter of time before they had enemies both in front and behind.

Stev and Mercy shoved through the doors first; Kit and Avin followed, carefully keeping Carrie in the center of the group. Kit had expected hordes of shamblers, all the first victims who had started the epidemic. She was ready to open fire, ready to make a stand against the mob. What awaited them was a different scene entirely.

There was only one shambler in the room—if it could be called that. It couldn't actually shamble anywhere. Its massive bulk filled the room, flowing over cots and tables, shoving up against walls and cabinets. The only signs it had once been human were a swollen head and huge, bloated arms perched atop the fleshy mountain. Most of its body was a pinkish-gray mound, covered in fist-sized lumps like massive tumors under the skin. The whole creature heaved and rolled in reaction to their abrupt entrance, and horribly veined, bloodshot eyes focused on their little group. With a groan, the distended arms reached forward to grasp handfuls of its own flesh, and the creature pulled its head and arms forward, rolling over its body like a great wave.

As one, they opened fire, but a couple bullets weren't enough to stop this monster. They had to pulp the entire head, and then the arms and trunk exploded like a popped zit, leaving behind a sea of flesh. Kit lowered her gun with a sigh of relief. Disgusting, but not as dangerous as she'd feared.

Before she had finished congratulating herself, the swell of flesh began to quiver. At the top, a larger lump appeared. It grew at a startling rate, humping itself up into a huge, tumescent growth, and then it opened its eyes. The tumor sprouted a head and a new set of arms. A crease in the head split into a new mouth, emitting a threatening, guttural noise, and it rolled toward them again.

Once again, the head was pulped before it could reach them, but while they were taking care of it, three more tumorous heads were growing behind it, and a roiling behind that indicated that an even greater assault was to come. Considering how long it was taking to destroy one head, there was no way they could hold off many more.

Kit's brain kicked into high gear. These nano-machines still needed energy to replicate themselves, so this thing must be using a massive amount of energy in order to build multiple heads and torsos. If they could hold out long enough, they might actually starve the thing—but they needed a way to quicken the process. She glanced at the first head they had destroyed. Its remains were disappearing under a fold of flesh, the blood and pus absorbing into the greater mass. She darted forward and yanked the hunk of blood, bone, and brain matter out of its crevice, then chucked it out the door behind her, straight into a group of milling shamblers who had stopped a few feet outside the door. They fell on it like it was a delicacy, but showed no interest in coming any closer or attacking Kit.

"Oy!" Stev yelled at her. "What are you doing? Eyes forward!"

"Remove any pieces you can!" Kit yelled back. "It's eating itself!"

Stev looked at her as if she was crazy, but Avin immediately darted in with lightning speed, farther onto the heaving sea of flesh than Kit would have felt comfortable venturing, and tossed a severed head to her. She, in turn, fed it to the shamblers outside.

The only good thing about the monster's multiple heads was that it seemed to have a very difficult time coordinating all of its torsos and arms. The groups of heads rolled at them much more slowly than the single ones had. The bulk of the monster became noticeably smaller, giving them more room to maneuver and making it easier to stay away from the heads. This advantage was counterbalanced by the fact that the whole team was tiring quickly. They had been fighting for a great deal of the day, and however seasoned and fit they were, it was draining. There were several near-disasters. Avin actually stumbled once, and Kit had to jump in to drag him out of harm's way. A head didn't quite die as soon as it needed to, and Mercy punched it in the ear, knocking it away before it could take a mouthful out of Stev.

Finally, the creature had exhausted nearly all its resources. It coalesced its remaining flesh into a bulbous sphere in the center of the room that came up to Kit's waist. It didn't bother with growing a torso or arms or even a head this time. The entire sphere sprouted gaping mouths on every side. With a loathsome quiver, it rolled right at them, mouths agape. The hail of bullets had no effect, and they were forced to scatter, spreading out around the room.

No matter how many bullets they put into it, the sphere continued its pursuit, snapping after them with toothy mouths and lolling tongues. Nothing seemed to affect it, and it had no protrusions for them to remove. There were more stumbles, more near misses, until Mercy actually tripped and fell. The sphere bore down on her. Stev dashed in and tried to pull her out of the way, but he was equally tired and he slipped on the blood-slick floor, missing her hand entirely. Kit sprinted toward them, but there was no way she could make it to Mercy in time.

Suddenly, someone else flashed in front of Kit. Carrie moved with a speed Kit had never suspected she possessed. Gripping the lever like a spear, Carrie raised it over her head and lunged at the sphere, driving the long piece of metal through its center. Every one of the mouths keened at once, an eery, high-pitched sound that vibrated through Kit's head. Carrie held the thing pinned to the floor, writhing against the metal skewer. It wrenched itself around, trying to reach Carrie, then expanded, inflating all over. Carrie hung onto the lever, refusing to let go. The mouths snapped at her, but she gritted her teeth and held her ground. Almost without thought, Kit found her gun raised. Her MDU targeted the precise center of the mass. Four shots blasted into the pulsing sphere from all sides, and it burst into a spray of blood, pus, and tissue fragments. The only part left was a huge, blue-gray brain, pierced straight through by the lever.

For a moment, there was utter silence. Then Carrie groaned and fell to her knees, her fingers finally slipping from the lever. Mercy dove across the floor to her, cushioning Carrie's collapse before she hit the ground. The woman was now nearly as covered in gore as she had been when they first met her. Her eyes were closed, as if that last desperate action had taken every bit of energy she possessed. The rest of them converged on her slowly, almost reverently. Kit knelt down beside Mercy and tried to clean Carrie's face as best she could, gently dabbing at the bloody mess. As she wiped bits of gloppy flesh out of Carrie's hair, Kit tried to think of a way to say thank you. It wasn't something she usually had to say; when you were part of a team, looking out for each other was expected. But now a scientist, a civilian, had saved Mercy's life—possibly all of their lives.

Stev knelt down beside Carrie. "Can you walk?" he asked with a much gentler tone than he had ever used with her before. She weakly shook her head.

"We have to get out soon," Avin hissed. "What if the only thing keeping the other shamblers out of here was that? They could come down on us at any minute."

"You have to get up, Carrie," Mercy said softly. "Or if you can't, I'll carry you. I owe you."

Once again, Carrie slowly shook her head. "I'm sorry, Mercy," she said in a whisper. "I can't go with you." Trembling, she lifted herself away from Mercy and held out an arm. Underneath the residue of the explosion, Kit saw that there was a raw, bleeding set of toothmarks. Kit choked, suddenly unable to catch her breath. In all the chaos, she hadn't seen Carrie get bitten.

"No...no!" Mercy gestured wildly in denial. "Come with us anyway, we'll figure something out, we'll find a cure!"

Carrie looked past her to Stev. "Don't let me turn into one of those things. Please." Stev nodded grimly, stood, and raised his gun.

"No!" yelled Mercy. She leaped to her feet and shoved Stev's gun down.

"It has to be done," Carrie said with quiet force.

"But you saved my life. If this has to be done, then I should be the one to do it." Mercy's voice was tight with grief, but her hands were steady. Carrie nodded in relief. Kit backed away, her throat constricted with grief and horror, and Carrie climbed to her feet, trembling but determined. She looked at each of them in turn, and then closed her eyes.

Mercy's eyes were bright. "Thank you," she whispered, then raised her gun. The shot cracked through the silence. Carrie crumpled to the ground.

They straightened Carrie's limbs and lifted her body onto the cleanest of the infirmary's cots. Kit hoped that would be sufficient to stop the shamblers from feeding on her remains before the place was demolished. Mercy carefully crossed Carrie's hands across her chest, then covered her still face with a white lab coat she scavenged from a closet. It was a strangely ceremonial gesture, all but archaic, but it felt right. The whole team stood a moment more in respectful silence before they were interrupted by a tentative scrabbling at the door. The shamblers were figuring out that the monster had been killed. Kit suspected that it had been as happy to absorb other shamblers as its own decapitated heads. Now it was more than time to leave.

The portal to the emergency exit was in the rear of the room. It was sealed tightly and had a large wheel on the door that spun to open it. For once, there was no lock. Somberly, they filed through the portal into the small, concrete-lined room beyond. An identical wheel could be used to reseal the door from the outside. Stev was the last one through; he turned the exterior wheel as tightly as he could.

They stood inside a cylinder made of smooth concrete, floored in metal. Except for the door they had come through, the walls were featureless. The long shaft stretched upwards into darkness, its base illuminated by two bulbs set into the floor. It was impossible to see the top.

As soon as the door was sealed behind them, the metal floor began to move smoothly upward. The concrete walls whizzed by as they ascended into darkness. This elevator was a far cry from the clunky, creaky specimen that had brought them down into the lab.

Kit stood with her head lowered, staring determinedly at the swiftly rising floor beneath her feet. She didn't want to think about Carrie, about Rose, about Charles Greyridge, riddled with cancer and then pumped full of nanos. She wanted her room in the barracks and night watches and drills. She wanted nice, routine missions and thoughtless celebrations at the bar. Even as she climbed closer and closer to the surface, she knew that simple life wouldn't greet her at the top. Instead there would be closed gates, the Faithful waiting outside them, and the strangely opulent life of the Elite.

The concrete ceiling of the shaft approached with alarming speed, but despite Kit's fears of being crushed into a pulp, the platform decelerated smoothly enough, leaving them standing in a pool of light, one trap door away from the outside.

The door looked like a manhole cover and was painfully heavy to their exhausted muscles. It took Kit, Avin, and Stev all heaving upwards to budge it. Mercy was too short to reach the ceiling, so was spared. A breath of fresh night air caressed Kit's cheeks when they finally managed to push the stubborn cover to one side. Kit reached into the circular hatch and hauled herself out like a shipwrecked sailor crawling out of the sea. Her muscles were screaming with fatigue, and even her climbers didn't help much. She immediately turned to help the rest, knowing that if she stopped moving at all, she wouldn't be able to keep going. It wasn't until everyone was outside that she took a moment to look around.

The laboratory was nowhere in sight. They stood on a rain-slick sidewalk. Close-set buildings towered over them, their mirrored sides reflecting a multitude of neon signs, flinging splashes of pink and green into the purple dusk. Steam wafted from dingy grates, giving the whole scene an air of the otherworldly.

The damp air crawled up Kit's spine like skeletal fingers. There was nothing familiar about this place. Bits of crumpled refuse blew about the street, landing in the puddles that filled the cracks and potholes. No bots appeared to collect them. No sentries came to accost the unit, despite the lateness of the hour. An eerie silence blanketed this place—the absence of a background buzz that Kit had taken for granted her entire life. Her heart began to pound. For once, her fight or flight response was tending heavily towards flight—but there was nowhere to run. She looked up, hoping that she would see a ceiling, confirming that they were still in the lab. Then they would just have to keep looking for the exit and everything would return to normal...

Beyond the mirror-sided buildings, far distant stars peeked through wisps of cloud. It could be an illusion, she desperately thought. But the lab had been way too small for anything of this size, even with the aid of optical illusions.

The faces of her teammates were equally unsettled as they took in their surroundings.

"Where are we?" Mercy whispered, her eyes wide. Kit could hear the vague hope in her voice. She was so new; maybe one of the veterans knew the way home. The hope died as no one answered.

Despair washed over Kit. For a brief glorious moment, she had thought they were done. Climb out, report, let someone else handle bombing the lab into rubble, go to sleep. She sat down on the sidewalk, pulled the biofilter off of her face, and closed her eyes for a second. When she opened them, the others had joined her on the ground.

"What do we do now?" she asked.

"We go on?" Stev said uncertainly. Then with more surety, he continued, "We've been all over the city on missions. If we keep walking, we're bound to come across something we recognize." He stood up. "Come on, everybody on their feet, let's move out."

No one moved. Stev's face turned red.

"Sit back down, Boss," Kit sighed. "We're all so tired we wouldn't know east from west right now. We have—" she checked her MDU. "Fourteen hours before our deadline. Plenty of time to get some rest before we start scouting out the area. If we can't make it back in fourteen hours, we'll have bigger problems to deal with than a missed report."

Anger and fear flickered across Stev's face in turn. Kit knew she shouldn't have countermanded his order, but she was too tired to care. She doubted Mercy and Avin were in much better shape, and Stev was still trying to process how he should react through the fog of his own exhaustion. Then Avin sat up sharply.

"Report," he repeated her last word as if it was a revelation. "We have to report as soon as possible."

"We will," Kit agreed, "after we get some rest."

"We have to report as soon as possible," Avin repeated stubbornly, a hint of panic coming into his voice, his eyes wide.

"We have fourteen hours," Kit said as patiently as she was able. "They won't even think to worry before that time is up." Gradually, the panic left his face and his posture relaxed. Kit looked at him askance. She'd never seen Avin lose his cool before—but today was full of firsts.

"I'm with Kit," Mercy said groggily. "I think if we tried to go on, I'd just end up sleepwalking." Stev, still standing, looked down at each of them in turn. Then, grudgingly, he sat down.

"I can see that none of you will be any use without some sleep," he said, as if the whole thing had been his idea. Kit barely stopped herself from rolling her eyes.

"What have we got left for food?" she asked instead. She produced her half-eaten jerky bar and a grain bar. They each still had their water ration, a little bubble of liquid encased in a soft plastic packet, but most of them had eaten at least a little bit of their two bar ration during the mission. They ended up with four whole bars and two halves—certainly not enough for a full meal for four very tired people. After careful consideration, Kit took one jerky bar and one grain bar out of the pile. She used her knife to slice each one into four pieces and distributed one quarter of grain and one of jerky to everyone. One water bag was torn open and passed around between the four of them. It was barely enough to dull the hunger, but their circumstances were uncertain, to say the least. No one protested.

They agreed on a four hour rest, leaving them ten hours leeway the next day. Since no doors were evident in any of the buildings, they set up a rudimentary camp around the manhole cover. Kit volunteered for first watch. She hated having her sleep interrupted. She loaned Mercy her field blanket since Mercy's had been lost somewhere along the way after it was given to Carrie. Soon, quiet breathing emanated from all three blanketed cocoons. Kit stood with her back against the building, leaning just enough to take the weight off her aching feet, but not so much that she could relax. She'd never fallen asleep standing up before, but it was fast becoming an option.

The quiet of the damp street was oppressive, to the point where the occasional buzz or flicker of the neon signs made her jump. To pass the time, she looked at the ones nearby. Most of the signs were only pictures—a palm tree, a star, a pirate ship. Kit was baffled. Another fizzle from an orange octopus made her start. She glanced down at her comatose comrades, splayed out around the manhole cover as if it was a campfire. Something about the glow from the lights inside the hole unnerved her. She didn't want their position to be visible. Yes, that must be it. She pushed off from the wall and dragged the cover back into place as quietly as she could. Then, activating a clock display on her MDU, she leaned against the wall and waited.

Chapter Seven

Three hours of sleep felt like three seconds. The concrete of the sidewalk wasn't the most comfortable bed, but the field blanket swathed around her was warm and her pack had made a serviceable pillow. And moving seemed like far too much effort.

Kit heard her teammates beginning to stir. Loathe to be the last lazybones to get up, she started to carefully limber up her stiff muscles. She couldn't suppress a groan when she heaved herself upright, though. Every part of her body felt abused.

She stretched her arms as far over her head as she could, feeling her shoulders pop satisfyingly, and surveyed their surroundings again. Everything looked exactly as it had when she'd gone to sleep, still shrouded in early morning darkness. Avin had taken fourth watch, and stood stoically, staring at the rest of them as they tried to coerce themselves into coherence.

"I woke up hoping yesterday was a dream," Mercy grumbled, yawning hugely.

"No such luck," Stev said.

"We need to get moving," was all Avin contributed.

Kit dug into their stores and handed out another two bars, divided into quarters. Stev looked irritated and Mercy glum, but there simply wasn't more to give. After this meal, there were only two half-bars left. Kit ate her ration slowly, trying to make it last, and Mercy and Stev did the same. Avin, on the other hand, inhaled his portion and then watched each bite the rest took, shifting his weight restlessly from one foot to the other.

"We have ten hours," Kit reminded him, keeping her voice as calm and patient as possible with only three hours of sleep and barely any food.

"We have to report as soon as we can," he replied.

Mercy snorted. "They don't care when or if we report. They'll probably torch the building one way or another."

"If we don't report, they'll think we've deserted!" Avin said, with some heat.

"Oh, I doubt it," Mercy replied offhandedly. "They'll just think we died in the lab."

"We have to report," Avin growled, his agitation growing.

"Don't you think we have bigger issues than reporting right now?" Mercy shot back, her temper roused.

"We have to report!" Avin repeated.

Kit looked at Stev, hoping he would defuse the situation, but he was simply watching, his jaws working methodically on a bite of jerky, brow furrowed. So...

"Settle down, you two," Kit said instead. "Priorities. First we figure out where we are, then we figure out where to go, then we report. Right?"

"Exactly," said Mercy triumphantly.

"That is logical," Avin agreed after a long pause.

It sounded simple when you spelled it out like that, but the truth was that Kit had no idea how to even begin figuring out where they were. She glanced up. Even if she had been able to gain any guidance from the sky, no stars were to be seen. The darkness of the early morning was compounded by low, heavy clouds. Once the sun came up, they might be able to get a sense of direction.

A thought occurred to her. "Do any of you have maps or navigational aids loaded in your MDUs?" she asked, her gaze turning hopefully towards Stev. After all, he had been in charge. She had never bothered with that stuff and only uploaded mission specific directions into her MDU—and promptly deleted them afterward. Stev shook his head, though. To her surprise, it was Mercy who answered.

"I have a compass app and some star charts," the younger girl volunteered. She flushed under their surprised glances. "I, uhm, took a bit of astronomy as an extra in school. And I like to collect unusual apps."

"Well, if the stars ever come out, the charts will be useful," Kit said. She hadn't been aware that astronomy had been an option in school, but she'd never been very scientifically-minded. "If they don't, the compass will at least make sure we don't wander in circles. Which way is north?"

Mercy's eyes unfocused for a moment, then widened. "Uhm, I don't think this was a very good app," she stammered. "It's just spinning all over."

Kit's eyebrows raised involuntarily. Compass apps were generally infallible, homing in on directional beacons maintained by the Congress at the four corners of the city. They weren't much use to the ORG, but regular law enforcement depended on them for quick guidance to crimes in progress.

"How...unusual," Avin said, narrowing his eyes at Mercy.

"Oh, lay off," she scowled back at him.

"We're no worse off with a malfunctioning compass than we were without any compass," Kit pointed out. "It's not Mercy's fault if she got a bugged app."

"I can take a look at the source code and try to fix it, but it'll probably take too much time," Mercy offered. Kit suddenly remembered her drunken ramblings about MDU programming, what seemed like a lifetime ago in their suite at the Congressional Seat. Apparently that hadn't been just theoretical knowledge.

This offer didn't diminish the suspicion on Avin's face in the least. Kit glanced at Stev again. She kept expecting him to chime in. She wasn't lead—nor did she want to be.

"We should probably be heading out soon. Right, Boss?" Kit placed just the slightest stress on the last word. Stev was stubborn and recalcitrant, but he wasn't stupid. He roused himself with a twitch and glanced around, noting everyone's readiness. He straightened his shoulders, thrust his chest out, and started in on his most unconvincing bluster as he went through a final inspection, exactly as if they were in the ORG courtyard about to leave on a routine mission. Kit kept from rolling her eyes through force of will. Mercy didn't bother.

"Ok, let's move out," Stev barked finally, his voice echoing strangely in the quiet, dark street. He set off down the street quite as if he knew exactly where he was going. Kit figured it didn't matter. One way was as good as another right now. She would have scouted in each direction first to see if there was any difference, or perhaps scaled a building for a better view—but it wasn't her call.

They came to first one cross street, then another. Both looked exactly like the street they were on, lined with mirrored panels that warped their reflections disconcertingly as they passed. At each intersection, Stev waved them forward. At the third intersection, the road they were on ended. Faced with a choice of going left or right, Stev hesitated. They paused for a long moment behind him, their terrifyingly tall and slender reflections staring down at them from across the street.

Losing patience, Kit stepped forward to get a good view down the perpendicular road. She couldn't see an end in either direction, nor a shift towards more normal city architecture. No wonder Stev had frozen.

Suddenly, soldiers were all around them. Kit's first thought was that they had sprung out of the reflective walls of the buildings. Then her brain caught up, and she saw that they were wearing, of all ridiculous things, rocket packs. They had dropped from above, catching the team entirely by surprise.

Kit's hand flickered towards her weapon out of habit, but she forestalled the motion immediately. They were completely surrounded, and if these people had meant them immediate harm, they'd already be dead.

The soldiers looked very well equipped, though none of their armament was even vaguely familiar to Kit. They were outfitted in something that looked like a slimmed down version of police exo-armor. Thick, shiny blue plates covered them from head to foot, clinging to some sort of flexible bodysuit underneath. It looked impressive, but to Kit's trained eye, it seemed like it would be heavy and awkward to move in. Still, their ambushers moved as freely as if they wore regular clothing. Heavy helmets with reflective visors covered all but the lower halves of their faces, leaving her with few clues about their intentions. Their guns were large and threatening, covered with little knobbly bits and flashing lights that seemed to have no purpose other than to evoke mechanical menace.

"Red or blue?" barked one of their mysterious assailants.

Stev moved to the forefront with a creditable imitation of his normal swagger, but Kit could tell he was badly shaken.

"We are the Elite of the ORG," he said importantly, squaring his shoulders. "We demand to be taken to the Congress. We have an urgent report."

The spokesman's lips tightened with disapproval beneath his visor. "Red or blue?" he asked insistently. "Are you rebels or loyalists?"

"We are loyal to the Congress," Stev said, sounding confused and affronted.

Suddenly, the guns were put up. All the soldiers relaxed. The leader pushed up his visor, showing a strong, square-jawed face with slightly squinty, deep-set eyes. A shock ran through Kit when she realized that he wasn't fitted with an MDU. He didn't even have the connectors installed. As more visors retracted, she saw that the lack was universal. They couldn't simply be a division of the police, then. Kit doubted any of the police officers could even get dressed without directions from their MDU.

"Here, soldiers," said the leader, holding out a handful of blue bands. "Put these on. You don't want to be mistaken for rebels. It's bad for your health."

Warily, Kit accepted one of the bands. What was she supposed to do with it? She glanced around surreptitiously, but the rest of her team were standing around awkwardly, equally unsure of what to do next.

"Let's head back to base so you can report," the leader continued, oblivious to their confusion. Avin's eyes lit up. Kit looked at Stev questioningly. Were they really just going to go along with this?

Apparently they were. He set off after the strange soldiers without even a token protest. She shrugged and followed. At least they were heading towards someone in authority who would, she hoped, be able to point them towards home.

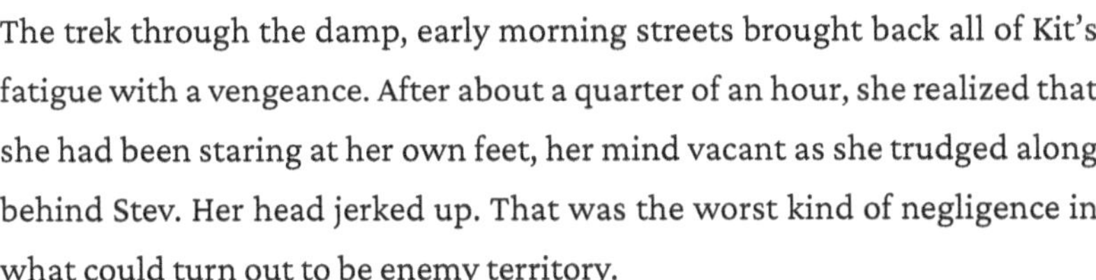

The trek through the damp, early morning streets brought back all of Kit's fatigue with a vengeance. After about a quarter of an hour, she realized that she had been staring at her own feet, her mind vacant as she trudged along behind Stev. Her head jerked up. That was the worst kind of negligence in what could turn out to be enemy territory.

The view had changed. Instead of endless rows of reflective towers, there was now a great deal of variation, in building height and design if not color or material. The flat roofs of the buildings looked almost like stairs. Now there were doors and windows scattered amongst the shiny panels, and the panels themselves looked less black than blue. Some of the buildings had square columns supporting balconies or incongruous rotundas. Kit itched to turn on her climbers and scamper away to explore, her fatigue momentarily forgotten. It looked like a playground for someone like her.

In another few minutes, they came to a tall barricade with a wide gate, both made of the same material as the buildings.

"Make sure you're wearing your armbands," their leader admonished. Kit still had the blue band in her hand, and she looked down at it skeptically. She doubted she could get it onto her arm with one hand, and their escort was already striding up to the gate ahead. Intending to loop it around temporarily, she raised the thing to her upper arm. To her dismay, it began to writhe. Before she could react, it had tied itself in a secure but comfortable knot above her bicep. The team looking equally surprised—but the gate had swung open with startling speed for something so large, and their escort was already moving through it. There was no time to ponder the armbands, nor question whether following people they didn't know inside a fortified compound was a good idea. It was either rush to catch up or made a break for it in the opposite direction. And Stev was already hurrying forward, slapping on his own armband as he went.

Within the walls was a small town in itself. The designer of these buildings had eschewed the mirror tiles of the towers outside for a more practical
concrete and metal girder construction. To the left was an armory, where a
steady stream of soldiers went in empty handed and came out laden down
with guns, rocket boosters, and those heavy-visored helmets. On the right
were two linked buildings which Kit suspected were living quarters, since
those lounging outside had an off-duty attitude about them. A surprising
number of people swarmed throughout the complex, despite the early hour.
By Kit's MDU, it was about three in the morning.

All of those details only registered in her peripheral consciousness,
though. At the end of the central path, unmistakably the centerpiece of the
whole operation, rose a building so baffling, so impossible, that Kit's mind
refused to grasp its existence.

Its snowy stone walls towered over the other buildings inside the complex. Intricately carved stone columns lined its steps. Massive wooden doors
bound in shining silver metal stood open to the world. Light flooded from
windows made of hundreds of tiny panes of sparkling glass.

Kit blinked until her eyes watered, barely aware that her entire team had
stopped in their tracks. Reality had just spun around a few times and then
folded in on itself. The Congressional Seat was the single most iconic piece
of architecture in the entire city. It was impossible not to recognize it.

Mercy edged closer to Kit. "Am I dreaming?" she whispered out the side
of her mouth, without taking her eyes from the building before them.

"If you're dreaming, I am too," Kit murmured.

Unnerved by this new development, the last thing that would have
crossed Kit's mind was confronting any of the soldiers that buzzed around
them with a demand for answers. She firmly supported the strategy of keeping her mouth shut until she knew what was going on. Stev, predictably, did
not agree.

"What are you people playing at here?" he demanded angrily. Kit winced
as his voice boomed around the courtyard. She had a sudden flashback to

the yard at the ORG, watching the new recruits flush with embarrassment. How the tables had turned...

All but the spokesman for the soldiers that had captured them had skittered off to other business while she had been distracted. She still didn't know his name—or anything about him at all.

"I don't understand your terminology," he responded politely, brow furrowed mildly.

"I want to know what is going on, and I want to know now!" Stev bellowed.

"I am escorting you to our superiors so that you can make a report," was the only response, then the man turned and continued towards the Congressional Seat.

Kit could see Stev's jaw jutting stubbornly, his shoulders tensing, and she was sure that he was either going to plant himself obstinately in the courtyard and refuse to follow or actually attack the man. She tensed, ready to react, though she had no idea what she would actually do.

Luckily, before she had to make that decision, Avin swept in, murmuring soothingly to Stev.

"He said *our* superiors," Avin pointed out quietly. "And he relaxed immediately when you told him we were loyal to the Congress. This has to be some sort of Congressional outpost. Who else would dare to replicate the Congressional Seat?"

He had a point. There was no way someone could replicate the building in this sort of detail without an intimate knowledge of the original—and this one was much newer. It seemed that, against all odds, even this strange place was under the power of the Congress.

She should feel relieved. This was what she had so ardently hoped for when she was stuck underground in a laboratory overrun by monsters—to just go home. But her nerves refused to settle. The thought that they were soon to be loaded into a transport and shipped back to the real Congressional Seat brought no comfort. Instead, she thought of that bug she had found in their room, right before they had been shipped off on this impossible, inexplicably hellish mission with no information, no backup, and no special equipment to speak of. Somehow she didn't feel any less scared knowing that this place was Congress-run.

Stev's face relaxed. He obviously didn't share her apprehension. Avin looked like he had been spared an execution. The two men now followed behind their escort with no hesitation. Glancing sideways at Mercy, Kit was surprised by her blank expression. She had expected at least a grimace or eye roll at Stev's behavior, but there was not even a flash of her usual mixture of temper and humor.

Kit was assailed by a sense of the surreal as she climbed the stone stairs of the building. They were much lighter than the original, unstained by years of dirt and wear and war. This must be a fairly new outpost, she thought with a frown, for this many soldiers to have left so few signs of their presence.

The entrance hall looked the same, though Kit couldn't be exactly sure. She had never expected to see another building like this. Portraits lined the hall, sans the protective cases. She wasn't sure if they showed the same people, but she felt like she remembered the one that featured a rather rotund little woman in a purple blazer. Why would they have bothered duplicating the artwork in an outpost of soldiers? She couldn't shake her suspicion, nor her unease.

Her heart skipped a beat as the realization hit her. It was the colors. There was no black or gold anywhere! No banners outside, no drapery inside, nothing. Everywhere, from the decor to the armor of their escort, was blue and silver. Why would Congress change the palette that symbolized their control for the benefit of a single outpost?

She forced herself to keep walking. If there was ever a time to keep her mouth shut and her eyes open, this was it. Let Stev and Avin believe that they were returning to the welcoming arms of the Congress and the ORG. That would lull their hosts into a false sense of security. She would keep a suspicious eye out and discover the truth. And so, she suspected, would Mercy.

They were escorted into a room that dwarfed anything Kit had seen before. It had a staggeringly high, vaulted ceiling supported by rows of columns that marched beside a center aisle. People scurried all around like insects within a giant nest. At the far end of the room, several steps led up to a raised dais with a blue carpet. A massive metal octagon, gleaming a deep brushed silver, stood on the platform. Its surface radiated a soft blue light, casting eerie shadows and deep hollows on the face of the man behind it.

"General Westen, sir," their escort barked, saluting smartly. "Four new recruits, private level."

Kit bristled. She didn't know much about old fashioned military ranks—she'd memorized them for a military history quiz back in school, but then had promptly forgotten the difference between a lieutenant and a corporal and a captain—but she did know that a private was the newest and greenest of them all.

The General's eyes raked over them. "At ease, recruits," he said in a voice like gravel rolling down a hill. "From the looks of you, I doubt you'll be privates for long." Kit forced herself to outwardly relax. She couldn't afford to take offense over a rank that meant nothing to her and possibly arouse suspicion.

Stev stepped forward and imitated the other man's salute. Kit cringed inwardly; it looked unnatural and awkward when Stev did it. Saluting was as outdated as the military rankings. General Westen didn't seem to mind, however. With a gracious nod, he allowed Stev to address him.

"Sir," Stev said confidently, "we are the Elite of the ORG. We will require transport back to the Congressional Seat. We have an urgent report to make." Stev was practically smiling by the time he finished, so sure and so relieved that things finally were making sense again. Kit had to stop her lip from curling in frustrated contempt. This place only made sense if you willfully closed your eyes to everything around you.

"So you are not here to join our fight?" The General frowned.

"Unfortunately, sir, our other duties prevent us from assisting you, unless ORG headquarters or the Congress reassigns us here," Stev answered smoothly,

"That is unfortunate," the General responded, still frowning, "since I've never heard of either this ORG or the Congress." Confusion and unease replaced the surety in Stev's expression, and Kit felt a little guilty for her earlier condescension. Not a lot, but a little. That was the face of a man who was out of his depth and knew it. But would never admit it.

"You must have!" Avin cried, his voice crackling with panic. Kit glanced at him in surprise. She had been too caught up in watching Stev's reaction to notice Avin's. Confront the man with the walking undead, tumescent monstrosities, and bizarre spacial anomalies, and he didn't bat an eye. Tell him you'd never heard of the Congress and—well, it looked like he was on the verge of a meltdown. His eyes were wide, his jaw clenched, his nostrils flaring with each heavy breath. Now Kit felt like she might have to restrain *him* from physically attacking the General.

Stev stepped back in before General Westen, who was staring quizzically at Avin, could even formulate a reply. "This building is an exact replica of the Congressional Seat. You can't tell me that you don't know where the original is."

"No, I can't say that I've ever heard of this Congressional Seat. But Azure Hall is a beautiful piece of architecture. Maybe your Congress copied it from us," the General chuckled. No one else found it funny. He sighed. "I shall try to locate this Congressional Seat for you—and you may fight with the Blues until they find it."

"I'll...have to discuss your proposition with my team," Stev said quietly. "In private."

General Westen looked surprised. "Of course. You may report to me whenever you decide to accept my offer." His tone was mild, but Kit had been an operative long enough to know that he wasn't really leaving them a choice. He turned away from them in clear dismissal and pressed a square on the glowing blue tabletop. A holographic representation of the city sprang up, and he immediately lost himself in its perusal. They had no choice but to go with the escort that appeared and nearly shoved them off the dais when they hesitated. The General would be answering no more questions right now.

They were escorted to a small barracks room with six beds, three against each wall. The whole room was lined with panels of brushed silver metal secured with matching rivets. Metal chests were positioned at the foot of every bed to hold personal belongings. Other than that, the room was featureless.

Their escort followed them inside as they filed along the center aisle, dropping their packs with careless thumps.

"I will need to collect your weapons now," he said serenely, as if he'd merely asked them for a spare uniform. Mercy was standing nearest to him, and he turned to her, shaking out a collection bag.

"Oh, no you don't!" Mercy backed away, hand on her gun.

"You will be issued regulation weaponry," the aide responded calmly. "Your own items will be kept safe until you leave this service."

"Are you crazy?" Stev bellowed, finally finding his voice. "We're not giving up our weapons!"

"If you wish to enjoy our hospitality, you must surrender your weaponry," the aide said, voice still perfectly even and unbothered. At that moment, a three-man patrol marched past their open door, their imposing guns held at the ready, little lights flashing like a countdown. Stev deflated abruptly. They were deep within not only the territory, but the headquarters of an entirely unknown power. They really had no choice but to comply.

Still, Kit didn't turn over everything, and she knew the others didn't either. The very differences in their equipment seemed to be an advantage. Their guns were obviously weapons, but the knives, with their retractable electric blades, looked like no more than thin rectangles of plastic and metal tacked onto their clothing. To the ignorant, they probably looked like decoration. The aide also failed to confiscate her climbers, which meant she retained her gloves and her lock picks. He only took their guns and everything out of Avin's pockets. Even though he clearly had no idea what any of Avin's toys were, he seemed convinced they were dangerous. Kit didn't know what half of it was either, but she was pretty sure dangerous was an understatement.

"Breakfast will be served at 0800 hours. The next battle will be joined at 0900 hours, unless you specifically request an assignment to our force before then. Wandering the complex is not permitted." The aide spun and exited the room promptly after delivering this extraordinary speech.

"Who schedules a battle?" Stev asked the closed door in disbelief. As if in answer, there was a clatter and a thunk from outside. In a flash, Avin was at the door, trying the handle, but it stuck in his hand. They had been locked in.

Kit scanned the room cautiously. She didn't see anything that could be bugged like that creepy cat from the Congress's suite. Could they have hidden cameras in some of the rivets? Listening devices under the beds? Her paranoia sat like a weight on her chest. No matter how unlikely, she still did a quick sweep of the room, prowling suspiciously around every piece of furniture while the others watched, not sure whether to join her or laugh. They didn't know about the other bug yet, though.

She found nothing. Either there were no bugs here, or these people were much better at concealing their devices. Either way, it was worth an attempt to unlock the door. She hadn't wanted to give away their possession of the lock pick if they were being monitored. No one said a word as she approached the door, but she quickly retracted her pick in disgust.

"With all their big, flashy guns and rocket packs, they still lock their doors mechanically? What is wrong with these people?" She turned and kicked the nearest chest dispiritedly, thoroughly disgruntled with her uselessness. Mercy and Stev turned to look at Avin hopefully, but he also shook his head.

"They might not have known what it was, but they still took the plasma torch and anything else I might have used. Our knives aren't strong enough to cut metal; it would only fry the electronics if we tried."

Mercy groaned and flung herself onto the bed opposite Kit. Then immediately jumped back up. The blood and dirt didn't show all that much on their dark gray uniforms, but it smudged disgustingly on the white blankets.

"Hey, look!" she exclaimed, pointing. Kit followed her finger and saw that one of the panels of the rear wall was a different size than the others. About the shape of a door, in fact. A knob had nearly blended in with the rivets, but was obvious now that she was looking for it. Before she could speak any word of caution, Mercy had bounded across the room and yanked the door open.

"Oh, heaven," Mercy breathed. The door opened to reveal a small but thoroughly functional bathroom, complete with a tiny cubby of a shower. "I found it, I call first shower!" She darted in and slammed the door behind her before anyone else could make a move. Kit couldn't help but crack a smile. Stev scowled at the closed door, probably peeved that his rank hadn't gotten him the consideration of being first. Too bad for him.

"I call next," Kit said, shooting a sly look at him. His scowl deepened, but he didn't dispute it. Instead, he flopped down on the bed that Mercy had already inadvertently dirtied, defiantly putting his booted feet up on its white covers. Kit couldn't find the energy to care if he was grumpy. All she wanted was a shower and a couple more hours of sleep, since it seemed like nothing else was going to happen until breakfast.

When Mercy came back out after a thankfully brief period of time, Kit sprang for the door before Stev could make a move. She didn't glance behind to see if he had even tried. Avin seemed to have resigned himself to going last. He was sitting cross-legged on the ground in front of the locked door in an attitude of guardianship. They might be prisoners, but he still wasn't going to let anyone get the drop on them.

The shower was everything Kit had dreamed of, a tiny haven of steam and warmth. She closed her eyes blissfully and, just for that moment, let her fears wash away with the blood and sweat. Her shoulder burned under the hot water, but when she opened her eyes to inspect the gouges, they weren't nearly as bad as she had thought. Not much more than scratches, really.

When she came out, Stev swung himself slowly out of his reclining position, looked penetratingly at Avin as if he expected him to make a break for the open door, then sauntered past Kit into the bathroom, pleased that he had managed to exert his authority over at least one member of the team.

Mercy was already asleep, and Kit, relaxed from the warmth of the shower, could feel her own eyelids sagging. Instead of an air dryer, this bathroom had held a stack of fluffy, white towels—old fashioned, but sensible in a room that small. Kit had one wrapped around her now, and she glanced from it to her soiled uniform. This was supposed to be a one day mission, and no one could have predicted the need for a spare uniform within that time frame. Not only was the uniform dirty, but it was slightly damp from the shower's steam. There was no way she was putting it back on. She carefully laid it out over the chest at the foot of her bed, entertaining some vain hope that it would air out before she had to put it on tomorrow. A critical look, however, convinced her that an early morning wash was in order. She dropped the blue armband, which had thankfully come off with only a tug, next to her uniform, then hung the damp towel over the bar at the foot of the bed and crawled naked between the sheets. It was slightly awkward, but at least Stev hadn't been here to ogle her, and Avin's eyes were tightly shut. She couldn't tell whether he was meditating or had fallen asleep sitting up. She pulled the covers up to her chin, reveling in clean cloth against her skin. When she closed her eyes, she could imagine she was at ORG headquarters, safe in her own bed, and the Congressional Seat, the lab, this bizarre cityscape had all been nothing but a series of particularly vivid nightmares. In the back of her mind, she knew what she would see if she opened her eyes (the bed was a smidgen softer than she was used to, the covers of a different fabric, the acoustics of the room slightly off) but she decided to keep them closed. It would be time to wake soon enough. She would face the truth then.

CHAPTER EIGHT

Kit's MDU woke her an hour before breakfast with a low, pleasant chime. At that particular moment, it sounded like the most obnoxious thing she'd ever heard. She groaned and thought about going back to sleep, just for five minutes. Maybe ten.

But then she remembered why she'd left so much extra time before breakfast. Clothing was an issue. A quick glance through bleary eyes told her that everyone else was still asleep. As quietly as she could, she swung her feet down to the cold floor, grabbed her grungy uniform, and made a dash for the bathroom.

As she had suspected, very little airing out had occurred overnight. The dampness had subsided into a sort of stiff, crunchy feeling. The others had been able to bring their clothing into the shower with them and wash the worst of the gore out of it. Kit's uniform had electrical wiring running all through it, so it was a bit more of a project to clean. She sat down cross-legged in the tiny bathroom and began to remove the power source and its associated wiring from the cloth conduits that held it in place. About a quarter of an hour later, everything was safely removed, and her dripping uniform, now vigorously scrubbed, hung over the shower door. She looked at it dubiously, hoping it would be dry enough to wear without too much discomfort soon. It would need quite a bit of time before she could replace the electronics. With luck, there would be no emergency climbing needed today. She gnawed on her lip a moment, then wrapped another towel tightly around herself, grabbed the uniform, and repaired to the outer room, fanning the clothing back and forth in a futile attempt to dry it more quickly.

Stev was awake, yawning hugely as he pulled on his boots. Avin, despite being somewhat rumpled, looked his usual alert, professional self. Mercy hadn't even managed to get out from under the covers yet; she grumbled something incoherently and pulled the blankets up over her face. Kit didn't blame her; she didn't want to face any of this either.

"Everyone up!" it wasn't quite a bellow, but Stev's voice boomed through the little room with too much force for Kit's liking.

"Alright, I'm up!" Mercy bellowed back, sitting up and tossing off the covers. She, too, had slept naked, and Stev's eyes bulged a little as she got out of bed and began to dress, muttering about the dampness of her uniform with no sign of self-consciousness. And Stev showed no sign of embarrassment for his lewd stare. Kit turned her back, disgusted at his shamelessness.

Once Mercy was dressed, Stev's brain clicked back on. "We need to discuss our answer for the General," he said gravely, as if this was the most important thing in the world. "Do we fight for the Blues or not?" He looked at his three subordinates expectantly.

"Is that really all you've taken away from this? A yes or no question?" Kit blurted.

"I'm prioritizing!" Stev blustered, but there was uncertainty in his tone.

"We have no idea where we are," she pointed out, brows furrowing. "We went into a laboratory in the middle of a very recognizable part of the city—a laboratory that was not that big, I might add—and came out in an entirely different city." Nods of agreement all around, though Stev looked doubtful.

"This leads us to several very important questions," Kit continued slowly, working it out as she went along. "Where are we? How did we get here? How do we get home? And perhaps most importantly, did we ever actually leave the lab?" She paused, letting the import of that sink in.

Mercy blanched. "If we're still in the lab, we're going to get blown to a bloody pulp in less than five hours."

"How could we still be in the lab?" Stev scoffed. "We could see the sky outside. There's a whole city."

"How could we exit the lab in an entirely different city than where we went in? One where they've never heard of the Congress?" Kit countered. "Maybe we were drugged somehow, maybe it's some sort of crazy travel apparatus, maybe it's something weirder. All I know is things aren't normal, and that makes me nervous."

"What if we're all dead already?" Mercy said hesitantly. A thick silence fell across the little group for a moment.

"I don't believe it," Kit said finally. "The Congress has executed so many people that I'm pretty sure the entire afterlife, if it exists, would be very well acquainted with them." That got a weak chuckle out of everyone.

"I still don't see how any of those questions are going to help us," Stev protested plaintively.

"Maybe they won't help," Kit admitted, "but it makes me feel a lot better to have them out in the open."

"Logically," Avin said slowly, "there are only two choices. We are in the lab and what we see around us is not real, or we are not in the lab and this is reality." He glanced at Kit for confirmation, and she nodded hesitantly in assent. She couldn't think of another option. He continued, "We do not have the option to retrace our steps to a point we are sure is reality. Therefore we only have one way to ascertain the difference. If, at noon, we die, then we are still in the lab. If we survive, then this is reality."

"I could really go for another way of testing this," Mercy said, trying to smile.

Avin just shook his head, not noticing her attempt at levity. "I can't think of another logical avenue for determining our location. However, we should act under the assumption that we will not die. If we are in the lab, nothing we do from this point on matters; our destruction is assured. If, however, we have found ourselves transported to a new and unknown location, then our actions within the next several hours may be critical."

"That makes a lot of sense," Kit agreed with relief. She didn't fancy sitting around here for hours, waiting to die. It wasn't her style. "So assuming this is reality, the ultimate goal is, of course, to find our way home."

"Which leads us back to my question!" Stev jumped in. "Do we fight for the Blues or not?" He shot a glance of triumph at her, as if he had somehow scored a victory.

"It's not quite that simple," Kit disagreed tiredly, rubbing her forehead. "We have to consider our position with the Congress." Avin turned pale, and Kit could see that he'd clenched his hands into fists. She frowned and continued anyway. "If we don't fight for the Blues, we might never be able to find our way home. We don't have their resources and aren't familiar with the territory at all. But if we do fight for the Blues, and they find us a way home...will the Congress consider us traitors to the ORG for fighting at the command of others?"

"It's all in the line of duty," Mercy protested. "We're trying to follow orders, which were to get back and report."

"They aren't always....reasonable," Kit said, shooting Avin another look. His jaw was clenched tightly as if he was trying to control himself.

"Even with help, there's no guarantee that we'll ever find our way back," Mercy said, a tinge of despair coloring her voice.

"It's our best shot, though," Stev said, finally weighing in.

"Getting back isn't going to do us much good if we're branded as traitors when we get there," Kit disagreed.

"What would you rather do?" Stev shot back hotly. "Sit around here as prisoners? Plan an escape attempt? This place is a fortress!"

Kit could think of no way to dispute that.

"As much as I hate to agree, I think Stev is right," Mercy said reluctantly. "At least if we fight for the Blues in exchange for navigational assistance, we can claim we did everything in our power to find our way back."

"It's not a great choice, but I guess it's the best one we have," Kit conceded reluctantly. "But make sure you demand regular progress reports on their search," she said fiercely, turning on Stev. She didn't want to get stuck here fighting someone else's war until she died. Getting killed in the line of duty was one thing; she had no obligation to these people other than convenience.

A knock on the door, followed by the thunk of the mechanical lock opening, interrupted their conversation. Kit hadn't minded sitting around in a towel amongst her teammates, but now she felt exposed. If she had to move quickly or fight, she had nothing close to hand. How could she have been so careless?

But it was merely an expressionless soldier with a rolling cart, delivering their breakfast. He dumped the cart in the middle of the room without saying a word and made a beeline for the exit. He locked the door behind him.

Cautiously, they moved to investigate the cart. It held a large, covered pot, a pile of bowls, and a stack of spoons. Kit eyed it dubiously. Who knew what the food was like in this place? But her stomach wasn't nearly as suspicious as her mind; it let out a loud, rumbling growl.

Mercy, more daring than the rest, lifted the pot's lid to peer inside, sniffing experimentally. "Some sort of porridge, I think," she declared. Unconsciously, they all turned to look at Avin. He shrugged.

"I don't have any means of testing it for poison, but I can't see why they'd bother. If they wanted to get rid of us, they have plenty of other options."

"What about drugs? Truth serum or something?" Kit asked, wracking her brain for any recollection of such a thing.

"If they have anything like that, it's unlikely they'd need to use it on us. We're already entirely in their power, and I don't think we have any information they want that badly. It's not like our political information would be of any use to them," Avin pointed out.

"Fair enough," Kit said, staring greedily at the pot.

"Well, dish it up, then," Stev said heartily, grabbing a bowl and heaping it full.

The porridge had a strange, lumpy texture as Kit spooned it into her bowl. She was used to porridge made from the highly processed and compacted grain bars that were the staple of the city. The grain in those was usually the consistency of wet sawdust once it was stirred into water and heated, and the resulting glob was sickeningly sweet from the syrup used to hold the bars together. This...she poked at it experimentally. This was made of actual, whole oats! It might just be porridge, but it was porridge fit for a king, by her standards. She tasted it carefully. It was richer than she was used to, and only lightly sweetened. She hadn't known porridge could taste so good.

Apparently the others shared her high opinion of the meal, since they were scraping the bottom of the pot in no time at all. They stacked their used bowls beside the pot and rolled the cart neatly by the door.

There wasn't much time left before the start of the scheduled battle. That concept still sounded strange to Kit. Did they send out invitations? She nervously tested her uniform and found it still thoroughly wet, but at least no longer dripping. It would be more comfortable to wear wet clothes than obsessively worry about when to dress. It wouldn't dry appreciably more in the next fifteen minutes anyway. With a wary glance at Stev, she grabbed the uniform and went into the bathroom to dress. She regretfully deposited the electronic components of her climbing gear in her pack; they had enough waterproofing to stand up to weather, but there was no point in taking chances.

She returned to the outer room to find a thick, uncomfortable quiet cocooning her teammates. Loathe to break the silence, she stood at the back of the room, shifting awkwardly in her wet clothes. As the time ticked down towards 0900 hours, the glances toward the door became full-blown stares.

Even though she was expecting it, she started when the door opened, nerves prickling, hands grasping after weapons that weren't there. She forced her fingers to relax and met the aide with an impassive gaze.

"You may see the General now," was all he said, and he glanced over all of them with supreme disinterest. He barely checked to see that they were following him, but there was little chance they wouldn't. Kit, at least, was thoroughly sick of being stuck in that one small room. Sure, she'd spent longer in smaller places, but she hadn't been a prisoner. That made a huge difference.

They were again brought to General Westen's command center. He looked as if he hadn't moved since last night, still perusing holographic maps at his table. As the aide approached, he took a step back, and the images disappeared.

Kit had been too tired and befuddled last night to take a good look at the man who currently held their lives in his hands, but now she scrutinized him carefully. He was old—older than she was used to seeing. ORG operatives were retired some time in their thirties, if they survived that long. Most didn't. And no one really knew what retirement involved, since those so discharged were never seen again. Half the operatives claimed that retirement was paradise, that you were given everything you could ever desire in gratitude for your service. There were rumors of golden floors and rare foods and servants like ancient kings used to have. The other half whispered that operatives who got too old were simply...disposed of. They knew too much to be released into the population as ordinary citizens. Though Kit couldn't imagine that the ORG was killing its own for no reason other than age, she certainly didn't believe all that stuff about gold floors. If nothing else, it would be horribly impractical. Gold was far too soft for flooring.

Except for civilians, Kit had rarely seen gray hair such as the General sported, and her contact with civilians was usually limited to either arresting or killing them. Nor was facial hair acceptable in the ORG, but this man sported a short, neatly clipped white beard over his strong, tanned jaw. His dark, deep-set eyes bored into her until she felt tiny, like a child being confronted by an adult over some wrongdoing.

"Well?" his deep voice rumbled after a long moment. "Will you join the fight?"

Stev, usually so eager to put himself forward, was reluctant. He literally dragged his feet, scraping them against the floor as he stepped forward.

"We will fight with you," he said monotonously, as if he had been practicing these words in his head for the past half hour. "But we have conditions of our own that must be met." Westen's bushy eyebrows rose, but he nodded for Stev to continue. Stev glanced at Kit, as if for reassurance, and she gave him a little encouraging nod. Just spit it out.

"You have promised to assist in locating our home base of operations," Stev continued, less than confidently. "We require regular updates on this progress."

"That seems reasonable. Anything else?"

Stev hesitated, brow creased. They hadn't discussed anything else explicitly—and such an obvious requirement jumped into Kit's head that she wanted to smack herself for not bringing it up earlier. Surely Stev would think of this, surely...but no, she could see in his face that he was about to clinch the agreement. Despite the tremendous breach of protocol and possible undermining of her own lead, she had to speak up.

"Please excuse the interruption, General and sir," she said, nodding respectfully to Stev in an attempt to minimize the damage. His shocked expression hadn't yet given way to anger, but she was sure it would. Any second now. Westen, at least, merely looked interested. For a General, he seemed strangely indifferent to military protocol. Kit took a deep breath and continued.

"I would like to add an addendum. We require assurances, preferably digitally signed, that we will be released from your service once our home base has been located, and we reserve the right to terminate that service if we do not receive adequate evidence that a search is being made."

Stev's eyes widened as he realized what they'd almost gotten themselves into. Regular updates did nothing if they had no right to terminate their contract. They could get updates weekly, daily even, stating that nothing had been found and be bound to continue fighting.

The General frowned, but Kit wasn't sure whether it was because he was annoyed at her suspicions or because she had foiled his plans. She didn't care as long as she and her teammates were safe.

"We should be able to comply with that condition," he said, crooking a finger at his aide. The aide handed him a small black hemisphere. It projected a holographic document out of its top, splashing a blue glow across Westen's face. His eyes scanned it quickly, then he used his finger to sketch a signature in the air. A luminescent blue line flowed out of his fingertip onto the document. He spun the hemisphere so that both Stev and Kit could inspect it. This hadn't been exactly what she'd had in mind when she'd requested a digital signature, but in retrospect, it hadn't been a very well-thought-out request. To her, a digital signature meant using a citizen's Congress-granted code to tie a document to their personnel records in the Congress's files, thereby making it a permanent part of their identity. Obviously that wasn't possible out here. Instead, she skimmed the writing, found only what they had discussed, and kept quiet while Stev awkwardly scrawled his Congress code next to the General's flowing signature. To her surprise, once Stev had finished signing, the General proffered the document in her direction.

"Since you have set some of the conditions, I would like to have a record of your agreement, as well," he said gravely. And uncomfortably, just as awkwardly, she used a finger to print her Congress code under Stev's. When she glanced sideways, Stev's jaw was tight, his brow furrowed, but his gaze was introspective.

"Now that's settled," Westen said, suddenly all genial smiles, "would you like to join the battle immediately? I'm afraid you're slightly too late to join the 0900 fight, but you'd be welcome to join the round at 1000 hours. If you'd rather simply get a feel for your surroundings, we can also offer you a tour of the compound, preliminary weapons training, a territory briefing that will give you an idea of the surrounding area, or even a holographic practice round. You can join up with the real fight any hour, on the hour. Lunch will be served between 1100 and 1400 hours."

This rather bizarre menu of options left all of them rather taken aback. Stev opened his mouth two or three times before he got any words out, even glancing at Kit to see if she might step in, but there was no way. She'd taken as much responsibility as she could handle today.

"I—Perhaps the tour and weapons training?" Stev finally replied uncertainly.

"Very good," Westen responded, for all the world as if Stev hadn't stood there gaping at him for a solid minute. As if this was all very routine. The aide stepped forward to lead them away, and the General turned away from them, once again perusing the holographic display from his table. Exactly as he had before. Kit wondered if he ever left that table, but kept silent and followed the aide away.

⸺◆○◆⸺

The aide began the tour by leading them out of the headquarters and towards the two linked buildings Kit had noted the night before. He steered them towards the larger entrance, where huge glass doors led into a strangely opulent foyer. Everything had a very high-tech, military ambiance, to be sure—there was a nearly overpowering amount of polished stainless steel and rivets in the decor—but it lacked the simplicity that Kit associated with the ORG. It was the sort of high-ceilinged, spacious room that screamed *display*. What could this room be used for? The seating was all arranged in scattered clusters, too far apart for a large group briefing, but too close to keep small meetings private. And the chairs themselves...they hovered. A vague blue flame flickered underneath the legless, riveted metal frames, each one softened by velvety blue cushions. They floated a good foot and a half above the floor. Kit wondered if they would adjust to the height of the person sitting in them.

The wall to their right was set with large, shiny elevator doors, and the elevator itself made its stately way up and down a transparent shaft. Beside the doors, a robotic attendant waited patiently. What purpose it served was unclear, since the whole space was echoingly empty of human life. There was no one to be attended to.

At the far end of the room rested a holo-table, much like the one in such constant use by General Westen, and it was to this that the aide led them.

He snapped his fingers, and the holograph unfolded itself into brilliant 3D, beginning a prerecorded sequence.

"Welcome to the Blue Barracks!" chirped a female voice, thick with electronic twang. "As a private, you will be placed in basic group housing." A re-creation of the room in which they had spent the last night popped up over the table, slowly rotating in bright blue light. "As your rank increases, you will gain the opportunity to move to premium or deluxe group housing, or even officer suites!" As the voice twittered on, increasingly luxurious rooms flashed into the hologram. It began listing all of the amenities in each style of room, and Kit shifted impatiently. She wasn't really that concerned with their housing as long as there was a bed and a bathroom. She didn't care if the premium suite came with something called a "hot tub" or if the deluxe upgrade got you a "surround sound system."

The next stop on their tour brought them across the path to the armory, a heavy, two-storied concrete bunker. But once they had pierced that concrete shell, it looked surprisingly like the barracks across the way, all silvery metal and rivets with splashes of metallic blue. Something about the whole place set Kit on edge. Then, as she scuffed her toes against the spotless floor, it hit her that there were no scuff-marks on anything, no imperfections, scratches, dings—nothing. Any room used by this many soldiers should show some signs of wear; even the most disciplined soldier might slip up if he needed to arm in a hurry. It all felt utterly unreal.

The weapons were just as odd as their surroundings. Kit had expected them to be highly complex, advanced, and require quite a bit of training to use. They were practically coated in little indicator lights, switches, tubing, knobs—anything that could be tacked on. But from the explanation they were given, the actual operation of these guns was as simple as point and shoot. Some types had old-fashioned targeting aids attached—lasers and scopes, the sort of things that hadn't been in use since the invention of the MDU. And they needed to be reloaded with solid metal bullets, of all things! They would have to cart around extra ammunition to use these relics. Kit hefted an ammo pack in her hand and was dismayed. Even a few of these things could weigh her down enough to stress the climbing equipment. It probably wouldn't over-stress to the point of shorting out, but there was always the very real possibility of the adhesion failing. Falling to her death was as unpleasant a prospect as electrocution.

Even the weaponry itself was heavier than she was used to. She was glad pistols tended to be her weapon of choice; anything larger than a pair of these pistols would be unwise, and maybe just one would be safer. She thought longingly of her own lightweight, sleek weaponry, confiscated and shoved who knew where. It didn't require reloading; it manufactured its own ammunition right in the barrel. The bullets were essentially tiny electric force-fields, made of the same tough but immaterial power as the blades of the electro-knives. That stuff had the added benefit of giving living targets a mild, stunning shock at low calibers—or permanent nerve damage at higher ones. All you needed to do was charge the gun up every once in a while.

That brought up another disturbing issue. There was nowhere in this bizarre armory to charge their own weapons. Kit tried to remember what sort of power her pistols had left. She thought they still had about three quarters after the whole shambler fiasco, but she hadn't exactly been clear-headed by the end of it. She could be wrong. As another one of those holo-tables explained how to reload these anachronistic weapons, Kit tried to wrestle her straying attention back to the lesson.

To her great surprise, they were allowed to inspect their own weapons after the hologram had finished its speech. The aide led them into a back room lined with safes, each carefully locked with old-fashioned numerical locks. Perhaps they used that sort of lock because they knew how difficult it was to pick with modern skills—or maybe it really was the best security they had.

The aide approached four of the safes in turn, opening each to reveal all of their weapons, carefully sorted.

"Please do not remove the weapons from this room. At least, until you take your leave of us," the aide requested, stepping back to allow them to approach. Kit went eagerly to the locker with her items, running her fingers over her pistols to check for damage—and, if she was being honest with herself, just for reassurance. It was nice to see something familiar, especially something as comforting as her weapons. It would be so easy to turn around, put a couple bullets in that aide...

And then what? Fight their way out of a compound full of soldiers? And go where?

Stupid brain.

The aide seemed totally unfazed by the fact that he had allowed four highly trained commandos access to their weaponry of choice. He had more faith in their intelligence and impulse control than she would have, had their positions been reversed.

Besides, this check was more useful for strategy than actual escape. Her eyes ran over the charge indicators: 67% on one pistol, 74% on the other. Hopefully that would last long enough. With a regretful sigh, she replaced the pistols in the safe and turned away.

Chapter Nine

They were promptly hustled off to a session of hands-on weapon training. The range attached to the armory was expansive and gleaming, as if it had never been used. The training was overseen by another holograph, a transparent blue man who looked like a younger, clean-shaven version of the General. Their escort had dropped them off and then left the range. Kit was sure either he or another guard was keeping an eye on the exit, though.

The holograph was a decent, if unimaginative, instructor. He would answer questions regarding the weapons and their use intelligently enough, but any other attempt at communications would be greeted with a blank stare. He methodically walked them through loading, aiming, and firing the weapon, presenting everything as if to the barest beginner. Kit found it frustratingly boring, but if you tried to skip a step in his instructions, he would just repeat it until you complied.

After the training was over, they were turned loose in the range for free practice. Kit breathed a sigh of relief. Finally, she could really get a feel for these weird weapons without someone looking over her shoulder. She spent most of her time working with a pistol, adjusting to the difference in weight and the massive increase in kickback, but she did set aside a little time to try out the other options provided. It wouldn't hurt to be comfortable with the larger weapons, even if she couldn't carry one and still climb. The assault rifle was actually a lot of fun, though still inferior to the ORG's current model.

She couldn't help wondering how these Blues had maintained their independence with this level of weaponry, though. Especially if they were in the midst of a war. If they had come up against the Congress, the ORG would have had them for lunch. They were lucky that distance had protected them.

Though...now that Kit thought about it, she had no idea how far away they might be or what was in any of the territory past the Swampies' domain. Were there neighboring cities? Obviously other people, other cultures, existed, or they wouldn't be in this fix. But she had never heard even a whisper or a speculation about them. For the first time in her life, it occurred to Kit that there was a whole world outside her city, and she didn't know how she felt about that. She squeezed off a few more shots with the pistol, trying to take comfort from her aim's steady progression towards the center of the target. She should be able to defend herself effectively, at least.

Right as the time on her MDU ticked over to 10:45 am, the holograph clicked back on. After a short lesson on the correct cleaning and maintenance of these weapons (far more involved with the metal bullets than with electric ones, Kit was dismayed to find), they were directed to exit the range. Their guide was waiting for them in the outer room, and pointed them to the correct racks for their weapons. Vaguely resentful at being herded around this way, Kit stashed the pistol and assault rifle as directed.

"The tour will conclude at the cafeteria, where lunch will be served from 1100 to 1400 hours. You may choose to stay there for lunch, join the next battle at 1200 hours, or continue with the territory briefing or practice round," the aide told them expressionlessly. Kit's stomach grumbled, and she fervently hoped that Stev would opt for lunch. Maybe there would be more of that porridge.

The building attached to the barracks turned out to be the cafeteria. Kit could see people wandering back and forth between the buildings inside the glass-paned connecting walkway. Strange—the barracks had seemed so empty inside, but she could have sworn that passageway had been just as bustling before they'd gone in. Perhaps it let out somewhere other than the main hall.

The "tour" of the cafeteria was nothing more than their guide walking them to the building. Inside, a maze of tables and chairs dominated. Some few of these were occupied, but there were plenty of empty seats—seats which, Kit was relieved to see, sat on the floor in a perfectly pedestrian way. At the far end of the room was a door flanked by carts heaped with trays and clean dishes. A sign beside it said "Line Starts Here" with a big red arrow.

"Lunch, battle, territory briefing, or practice round?" their guide asked with no preamble.

"Lunch," Stev replied just as shortly.

"I will return when you're done." And with that, they were alone. No one else even glanced at them; everyone moved purposefully and disinterestedly through their routine. A slow but steady trickle of people came out of a door opposite the one with the red arrow, each with a tray full of food. They sat by twos and threes and ate methodically, occasionally looking up to converse in low voices. Kit couldn't hear what they were saying. Others, earlier to lunch, finished up their trays and dumped their trash into another counter with a hole cut into the top. No one looked at them.

Stev squared his shoulders and strode purposefully across the room towards that prominent red arrow. He grabbed a beige plastic tray, a spotless white plate, and a napkin-wrapped package of utensils, and the team followed suit. Kit was shocked to find that the napkin was made of paper. Who wasted paper on a napkin?

Through the door, they found a long counter with a ledge for their trays. Food was laid out in bins along the counter; each station had its own server, all of whom looked eerily alike in their white caps and aprons. Kit put her tray down and slid it along the ledge, collecting food as she went. Her eyes got wider with each item that was served. She couldn't even identify most of it, but it smelled like heaven. She was first given a large hunk of pale meat covered in a dark red sauce. It smelled...a little like smoke, but with a strange, tangy tone. Something orange and lumpy landed beside the meat with a splat, followed by a double handful of long, thin sticks of - was that potato? The golden brown slices were a far cry from dehydrated potato chips, which were most reminiscent of dry slabs of cardboard and disintegrated slowly into a soggy mass as they were chewed. These sparkled with a faint sheen of grease, and when she poked a finger at one experimentally, she found a shell that crunched inward to reveal a soft, fluffy interior. And they were hot! She stuck her scorched finger in her mouth and tasted salt.

A white plastic container was plunked onto her tray, interrupting her contemplation of the potatoes. She didn't get a chance to peek at the contents, though she was consumed by curiosity. Then, just as quickly, she was distracted from the mysterious container. At the end of the counter rested a large basket of assorted fruits. Kit was shocked to see that everyone was taking a whole fruit for themselves. Stev tried to do the same nonchalantly, as if this wasn't the greatest wealth of food he'd ever seen. Kit could see his hand shaking slightly as he reached for the bowl. When it was her turn, she looked over the array of choices, baffled; she'd hardly ever been given a bit of fruit, and it had been either dried and ground into tough leather or chopped into tiny bits and suspended in cloyingly sweet syrup. These were fist-sized globes of red and green and orange, and she had no idea what any of them were. Afraid of holding up the line and looking like an idiot, she grabbed at random, and came up with a round, green fruit. It was streaked with uneven red stripes, and a short stem protruded from the top, as if it had just been picked. As she shuffled forward in the line, she surreptitiously sniffed it, savoring its remarkable perfume.

Next the line brought them to an enclosure with glass doors, each shelf stacked with small, many-colored cartons. Again, she grabbed at random, and felt liquid sloshing around inside. A wave of cool air swept over her when she opened the glass cabinet, and the liquid inside the carton seemed to be chilled, but not frozen. She was more used to drinking beverages at room temperature or partially frozen – usually due to impatience when she didn't want to wait for her drink to thaw. She wiggled the carton side to side cautiously, but couldn't determine anything else about its contents.

The line broke up after that, and she followed her team to an unoccupied table. They exchanged slow, uncertain looks across the food-laden expanse, both nervous at the bounty before them and sharply aware that this could be their last meal. The time was ticking down towards noon—twenty-four hours since they had entered the laboratory. Stev broke the pause by grabbing for his fork and aggressively attacking his plate. Everyone else followed his lead, albeit less energetically. And suddenly, Kit didn't care that the clock was ticking down the minutes until her possible demise.

She had never tasted anything so wonderful. The meat was tender and juicy, and definitely fresh rather than re-hydrated; the red sauce had a complexity beyond anything she had ever experienced, tart and spicy and slightly sweet. The orange, lumpy stuff proved to be pasta coated with a sauce that tasted vaguely like the dehydrated cheese powder that was occasionally sprinkled on frozen vegetables or into a stew made with meat jerky. The cheese powder had grown increasingly scarce as Kit had gotten older, and she hadn't had any in a very long time. She had really enjoyed it as a kid, but suddenly it paled in comparison with the plate in front of her. The cheese sauce was almost unbearably rich to her inexperienced palate, and she had to eat it slowly to keep from being overwhelmed.

The potato sticks had cooled now, and while still recognizable as what she considered potato...there really wasn't any comparison. The texture—she'd never experienced anything like it. The crunch as she bit down, the soft, fluffy center that melted on her tongue—and they were even better when dipped in the cheese sauce. Though on reflection, Kit suspected nearly anything would be better when dipped in that cheese.

She was halfway through her plate before she remembered the mysterious white container. When she popped it open, she gasped aloud at the bounty it held. Carefully, delicately, as if it might disappear, Kit brought one of the dark green leaves to her lips. It was crisp and thick, almost spongy, and had a slightly bitter, mineral taste. The next, slightly lighter in color, large and frilly, had a mild, sweet taste and a crunchy, juicy stem. She tried a dark curly-edged leaf that tasted vaguely of pepper, a pungent sprig of something with small, feathery leaves, a crunchy purple leaf with bright white veins. There were small, red orbs in with the leaves that exploded when she bit into them and filled her mouth with a fresh, acidic sweetness, completely different from the sickeningly sugary syrups of her usual diet.

By surreptitious observation, she was able to figure out how to correctly open the paper beverage carton. Stev had given up in frustration and ripped the whole top of the carton off. Kit had gotten an orange-colored carton, and when she pried the paper lip open, a sweet, fruity scent wafted over her. She sipped the orange liquid hesitantly, and was met with a refreshing tartness. It was all she could do not to drink the whole thing at once.

"What did you get?" Mercy asked. She was holding a blue carton, and looking at Kit's curiously.

"Orange," Kit shrugged, not knowing what else to call it.

"I think mine's real milk," Mercy said, eyes shining. "Want to try?" Eagerly, Kit handed over her orange drink in exchange for a sip of the creamy milk.

"What about you?" Mercy asked Avin, excitedly eying his red carton. Wordlessly, he proffered it to her, and soon they were all sipping from the different colored cartons. They had long since stopped caring about making a spectacle of themselves. The red had a tangy, dark juice that was almost sour, but still delicious, and Stev's brown one had a sweet, richly flavored milk that sort of tasted like chocolate, except it was so much better than anything chocolate-flavored she'd experienced before that Kit hesitated to use the word for it. She resolved to try every color the next chance she got.

The only thing left on her tray now was the fruit. Again, she had to glance around to try to determine the best way to eat the thing. Did she just bite into it? At last, she saw someone with a fruit like hers, mostly eaten, gnawing on a center core. She picked up the fruit as if it was made of glass, looked at it nervously for a moment, then bit into it.

Juice filled her mouth. The crunchy skin gave way to tender flesh inside. It was sweet and tart and so delicious that it nearly brought her to tears. In that moment, she would gladly have fought through twice as many shamblers just to get to this table with this meal. She looked up and met Avin's eyes; he held a slightly more oblong fruit, so dark a red as to be nearly purple, with a crisp, white interior exposed where he'd taken a bite. His face was full of awe, and he met her slow grin with a rare smile of his own. A grunt of frustration from Stev drew her attention, and she nearly laughed aloud as he tried to gnaw a bite out of his lumpy orange sphere. When his teeth broke the thick rind, juice sprayed out, covering Mercy in a fine mist, and he cursed heartily at the fruit - until he licked up a drop of juice off his hand. His expression transformed to something rapturous.

"Well, it could be worse," Mercy said philosophically as she used her napkin to wipe the sticky spray from her arms. "At least it smells fantastic." Kit giggled and Stev studiously ignored her as he peeled away pieces of the rind, digging for the tender fruit underneath. Then juice dripped down Kit's fingers, reclaiming her attention.

In what seemed like a fraction of a moment, the fruit was gone, and she was licking the last of the juice from her fingers. She was completely stuffed, more satisfied than she ever remembered feeling after a meal. Perhaps she shouldn't have gorged herself so much, but she couldn't bring herself to regret a single mouthful. Her senses had been assailed and overcome. More than anything, she wanted a nap.

Then her MDU sent a quiet ping reverberating through her senses. 11:55 am. She had forgotten she'd set that reminder. How bizarre, to set a reminder for your own destruction. She found herself sitting bolt upright and forced herself to relax into a parody of her previous comfortable slouch. But everyone else was just as tense now, and her food sat in her stomach like a lump of clay.

Five minutes. She knew what death looked like for other people. What would it look like for her? If they were close enough to the detonation point, the explosion would tear them apart, and what was left would be battered by shrapnel, crushed by debris. Anything that made her recognizable as herself would be pounded into a red pulp. She would become nothing but a piece of meat.

If they were far enough underground, they might merely be caught in the collapse. Trapped by falling walls and ceilings, tons of concrete and metal between them and the surface. It was the recipe for a slow, painful death.

And who would notice? The only people who cared if she lived or died were right here with her. It dawned on her that if she died, the ORG would take one of those awestruck, fresh-faced recruits and stick them in her bunk with her uniforms and her gear. And no one would know the difference.

She had always felt important in the ORG, like she was in a class above the people they policed. She, as the ORG was so fond of saying in their speeches, would "really live before she died," unlike those poor sods who had no choice but to be civilians. But in the end, she was just as expendable as they were, with no more merit attributed to the days she'd had. Maybe less. All she'd done with those days she'd "lived" was follow orders. She felt uncertain and very small; her shoulders hunched and she shoved her hands in her pockets to hide their trembling.

Her cold fingers found the gold ring she'd taken off Rose Greyridge's corpse. Its smooth roundness was strangely comforting as she turned it over and over in her pocket. *For my summer Rose.* Did Rose have someone who missed her, who still wondered what had happened to her? Or had every memory of her been wiped clean in that lab?

Kit glanced around the table, but only Avin would meet her eye. His face was blank, impenetrable. As usual. She suddenly had the urge to throw her tray at him, make him show some emotion. Didn't he realize they might be dead in—she checked her MDU—two and a half minutes?

They might all be dead, and would any of them be remembered? She realized that she had no idea. She spent nearly every working moment with these people, but she didn't know anything about their personal relationships. She'd barely had time to get to know Mercy as a teammate. Avin was not only a closed book, but one whose cover was blank, and the title page torn out for good measure. And Stev—well, he was known as a womanizer far and wide (and how he hadn't gotten nabbed for illegal fornication boggled her mind). But she didn't know if he had any lovers currently, or even any friends. She'd always made a point of remaining ignorant of Stev's social life, whenever she'd had a choice in the matter.

Kit had been teamed with Avin and Stev ever since she'd become a full member of the ORG. She tallied up the time in her head and realized it had been a little over two years. For the first year and a half, they'd been teamed with a nice older woman, but time wasn't kind to ORG operatives. Merdith had been sweet and soft-spoken, reliable in a fight, but pushing thirty when Kit joined at eighteen. One day she simply hadn't shown up for the briefing, and the next day, they'd been assigned Lis as her replacement. That was how retirement went. Kit hoped that she'd gotten her golden floors and servants and not...the other option.

Lis and Stev had hit it off immediately. She'd had none of Mercy's shyness, all freckles and chestnut curls and easy smiles. Nothing he said could shock or annoy her; she'd laugh it off or give as good as she got. The whole ORG seemed brighter with her in it, less boring, less bloody. Kit had even been able to tell which girls from other units had been involved with Stev before she came along because every one of them would glare and growl at Lis. Stev was entirely fixated on her, and Lis reacted to all that attention in a way that Kit saw, in hindsight, was inevitable. She fell hard.

Kit had shrugged and let it happen. The rules about love and sex were utterly draconian, she'd thought. She wasn't going to report her own team-mates. And what harm could it really do?

And then they'd gone on that mission. That stupid mission—it shouldn't have been anything especially hard. It was just a couple of squatters who weren't even reported to be armed. Stev had walked right up to them, all swagger and bluster, and grabbed the arm of the older man to pull him out of the abandoned apartment, toss him into the street. He hadn't seen the younger one grab for a gun—a gun so old and battered that it was almost unrecognizable. He didn't notice anything until Lis had already jumped in front of him, bearing the young attacker to the floor even as he pulled the trigger—and the gun exploded. Kit was no stranger to death, but she'd never forget Lis toppling forward, falling to the floor tangled with the body of the young squatter, both of them torn to shreds by shrapnel. A piece of the gun had sliced a diagonal swath through Lis's face, right down to the bone.

Another shard had gone through her throat. She died choking and writhing, tangled in the lacerated arms of her murderer.

Stev had killed Lis, just as surely as that squatter had, by clouding her mind with the idea of "love." If she'd been thinking clearly, she would have held back, trained a gun on the kid, threatened him or even shot him point blank. Instead, she tried to shield Stev with her own body and died with her lungs full of blood. And how had he repaid her? By immediately flirting with her replacement. If he had grieved, Kit hadn't seen it.

And as surely as blame lay on Stev, it also lay on Kit. She had been fully aware of what was going on. She could have stopped it. She needn't even have reported them, only threatened to. Stev was hopeless, but she probably could have convinced Lis that the affair was a bad idea, if she'd just tried. But she hadn't. She clutched the gold ring in her pocket until it dug into her fingers. It had been the same with Rose—rushing ahead in science rather than battle, but still jumping blindly forward to save the one she loved. And ending in disaster. It was all so stupid, so pointless, and yet—there was still something so beguiling, so tempting in the idea. She could see now why such affairs had been outlawed.

Half a minute left. Abruptly, Kit shoved away from the table and stood. If she was going to die, she wasn't going to do it slouched over the remains of her lunch. A heartbeat later, Avin, Stev, and Mercy joined her. They stood in a small, tight circle, backs straight, eyes not meeting as they focused inward on the MDU countdown. The Congress and the ORG were punctilious in their timing. If demolition were to take place, it would be to the second.

3...2...1...

Nothing.

Chapter Ten

There wasn't even a shudder. Outside the bubble of silence surrounding them, life went on with a steady, purposeful stride. Kit couldn't breathe for a moment. The air froze in her lungs and it felt like her heart couldn't bear to contract again. It was going to keep swelling and burst out of her chest.

Stev let out a loud whoop and punched the air exultantly. And then they were all unfrozen, laughing, jumping up and down, slapping each other on the back. Stev swooped Mercy up in a hug and whirled her around wildly; she didn't even protest. She staggered a little when he dropped her and laughed, her wide eyes sparkling. Kit grinned as she steadied the smaller girl, and her eyes met Avin's over Mercy's shoulder. He was smiling broadly, all the harsh lines of his narrow face softened in that moment. He looked like an entirely different person. She wished he would smile more.

Then the smile melted off his face as if it had never existed. Kit's muscles all tensed and she scanned the cafeteria, looking for the threat that had caused Avin's wariness. Nothing. Everything was exactly as it had been before.

Wait. Exactly as it had been before. They had been carrying on and making great, big, loud fools of themselves for a reason that no one else could be aware of. Someone should have noticed, should be eyeing them with curiosity or disdain for causing such a disruption. Instead, everyone, every single person in the cafeteria, continued on with their meals as if nothing out of the ordinary had happened. They ate methodically, rhythmically, walked with a steady pace between the serving line and the tables and the trash bins. They stared straight ahead. The groups at the tables spoke at even intervals, never seeming to respond to each other with either word or expression. The unreality of it crashed over her like freezing water.

Stev and Mercy were looking at her and Avin questioningly. They didn't seem to notice how the entire illusion of normalcy had suddenly been stripped away. Kit frowned. Could she be mistaken?

That was it. She was tired of it. All of the uncertainty and confusion and frustration of the past 24 hours boiled up and she took a step towards the nearest table. She was going to ask those people what was going on, and she was going to get some answers if it killed her—

"Was your lunch satisfactory?" The aide's voice stopped her in her tracks before she'd gone more than a step. Slowly, she turned to face him, standing shoulder to shoulder with the rest of her team, all of them inspecting him with various levels of suspicion.

"Um, yeah...yes," Stev stuttered.

"Very good. Battle, territory briefing, or practice round?" The aide gave no indication that he found anything unusual in their behavior, but Kit felt there was a glint of suspicion in his eyes. Was it her imagination? Her heart was fluttering wildly. She had no frame of reference for this situation. A battle, a hostage situation, an infiltration—there she was entirely comfortable.

Stev glanced nervously at her, not answering the aide's question. From her behavior and Avin's watchfulness, he knew that something was wrong, but it was beyond his perception. She steadied herself, reversed the step she had taken, and addressed Stev rather than the aide.

"I believe that an overview of the surrounding territory would be very helpful to us," she said, keeping her voice expressionless and hoping he would catch the significance of her request anyway. Something was very wrong here and they needed to be ready—ready for an attack, ready for an escape, ready for anything.

Kit had fallen asleep instantly the first night of their captivity, but the second saw her wide awake, listening to the thoughts buzz around in her head like trapped flies. The territory briefing had only confirmed her suspicions—or confirmed that there was something to be suspicious of, anyway. She still had no idea what was going on here.

No one in their right mind would choose this place as a battlefield. It was full of twists and turns, every corner ideal for an ambush, almost as if it had been designed that way. And the area of battle, they had been informed, was restricted to the strip of land between the two factions' bases. What kind of war had such stringent boundaries? How could they possibly be enforced? But their instructor, another amazingly unremarkable aide, had been very firm on that. The enemy would not go outside those parameters, and they were not permitted to either.

When Kit had ventured a question about the cause of the war, the aide had shot her a bland look and replied with only, "They're rebels."

Kit chased one stray thought after another, but no matter how she worked it out, she reached the same conclusion. Someone had to go out there and observe the situation, perhaps even capture an enemy combatant to question. If they were going to be caught up in this, they needed far more information than they had been given.

She was the best candidate for the mission. She was more subtle than Stev, more experienced than Mercy, and more mobile than Avin. But Stev would never approve such a mission. He wanted to stay on their hosts' good side in the hope that they could locate their home city. He would consider it an unnecessary risk. And Avin would never support a mission without approval. Mercy...Mercy might be counted on as backup. She had seemed a bit timid and overawed when she had first joined the unit, but she'd shown an impressive, though sometimes ill-advised, ability to stand up to Stev since they had embarked on this mission. She almost seemed like a different person, but Kit liked this version better. She resolved to share her plan with Mercy if she got the chance, then drifted off into a restless sleep.

Kit was, once again, the first one out of bed. She needed extra time to rewire her uniform. She was relieved that she hadn't needed any of its extra capabilities yesterday, but didn't think she'd be so lucky again today. There were only two items left from their list of options: battle or practice round. Either way, she wanted to be able to climb.

As she sat and fiddled with the wiring, she came to the conclusion that the best course was to sneak away during the heat of battle. Surely there would be enough confusion and clutter in that weird cityscape to allow her an opportunity. She had hoped that Mercy would be up before Stev and Avin so she could have a quiet word with her, but Mercy was nearly always the last one out of bed. It seemed to be one aspect of military discipline she could never come to terms with. Instead, Avin rolled out of bed and stalked into the washroom. In a minute, she heard the water come on; in five, he was back, rubbing his short, dark hair with a towel. Kit had no idea how he'd done it, but his uniform looked completely clean and wrinkle-free. He took a cross-legged seat on his bed and regarded her steadily, watching her fingers as she slowly urged the wiring back into its pathways. It was unnerving. Did he suspect what she planned? He had picked up on the inconsistencies before she had, and he was a brilliant strategist. How could he not suspect? He must be planning to report her to Stev—but he only sat there, staring. She lowered her head to her work.

When breakfast arrived, the aide who came with it issued the promised daily report: no sign of the Congress had been found. Well, it had only been one day. Today's porridge had a spicy scent and bits of dried fruit mixed into it. However weird this place was, there were worse places to be held prisoner.

As Kit had expected, there were only two options provided for their daily activities. Stev chose the practice round, probably acting on the theory that they should stay out of real combat for as long as possible. This, of course, kept them within the compound's walls, and Kit chafed at the delay. They fought four-on-four against blue-uniformed soldiers wearing red armbands. Both sides wielded mock weapons, and if a combatant was hit, their armband would slither off their arm. How or why, Kit had no idea; the technology of this place seemed to function on an entirely different level than their own. Regardless of the unit's inexperience with these weapons, they still took down their opponents without a single loss. Kit couldn't tell if they were really that much better or if the natives were going easy on them. If they were, she thought sourly, it wasn't going to be to anyone's benefit once they got out into the real fight. And if they weren't, well...their training was severely lacking. Unfortunately, the brevity of the fight meant that she didn't have a chance to pull Mercy aside.

Kit's nerves jangled as they were issued fully functional weapons in the armory. Supposedly this was a war fought in hour-long shifts, and they were informed that they could retreat to the main complex at any time if they were injured or felt too fatigued to continue. Kit's brow furrowed at that. What sort of war was this, where soldiers could come and go from the field of battle without a commander's orders? Still, if there was no commander overseeing the attack, that would make it easier for her to slip away.

The armorer also issued those bizarre rocket packs to Stev, Avin, and Mercy and gave them brief instructions on their use. He didn't bat an eye when Kit refused hers, which unnerved her even more. She was starting to wonder if everyone here was actually some form of robot or android. It wouldn't be any weirder than the shamblers.

They joined a group of six other soldiers at the main gate—the rest of their shift, apparently. Kit supposed that a smaller group of guerrilla operatives would be more effective in the warren of streets than a full-on assault. But then again, there were a lot of soldiers in that compound. Kit had never been involved in a real war before, but she had somehow thought they were...bigger. Messier. Not fought by ten soldiers in hour-long shifts.

The gates opened. The other six soldiers moved out at a purposeful trot. Kit's unit followed, none of them entirely sure what to expect. And Kit's next big surprise was waiting right outside the gate. Once they were outside, all six of the soldiers just...scattered. There was no cohesion, no strategy, as they charged ahead, each one looking around for enemies as they went. Some used their rocket packs to boost up to the roofs, others crept into the shadows and concealed themselves in nooks, and still others ran straight up the middle of the street. To an experienced fighter, there was no doubt these soldiers were improvising.

The team exchanged disbelieving glances, then Stev took over. Soon Kit was scouting the rooftops ahead, while the other three moved between bits of cover on the street below her. This made her plan more difficult. She had expected more coordination, more support from the other fighters. She couldn't leave her team when they needed her skills.

A flash of red ahead caught her eye, and a quick ping brought her teammates to a halt below. She wasn't sure they needed to be so cautious, though. The enemy, a lone soldier, ran straight at them without any caution whatsoever. From above, she watched Stev raise his weapon hesitantly. She scanned the streets in the distance, but saw no one else. The soldier was well within range now, but still no one opened fire. It felt so wrong, like shooting someone who was just strolling down the street.

When he could no longer wait, Stev fired into the ground in front of the soldier. Immediately, the man shifted to an exaggerated fighting stance, scanning his surroundings, but he didn't do the one thing that made sense. He didn't dive for cover. He stood stupidly in the middle of the street, until he caught sight of Stev and opened fire. At that moment, bullets from three guns converged on him, and he dropped where he stood—and disappeared.

Kit couldn't believe her eyes. There wasn't even a smudge of blood left where the man had stood. Before she could come to terms with what had happened, Avin gave a warning shout and opened fire on a pair of approaching Reds. Kit swung into action. Once again, survival had to take precedence over thought.

After that, there seemed to be a never-ending stream of enemies coming their way. By the time their hour was almost up, Kit understood why there were shifts. While there were many enemies, they were woefully incompetent. They never changed their strategy or tried to come at them from a different angle. They ran down the street, were mowed down by bullets, and disappeared, leaving the pavement still flawlessly clean. At this point, killing them felt like a chore. No one had sustained any injuries, and Kit suspected their most dangerous enemy at this point was boredom, and the carelessness it brought.

Kit, however, had her steadily increasing level of anxiety to keep her sharp and focused. As the minutes ticked down to the end of the hour, she wondered if there would ever be an opportunity for her to slip away. And then, at five minutes to the hour, her chance arrived from the sky on big, whirring propellers.

What the craft was, Kit couldn't say for sure. But it was big, it was loud, it was mounted with guns, and it was full of soldiers. The soldiers dropped out of it, dangling on lines like awkward metal spiders. Kit and Avin picked many of them off before they even reached the ground, while Stev and Mercy emptied what was left of their ammo into the flying machine itself. It wavered and yawed erratically, losing altitude, and Kit had to retreat from the edge of the rooftop to escape the strength of its downdraft, moving out of sight of the street below.

An explosion rocked her onto her heels. Fire blossomed out of the aircraft as it plummeted out of the sky. She stood for a moment, mesmerized, before she realized that it was headed squarely for her. She spun and sprinted across the rooftop, activating her climbers as she went, and launched herself at the next building. It was taller than this one, with only a small gap between, and she landed spreadeagled against its mirrored wall. She scampered up and turned just in time to see the machine plow into the rooftop she had vacated a moment ago, propellers still flailing dangerously. Its tail skidded to the side and crashed into the building she was perched on, making her stagger. That thing had been more dangerous in its destruction than it had been when functional.

The end of the hour ticked down on her MDU. Three all-clears pinged. Kit looked around. Without realizing it, she had fled further down the road toward enemy territory. It was now or never. She pinged the all clear back to her teammates, then added the ping codes for "regroup" and "base." Hopefully that would keep them from waiting for her. It would have been nice to tell Mercy her plans, to have some backup if things went wrong, but that hadn't been possible. She was on her own.

As she set off alone towards the enemy base, smoking machinery at her back, silence settled on the city. The streets below were empty. She wondered if the Reds worked on the same hour-long shifts as the Blues. That could make it very difficult to snatch one for interrogation before the battle was rejoined. Behind her, even the smoke was dissipating, as if it had finished its job. A flicker of movement in the street below caught her eye, but when she froze and surveyed the area, there was nothing. It was likely her nerves had gotten the better of her. None of the Reds had displayed any initiative for stealth thus far. Still, it could be fatal to underestimate them. She moved even more slowly and silently, but she saw nothing else—until thirty seconds later, when a fully-armed Red soldier clomped heedlessly down the middle of the street. A quick glance showed no other soldiers in sight. She grinned. Easy prey.

She dropped down behind him, using the force of her leap to bring her larger opponent to the ground. Before he could cry out, she had a knee on his back and her knife to his throat. A flicker behind her distracted her for a fraction of a second—and her captive moved with a speed that she never would have anticipated, blurring her vision. Suddenly, her knife was gone, and she was on her knees, unable to move. If she looked out of the far corner of her left eye, she could see Avin, also on his knees, encased in a blue glow. His muscles stood out in cords as he strained against the invisible force holding them both motionless.

The Red soldier stood over them, finger pressed to a button on his wrist-band. Kit could only assume that this was generating the force field that held them helpless. She stayed still, watching Avin struggle at the periphery of her vision. A dull anger burned in her stomach.

"First warning: unauthorized weaponry on field of battle. You are disqualified from participation for twenty-four hours." He touched another button next to the first, which opened up an ominously glowing red portal, and with a flick of his wrist, sent both of them hurtling through it.

They landed more softly than Kit had feared. The paralysis lifted before they hit the floor, allowing them to tumble with more control. Avin, predictably, rolled gracefully to his feet and sprinted back towards the closing portal, but he was still too slow. Kit glared and rubbed a bruised hip. Her knife was gone, and neither of their guns had made it through the portal.

"What the hell did you think you were doing, following me like that?" Kit growled. If he hadn't come up behind her and distracted her at that one critical moment...

"What the hell did you think *you* were doing?" he responded with surprising heat.

"I was going to get information. You saw it, there in the dining hall, I know you did! These are not normal people."

"You were sneaking off, without orders or the permission of your superior officer," he retorted coldly, eyes flashing. "It was my duty to find out what you were up to and return you to face appropriate discipline."

"From who? Stev? What discipline could he give out, when he's as much of a prisoner as the rest of us? The Congress has no power here."

"The Congress has power everywhere." His tone had gone very flat. If she had been less angry, she might have taken that as a warning, but the rage burned in her gut.

"Not here! These people don't even know what the Congress is. If we don't take some steps—outside the chain of command, if need be!—then we will never get back to our normal lives."

Avin's eyes widened. It wasn't possible that he hadn't considered the prospect; they'd discussed it amongst themselves before. But he looked stunned.

"No, we have to get back. There's a way back." His voice had a tinge of shakiness. Kit peered at him, His pupils were completely dilated, as if he was in shock, and his fists were clenched.

"Well, yeah," she agreed, confusion chipping away at her anger. "There has to be a way back somewhere. We just won't find it if we sit around in the Blue camp surrounded by...who knows what these people are. Androids or robots or something..."

He calmed a bit. "There has to be a way back somewhere. We have to find it. I have to go back." He began scanning the room they were in, stalking along the walls like a caged animal. Kit watched him with growing concern.

"Avin." She called his name sharply, but got no reaction. "Avin, what's wrong with you?" He didn't even look at her, just prowled ceaselessly around the small room in which they were being held, running his hands along the walls. Kit followed his rotation, realizing for the first time that there was no door. This room could only be accessed through that strange portal, it seemed. Escape was impossible.

After several more attempts to get Avin's attention failed, Kit sat cross-legged in the center of the room where she wouldn't be in the way of his circling. She checked her pockets for anything useful, but came up with only a few tranq stamps, the two half-eaten ration bars, and Rose's gold ring. Everything else had either been confiscated or left in her pack at the Blues' base. There was no furniture in the room, only featureless gray walls. She wondered if they would be fed. If they would actually be released at the end of twenty-four hours. If they were released, what welcome would they have at the Blue complex? She had counted on returning with vital information. If she returned with nothing, Stev might decide to expel her from the team, or leave her behind if they found a way to return. Or worse yet, bring her back for discipline from the ORG and possibly the Congress itself. That would mean—

Psychosomatic inducement. Conditioning, brainwashing, until she'd never dare to disobey an order again, couldn't bear to think for herself...

What would happen to such a person if they were physically prevented from doing what they perceived as their duty?

She shot to her feet. Avin was still circling, as if a door might suddenly materialize in one of the walls and he had to be ready for it. Calm, collected Avin, the best strategist she'd ever seen. She darted in front of him, reached up, and grasped his cool face between her hands, forcing him to look into her eyes. There was only a sliver of silver iris around the black well of his pupil, and he looked past her blankly. With an absentminded swat, he pushed her hands away and went on, mindlessly, wall after wall.

"Avin," she called after him more softly. "It's okay. We're going to get back. We're going to go back and give our report. Avin?"

He paused, as if her words needed time to seep into his mind, past the layers of panic.

"We're going to report," she repeated firmly. He sighed, still facing away from her, and his shoulders drooped. She approached him cautiously, grasped his shoulders, and turned him to face her. His eyes focused on her.

"We're going to report?" His voice was very low, plaintive.

"As soon as we can," she promised.

He took a step back, leaned against the wall, and slid down it, his eyes closing. Kit knelt next to him, ready to catch him if he kept falling, but he just sat, head on his knees, for a long moment.

"You figured it out." It wasn't a question. She nodded anyway. He raised his head and looked at her, silvery eyes intense. "We've been working together so long. I hoped you never would." Kit made a strange gesture, half head-shake, half shrug, trying to dismiss everything that had just happened as insignificant. As if inducement could ever be shrugged off. He frowned. "I don't want your pity."

That stung. "As if I could pity you. You beat me eight times out of ten in practice, and you can practically keep up with me in scouting even without climbers."

"Eight out of ten?" he asked, eyebrows rising.

"I counted." She thought she saw the corner of his mouth quirk upward, but then he turned his head away, resting it on his knees again. Silence lowered around them like a curtain. A thousand thoughts bobbed through her head like leaves on water.

"It took me a year to even beat you once." Kit wasn't sure why she had said that. Avin raised his head and looked at her. Perhaps he hadn't noticed that she'd always judged her own progress against his skill. "Then it took me another two months to do it again. Two out of ten is only my record so far this year."

"You shouldn't judge yourself against me."

Kit raised her eyebrows, surprised. "Why not? You're the best of us in combat, no question." He shook his head stubbornly.

"You're a better operative than I'll ever hope to be."

"That's not even close to being true."

"You never tried to desert." Any attempt at mirth slid off her face. Avin wouldn't look at her.

"So that's why..."

"That's why," he said bitterly, staring at the far wall. "That's why I can't even think of disobeying orders without turning into a mindless animal. That's why I can't put a toe out of line. That's why I had no choice but to follow you." He turned a burning gaze on her, and she shrank from the anger and pain in his eyes. "You fear the people here because they might be robots, just faithfully following some program. But I'm no better."

Her heart felt like it was bursting in her chest. All of this inside, and she had never seen it, never looked past the cool and collected exterior. She reached out a tentative hand and laid it on his shoulder. He shrugged it away.

She knew it wasn't about her. She knew he was suffering with her knowledge of his past misdeeds. The rejection still stung. She stood up and walked several paces across the small room. Then, with a sudden surge of mingled anger and courage, she spun to face him.

"You know, you're not the only one who's messed up. Do you realize, this—all of this!" she gestured expansively, taking in their imprisonment, their displacement, all of the danger and confusion of the past few days, "—could be my fault?" Avin looked at her silently, and she plowed on. "The morning before our mission, I found a listening device in our apartment. A bug. They were spying on us." Her heart was pounding. Already she regretted this, but it was too late to reconsider.

"What were they hoping to hear?" Avin asked reluctantly.

"The night after we hit the orphanage, I had guard duty. I saw the children escape. I didn't raise the alarm." She said it as calmly as she could. Kept it simple. Discarded any doubts or inner turmoil about what she had or hadn't seen, what action she might have taken.

Avin didn't respond for a moment. He tilted his head back against the wall, stared at the ceiling. She stood in the center of that small room, waiting for his disapproval, anger, reprimands.

He stood up slowly, a bit awkwardly, and came to stand in front of her. She wondered if he would try to take her into custody, even though they were both prisoners. Maybe he would hit her. How would his programming respond to this damning admission? She looked at her feet.

Cool, long-fingered hands cupped her cheeks, tilting her face upwards in the reverse of her earlier gesture. Her eyes flew up to meet his in surprise.

"Thank you." His expression was more open, more honest than she had ever seen it. "You spared them what I went through. If we get back, I will do everything in my power to leave this out of my report." He leaned his forehead down to press it against hers. She was suddenly, startlingly aware of how close their faces were. Her heart was pounding again. His thumb moved across her cheek in the barest suggestion of a caress, and then he turned away.

Kit's fears proved to be unfounded: they were, it appeared, to be fed. At noon, a portal opened up near the ceiling, and a basket of food was lowered down to them. Sitting side by side on the floor, they watched it land with an encouragingly weighty thunk. The portal closed, slicing off the cord the basket had been lowered on. The end snaked down at their feet, leaving no doubt as to what would happen if they tried to make a dash through a portal, come next mealtime.

Wordlessly, they stood and investigated their meal. Not only were they not to be starved, they were apparently not to be stinted either. Inside the basket, they found several plastic-wrapped stacks of fluffy bread, meat, cheese, and vegetables. Each one had a little printed label proclaiming them to be different types of "sandwiches" - Ham and Swiss, Egg Salad, Roast Beef with Horseradish, and Turkey Club. There was also a large bag of something called "potato chips," several pieces of fruit, and a couple of the paper containers of liquid.

They opened each of the sandwiches and sniffed them experimentally. Avin offered her first choice, and she decided to try the turkey club. It had the least pungent smell. Avin, probably deciding to take one for the team, tackled the appallingly smelly egg salad sandwich.

"How is it?" she asked doubtfully after his second bite.

"Not bad," he replied laconically. Kit continued to be doubtful. Hers, at least, was milder, with a pleasant crunch and a tangy, creamy spread.

Unsure whether they would get dinner, they decided to save the fruit and potato chips for later. The sandwiches seemed perishable, so they each chose a second to eat now. The roast beef looked more questionable, and Kit decided to save Avin from it. It had a strange, bitter scent, but nowhere near as overwhelming as that egg salad had been. Trying not to show her reluctance, she took a big bite, and gasped in surprise at the pungent spiciness of it. It didn't burn, it just sort of tingled in her nose. It was one of the oddest sensations that she'd ever felt. She hastily swallowed—and sneezed.

"Are you okay?" Avin asked, torn between concern and amusement.

"I'm fine," Kit spluttered, taking a swig from her carton of red juice. "Just surprised."

"Can I try a bite?" he asked. She shot a surprised glance at him, and he smiled. That surprised her even more. "I'm curious," he admitted.

"Be my guest." She handed the sandwich over to him, and he took a careful bite.

"Whoo!" he exclaimed. "No wonder you were surprised. That sandwich bites back. Do you want the other one?"

"No, it's fine. Now I'm forewarned." Kit reclaimed the sandwich, grinning. His eyes crinkled at the corners when he smiled. She wondered if he had been more like this, before...

The day crawled by. Kit was tempted to eat the fruit out of boredom. She and Avin chatted occasionally, with greater ease than she had ever conversed with him before, but as the day passed, they transitioned into quiet. Avin's tension was rising, though she could tell he was trying to suppress it. Dinner came and went in silence. It turned out they hadn't needed to save the food after all, but it had made both of them feel better. After they had eaten, Avin sat down with his back against the wall and closed his eyes in meditation. Kit didn't begrudge him that, but she felt strangely lonely. There was nothing to do except wait and hope that, should their captors break their word, Stev and Mercy could find them, perhaps bargain for their release. She paced up and down in the tiny room until she began to feel tired, then laid down on the hard floor and tried to sleep. Her mind wouldn't stop racing, and the floor was cold. She shivered, wishing she had thought to stick her field blanket into a pocket instead of leaving it in her pack. What a stupid oversight.

A warm weight settled over her. Her eyes flew open to find Avin settling his field blanket over both of them.

"I hope you don't mind if we share," he said with a tentative, crooked smile. She shook her head, and he laid down beside her. The blanket captured his warmth and reflected it back to her. The soft sound of his breathing lulled her to sleep.

Chapter Eleven

There was no change in light to signal the coming of morning, but Kit's MDU didn't care about that. Its alarm restored her to consciousness right on time, even though there was nothing for her to do. As wakefulness reasserted itself, she realized that she was stretched out on her side, head pillowed on her arm, and there was something very large and warm pressed up against her back. And—was that an arm wrapped around her waist?

Avin's alarm must have gone off too. He stirred sleepily, pulled her closer—and then launched himself away from her, rolling to his feet. Kit rolled over, laughing at his distraught expression.

"It's not a big deal," she said, waving a hand dismissively, and stood stiffly to fold the blanket. His cheeks flushed bright red, and he turned his back to her, hiding his face in his hands. She laughed again. It felt nice, having something to laugh about in all this. She put down the folded blanket, and laid a hand on his shoulder.

"Really, it's fine. Warmer that way, anyway." Finally he lowered his hands.

"Sorry," he muttered. She shrugged. She'd already said it was fine.

Breakfast arrived in the same way lunch and dinner had. The baskets were starting to pile up in the corner of the room. The newest one contained a pot of porridge that tasted nearly identical to the stuff served at the Blue complex. The only difference was that the dried fruit was orange instead of brown this morning.

By the time they had finished eating, Avin seemed to have gotten over his embarrassment. "Almost time for our release," he commented with a crooked smile, his eyes flickering around the bare walls of the room. Kit knew he was awaiting that deadline with even more trepidation than she was. If escape started to look impossible, his conditioning might kick in again, whether it was useful or not.

"If they don't release us, I'm sure Stev will come looking. I assume you told him you were following me. Authority figure and all that."

Avin shrugged. "I sent him a team retrieval ping. He thought I was going to meet up with you and help you clear a way through the rubble." Kit raised her eyebrows and he chuckled. "I can't disobey, but I've found ways of omitting information unless directly asked. The less I say, the less people expect me to say." Kit's respect for him increased. Even with the inducement, he was finding ways to work around it. That was...unheard of, actually.

"Thank you." Knowing what he'd done for her, even against his conditioning—she no longer had to fear discipline when they rejoined the team. If neither of them disabused him of the notion, Stev would believe that they had been captured while making their way back to base.

He shrugged again. "I don't believe in subjecting anyone to unnecessary punishment. I understand what you were trying to do, and why. I just—couldn't—" He gestured helplessly.

"I bet it's worse when someone's not just breaking rules, but also going off by themselves. I could easily have been deserting." He nodded. She took a deep breath and asked, "What made you desert in the first place?" She couldn't imagine deserting. The ORG had been her home, the home of her friends. Where else would she have gone? What else would she have done with her life?

Avin opened his mouth to reply—and choked. "I—can't," he gasped.

"Sorry!" she exclaimed. "Of course you wouldn't be able to—sorry!"

He wiped his watering eye with the heel of his hand. "I shouldn't have even tried. I know better. But I thought maybe this time..."

"Does Stev know?"

"No. I was assigned to his team after. A fresh start." His mouth quirked bitterly. "It wasn't so bad, taking orders instead of giving them." Kit's eyes widened. So he had been a unit lead? Or higher? He realized what he'd said, and coughed, as if his throat had tried to retroactively close. Then he chuckled. "Well, that just sort of slipped out."

"Let's change the subject," Kit suggested. Before he accidentally asphyxiated himself. He shrugged noncommittally, but before Kit had even started to mentally grope for an appropriate subject to switch to, they were interrupted by the glow of a red portal. This one was in a wall, rather than the ceiling, and easily situated for walking. They both stood and faced it. Avin sidled behind her, covering her back should they be attacked.

Instead, the Red soldier who stepped through addressed them neutrally. "Your sentence has been served. Please proceed to No Man's Land."

What an absurd name. Kit recognized it from military history courses and books, but it had never made sense to her. If it was no man's land, why were there always so many people fighting over it? But she had been a mediocre student, at best. She shot a glance at Avin, who nodded her ahead.

She steeled herself, but the passage through the portal felt like nothing. One step she was in the cell, the next in a park-like square surrounded by buildings. A group of bushes stood in the center, open to the sky. Kit glanced up to make sure, but it was true. There was greenery and plant life out in the open with no protection. There wasn't even a barrier around it; in fact, there were benches set amidst it, as if anyone could wander up and sit. She glanced behind to make sure that Avin had followed her through. The portal zipped closed behind him. She jerked her head to the left. He nodded and began to scout the perimeter to the right.

Kit felt exposed. None of their weapons had been returned to them—not that she had expected it. But she hadn't been this completely unarmed since her early training. It was uncomfortable.

Nothing threatened around the perimeter, nor were there any exits. She met up with Avin, who had similar non-results, on the far side of the square. There, they discovered two more portals, one red and one blue. Between them was a little table with colorful signs and brochures that read things like "Join the Blues, Fight for Right!" and "Rebel with Red, Take Freedom Back!" Avin picked up one of the brochures and leafed through it.

"I think we're supposed to choose," he murmured. "Go back to Blue, or turn on them."

"We have to go back to Blue, though. Stev and Mercy..."

"You were willing to go your own way once, to get more information. We might be able to learn something valuable in the camp of the Reds," he countered.

"Isn't that...disobedient?" she asked, concerned for him. And for herself. What if, in the middle of enemy territory, his conditioning decided that he had to bring her to Stev for disciplinary action?

"Oh, I fully intend to return to the unit, and clearly you do too. That's enough to satisfy me for now. It's all about the belief." He idly turned the brochure over in his hands—and froze.

On the back of the brochure was a crudely drawn but still very recognizable design in heavy black ink. The Congress Seal. Beneath it was a set of coordinates.

Conflicting emotions flooded Kit. Elation—here, finally, was evidence that their home still existed and that they weren't crazy. Dismay—in the wake of the things Avin had told her, the things that she had told him—returning seemed nearly as scary as staying. Doubts gnawed at her. What did she have to go back for, really? Her closest friends, her teammates, were here. Was fighting for the ORG actually any better than fighting for the Blues? Or even the Reds? She had no idea why or who she fought, either way.

Was she really considering the idea of not returning to the ORG? That was insane.

And yet, the little whisper insisted, Avin had tried to desert. He, of all people, must have had reason to take such a risk.

Kit glanced at her teammate. His eyes were fixed on the Seal, shining with fanatic zeal. She realized that her wishes were irrelevant anyway. Avin would have to go home or go mad.

"We need a point of origin to find those coordinates," she pointed out, moving on to more practical concerns.

"They're very low numbers," Avin commented, a little sense reappearing in his eyes. "Perhaps the brochure itself is the point of origin." He replaced the sheet of glossy paper on the table, and Kit focused on it, setting it as the center of a coordinate grid. Then to match the written coordinates...

She and Avin moved together towards the park-like center of the square. She took care not to brush against any of the bushes, which were set in little planters surrounded by a sea of light gray gravel; she didn't want to damage them with her passing. She had no idea how delicate an actual living leaf might be.

They neared the center of the square, but saw nothing unusual. Then Avin's foot came down with a hollow clunk. He knelt and brushed away the gravel, revealing a large, thin metal sheet with a mirror sheen. It might have been scavenged from the side of a building. He dug his fingers under the edge and lifted experimentally. It hinged upwards, revealing a gaping hole in the ground and a rickety ladder descending into the depths. Kit looked toward the blue portal. Who knew what was happening to Stev and Mercy right now? By the time she turned back, Avin's dark head was already disappearing down the ladder.

Once on the ladder, the hole seemed claustrophobic and cramped, in a way that even the vents in the lab hadn't. Its walls were made of some muddy dark brown substance. It didn't seem to be either dirt or wood, but something in between, like rubber that had been stretched too far. Kit couldn't bring herself to touch it. At the bottom, a low-ceilinged tunnel ran a short distance, then curved sharply to the right. By the time she was off the ladder, Avin was already turning the corner, head and shoulders hunched to fit through the narrow aperture. She hastened to follow, loathe to let him out of her sight in this unfamiliar territory.

Kit turned the corner, and was forced, not for the first time in recent memory, to confront the possibility of encroaching insanity. She shoved her way through the rough concrete that edged the end of the tunnel and emerged into the cool white lighting of a different world.

She stood in a much larger shaft, walled and floored in smooth, gently curving concrete that met in an arch far above her head. In the center of the floor was a canal, roughly as deep as she was tall, filled with mossy green water. White bridges with metal railings spanned the canal at regular intervals, and people bustled to and fro across them.

Everyone here wore the ORG uniform.

Even as she gaped in astonishment, a crisp order came from her left. "Hands up! Drop your weapons!"

That last wasn't necessary. She'd been too shocked to think about pulling a weapon even if she'd still had one. She raised her empty hands.

"No need to worry," the voice from her left came again, more cheerfully this time. "Only a precaution. Some of our new members are a little confused at first." The owner of the voice, a tall blonde woman, edged into her line of vision, keeping a pistol trained steadily on them. When it became apparent that neither of them was about to go ballistic, she lowered—but didn't holster—her weapon.

"Unarmed?" she asked. When they both nodded, she sighed in disappointment. "Too bad, we could use more new tech. You can put your hands down now. Your escort will be here in a moment, and you'll get some answers."

Answers? Kit couldn't imagine how this place could be explained. Still, someone had better try.

In the promised moment, two new ORG operatives marched up. They were a strangely mismatched pair, a tall, thin man and a surprisingly short, heavyset woman. The woman winked impishly up at the blonde who had so carefully greeted them.

"Two more new recruits? Let's get you to the Commander for debriefing." The heavyset woman's voice and bearing were relaxed, as if she handled this situation every day. Her weapon was held ready, and Kit had no doubt that if she or Avin were to make a false move, it would be used, but her attitude said that she did not expect that scenario. A sideways glance at Avin showed that his eyes had gained a manic gleam at the word "debriefing." He must believe that this was a legitimate outpost of the ORG.

Kit docilely followed the shorter woman, but her eyes were busily flickering from one detail to the next, taking in this newest oddity. She quickly realized that while everyone wore the uniform of the ORG, not all the uniforms were the same. The cut varied, not enough that it was immediately apparent, but enough that it was odd. The fabric was often faded or patched, as if the owner had no access to replacements. Even the MDUs showed a surprising variety of form. Some of them looked like miniature telescopes, others were reflective where they should be matte, and still others were frankly grotesque. Instead of discreet, flesh-toned plugs, they had been stapled directly into the skin, leaving puckered scar tissue along the edges. These seemed to be rare, but often worn by people with the attitude of command.

The tunnel was lined with doorways, some real frames with actual doors in them and others simply crevices like the one they had entered by. They were escorted to a metal door that swung open on nicely oiled hinges. The walls were lined with metal shelves, as if for a storage area, but the center of the room was dominated by an aluminum table, balancing on spindly folding legs, and a semi-circle of stools. The layout was reminiscent of the briefing rooms back at the old ORG.

The woman behind the desk raised her head, tossing aside shaggy brown bangs to reveal a deeply lined face and a bulky MDU that was a dark, smudged silver rather than black. It was surrounded by thick, rippled scarring, and seemed to pull heavily on the woman's skin, sinking into her cheek and pulling down on her brow, giving her entire face the impression of being lopsided. She folded her hands on the table and frowned. The corner of her mouth beneath the MDU didn't curl downward as sharply, and when she spoke, it became evident that she had limited movement in that side of her face.

"Welcome to the ORG Extension Headquarters. I am Elite Commander Tera. Your designations?"

"AVN1424," Avin responded promptly, standing at attention. The Commander's stony gaze flickered to Kit.

"KIT1642." She tried to mimic Avin's confident acceptance of the situation, but her patience was wearing thin. Yet again, she had to pretend that the bizarre situation around her was normal, and frustration crawled up her spine like a many-legged insect that begged to be swatted.

"Weapons? Equipment?" She tapped a commanding finger on the table-top. Both operatives advanced and turned out the contents of their pockets. It was a meager array: Avin's blanket, her tranq stamps, and the two half-bars of rations that Kit had managed to save all this time. She left the gold ring in her pocket, as it was neither weapon nor equipment. Avin, burdened by no such concerns, turned out his pockets down to the lint. It looked like he had been collecting loose screws and bits of metal, though Kit wasn't sure what he'd intended to do with them. With their original equipment confiscated by the Blues and their newly issued weaponry taken by the Reds, there wasn't a whole lot left that was useful. The frown on the Commander's face deepened—on one side, anyway.

"At least we'll have more tranquilizers," she grumbled. "These will be added to our communal stores." Resentment flooded Kit, but she kept it to herself. Again. The Commander's eyes flickered up to Kit, and for a second she feared that the older woman could read her disobedient thoughts. Instead she grunted, "Climbers in working order?"

"Yes, Commander," Kit replied as respectfully as she could.

"That's something." She didn't seem impressed. "Repeat the last orders you were given."

Without hesitation, Avin rattled them off. "Research Laboratory #24. Contact has been lost. You will enter the lab, ascertain their status, and destroy any hostile forces. If you do not report within 24 hours, the facility will be deemed lost and the entire structure leveled."

The Commander nodded, as if that was exactly what she had expected. "State the year, per your MDU, in which these orders were issued."

"947," Avin answered promptly. Kit fought to keep her face from showing the warring puzzlement and suspicion that raged through her.

"Sit."

Kit and Avin moved forward, leaving their two escorts guarding the door, and seated themselves on the stubby stools. These seats, made of dented metal and several inches shorter than the stools in the ORG briefing rooms, made her intensely uncomfortable. The Commander steepled her fingers and eyed them contemplatively before she spoke.

"You have found your way, as I said, to the ORG Extension Headquarters. You were chosen by the ORG as our newest elite soldiers, and you have passed the tests that are set to new members. You will enter service here, awaiting the day we are called, by the will of the Congress. Any questions?"

"No, Commander!" Avin answered immediately. Kit had a great number of questions, and that number was growing every second, but asking the Commander straight to her face, well, that was a good way to end up in the exact same position as Avin, completely unable to question what he was being told. A whisper of despair tried to creep into her mind; she could no longer count on Avin's strategic acumen. He would not be applying it here. She was effectively on her own.

Commander Tera stood, towering over them. Avin sprang to his feet also, and Kit hurried to follow suit, but she was sure that the Commander had noted even such a slight hesitation.

"Do you accept your positions, by the will of the Congress?"

"By the will of the Congress!" Avin replied. His voice was quiet, but sure. Kit envied him that. Her limbs felt as if they were filled with lead. She was no longer sure whether her next words would be truth or subterfuge, or what her reasons would be for either.

"By the will of the Congress," Kit said.

Chapter Twelve

K it and Avin were escorted into the main tunnel and across one of the bridges to the other side of the canal. Kit's mind was buzzing with all the new concepts that had been piled into it.

This place was supposedly the staging ground for some great army that the ORG was building, made up of its former Elite units. That raised the question of why the Congress felt the need for such an army. The ORG and regular police force were completely adequate for keeping control of the city, at least inside the Limits, and as far as she could tell the Congress didn't much care about the Limits. That meant that this could only be intended for some military action outside the city. Invasion of—or defense against—a foreign power. Kit had no idea what would be needed for such an action. Until this mission, she hadn't considered that any such foreign power might exist, but this army seemed to indicate that someone else—someone more powerful than the Blues—was out there.

The subterfuge of getting them in here, though—well, she supposed they couldn't just be told of the Congress's plans. If the army was being built in such a secret location, it was likely that none of the flunkies who would be talking to someone of her rank would be in on it. It was essentially a transfer of command where no one knew the new recruits were coming until they arrived.

The Commander had mentioned that they had passed their tests. The lab, the shamblers, the Reds and the Blues—could those really all be tests set in place by the ORG? That would explain the inexplicable. All the monsters and the enemies must have been some sort of advanced bot. She had never really left the ORG. Now she was glad she hadn't voiced any specific doubts.

But she had told Avin of her indiscretion on guard duty. She had no idea whether they would have waited this long to apprehend her if they had overheard that conversation. She didn't think so, but she was unsure of her own judgment at this point. And there was always the chance that he would reveal it, if he was questioned closely enough.

A horrible thought crossed her mind. Could Avin have deceived her? He could have made all of that up, put her in a situation to trade confidence for confidence, all with the plan of reporting whatever she said to the ORG. She glanced at him, walking placidly at her side. If he had any fear of what was to come in this place, he didn't show it. Was it only the inducement—or true, bone-deep loyalty?

Why couldn't she feel that loyalty anymore?

Her anxious thoughts were cut off by their arrival at a new door. This one was nothing more than a curtain hung over a length of pipe that spanned the doorway. For an Elite ORG army, this place was surprisingly shabby. Behind the curtain, they found a narrow, concrete room with four cots pushed against the walls. Each cot was matched with a crate for storing personal belongings. One of the beds had a field blanket folded at its foot, and its crate had an old-fashioned padlock dangling from the clasp. The other three were bare, but for some dingy sheets and a thin pillow each. Once again, Kit regretted forgetting her field blanket. She had doubts about whether she would be issued a new one.

"Your new lead will be here soon," one of their escorts told them. Then, to Kit's surprise, she gave them a saucy wink before both the guards walked away. They were left to their own devices.

Avin moved to the bed across from that taken by the mysterious third occupant, whipped his field blanket out of his pocket, and began to refold it meticulously. He concentrated on every crease as if it was a work of art. When he was done, he laid it at the foot of the bed, and dumped his screw collection into the metal box with a decisive clatter. Kit stood watching him. Even her half-eaten ration bars had been claimed for communal stores.

Still, she should choose a bed. With resignation, she sat down on the bed next to Avin's. Maybe he was trustworthy, and maybe he wasn't, but at least she knew him.

As Avin finished storing all of his gear, the curtain across the doorway was pushed aside. The man who entered was tall and well built, but slightly unkempt. His sandy brown hair was long by ORG standards and it looked as though he hadn't shaved in a couple of days. His MDU was the same type as the Commander's, though his scarring was less pronounced, blending into the deep smile-lines creasing his face.

"Hello recruits," he said with a crooked grin. "I'm Jak, and I'll be your unit's lead and guide, at least until we get some recruits newer than you." He shook hair out of his startlingly blue eye and peered at them. "We've got a climber and a—no, no, wait, let me guess—equipment specialist?" Avin nodded respectfully, though his slightly furrowed brow indicated that he was unsure of this informal welcome. Kit wasn't sure of it either, but still—Stev was very informal when they weren't out on a mission. Many leads integrated very closely with their units. After all, they only had three subordinates.

"Good, that'll round out this unit nicely. No need to do any swapping with other units. It's always nice to keep teammates together." Jak smiled and rubbed his hands together, as if he was bracing for something.

"Now for the difficult part. I swear by the Congress that what I'm about to tell you is true." He was still smiling. Kit's nerves vibrated in warning, but she stayed still and silent, waiting. "What year is it now, according to your MDUs?"

There it was, that question about the year again.

"947," Avin answered, just as promptly but more warily.

"Time flies," Jak said with another crooked grin. This time the expression seemed tinged with melancholy. "This is where I have to request the suspension of your disbelief. I left regular operations in the year 695."

Kit shook her head, thinking she hadn't heard correctly.

Avin frowned. "That would make you over two hundred years old." Both of them eyed Jak's deeply lined face skeptically. He was older—certainly older than she was used to seeing on active duty in the ORG—but nowhere near that old. Jak grinned again, crinkling the creases at the corners of his eyes.

"No, I'm not quite that old, though I'm sure you think being in my fifties is old enough." Kit gasped and then tried to turn it into a quiet cough. Fifty? That was so far past the usual retirement age that she hadn't ever considered growing that old. "Due to some sort of anomaly, time runs differently here than it does back home. We believe that the ORG created this time distortion so that it could collect its very best soldiers from all time periods. So I've only been living here for about thirty-six years, but two hundred and fifty have passed outside." He paused to see if they were accepting his explanation. Kit's head was spinning; she didn't think she could have responded if she wanted to. And Avin would probably have rather cut off his own arm than tell a commanding officer that he was lying. Jak seemed to take this silence for acceptance.

"We have operatives from all time periods here," he continued. "Tera—Commander Tera to you—and I are from the oldest unit still on active duty. We try to follow the most recent form of ORG regulations, so you should be familiar with most of our operating structure. If you see someone doing something that seems irregular to you, don't hesitate to come to me. I'll let you know whether it's acceptable behavior or not. The ORG used to be more...hmm...relaxed in its requirements of its operatives, and a lot of us older ones have a hard time with the new, stricter rules. You'll pick it up as you go along."

Pick it up as they went along? Kit shot a nervous look over at Avin, who looked frankly terrified. In this they could agree. How could they follow rules when they weren't sure what the rules were?

"You'll find the schedule here is also similar to what you're used to. You'll still train with your unit, but you'll also be expected to learn how to function as a foot soldier in a larger army. We don't run missions, as such, but we do keep an eye on the surrounding territory, and we do supply runs. I have other duties as both Recruit Commander and as the ORG Historian, so I won't always train with you. Your other team member should be here soon, and she'll show you the ropes and give you a tour of our facilities." Jak chattered on, seeming not at all put off by their blank stares. If he had the dubious honor of explaining things to all the new recruits, he was probably used to gapes of disbelief.

In a moment, the door curtain stirred, and the previously mentioned new teammate stepped through. Kit was hit by a stab of resentment. This person was being shoved into her team, taking Mercy's place, as Jak was trying to step into Stev's. Her team was still out there, and she was being forced to work with strangers!

As quickly as the resentment had arisen, it withdrew, to be replaced with relief and delight. She recognized those dark brown curls, the sweet heart-shaped face with its heavy-lidded eyes...

"Merdith!" she exclaimed.

"Kit! Avin!" Her former teammate broke into a wide smile and rushed forward to give her a hearty hug. Rather than a hug, she offered Avin a reserved handshake, but she seemed pleased to see them both. Kit, for her part, was so relieved to see a familiar face that she felt like crying. She swallowed repeatedly to clear the lump in her throat.

"I see you know each other," Jak said. "I'll leave you to get reacquainted and up to speed. If you need me for anything, I'll be in the archives." He directed this last to Merdith, then threw a careless wave at the group and departed.

The joy of reunion quickly faded into awkwardness. Merdith shifted uncomfortably from foot to foot, then decided it was her job to break the ice.

"I'm glad you two made it through the testing. How have you been? Did Stev come with you?"

Kit judged by Avin's closed expression that she would have to be the one to carry the conversation. "We're...in one piece. As far as we know, Stev is still in the Blue compound. So is our fourth."

Merdith's smile faltered. "Been replaced already, have I?"

"Twice, actually," Kit admitted. "I know it's only been a little over half a year, but your first replacement was killed in combat." She winced away from that memory again. "Mercy is brand new."

"Oh! The time difference," Merdith exclaimed. "I keep forgetting. I've only been here for a month."

Kit's eyes widened. "So it's really true? Time is different?"

Merdith nodded. "As nearly as they can figure, one day here is equal to about a week outside. It seems to be fairly constant." She shrugged non-committally, but Kit detected disquiet in her manner. "Come on, let me give you the grand tour."

Merdith started the tour with the mess hall, which was a cavernous room full of drab metal tables and benches. "We intercept food caravans headed for the Blue and Red complexes in turn," she told them. "They don't seem to mind too much, so while everything else is a bit makeshift, we still eat like kings."

Across the canal, there was a large, open space set aside for combat training. One of the walls had been meticulously paneled with mirror tiles scavenged from the buildings outside. A guard stood at attention outside a nearby door—the armory, Merdith informed them. Weapons were kept communally, since there were relatively few of them. The operatives trained with everything available, both old and new ORG tech and weapons acquired from their neighbors, but there was also a heavy emphasis on unarmed combat. There was a firing range set up behind a carefully constructed barricade, but most of the available space was occupied by dueling combatants, hand-to-hand drill, and handcrafted dummies.

"We haven't figured out how to recharge the newer weapons," Merdith commented, "so we mostly train with weapons we've captured. We can always get more ammo on the next caravan raid."

The neighboring washroom and laundry were even more rudimentary. The location had been chosen for one reason: a long, exposed length of pipe ran across the ceiling. At the far end of the room, the pipe had been severed, pouring a steady stream of water into a pit lined with a large sheet of black plastic. A channel carved into the floor caught the overflow and directed the water back across the room and out the door, finally emptying into the greenish drainage channel in the main corridor. Near the pit, several operatives were stoically scrubbing away at a pile of dirty uniforms, sleeves rolled up past their elbows. Kit felt as if she had jumped into the far past. Then she realized that she was actually living in the past. For every day she had been here, a week had passed at the real ORG headquarters. Time was moving on without her.

The part of the room not taken up by laundry facilities was open space, crisscrossed by shallower channels. In each block of space, a hook had been driven into the concrete of the ceiling, and each hook had a bucket. The buckets were partially covered with pieces of thick, perforated fabric, and Merdith showed them how to pull on a rope to create a cascade of water. The buckets had to be manually refilled before each shower, but it was still better than going dirty. Then Kit got hit by a spray of freezing cold water and had second thoughts. There was a walled-off area towards the rear for private functions that wasn't much more sophisticated than the showers. It also involved buckets.

"It's a good thing a sewer line runs right under us, or I don't know how we'd get rid of all the waste," Merdith noted, wrinkling her nose.

Most of the other rooms and cubbyholes were living space except for the archive, which Merdith pointed out with careless wave. Kit wondered if she could obtain permission to access it. Maybe if she could read the history of this place, more things would make sense. Maybe she would feel more comfortable.

The tour concluded at two branching tunnels. One, Merdith told them, ran to the Blue territory and the other to the Red.

"I don't suppose they'd let us contact Stev and Mercy?" Kit said as casually as she could, eyeing the tunnel that ran towards the Blues.

"Nah, they say everyone has to pass the test for themselves." Merdith frowned.

"Doesn't seem quite right. Avin and I got here because we got ourselves captured." Merdith shot her a sharp glance, and she hastily added, "But that's the way it is. I understand." Avin nodded agreement, and Kit wondered if there was any way she had imagined that exchange during their imprisonment.

Without another response, Merdith turned and led them back the way they had come. Kit couldn't help glancing over her shoulder at the tunnels as she walked away. They looked unguarded from this end, but Kit was willing to bet that wasn't actually the case. With a sigh, she followed Merdith.

The last stop before lunch turned out to be a visit to the officer in charge of the duty roster. There was a great deal of work that had to be done by hand in this place—cooking, cleaning, maintenance, repairs—and no one but operatives to do all of it. She, it turned out, would be expected to take her turn in the laundry room, learn how to cook, and even scrub out the bathroom buckets.

If this was how the ORG expected their best operatives to live, then Kit thought she could have dealt with being average. It didn't make sense.

The sergeant looked her over, asked her specialization, and then assigned her to an excavation crew that was building new rooms to expand the compound. Kit gathered that they needed a climber to help finish the ceilings. Avin was told to report to the kitchen.

"Spend the afternoon as you see fit," he told them expressionlessly. "Just report on time tomorrow."

In the mess hall, Merdith led them through the same sort of line with trays and dishes that they had experienced with the Blues. The food wasn't quite as mind-blowing, but the stew was hearty, and there was fresh fruit available. Showering out of a bucket might be worth it for fresh fruit every day.

"I have guard duty this afternoon," Merdith told them after lunch. "I'll meet you back here for dinner. You can do whatever you want until then. Just don't try to leave the compound."

"Are we allowed to access the archives?" Kit asked tentatively.

"Not really," Merdith replied, "but you can ask Jak for a tour. I'm sure he'd be glad to find someone who's interested in those stacks of dusty records."

"I'm going for a workout," Avin said brusquely and disappeared.

"Hah! Same old Avin," Merdith laughed. Then she was gone as well.

Kit found herself alone outside the mess hall. Everyone but her had somewhere to go. She set out toward the archive, though she no longer had any real enthusiasm for it.

The door to the archive was another of the few metal doors in evidence, carefully locked and guarded. Apparently they took their record keeping seriously. She approached the guard cautiously.

"I was told that Jak would be here."

"Sure he's in there. Who's asking?"

She frowned at his casual manner. He was on duty. Surely a little more formality was called for. She gave him her name regardless.

"Kit, huh?" He bit off the 't' with an unsettling intensity. "Sure you wanna go in there? It's all dusty, boring books. I go off duty soon, I could make sure you see something really interesting." His friendly smile slipped into something closer to a leer, and his gaze ran over her body a little too obviously.

Kit flushed red with a mixture of rage and embarrassment. It wasn't that she'd never been propositioned before, but no one had ever been quite this obvious about it—and on duty at the time. She desperately sought for an appropriately acidic refusal, but came up empty.

The metal door swung inward, and Jak's shaggy head emerged. "Wil, are you hassling someone? Oh, hello Kit, is something the matter?"

"I came by because I had a free evening and was interested in touring the archives," Kit replied somewhat stiffly. "Merdith said it would be alright to ask."

"Of course! Come in."

She walked toward the door, trying to seem unconcerned while still keeping as much distance as she could between her and the lecherous Wil. Even with that distance, he leaned in as she passed.

"Remember, if you get bored, you know where to find me." His eyes lingered somewhere lower than her face.

"Soldier!" Jak barked, and Wil snapped to attention at his post. Jak gestured her inside, and then stepped out to address the guard in softer tones.

"New regulations, Wil, remember. The new ones aren't used to familiarity. If you aren't careful, you're going to regret it."

"Used to be you could flirt with a pretty girl without worrying about a knife showing up in your throat," grumbled the guard.

"We're from a simpler time. Still, keep it to yourself." Jak gave the guard a friendly pat on the shoulder and closed the archive door. "Sorry," he told her. "Not everyone is on board with the new rules on....fraternization." He said the last word delicately, as if afraid that he would offend her.

Kit shrugged, trying to alleviate her discomfort. "It's not unheard of in my time either. Just not so...blatant. Is that really how it was in the ORG in your time?"

"Wil is a little more...forceful in showing his interest than most," Jak admitted. "But there were no laws for either the ORG or the general population in my day. We flirted, we had fun, we fell in love. Sure, there was a prohibition against illegal pregnancy, but we had ways around that. Ways that, I hear, have long since been outlawed and taken off the market. And back then the world didn't end, and society didn't collapse, and people were a lot happier, from what I can gather." He shook his head sadly. "I have a lot of trouble imagining a world where no one's allowed to screw without the government's say-so."

Kit shrugged and let the subject drop. It was the only way she had known, and it didn't seem that bad to her. She had never really gotten the big fuss about sex, anyway. She had given in to pressure from her friends once when she was younger and visited a prostitute—back while she was still at the Academy, in fact. He'd been government licensed, properly sterilized, and quite good at his trade. He'd taken care of physical needs she hadn't even known existed before then, but left her feeling awkward and uncomfortable after the act was done. She'd dressed, paid him, and scurried out the door. She'd never returned.

"So, what was it that you wanted to know about the archives?" Jak asked, jarring her out of her thoughts.

"Um," Kit replied eloquently. She had mostly been following a vague hunch that information was important, and this was where the information was stored. But she couldn't tell Jak that she was suspicious of everything about this place. She glanced around for inspiration—and froze.

All around were shelves, dozens of shelves, lining every wall, marching in straight, well-ordered rows down the center of the room, every one of them full of—

"Are those...books?" she asked, awestruck.

"We don't have the sort of digital resources you're used to," Jak said apologetically. Kit shook her head wordlessly. She'd never seen a real, paper book before. It made no sense—they took up an absurd amount of space when compared to a datacell, they were harder to search through, they would decay over time—but somehow she was awed by the visual representation of so much knowledge in one place.

"Where did you get them all?" she asked in a hushed tone.

"We found a section of the city where the Reds and Blues never go," he replied. "It's...unfinished. That's how we've gotten a lot of the furniture that we have here, scavenging those buildings. One of the places we found looked like a library, full of shelves and books, but all the books were blank." He pulled one of the books off a shelf and opened it, revealing carefully hand-written pages. "So we started taking the books and filling them in ourselves. Most of these are records for the Extension, some of them are personal journals written by older operatives and donated upon their deaths, and a few are hard copies of digital files that new members had saved on their MDUs when they arrived."

"What's the oldest file...book...that you have?" Kit asked, scanning the array of blue, red, and green spines. There were thin books and thick books and rows of identical books that looked like part of a set. She flexed her fingers as she looked around, marveling at the time and effort it must have taken to write all of them.

Jak gestured that she should follow, and led her to the farthest corner of the room.

"This is the section for personal journals, and here are the earliest ones we have. The unit that founded the Extension, the First Elite, each left a journal." He pointed to each book in turn. Kit eyed them greedily. The first ORG members to arrive here—surely there would be answers within those pages...

Jak eyed her with an odd expression that could have been either suspicion or speculation. She blanked her own features as best she could.

"I could...lend you one of them to read, if you'd like," Jak offered in a purposefully offhand tone. "It's not precisely regulation, though, so I'd appreciate it if you didn't tell anyone." Kit's eyes narrowed. This could be a trap. If she accepted, he could report her for breaking regulations. Sure, he had offered, but who would accept her word against his?

He picked one of the books off of the shelf. "Please, I'd love to be able to discuss these with someone else who appreciates history."

Kit hadn't really considered herself as a history enthusiast, but for the sake of discovery, she thought she could become one. Her hand crept out and grasped the book. The cover was rough and hard under her hands, and the book was heavier than she'd expected. She gripped it more tightly, afraid to drop it.

"Bring it back here when you're done. I'm here most evenings. Please don't leave it with anyone else, though. As I said, this isn't strictly regulation, and that's a valuable bit of history. But what's the point of history if no one's allowed to learn from it?"

The portraits of those forgotten people hanging in the Congressional Seat swam into Kit's mind. They had been important once, and now their names, their significance, any actions they had taken in life were wiped from the face of history. Maybe those in the upper echelons of rulership remembered. Kit would never know. The unmarked green cover of the book in her hands stared up at her. The First Elite—and she had never heard of them either. She looked up and met Jak's steady eye.

"Thank you."

He broke into a wide grin. "Here, let me get you a cover for that." She followed him to the front of the archive, where he pulled out a piece of canvas and expertly wrapped up the book. "Protects the book from damage, and you from prying eyes," he explained. Then he ushered her towards the exit and waved a cheery goodbye. Kit felt self-conscious walking past the guard, worried that he would comment on the package she carried under her arm. A quick glance, however, showed that this worry was baseless. He was much too busy staring at her backside as she walked away.

Still nervous that someone would question her, Kit made a beeline to her bunk. Amongst so many people walking with purpose, her hurry didn't look out of place. When she drew aside the curtain, she was unsurprised to see that she was the only one back. Merdith would be gone until dinner, and Avin took his workouts seriously.

Some items had been laid out on her bed, and another set was on Avin's. Upon inspection, it turned out to be a second set of clothes and a sparse set of toiletries. She was especially grateful for the hair brush. The clothes were also very welcome, though they weren't anywhere close to an ORG uniform. Uniforms seemed to be in short supply, which was no wonder if everyone who showed up was as under-equipped as Kit. The loose beige pants and white shirt looked casual, but serviceable for off-duty wear. All the people in the hall had been wearing uniforms, so she gathered these were for private use only.

The feeling of clean cloth in her hands reminded her how long it had been since her last shower. She was still covered with the sweat and soot of yesterday's fight and the flying machine's explosion. The book beckoned, but she decided she would never be able to concentrate properly without a shower and clean clothes, cold water or no. She bundled up her new outfit and set off for the washroom.

When she entered, somewhat hesitantly, the showers were more populated than before. That actually made her more comfortable. There was no attempt at privacy, but at least she wouldn't be the only person stripped to the skin and shivering. And that was a blessing of the cold water, as well. At least no one would be loitering around and leering like that guard had. Everyone was rushing through their bathing as quickly as possible. Kit claimed a shower towards the back, stacked her clean clothes on a shelf that ran the length of the nearby wall, and grabbed the bucket off its hook.

As it filled with icy water, Kit eyed the laundry workers. She really wanted her uniform washed for the next day, but she couldn't very well skip in line. They had a veritable mountain of dirty laundry to get through. When her bucket was filled, she approached the most friendly-looking of the washers.

The man laughed when she haltingly framed her request. "Sure! Bring your stuff over here when you're done and I'll show you the ropes. It'll save time whenever you're assigned laundry duty anyway." Kit thanked him gratefully, and hauled her filled bucket to her corner.

On the same shelf where she had placed her clean clothes sat bins full of shower necessities and stacks of the same fluffy, white towels that she had used in the Blues' complex—scavenged from one side or the other, she assumed. When she peered into the bin, she found that it was half full with tubes of the soap pellets she was used to and half full of strange white blocks. She wasn't sure what those were for, so she ignored them and popped open one of the tubes. She carefully poured one of the spongy pellets into her palm and replaced the tube. Like everything here, these seemed to be stored communally due to limited supplies. Now that she thought about it, she recalled seeing one of those white blocks in the bathroom at the Blues' complex too, but she hadn't known what it was for there either, and had used one of her own soap pellets from her kit.

The sense of relief as the sweat-soaked uniform peeled away from her skin was intense. She dumped the rank uniform in a crumpled pile on the shelf so that the electronics wouldn't get accidentally soaked. Her covert glances told her that the half dozen other men and women using the showers were paying her no attention at all. She wasn't generally body-shy, but the guard's blatant ogling earlier had made her wary.

She nerved herself and gave the shower pull a sharp tug, dousing herself with chill water. Despite being prepared, the air was driven from her lungs, and her entire body broke out in goosebumps. She held the soap pellet under the water for a moment, then let the bucket swing upright again, cutting off the cold deluge. The pellet hydrated swiftly, growing into a large, soft sponge that dripped suds onto the ground. She soaped her body quickly but thoroughly, and worked the suds through her hair with rough efficiency, determined to get every bit of grime. She wanted to repeat this experience as rarely as possible. With another tug on the chain, she rinsed away the suds hurriedly, scrubbing roughly with her free hand, as much to warm her limbs as to get rid of the soap. Her scalp prickled as icy water ran in torrents through her hair.

She managed to rinse away most of the soap before the bucket ran out of water. Despite a few scattered bubbles, she didn't even consider refilling the bucket, and instead made a mad dash for the towels. She toweled herself off vigorously, trying to urge her circulation back to normal so that her toes would no longer verge on blue. When she pulled on her new clothes, they seemed painfully flimsy. She was used to the sturdy, form-fitting fabric of her uniform. The new pants were sized to fit a variety of forms, with wide legs and a drawstring waist. She pulled the string as tight as she could to fit her slender midsection, but still felt as if the pants were going to end up around her ankles. The shirt wasn't much better, with a loose, billowy fit that made her feel as if she was wearing nothing at all. And the white fabric was so thin it was practically translucent. She tossed her used towel into a bin underneath the shelf, then grabbed her dirty uniform and held it in front of her chest.

The friendly washer showed her how to clean the uniforms, and incidentally explained that the white blocks were solid bars of soap. If there were no pellets at some point, which he said often happened, she now knew to just wet the blocks and rub to lather. As with everything old fashioned, it was very space-inefficient, but still effective. Her uniform was soon dripping wet and sweet-smelling. She carefully wrung out as much water as she could, then gathered the damp cloth in one hand and the uniform's wiring in the other. She felt exposed as she rushed back to her room. The wet uniform couldn't be held in front of her without wetting her current clothes, and the wiring didn't make enough of a shield to be bothered with.

She relaxed once she reached the safety of the room. A curtain across the door wasn't much privacy, but it was enough. Even when Avin and Merdith returned, they were from her time. They wouldn't be staring at her chest. She draped the wet uniform over the box near her bed, then settled down with the book.

Chapter Thirteen

A whisper of sound wrenched her from her reverie. She realized by the volume of pages to the left that she had been reading for much longer than she'd realized. And the sound had been made by Merdith sticking her head through the curtain.

"You weren't at dinner. Is everything okay?"

Kit hurriedly closed the book and shoved it behind her as she sat up. "I must have forgotten to set an alarm. It's so strange to not have a scheduled duty that I lost track of time. Is there any food left?"

"Yeah. Don't wait too long though," Merdith advised. "They'll start cleaning up soon."

Kit rolled off her cot as Merdith's head retreated behind the curtain. The book went into her box, followed by her extra clothes. She wasn't going to the mess in that outfit, even if her uniform was still quite damp. She artfully arranged the cloth over the book so that it was completely obscured, then took a screenshot with her MDU so she'd be able to tell if the clothing had been moved. Only then did she move purposefully in the direction of the mess, trying to look as if the last couple hours of reading hadn't shaken her to her core.

She moved automatically through the line, projecting a sense of familiarity that she in no way felt. Her mind worked furiously, trying to process what she had read, while her body moved forward mechanically.

It was nothing she couldn't have figured out on her own, if she had only thought about it. The tumultuous early history of the Congress. Their desperate attempts to stay in power over an unruly populace, with increasingly dictatorial methods. And the First Elite—of course, they hadn't been part of the ORG. They had been part of the army, a group of friends rather than a formal unit. The journal had been written by a woman named Zo, an infiltration specialist with much the same skill set as Kit.

I supported the Congress, Zo had written. *I fought for freedom. But now I question whether we have simply turned our poor city over to a new dictator, worse than the last. Power may have passed to new hands, but people are still rioting in the streets. New laws are being passed left and right, with no input from the people they most affect. Curfews. Dress codes. Restrictions on movement. What will be next, I wonder? Will they try to tell us where to work? How to spend our free time? Which people we can associate with? How to raise our children?*

Those questions were telling. It sounded as if, in that far past time, it had been possible to choose so many more things, even down to where you traveled and what you wore. Kit's first thought was that such freedom was uncivilized—barbaric, even. How could the general population be trusted to decide what work they were best suited to? How could they possibly raise their own children? Clearly the society where that had been normal had not worked.

But the people of that time had not craved the rigid control that they were forced into. Even those who had fought for the Congress hadn't liked the outcome. It wasn't a gradual climb into a more civilized society. It was an imposed control to keep them under the thumb of new and unstable leadership. How, then, could she claim that her way of doing things was better? Unruly memory supplied the images of a hundred missions. People were still fighting against the Congress, against the ORG, for just a taste of the freedom of choice that those long ago people had been accustomed to.

Kit had always seen the city's population as a nebulous cloud of untrustworthy people, separate from herself. Now she twisted her thoughts, rearranging them to place herself within that cloud, as a citizen of the city, no more virtuous or special than any other. If she were honest, would she have preferred a life other than the ORG? She couldn't imagine another one.

There had been no other choices laid before her, but if there had been, she might have chosen differently. Perhaps she would have chosen to associate with different people. Or with the same people in different ways. If she had been given a choice. If she'd had the courage to make a choice.

It dawned upon her that she had been taught to think of the general population in a very specific way: stupid, stubborn, unable to make good decisions for themselves. And yet, when she had been in school, she had not found herself to be any more proficient than her peers. They had gone on to become part of that general population in one way or another. She, in her position of relative power, had been looking down on them and denying them the ability to make their own decisions—because those in power told her to.

She had not been the peacekeeper. She had been the oppressor.

It was not a sudden revelation, a bolt of lightening that struck her as she sat in the mess hall listening to the ambient buzz of electric lighting. It was the blossoming of an idea that had slowly been taking root in her mind—that freedom, that choice, was important. She had the ability—no, the *right*—to decide within her own mind what was good and what wasn't. It was a right that she had never thought to exercise before. And as she looked around the regimented rows of mostly empty tables, she realized that she would never truly fit in here again.

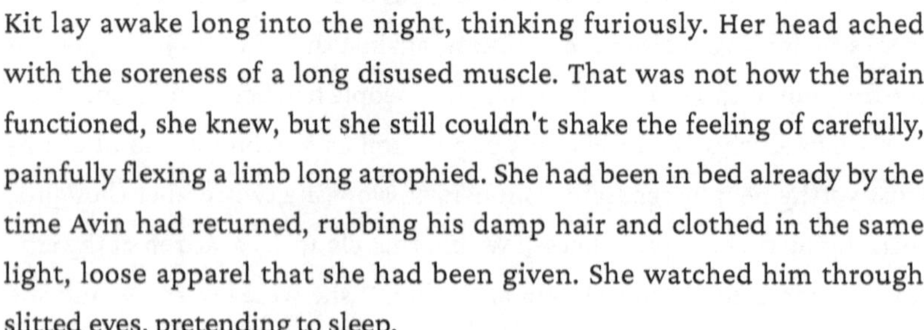

Kit lay awake long into the night, thinking furiously. Her head ached with the soreness of a long disused muscle. That was not how the brain functioned, she knew, but she still couldn't shake the feeling of carefully, painfully flexing a limb long atrophied. She had been in bed already by the time Avin had returned, rubbing his damp hair and clothed in the same light, loose apparel that she had been given. She watched him through slitted eyes, pretending to sleep.

She wondered how much he had already figured out. He had to have some idea of what she had learned. He had tried to desert. He had known this wasn't the place for him, and he had been dragged back in, because once the ORG claimed someone, it never let go.

She turned her questing mind in his direction. There were two sides in this battle—Avin and the ORG—and she had already decided that the ORG was not, in the simplest terms, good. But did that mean that Avin was necessarily in the right? She squeezed her eyes more tightly shut, as if she could simplify the problem by removing the input of her own senses. No, she finally decided. One thing being bad did not make its opposing force good, as much as that simple solution would please her.

Avin, then, needed to be considered as his own separate entity, outside of the ORG. She had seen two sides of him now. The one she was most familiar with was efficient, dedicated, utterly ruthless when the situation called for it. She had been both admiring of that ruthlessness and repelled by it in equal measure. It could mean that the second side—conflicted, rebellious, strangely vulnerable—that could have been a contrivance. The one thing she was sure of was his tactical skill, and what was manipulation, if not the tactics of emotion?

But as she poked and prodded at the memory, she couldn't bring herself to believe that it had all been an act. She had no good reason to trust that he had been genuine except her own conviction.

It came down to consequences, in the end. If he had been manipulating a confession out of her, he had already achieved that goal. She was already in such deep trouble that it didn't bear thinking about, and there was nothing she could do to fix that.

If, however, she believed he had been manipulating her when he hadn't, she would be abandoning him to fight his conditioning alone. That would be a terrible betrayal on her part. If a person didn't even have freedom within their own thoughts—that was horrifying, the deepest form of violation. She owed it to her teammate, her friend, to help him gain the upper hand in any way she could. But she had no idea what to do.

Inducement was considered a final, irreversible punishment, and yet it seemed he was already fighting it. There had to be some assistance she could render, but whatever it was would have to be subtle. His conditioning would not allow him to accept an open offer. It could not be fought head on. She would have to follow Avin's own example: opposing through omission and manipulation, circumventing when possible. Knowledge would be her best ally. Right now, she had no idea how the process of inducement was even carried out, let alone how to reverse it. She would return to the archive as soon as possible.

It was disturbingly easy to fall into the new routine of the Extension, and frustratingly hard to find time either to read or visit Jak in the archives. Kit found her days eaten up with training, chores, and meals, and her free hours were expected to be spent with her fellows. It would have been highly suspicious if she'd absented herself, especially to Merdith, who knew her well. So instead of spending her off hours in reading and contemplation, she found herself in a dimly lit corner of the Extension, surrounded by rowdy operatives, sipping some sort of fermented fruit juice. There didn't seem to be any beer on the premises, which was disappointing. Considering how much better all the food was here, Kit couldn't help fantasizing about the wondrous things they might be able to do with beer. Still, the alcohol they did have wasn't horrible, just weird. Apparently a group of operatives used their free time to make the stuff out of the fruit they captured in their supply raids.

She nevertheless found a few moments to read here and there, carefully concealed from both Avin and Merdith. Perhaps Merdith would be on her side, but perhaps not. Kit couldn't decide whether to trust the older woman.

Much of Zo's journal was everyday events and random musings, but every so often Kit stumbled across things that shocked her. One day, she realized that Zo was in a romantic relationship with another soldier, Parik.

And they had children—children that they were raising together. Openly. As if it was nothing to worry about. While much of the journal was work-related, a few anecdotes from Zo's family crept in—a quarrel between siblings, how her oldest was taking an interest in joining the army, how Zo's sister cared for the two children when she and Parik were away on a job. Kit found herself wondering what it would have been like to grow up in such a place, where everyone around was directly related to her, directly invested in her future. For the first time in her life, she wondered who her mother and father had been, and if either of them had other children. No one would be allowed to procreate with the same person twice, but she could have half-brothers or sisters. She had never cared before, but now...the ORG no longer felt like her family.

As her reading progressed, there were fewer and fewer family anecdotes, and a growing sense of disquiet. Zo wrote of increasingly draconian punishments, and confided that she had hidden her writings away behind a screen of encryption on her MDU. She had burned the original hard copies. She was terrified that her family would pay the price for her dissension.

Kit began to wolf down her meals in order to steal a moment alone in her bunk to read. One day while Merdith was enjoying a more leisurely lunch and Avin had mid-shift guard duty, she sprawled on her cot with the open journal before her. Her storage box lay open beneath her hands so that she could drop the volume into it at a moment's notice and pretend to be napping, should anyone pull aside the curtain unexpectedly. Still, with the passage she had just found, it would have taken an explosion to dislodge her from the page before her.

The Congress has begun to use a truly horrific method of keeping us in line, Zo wrote. *They call it "loyalty training," though the medical term is psychosomatic inducement, or so I've been told.*

Kit's breath caught in her throat. She'd taken it for granted that inducement had always been around, but here it was. The starting point. She read on eagerly, hoping that its origins would give her some clue that could help Avin.

It's only training in the way that you would train a particularly dangerous dog. This is no procedure that any human should have to endure. I don't know whether to be relieved or outraged that this is limited to the military. At least I know most of my family is safe, and Parik and I are already watching our backs as best we know how.

Inducement had been limited to the military? Kit paused and looked up from the page. She had no idea whether that was still the case. Perhaps it had later been expanded to the general population, or perhaps there was a reason why it could only be done to operatives. She returned to her reading, and the next line jumped off the page to slap her in the face.

Those in power have found a way to subvert our own minds using the power of our MDUs. We chose to let these machines invade our brains in order to win the war for them, and now they can reprogram both the machines and our brains at the same time. The modifications to the MDU programming can create the sensations of pain, fear, joy...or remove emotions entirely. Playing God with the chemicals of our brains. Controlling what we think and feel. Parik has begun talking about fleeing to the swamps and joining what remains of the freedom fighters. I understand, but I wish he would shut up about it. Anji is too young to live out there. Even if he doesn't mean to follow through, talking draws attention we can't afford.

Kit sat up and slowly closed the journal. So that was the secret. It wasn't merely some crazy form of conditioning. There wasn't a great big machine where you went in one side as yourself and got spat out on the other as one of the Faithful. They reprogrammed the MDU to adjust your brain chemicals when you got too uppity. That was why inducement had been limited to the military and the ORG; only operatives had been fitted with an MDU.

Kit's stomach lurched with betrayal. Somehow it was worse to know that she could be reprogrammed like a machine. Just add a chip, upload some data, and she'd be forced to behave. But—and her stomach lurched in the other direction—surely if the MDU had been reprogrammed once, it could be done again. If she could figure out a way into Avin's MDU, there was a chance he could be freed from everything they had done to him.

Not that she had any idea how to do that. She needed someone more knowledgeable and tech-savvy than she was. Climb a wall, sure—but hack an MDU?

There was only one conclusion she could come to. She needed a technology specialist, a hacker who had experience with the inner workings of MDUs. The only one of those she knew was currently languishing away in the Blue complex because the Extension didn't believe that she was worthy of joining them.

Kit was done with sitting around and waiting. It was more than time for action.

Action, however, proved just as hard as inaction, in its own way. Kit was used to having a lead to provide orders and decisions. In combat, she had no problem being an autonomous unit, creating a plan and carrying it out with little to no feedback from others. In this game of subterfuge, she found herself at a loss. There was no one she could trust or turn to for advice. And the second she made a move on her own, the entire seething swarm of humanity that called the Extension home would turn on her.

She told herself that she was biding her time, gathering more information, taking advantage of the training the Extension offered. And she really was learning important survival skills.

Her first morning of training, she had reported to the armsmaster with a fair amount of confidence. The agility and precision that made her an excellent climber had always helped her make a good showing in combat training. And it hadn't hurt to have Avin to train against. An opponent so fast that he barely seemed human was a good way of sharpening your wits. So when she squared off against the unassuming armsmaster, she was shocked to find herself on her back a second later.

From the floor, she'd taken a dazed second look at the man who'd put her there. He was aggressively average—height, build, features, with brown hair, brown eyes, and a mild expression—but when he moved, he became anything but average. He nearly flowed as he moved over to give her a hand up.

"The human body is the most underestimated weapon," he told her. Then proceeded to prove it to her by handily defeating her, no matter what weapon she laid her hands on.

Later, when she was nursing her bruises in the Extension's impromptu bar, she was regaled with tales of all the impossible stunts that the man had pulled off. No one seemed to know his given name. They just called him Bullet. When Kit commented that it was a strange name for a man who never seemed to pick up a gun, her companions laughed.

"His name is the only bullet he needs," Merdith told her with a smile. She said it with the cadence of an oft-repeated adage.

There was no doubt that she could learn a lot from him. And she was learning things in other areas as well—how to thoroughly clean and mend her own uniform, how to cook the food that was available here, even how to light a fire and navigate without the use of a compass in this environment—for it turned out that Mercy's compass app was not unique in its malfunction. No compass, whether digital or physical, functioned properly here.

As she soaked up all the information she could, pushing herself to the breaking point in her training, Kit also used the time to observe Merdith carefully. Merdith had held Mercy's position in the team before her retirement: technology specialist. Kit had no idea if her former teammate had ever programmed for the MDU. It wasn't a common skill, and not overly useful to the average operative, but Merdith was far more available than Mercy was right now. If she was able to help...

But if Merdith had any idea that all was not right within the Extension, she gave no signs of it. She seemed much the same as she always had, cheerful, efficient, constantly finding little ways to make others comfortable. A thoroughly pleasant person to be around, but showing little initiative or ambition. If she was less than contented within the ORG, she was careful not to show it. As careful as Kit herself was.

Still, something nagged at Kit. She had been sent in here with her entire team. Merdith had once been part of that team, and she hadn't been reassigned, as far as Kit knew. How had she come to be here on her own? There was no way that she could have waded through the shambler-filled lab without assistance. Kit looked in vain for a casual way to bring up Merdith's arrival in conversation.

Over a week had passed before she found the part of the journal where Zo and her unit first entered the lab. By this point, Zo was nearly frantic with worry for her family and her teammates. Parik was becoming more insistent that they desert. Her best friend, Lena, had become withdrawn and uncommunicative to the point where Zo suspected she was being pressured to provide intelligence on her comrades. The only way Lena could make sure she had nothing to report was to have as little to do with her friends as possible. And Garet, the last of those who had come to be called the First Elite—it turned out that he had been part of the team that had originally created the MDUs. He was sickened and horrified by what had been done with his creation. He had designed the MDU to create peace through law and order, and it had been turned into a tool for brainwashing soldiers. Garet and Parik had taken to spending hours railing against the Congress, the military, and their inability to protect their loved ones.

The last straw was when Zo's sister was taken in for questioning. Zo described her injuries starkly, but Kit could tell there was a seething rage behind the clinical words. They began quietly stockpiling supplies and planning their escape from the city.

On the next page, a brief note mentioned that they had been tagged for a top priority mission and would have to leave the next day. Zo's sister was not yet recovered enough to watch the children, so they'd had to scramble to find neighbors who would be willing to mind the little ones. Zo wasn't entirely pleased with the situation, but she felt it was important not to argue with orders just then.

The next entry wasn't until many days later.

Lab was full of goddamn zombies. Idiot scientist sealed us in. Had to fight a goddamn flesh monstrosity to get to the emergency exit. No idea where we are now. Some sort of weird future city? Parik has a broken arm and Lena had some kind of breakdown. Wouldn't stop babbling until Garet gave her a good slap.

I think the Congress found a way to get rid of us. Please let the kids be okay.

Here was confirmation of all Kit's suspicions. The first unit to come here—they were given no orders. They weren't the start of some great army. They were inconveniently powerful war heroes who were about to desert and give their expertise and inside knowledge to a revolutionary faction. This wasn't a vault to preserve the best and most skilled of their people. It was their garbage disposal.

Kit's unit hadn't been qualified to be the Elite. Stev was a womanizing, power-grasping mess who'd recently gotten a teammate killed. Avin had already tried to desert once and been put through inducement—and was still fighting against it. Mercy was brand new—not a likely candidate for such an honor. And Kit felt that she herself, while good at her job, was not anything special. Not to mention her indiscretion on guard duty. Maybe they really had found out about it.

Merdith—she had been retired. How many other operatives were here because they'd gotten too old to be considered useful? Retirement had always been simply another fact of life in the ORG, but now Kit seethed. Merdith was no more in her dotage than Kit was. Was the benefit of her experience and knowledge worthless?

She thought of the other people she had met here, many of them wild and undisciplined by her standards. Perhaps that wasn't only a cultural difference between time periods. If the ORG was disposing of their most disruptive operatives by chucking them in here...

And then there was Bullet—a man so skilled in unarmed combat, so dangerously nondescript that he could only have been an assassin. What did you do with your best assassin when he started to slip his leash?

Even Jak did not strike her as an ideal operative. He was so relaxed, so dismissive of protocol, and so absorbed in his books and records that he rarely joined them for training unless reminded to do so. As a superior officer, he left much to be desired.

Something clicked in her brain. Jak knew everything that was in these books. She was sure of it. And he had given her this one in particular to smuggle back to her room and read. He knew exactly what was going on here, that there were no outside orders from the ORG and that the entire Extension was a farce. Was this book a message? An...invitation? Perhaps he had been waiting for her to approach him this entire time.

Only an effort of will kept her from leaping to her feet and charging out to find him immediately. That would look suspicious. And as much as this was not the "real" ORG, it was just as regimented and watchful, in its own way. It was a warped reflection, and she didn't expect that punishment for rebellion here was any less horrifying. If anything, the restlessness of the operatives, the defects in their natures that caused them to be sent here, would make even harsher punishments necessary to keep them in line.

And before she spoke to Jak—she couldn't tell Avin yet, obviously, but Merdith had a right to know. Maybe she already did, and had been waiting for Kit to learn the secret. But on the chance that she didn't, Kit's first loyalty now was to her friends. If Jak had a plan that he wanted to bring Kit in on, he could include both of them—or neither.

CHAPTER FOURTEEN

The next several days were taken up by agonizing over how to get Merdith alone, and what to say when the time came. *Hi, our entire lives have been a lie.* It just didn't have the right ring to it. And privacy was in very limited supply.

The end of the third day came, and Kit found herself sipping weird-tasting fruit juice in a corner of the bar without having found an opportunity to get Merdith alone. People flowed around her in groups of friends, units, the occasional pair of lovers. Her eyes traced them idly as the subtle buzz of intoxication invaded her thoughts. She absentmindedly fiddled with the gold ring in her pocket. This was about the time of evening when couples started sneaking away for a quiet moment together before the bunks were fully occupied...

All at once, she knew what she had to do. She began to drink with more purpose. This was going to be incredibly awkward.

When Merdith got up from her table, separating herself from the laughing group to grab another drink, Kit steeled herself and left her solitary corner to follow. She tried to look casual, as if she did this all the time. It was no big deal here, she reminded herself. She'd been propositioned several times since she'd been here, though thankfully most had a little more tact than the lecherous Wil. A polite refusal had been all it took.

With a deep breath, she came up behind Merdith and put a shaky hand on the bar, then leaned in to whisper in Merdith's ear, so close that Kit's lips brushed her curls. She couldn't risk being overheard, or this whole charade would be for nothing.

"There's something really important that I need to talk to you about. In private," she breathed.

Merdith turned to look at her in surprise, and their faces ended up uncomfortably close. Kit kept from recoiling by sheer force of will, and wrestled her features into what she hoped was a seductive smile. It wasn't an expression that had ever had a home on her face before.

Merdith would know how incredibly out of character this was for her, but no one else would. For all they knew, she and Merdith could have been lovers before they'd ever come here. While the operatives from earlier times seemed to prefer male/female couplings, most of the more recent additions tended toward same-sex, for the simple reason that there was no chance of an unexpected pregnancy and the horrific repercussions that came with it. The only one who would find this supposed liaison strange was Avin, and he was using his free time in extra practice, as always. The only question was whether Merdith would refuse her—or worse, call her out on her subterfuge.

But a slow smile spread across Merdith's face, and she slipped her arm through Kit's. "Sure, let's go," she said, loudly enough for those nearest to hear her.

They walked arm in arm back to their bunk, and no one bothered them except for the occasional knowing smirk. Kit began to fear that Merdith thought she was serious, but the second the curtain fell behind them, Merdith dropped her arm and the smile both.

"If you want me to help you get Stev and whats-her-name out of the Blues, it won't work," she said instead. "We'll get caught and tossed out of the Extension, and that won't help any of us. They're safe enough where they are."

"That's not—well, that sort of is what I wanted to talk to you about, but that's not nearly all of it," Kit said quickly. "I mean, I do need to get them out, but—" She stopped and tried to organize her thoughts. That last big gulp of booze was fast becoming a regret. She dropped onto her cot and put her head in her hands, wishing the persistent buzz would abate if she asked nicely.

The cot creaked as Merdith's weight settled next to her. "If that's not all of it, then what's the rest?" Merdith asked gently. The hand she placed on Kit's shoulder was soothing, rather than seductive. Merdith had always been good at the whole comforting thing. It was something that had always been lost on Kit.

Okay, she was listening. First step accomplished. Start at the beginning. Explain clearly. But before she went any further...

"I need your word that you won't tell anyone else what I'm about to tell you unless we both agree to. The consequences could be...extensive."

The lines of worry on Merdith's face deepened. "Will it compromise my loyalty to the ORG?"

Kit met her eyes squarely. "Yes." Merdith's face went slack with surprise.

"If it was anyone else, I'd tell you to take your secrets and shove 'em, but for as long as I've known you, you've eaten, slept, and breathed the ORG. Only person I've seen more dedicated was Avin. If it's made you change your mind, then it's got to be huge."

"It is."

"Okay then. I'll promise."

Haltingly, Kit explained everything, starting from when she received Zo's journal from Jak and ending with the discovery that the Extension was nothing but a farce.

Silence fell when she was done. Merdith stared into the distance. Kit didn't blame her. The muddle of fear, betrayal, and anger still threatened to overwhelm her when she thought about the situation too closely.

"I don't believe it," Merdith said abruptly. "If the First Elite were so anti-ORG, why would they pretend to have orders and create the Extension and all that?"

"The ORG didn't even exist yet when the First Elite were sent here," Kit pointed out. "The story must have been started some time later, probably by operatives who couldn't come to terms with the fact that they'd been abandoned. I'd need newer records to be able to say for sure. But I'm willing to bet that Jak knows the whole story."

"That bastard," Merdith said, but her anger was halfhearted. "Why didn't he give me a book when I got here?"

"How did you get here?" Kit asked, finally getting the opening she'd been waiting for. "We barely got through with a whole unit. Did they send you in with other people?"

"No," Merdith said bitterly. "And it's making more sense, now. They told me I was being moved to retirement barracks with full honors, had me pack up all my personal belongings, then escorted me to the door. I thought it was weird that the yard was so empty and unkempt, and that we were in the science district, but who was I to argue?" She stared into space for a moment, contemplating the memory. "I've talked to a bunch of people about how they came here, and it sounds like somehow the scenario adjusts depending on how many people are sent in at once. I didn't have nearly as many—what were you calling them, shamblers? I like that better than what they use here. 'Gatekeepers,' my ass. But everyone gets locked in by that same stupid scientist and has to fight that goopy monster at the end. We've figured that singles get an easier version of that, though. I've always wondered how they faked that thing."

Kit sat up straighter. That was something she hadn't considered yet. "If the ORG isn't in control in here...then who did fake those things? How do they reset every time?"

Merdith shook her head in bafflement. "No one has ever really figured out where this place is or why time functions the way it does. Just wrote it off as being the ORG's grand plan."

"Oh, it's a grand plan, alright," Kit retorted bitterly. "The grand plan of dumping us all somewhere we can't possibly make trouble. Who cares if we survive the experience. How many units don't even make it past the shamblers?"

"Impossible to say. But plenty of 'em show up missing members."

"It's not right," Kit said, barely remembering to keep her tone hushed. "It's not fair, and it's not right. They take us and use us up, and then they throw us away."

Merdith put her arm around Kit's shoulder and hugged her for a brief moment. "I don't doubt you, but it's so hard to believe. Can I—can I see the book?" Wordlessly, Kit reached down into her chest and fished it out from beneath the concealing layers of fabric. Merdith held it on her lap, staring down at its blank cover, then carefully began to rifle through it, reading passages at random. At first she avoided the page that Kit had marked with a scrap of plastic, but finally she visibly steeled herself and turned to it. Kit sat in awkward silence, waiting for her to finish and watching her face settle into a mask. Merdith closed the book and handed it back to Kit without a comment. They sat, still and somber, for a long time.

"What do we do now?" Merdith asked quietly. Kit pulled herself from her thoughts.

"We need to confront Jak, I think." Merdith frowned, and Kit explained swiftly. "He had to know what was in that book, and we need to know why he gave it to me. He offered it." She took a deep breath and turned to face Merdith squarely. "But first, I need to know how much you know about the programming of our MDUs."

Merdith's eyes widened in surprise. Obviously, she had not been expecting that as first on the agenda. "Uhm, a little bit. I know the language they use well enough to write a really simple app, at least, and I can do troubleshooting and maintenance if nothing too huge is wrong. Why?"

It wasn't her secret to tell—but if Avin's mind was going to be freed, then Merdith had to know. Tersely, Kit explained about Avin's situation and her own revelation regarding the MDUs.

"Just when I think it can't get any worse," Merdith said through gritted teeth. "That does explain his zeal for training. But—I don't think I have the skill to undo what was done to him. I'm not even sure where to start looking in the code for something like that, and there are bound to be safeguards in place to make sure whatever they installed isn't tampered with. And what if I found it and made things worse? That's his brain I'd be mucking up."

Kit was disappointed, but not entirely surprised. "Then we really do need to get Mercy away from the Blues. I don't know if she's up to the task either, but she seems like she's studied the MDUs a fair bit, and it's our best hope. If Avin finds out that this isn't an actual ORG sanctioned outpost, he's going to—" She thought back to his behavior in the Red's prison, the wild animal pacing and panic. She shook her head. "Well, it won't be good."

"Maybe Jak will know how to remove the programming, or know someone who can," Merdith suggested hopefully.

"Maybe, but I haven't even begun to think about trusting him yet. I don't know what he wants from us, so I'm not about to start asking favors. Mercy's one of us."

Merdith agreed regretfully, and Kit got the impression that she would have really liked to turn the problem over to someone with greater authority. Understandable, but right now that wasn't something Kit was willing to do. Those in authority hadn't been winning any points with her recently.

"When's your guard shift tomorrow?" Kit asked.

"Morning."

"I have mid. After I get off, I'll go by the archive before lunch. If I don't show up by halfway through, come to the archive. Act like we had plans to practice together in the afternoon unless I ping the all clear. If it turns out to be a trap, there's no point in both of us getting caught."

Merdith looked doubtful, but agreed.

Kit awoke the next morning in a cold sweat of nerves. She rolled out of bed before her alarm had a chance to go off, gathered her shower things with fingers that threatened to tremble, and went off to douse herself with ice water. At least then, if she was shaking, she could imagine it was from cold instead of nerves.

By the time she was done, it was still too early for breakfast, and her stomach was far too restless to be interested in food anyway. Instead, she took a turn for the training floor. Never mind that she had just showered. She could always shower again.

This area was even more deserted than the showers. In the washroom, a few hardy souls who preferred to bathe after night watch had been hurriedly dousing themselves, but no one else was interested in training at this hour. That was perfect, as far as Kit was concerned.

Two days ago, she had graduated from Bullet's initial training course, just behind Avin, who she suspected had been holding back the tiniest bit, waiting for her. As a reward (or punishment, according to the other operatives, but she didn't agree), she'd been introduced to a wonderful area that hadn't been covered in their general tour: the climber's obstacle course. Accessed through a narrow arch in the far wall of the training area, the course made use of a natural underground fissure. The natives had run huge pipes through it at some point, providing a perfect base for the course. The pipes had been used to support platforms, all built with a variety of scavenged materials—wood slats, tile, glass, concrete, metal—and arrayed at many different angles for the climbers to scramble over and leap between. The course ended at a hole in the training room ceiling. Unofficially, extra points were awarded if the climber could drop down and catch one of the other sparring operatives unaware as a finale to their run. Kit had silently awarded herself double points the one time she had managed to drop down behind Avin and get a touch on his shoulder—not a lethal blow, by any means, but she was proud nonetheless.

Besides practice, she hadn't had much to do with Avin since they'd been here. He seemed to be purposefully keeping to himself. Perhaps it was because of a conditioned distaste for the disloyalty she had confided to him. Perhaps he was trying to protect her. Either way, his usual detachment and reticence had increased a hundredfold. When they were both present, he sat with her and Merdith at meals, but ate in silence. He practiced with them in silence. Most evenings, he chose extra training sessions rather than joining them at the bar. Truth be told, Kit would have preferred to train, but she had to seem normal at all costs. She couldn't afford to stand out or be unusual in any way.

Kit began by moving through some quick stretches, a necessary warmup after her cold shower and the relative inactivity of her restless night. It felt good to move, warmth seeping into her muscles, knots unwinding themselves into fluid motion. When she was ready, she moved seamlessly into the unarmed combat exercises that Bullet had taught her, ducking and spinning. The goal was to never give your opponent a still target until you were too close to avoid—and then hit hard before you were shot at point-blank range. Speed was essential. Sweat beaded on her forehead and dripped down her nose. A timer on her MDU tracked each set, and she concentrated on repeating the motions, each time faster than the last. She was so focused that when a hand reached from behind to tap her shoulder, she spun without thinking, gripped the offending arm, and tossed the person attached onto their back. Avin blinked up at her from the mat in surprise.

"You're getting very fast," he said. It was a flat statement of fact, but Kit flushed in pleased embarrassment. He propped himself up on an elbow and continued, "I was going to ask if you'd like to practice together." In fact, Kit would have much preferred solitude at this particular moment, but there was no real reason to refuse him. And despite everything going on, she found his company strangely comforting. They had shared their secret shames with each other, and even if her secret wasn't exactly safe with him, it brought a silent understanding to their interactions.

Avin had grabbed a practice pistol from the armory, one of a few designated modern weapons with the power reduced to the lowest possible setting. That transformed the bullets from lethal capsules of electricity to little more than a static buzz that hummed unpleasantly against the skin and, if it failed to hit, dissipated harmlessly into the air within a couple of yards. At that level of power usage, the pistol's charge could last for years.

He squared off against her, and they went through the exercises several times. He was still faster, and managed to counter her each time as she grew increasingly frustrated. She hadn't been in the most stable frame of mind this morning to begin with. Being bested repeatedly was not what she had come here for. She held onto her temper with gritted teeth for a few more rounds before she snapped.

Avin was expecting a certain set of moves to counter. Instead, she ducked low under his shots and charged headlong, abandoning finesse in favor of speed and power. He adjusted enough to get one shot off before she hit him. Her shoulder tingled with the static buzz, but even if it had been a real bullet, it wouldn't have been enough to stop her from knocking him sprawling. She landed atop him, pinning him with her body weight as best she could, and grabbed at the pistol. To her surprise, she managed to swipe it from his grasp, and a second later, she had the gun aimed at his temple. He gaped up at her, then his face slowly flushed a bright cherry red—the same red it had been the morning after they had slept beside each other in the Reds' prison.

Awareness dawned. She was sprawled half atop him, her free hand pressing down on his chest. His very firm, solidly muscled chest. Her cheeks burned, and she hoped desperately that she wasn't as red as Avin. Maybe the flush of exertion would hide the blushes. She pushed herself off of him and stood hurriedly. What was wrong with her? Or him? Both of them?

"I'm going to run the obstacle course," she said flatly. She tossed him the pistol, which he caught while still lying prone on the ground, and turned her back on him. As if she had needed to feel any more unsettled today. Fantastic.

After several runs of the course, during which she broke her personal record twice, Kit felt a little more calm. She dumped some more cold water on her head to rinse away the sweat, ate as heartily as she could manage while steadfastly refusing to meet Avin's eyes, and then sped away to report for her mid-shift guard duty. Merdith would be leaving her own morning shift now. Kit was glad that the other woman hadn't been there to wonder at the strain between her and Avin. Then again, had there really been anything there besides the normal mealtime silence? She had been so busy not looking at Avin that she had no idea whether he had been looking at her. She didn't even know which option she preferred.

Guard duty passed uneventfully, which was unfortunate since it allowed Kit's thoughts to wander free. She had been placed at the mouth of the tunnel into Red territory for this shift. This wasn't the type of guard duty where she stood at attention on top of a brightly lit wall. The tunnel let out in a little park, much like the one she and Avin had been dumped in before they found the Extension. Her post was concealed by a blind of carefully woven vegetation, and she crouched, knelt, or sat behind it in rotation, trying to keep her back from cramping up in the close quarters. The tunnels that led down to the Extension were too long for unassisted pings, and there were no boosters here like there were in the city. Instead, there was a cord that ran along the ceiling, all the way to the interior. Tugging on that cord activated an MDU, scavenged from a dead operative and powered by the battery from a damaged gun. That MDU had been rigged to ping an alert to everyone within range, which could then be passed on to everyone outside its range.

It wasn't the most foolproof of arrangements, but it seemed to be adequate, considering the Reds and Blues left the Extension pretty much alone. They would retaliate when attacked or when the operatives got too confident about roaming their territories, but in all the years the Extension had existed, no one remembered or had heard of an actual assault.

It was a good thing that guard duty was largely useless and uneventful, because Kit paid very little attention to her surroundings on that shift. By the time her relief arrived, she was so tightly wound that she felt like she was vibrating with every step, but the man who showed up to take the next shift didn't seem to notice anything amiss. As she exited the tunnel into the Extension proper, she caught a glimpse of the relief guard for the Blue side as she disappeared down the other path. Kit paused, distracted for a moment from her tumultuous thoughts. The other woman looked vaguely familiar, but Kit couldn't place her. As her honey blonde ponytail bobbed out of sight, Kit shook off her puzzlement and went along her way. She had enough to worry about at this particular point in time. She walked quickly back to her bunk, snatched the book out of her chest, and left with a determined, purposeful stride.

Her steps slowed as she approached the archive. Maybe this was a horrible idea. Maybe she and Merdith could handle the situation on their own. But deep in her gut, she knew that she couldn't let this rest. She had to know the full story.

The same obnoxious guard was on duty at the archive. She had all the luck today. She approached cautiously.

"I'm here to see Jak. Please let him know I've arrived." There, that made it sound as if Jak knew she was coming. Hopefully that would head off any issues.

Her luck did not seem to be changing. Wil swept a glance over her that didn't pretend to be anything but lecherous. Her uniform suddenly felt too tight, too revealing. For the second time that day, she found herself flushing a deep red, and this time she had no doubt about her feelings on the matter.

"What's the password?" Wil drawled, shifting his position so he was casually leaning against the door. Now, if she wanted to knock or try the lock for herself, she would have to come within reach.

"I don't have time for your games." This was the last thing she needed right now.

"I promise, I'm more interesting than anything you'll find in there. Don't you want to get to know me better?" he asked in a wheedling tone that grated on her nerves in the least seductive way possible.

"Actually, I can't think of anything I want less."

"Don't be like that. I can show you a real, old-fashioned good time."

He pushed away from the door and moved towards her now, apparently under the impression that he was making progress with her. He was several inches taller than her. Perhaps he thought that was going to make a difference.

Kit took a deep breath, trying to keep her temper in check. If she lost it on this moron, the result would not be so benign as with Avin. "All I want you to show me is the inside of that room."

"Say please," he said, reaching for her.

That was enough for her, fellow operative or not. She evaded his grasp easily, knocking his hand away, then lunged. His body made a satisfying thud as it slammed up against the locked door, and he spluttered in shock, her forearm pressed against his throat. He raised his hands in a quick gesture of surrender as he choked and gasped for breath, but his eyes flashed with rage. She loosened her grip, but didn't remove it. He was taller than her, and bulkier. She didn't trust him. As she eased up enough to let him breathe, a strange smile, half desire, half anger, spread across his face.

"So you're the type of girl who likes it rough, huh? I can work with that."

She could feel his throat moving against her arm as he spoke, and involuntarily loosened her grip even more in revulsion. He chose that moment to break her hold entirely, using his superior size to his advantage. Abruptly, she was on the defensive.

He made a grab at her, trying to pin her arms to her sides, but she was too fast for him. As she danced out of the way, her eyes flickered side to side. No one was in the hallway to witness this. Everyone was either on duty or at lunch, and she didn't even know whether Jak was in the archive. It didn't matter, she decided as she dodged another swipe. She was going to teach this bastard a lesson he wouldn't soon forget.

Kit timed her move carefully. She dodged again, then pretended to stumble. He tried to correct his lunge to take advantage of her supposed misstep, in turn putting himself off balance. That was when she struck. A quick swipe with her foot took his legs out, and he tumbled to the ground. The time for fair play was long past. Kit landed a heavy kick to his midsection while he was down. Vindictive joy filled her as he curled into a ball, hugging his gut, but he still managed to snatch at her ankle, and she had to dodge away. In the time she took to retreat, he regained his feet and came after her again, yelling in blind, mindless rage. She stood her ground, dodged his wild swinging, then snapped a solid kick right into his gut.

He reeled backwards, falling into the archive door just as it was yanked open from the inside. He toppled inward, landing in a sprawl at Jak's feet. His body hit the concrete floor with a gratifying thump.

"You are dismissed from your post, operative," Jak said, his voice steely and quiet as he looked down at the crumpled heap of a man at his feet. His eyes were flat and hard, brooking no argument. Suddenly, the friendly, untidy scholar was gone, and Kit could see the resolve of a real warrior. Wil, too dazed for clear thought, opened his mouth for some sort of explanation or excuse. Jak interrupted him by reaching down and lifting the man to his feet. Eye to eye, they stared at each other, and the guard blanched.

"Dismissed," Jack repeated, biting off each syllable and speaking slowly and precisely, as if the other man was too stupid to understand him. Privately, Kit suspected that was indeed the case, but at least Wil had the good sense to shut his mouth and leave—very quickly, too. Only when the man was entirely out of sight did Jak turn to Kit.

"Thank you for showing restraint, operative," he said formally, then he cracked a grim smile. "I wouldn't have blamed you, incidentally, for doing some more damage. Wil has a...less than perfect record, and no one would have questioned it." Jak looked at her intently. "Though he's never actually attacked anyone before. Are you hurt?"

Kit mutely shook her head. Technically, Wil hadn't attacked her, but she was willing to let him take the blame for that. If he was stupid enough to claim that trying to grab her against her will wasn't an act that warranted aggression, she would be glad to teach him a second lesson to go with the first.

"Rest assured, steps will be taken." The menace in his tone belied his calm words and expression. Kit wasn't sure what sort of punishment was planned, but she was confident that Wil would find it exceedingly unpleasant. They might not have the knowledge for carrying out inducement here at the Extension, but she was sure that they had an equally harsh way to punish their transgressors. Discipline was paramount in the ORG. And she had more important things to think about.

Jak was watching her intently. "If you're alright...what brought you to the archive in the first place?"

With a start, she realized that the book, swathed in his canvas cover, was still clutched in her right hand. It was a good thing she preferred kicking to punching, or it might have sustained some damage. While it would have amused her to clobber Wil over the head with a book, she suspected Jak would not have been quite as concerned with her welfare after that. Guiltily, she held it out to him.

"Ah. Why don't you come in?" He backed out of the doorway, motioning her inside the archive with gentlemanly courtesy, as if determined to make up for his guard's misconduct. He closed the door behind her, and they exchanged a long, cautious look. Kit thought about forcing him to speak first, but then gave it up. There was no point in playing power games with a man who already held all the power.

"I read the journal. All of it. I know that we have no orders, that the ORG never intended to form the Extension, and that this place was founded by malcontents and near-deserters." She said these things as a statement of fact, as expressionlessly as she could manage. Let him try to decide how she felt about the information.

"Then you understand why we can't allow the current state of affairs to continue." His expression was open and affable, as if he'd just told her she must understand why they couldn't have warm showers. Except he was brazenly suggesting revolt.

There was still a tiny part of her that was horrified. She reminded herself that this wasn't even the real ORG, and even if it had been, they had thrown her and her teammates away like garbage. She owed them nothing anymore.

Still, she had decided. Just because you opposed evil didn't necessarily make you good. She didn't know whether Jak was worth following. Look at what had happened with Zo and her unit. They had defeated a government they saw as despotic, and replaced it with the Congress.

"What do you propose to do about the current state of affairs? Why do you consider it to be so awful?" she asked. "It seems to me that, while it may be based on lies, the Extension is functioning efficiently as a home for many people."

"First of all, I wouldn't say that it's functioning efficiently. We have only the most rudimentary of quarters, and we're rapidly running out of room. The Congress may only send in a unit or so every six months out there, but here we get a constant influx of new people. It adds up."

Kit nodded slowly. She could see how an extra four people every month would strain the resources of this space. She had helped in construction of new areas, and knew how laborious preparing even one new chamber was.

"But that's not the largest issue," Jak continued. "We are perpetuating the standards that the ORG has set, which become more draconian every passing year. We can't become a truly independent, functioning society if we are denied the ability to reproduce."

That surprised Kit. Reproduction wasn't something she often thought about, after all. Some people coveted the act, and made it their life's goal to prove themselves worthy of the Congress' permission. She had never been one of them. And if overcrowding was already an issue...

"I'm not sure I understand," she told Jak honestly.

"It's not about increasing our numbers," he told her earnestly. "It's about being human, having choices. My time wasn't as much of a free-for-all as the First Unit's. Reproducing was regulated—but plain old sex wasn't. And you may have noticed that many of the operatives here aren't that crazy about following the new regulations." Kit grimaced, and he frowned in turn. "Not like Wil. Consenting. But we don't have the resources here to prevent pregnancy in a safe, reliable way. So what did Tera decide to do? Not bend regulations, allow for families, allocate space for a nursery like I wanted to do. No, she decided that we would use what resources we had to induce miscarriages in the women unlucky enough to get pregnant. And if the mother died as well as the child, well that's one less person to house." His face had gone all flat and hard again, like when he had sent Wil away. Kit didn't want to be on the wrong side of that expression. And so far, she was in agreement with him, to her surprise. She had never been the sort to take chances on pregnancy, but for those who did, it shouldn't be a death sentence.

"So if you take power, that's what you'll do? Allow families?"

"That and more," he promised. "I want to expand the Extension into Red and Blue territory, take control of the region. They have more than enough resources to care for an expanding population."

"You're talking about starting a war."

"Yes."

Kit thought about that. Having choices was good. Protecting these people, who had been discarded by their own leaders, that was good. But a war, where people died, and over territory and resources that could be obtained in another way—she wasn't sure that was good. She also wasn't sure it was bad. Perhaps that was the natural order of things.

"If you win the war, take the territory controlled by the Reds and the Blues, what will happen to the people there?"

Jak shrugged with a certain indifference. "If they're not killed in the fighting, they can find somewhere else to live." He paused, as if considering this for the first time. "It would probably be best if they didn't survive the fighting to come back and contest the area, though."

Kit's stomach turned. For all his high-minded ideas, Jak was precisely like the others in the ORG. Only concerned with those he deemed important. His people. She would be the first to admit that the Blues were an odd bunch, perhaps not even fully human. But her ignorance about their nature didn't mean they deserved extinction. And who was to say they couldn't defend themselves when the time came? That Red had trussed her and Avin up in the blink of an eye. How many operatives would be lost in a head-on conflict? Perhaps by the time the war was over, they would no longer need the extra space.

This was not something she could support. But she needed to proceed with caution.

"What is it that you want from me?" She kept her expression guarded. Hopefully he would not read her refusal there.

"I want you to join me. Tera is a good woman, but a painfully narrow-minded commander. The time is quickly coming when she needs to be removed from power, and I need every good soldier that I can get on my side."

"And what if I refuse?" Kit tried to make the question sound as casual as possible.

"That's not really an option," he said, and there was a shade of apology in his voice. "Now that you know my plans, I can't simply let you walk away. And though Wil was in the wrong, I doubt he will come forward on your behalf if I claim you assaulted a fellow operative."

Kit went cold. "I understand." If there was a noticeable stiffness in her voice, she thought it was deserved. Clearly he only believed in the right to choose one's own path when it suited him.

At that moment, a knock sounded on the door. When Jak courteously excused himself and answered it, Merdith's curly head poked through.

"Sorry to disturb you, but Kit was supposed to meet me for practice, and someone saw her coming this way." Merdith babbled out her explanation just a hair too quickly, as if she had been rehearsing what to say the entire way over, but Jak didn't seem to notice. He glanced at Kit questioningly.

"Of course, Merdith. I'll be along in a minute." Instead of the all clear, she pinged a warning signal. Merdith's face fell. But all she said was, "See you on the floor, then."

The door closed, leaving Kit alone with Jak once more.

"Your orders will come. Until then, continue as usual." She nodded stiffly and turned to go. Outside the archive, a new guard was already on duty, this time a slightly-built woman with honey blonde hair, pulled back severely from her face. She looked an awful lot like the woman who had been going on guard duty for the Red tunnel. Strange, but Kit had bigger things on her mind. She went to meet Merdith for training.

No discussion could take place in the open, busy training area. Kit could tell that Merdith's frustration was mounting fast. As time went by, Merdith pulled her blows less and less. There would be some bruises from this. While

Kit could understand, it wasn't as if she could do anything about it. If she went straight from the meeting with Jak to closet herself with Merdith, it wouldn't take a strategic mastermind to figure out what was going on. Then Merdith would find herself as trapped as Kit herself.

Another cold shower, another silent dinner, and by the time it was over, Kit knew there was no point in going to the bar and trying to pretend that everything was fine. Merdith was a bundle of nerves, and Kit wasn't much better. By silent agreement, they went straight to their bunk afterward. Hopefully anyone who noticed their bad moods would think it was a lovers' spat, and that they were going to "make up," as it were.

As soon as the curtain fell behind them, Kit flopped down on her bunk. For one blissful moment, the insanity of the past weeks melted away. Nothing quite compared with the feeling of a good flop, letting her arms hit the mattress with a satisfying bounce as every muscle went limp. The force of her fall knocked a puff of breath from between her lips, and as she lay still, she inhaled deeply, taking pleasure in filling her lungs to bursting. Distracted by those tiny physical impulses, so trivial and yet so vital, she felt a fleeting peace.

But fleeting was all it was. Merdith was sitting gingerly on her own bunk across the way, radiating an almost palpable anxiety. She had waited long enough for an explanation. With a sigh, Kit heaved herself up and launched into an abbreviated version of her talk with Jak. Merdith's tension didn't diminish in the slightest once it was over. Not that Kit had truly expected it to.

"What do we do now?" Merdith's question was nearly as unsettling to Kit as the information that had precipitated it. The other woman was gazing at her, not without worry, but definitely with trust. She expected Kit to have a plan. Kit had no idea how she had become the de facto leader of this team of two, but it seemed to have happened.

What should they do now? They were caught between two opposing sides, and neither was interested in giving them a choice of which to support. Whose side were they on?

Their own, Kit decided. The Extension was a quagmire of hidden dissension that was about to burst into open conflict, and she wanted none of it. She would take care of her own, and that meant Merdith and Avin—and, once they had been retrieved, Stev and Mercy. Unlike the ORG she had come from, the area outside the Extension was wild and unknown. She thought of the area that the books had come from, where Jak said the Reds and Blues never ventured. Perhaps if they went far enough in that direction, they could escape all of this and find a way to live as they saw fit. Maybe they could even find like-minded people somewhere in this unknown vastness.

"It's time to leave," Kit told Merdith firmly. "I won't be coerced into fighting for something I don't believe in, and if you stay here long enough, you'll be forced into the conflict on one side or another too. But you have to decide for yourself. Do you want to come with me?"

"I don't really want to," Merdith told her frankly, "but you're right. Things are about to get bad here, and I don't see a good way around it. I'm with you."

Kit heaved a mental sigh of relief. She didn't know if she'd have the gumption—or the resources—to go through with leaving if she was on her own.

"Avin," Kit exclaimed suddenly. "He won't be able to come with us if we just ask him. The inducement—"

"We'll think of something," Merdith said confidently. Kit had the horrible sinking feeling that by "we," she actually meant Kit. Her growing trust was touching, but Kit felt a dreadful certainty that one of these days, she would let Merdith down. And that would be devastating.

Chapter Fifteen

The next day passed in a blur. Kit did her best to focus on the present, but she worried that she was making too many mistakes, looking too distracted, acting suspicious. She was great at not being seen, but here she had to be seen without being noticed. That was becoming increasingly difficult, as she had unintentionally gained a certain notoriety. Gossip spread quickly here, even faster than it had in the old ORG barracks, since this was a much smaller group. It only took until noon the next day for the entire Extension to know that she was the reason Wil, the lecherous guard, was no longer at his post. No one was sure what had happened to him, though there was plenty of speculation.

There were surprisingly mixed reactions about Wil's disappearance. There were more than a few dirty looks and some unkind words tossed her way by people she had never interacted with before. Doors were slammed in her face, and one woman even tried to trip her, which Kit found astoundingly stupid. If she wasn't agile enough to avoid an outstretched foot, she wouldn't have survived very long in her line of work. She suspected the woman of being one of Wil's (allegedly many) girlfriends—another piece of evidence suggesting her intelligence was shockingly low.

As difficult as it was to believe, the man had been popular, especially among the earlier (and therefore senior) members of the Extension. Their almost aggressive disregard for the newer regulations meant that this became more than a simple case of assault. It was a battle between the new rules and the old, and they were furious that the new rules had won. Kit was disgusted by the lot of them. She had asked for clarification on the old rules: could a man actually just grab any woman he wanted, whether she was interested or not? Of course not, was the reply, but...

There were no "buts" that could possibly justify that attitude to Kit. Old rules or new, what Wil had done was wrong and deserved punishment. They were making an excuse to stir up trouble. She wondered how many of the aggressors were already part of Jak's rebellion. It solidified her decision to have nothing to do with it.

The newer operatives were no better, for all that they were on her side. From them, she received congratulatory shoulder slaps and high fives, as if getting Wil thrown out had been the plan all along. At the time, her entire plan had consisted of not letting him touch her. She still got a sick, angry feeling in the pit of her stomach when she thought about what he might have done, given the chance.

So she tried not to think about it. Instead, she planned obsessively for their escape from the Extension. There were a million details to consider. They needed food, weapons, equipment, and ideally knowledge of the surrounding area. Kit's personal preference would have been to avoid Jak entirely unless forced into his company, but she needed information, and he was the keeper of that information.

She began to stop by the archive daily during her lunch hour. The new guard, a short, stocky man with disinterested eyes, started to let her in without question. Jak, seemingly secure in her compliance, allowed her to browse the shelves in peace. He appeared to think that whatever she found there would reinforce his point. He didn't realize that it wasn't his point she disagreed with; it was his methods.

The first book that Kit grabbed off the shelf was Garet's journal. Apparently, keeping a personal memoir had just been the thing to do in those days. Kit toyed with the idea of starting her own journal, but decided that no one would be interested in what she had to say. Garet, on the other hand, had hundreds of pages of useful information in his journal. Instead of familial anecdotes, he had notes and musings on his research and development of the MDUs. Nearly all of it went over Kit's head, and she desperately wished that Mercy was there with her. She kept hoping that Jak would offer to loan her the book, as he had Zo's, but he seemed content to have her lurking around the archive now that she was in on his grand scheme.

That was another way of obtaining valuable information, however. Jak held his clandestine meetings in the archive, and though he didn't exactly invite her to participate, he didn't kick her out either. Sometimes she was able to see the person who entered or overhear snippets of conversation. This was how she learned that the rebels were stockpiling food and weapons in a myriad of small caches outside the Extension. Those with frequent kitchen duties would hide a few nonperishable items each shift and stash them outside the next time they had guard duty. The stash's location wasn't explicitly stated, but that didn't bother Kit. She could find out. She risked a glance around the shelf and took a quick screenshot of the man's appearance—round face, longish light brown hair, a turned up nose.

She began lingering over her dinner. When she saw that man leaving with the rest of the kitchen staff after the meal one day, she switched tactics, and instead loitered at the edge of the training area around the time for shift changes, waiting for the next time he was assigned as tunnel guard. She had a pretty decent view of the tunnel mouths from there, and no one questioned her presence as long as she made a pretense of working out.

In the end, though, her stakeout was in vain, because luck granted her an even better opportunity. After several days of this, that particular man turned up to replace her at the end of her morning shift on the Blue side. She'd been watching him so long that it took all her self-control not to greet him like an old friend. Instead, she nodded stiffly and retreated down the tunnel, far enough that she couldn't be seen from the mouth. She paused there; he would bide his time to be sure she was gone before stashing the goods. After a decent interval, she crept up the tunnel, just in time to see him poking at something behind a bush several feet beyond the guard post. As he finished, she melted away into the shadows. That was all she needed.

That would take care of an initial supply of food, at least. She had no idea how they were getting weapons out or whether they were stashed in the same place, but they were issued a basic light armament for guard duty, so she would at least have access to that.

In the evenings, she and Merdith had returned to the bar, but instead of sitting in the midst of the rowdy conversation, they tucked themselves into a dark corner. They made plans and traded tidbits of information through a screen of flirtatious smiles, whispers, and giggles. After a few evenings of this, Kit even loosened up enough to find it genuinely funny.

They decided that their best bet was to wait until one of them had a night shift for guard duty, eliminating the need to sneak past a guard. If they were very lucky, the next guard might think that Kit had been the victim of foul play long enough to let them get a good head start. That assumed there would be pursuit. There might not be, but they couldn't afford to plan for the best case scenario.

The last stumbling block was Avin. They couldn't leave him behind, or they would never see him again. They certainly couldn't bring him in on their plans, since he would run to the nearest authority figure to report them. That left subterfuge. They finally agreed that whoever was on guard duty would go out first and gather supplies from the cache, while the other waited within. Then they would take a gamble and tell Avin that the one outside was thinking about making a run for it. That came with a certain set of risks, as Avin would need to be convinced that going after the offending party themselves was a better course of action than reporting. They had considered trying to convince him that they had an Extension-sanctioned mission, but there was a major problem with that. Avin was smart. They had to tell him as close to the truth as they could manage, or he would call them on it.

"We'd better make sure you're the one with guard duty," Merdith murmured to Kit one evening, batting her eyelashes.

"Why's that?" Kit returned, laying her hand over Merdith's on the table.

"I think he'd try to follow you anywhere," she replied, and Kit couldn't tell whether her teasing smile was a part of the ruse or not. Kit's blushes certainly weren't, though she still wasn't sure why they insisted on happening. She glanced around the room self-consciously to see if anyone was watching.

There was that woman with the honey blonde hair again, watching them sidelong. She kept popping up wherever Kit was, always for entirely plausible reasons, but it was making Kit jumpy. She could be spying for Jak, or for the Commander, or just for her own advancement. The woman's face tugged at her memory, and not only from the last couple of days. It was as if Kit had seen her outside the Extension, but that was impossible. She had one of the mid-range MDUs that, while not as old as Jak's, was certainly not from Kit's own time.

They planned until there was nothing left to plan—and no more excuse for inaction. Trickles of disquiet tingled across Kit's body and down her limbs as she left her bunk for what would hopefully be the last time. She tried to imagine that she was about to embark on nothing more than a normal mission. There was danger, yes, but she was prepared. There was a plan.

The fact that she had made the plan did not make her feel more secure. The opposite, in fact.

She glanced around for the honey-haired spy before she entered the tunnel to the outside world. Her pistol sat comfortably on her hip, and she had scavenged some other small items from the armory, tucked into various pockets while she was arming herself for duty: two electroblades, a handful of tranq stamps, and an antique version of a plasma torch. She had also managed to snag some medical supplies, and had pilfered extra soap pellets from the showers. If only there had been another field blanket available...but at least Merdith would have hers. She desperately hoped that the stockpile of supplies would include water, since she had found no good way to smuggle it along with her.

Kit greeted the guard she was replacing civilly, waved a goodbye, then settled down into the blind as if she had nothing on her mind except a long night of solitude and quiet. She stayed there for a solid fifteen minutes, then stepped out from the blind, not to investigate the stash, but to scout up the tunnel. No one would spy on her as she had spied on others.

The tunnel was empty. Kit padded silently back to her post, then past it to the bush that concealed the stash. She hadn't investigated it too closely before. If there were traps or safeguards in place, she didn't want to trip them before she and her teammates were on their way. She now had another fifteen minutes before Merdith started working on Avin. There was no telling how long it would take to convince him to go after her, and they wanted as much travel time as possible before anyone realized they were gone.

The stash wasn't booby-trapped, as far as she could tell. It was hidden under the bush, beneath a square of sod that peeled up like a carpet. Two of the metal chests that accompanied their bunks were nestled in the hole. They weren't locked in any way, but she supposed that Jak couldn't very well give a key to every operative who went to deposit items there.

The first box she opened proved to be food. Much of it was stored in metal cans or glass jars, not ideal for a small group on the run. She took a few of the smaller cans anyway. They were heavy, but not that heavy, and they could eat those first. Much more useful was the multitude of ration bars that littered the crate. Kit recognized the type that she was familiar with, in both meat and grain varieties, and shoved as many of those in her pockets as she could. There were also several types she didn't recognize with brightly colored labels. Bold print advertised things like chocolate chips and peanut butter. Kit took a handful of these as well, but they seemed squishier than the ration bars, and she wasn't sure how well they would hold up over time. And as much as she would love to take several of the bags of meat jerky, they were too large for her pockets.

When she moved on to the second box, however, she found that her problem was solved. Inside were several ORG pistols, a rifle of modern design, and a dozen pistols in varying shades of red and blue. The weapons weren't the real score, though. It was the ammunition bag underneath them that she coveted. Quickly, she dumped most of the ammunition out, added a pair of each type of pistol, and returned to the other chest. Those lightweight but bulky bags of jerky went in first, followed by any bars she hadn't been able to fit in her pockets. Then she started adding cans, checking the weight carefully as she went. And, joy of joys, at the bottom of the chest, she found a dozen small plastic water bottles. Regretfully, she decided to only take six. With a little luck, they would find a place to refill them. It was better than she had hoped for.

She sat back on her heels, zipped up the bag, and tossed it over her shoulder. She replaced the sod, and returned to her post for the last time. A nagging sense of unease gripped her. She was about to leave the Extension unguarded for the better part of the night. That was a dereliction of duty so severe that it made her earlier lapse seem like a trifle. But—this was not the ORG, and she had no loyalty to these people anymore. She would choose her own fate.

Kit found a stately tree at the corner of the park and swung first her bag and then herself up into it. One of the few times she had been able to surprise Avin had been when she dropped from above. She hoped it would work again, because even with two of them, subduing Avin in a fair fight would be difficult, loud, and probably messy. The dark, rough bark felt reassuring through her boots and gloves. It was a good climbing surface. The branches wound like a stairway into the higher foliage. She amused herself while she waited by clambering up a good distance to where the branches grew thin, but as the minutes ticked by, she returned to the lower limbs to peer towards the tunnel mouth with concern.

Maybe Avin had refused to come. He could have reported her. Merdith could have overestimated his concern for her safety.

Just as she was ready to vacate her perch and check the tunnel, she saw Merdith's curly head bounce up above a bush, craning around to spot Kit's hiding place. Kit sent a very tightly contained private ping to Merdith: direction, ten o'clock. Merdith's head swiveled in her direction, and Kit saw her point. In a moment, Merdith led Avin directly below her hidden roost. This was it.

Kit dropped down behind Avin, swift and silent, and tagged his exposed neck with a tranq stamp. He spun, clapping a hand to his neck, and staggered into her with a look of blank betrayal. She caught him as he slumped forward, easing him to the ground. Kit grimaced at Merdith. Avin might be slender for a man, but he was still no featherweight. They were going to have quite a time hauling his senseless form to a more suitable location.

"Need a hand, ladies?"

Kit spun, pistol instantly in one hand, knife in the other. Leaning against the tree, casual as can be, was the woman with the honey blonde ponytail. She inspected her nails with every evidence of unconcern, despite the weapons trained on her.

"Who are you? What do you want?" Merdith had tried her best to keep the tremor out of her voice, and Kit inwardly commended her for it.

"Kit knows me. Don't you, Kit?" Kit shook her head, keeping her pistol steadily trained. "Aw, really? Well, maybe this will help." She let her hair down, plucked the MDU off of her face as if it was nothing, and pulled something long and white out from behind the tree. Kit was positive there had been nothing that color behind the tree a moment ago. She was puzzled—until the woman put the thing on, and she realized it was a clean, white lab coat.

It was as if the woman's face abruptly came into focus. Now Kit knew exactly where she'd seen her before—but it was impossible...

"Carrie?" she gasped. "You...but...you...?" Kit had lost the ability to formulate sentences.

"Nothing here is as it seems," Carrie said as she took off the white coat and tossed it into the air, where it vanished.

Slowly, Kit lowered her gun and knife. If Carrie had meant them harm, they would already have been dead or captured. And a vision of Carrie's still form in the blood-soaked horror of the infirmary flooded her mind. Unexpected tears welled up in her eyes, threatening to spill over.

"How can you be alive?" Kit whispered. She was afraid that if she spoke any more loudly, her voice would crack or the tears would escape.

"Can't it be enough that I am? At least for now, anyway..." Carrie's voice trailed off as she registered the refusal in Kit's expression. Kit had had enough—more than enough—of mysteries. She was ready to punch any mystery that reared its ugly snoot at her. She glared at Carrie through watery eyes, and the other woman blanched slightly. "Okay, yes, I'll explain everything once we get to a safer location. Follow me, ladies." Without any sign of strain, Carrie heaved Avin's unresponsive body over her shoulder and strode off, away from the park, the tunnel, and the Extension. Kit and Merdith exchanged painfully confused glances and then followed. There was nothing else to be done.

Carrie led them along the border between the Blue and Red territories. Though they were still on the Blue side, they could see reddish-tinged mirror tiles across the way. Carrie walked boldly along the street with no attempt at discretion, and Kit followed in her wake, slowly pulling herself together.

It was not as if she had known Carrie well. Getting so emotional wasn't logical—but neither was Carrie's reappearance. Kit's ability to cope was bruised and battered at this point, reeling drunkenly from one inexplicable event to the next. Perhaps it was a wonder that she hadn't broken down before this, hardened soldier though she was. Nothing in her training or experience had prepared her for people coming back from the dead.

As they walked, the blue and red faded from the tiles around them. The buildings began to look more ramshackle. Not dirty, but incomplete. Tiles were missing on some sides, leaving an unidentifiable gray substance exposed. Even farther down the road, she spotted a building that was missing an entire wall. It didn't look as if the wall had fallen down, but more as if it had never been built in the first place. It made as much sense as anything else in this place.

The street was becoming emptier. The little details had disappeared at some point. The texture of the road was unnaturally smooth, the streetlights and neon signs were gone, and the light seemed to be emanating from some diffuse point directly overhead, throwing shadows that were somehow a shade too dark and moved a little too noticeably as they walked. Kit's unshed tears dissipated, replaced by razor-edge wariness.

"We can stash your friend here," Carrie announced, gesturing toward a large building on her right. She led the way up the wide steps to a glassy set of double doors. The building itself looked finished, but the steps were that indeterminate matte gray stuff, leaving no clue as to whether they were wood or stone or concrete. Her feet made no sound against them, regardless of how firmly she stomped. It was unnerving, but she followed Carrie, whose mere existence was far more bewildering, through the door without protest.

This was where the archive's books had originated. Shelves lined every wall and formed countless aisles in between, every one filled with red, green, and blue books. The archive's pilfering hadn't even made a dent in the number of tomes here. But as Kit's eyes brushed along the innumerable shelves, she realized that something was abnormal about their contents. In Jak's archive, the books had been arranged in sections by subject, then alphabetically by author. Here, they were arranged by color and size - not that all the blue ones were together, or all the large ones, or anything so regular as that. There was simply a pattern, arranged so that it looked intentionally random on a single shelf, but then repeated on every shelf thereafter. Medium-sized red, then large blue, then two small green and so forth, on the top shelf of every bookcase. Kit blinked rapidly, but it stayed the same.

There was a desk not far inside the doors that provided decent cover. Carrie lifted Avin from her shoulder, still with no sign that he was heavier than a spare towel, and laid him down behind it.

"He'll be safe enough there while we go reclaim your teammates," she declared.

Questions exploded through Kit's mind, but Merdith found her voice first. "Oh no, we're not leaving him here unconscious and helpless. And what if he wakes up while we're gone? He'll go straight back to the Extension. He won't have a choice."

Kit hissed a warning at Merdith under her breath, and she quieted down. Avin's conditioning was no one's business but theirs. Carrie, however, didn't seem in the least surprised or confused

"True," she agreed calmly. "It would be best if he could be kept unconscious until he's been de-programmed."

"What do you know about that?" Kit snapped.

"Everything you do, and no more," Carrie replied breezily. "I've read all the files on your recent activity."

"The Extension has files that extensive on us?" Merdith sounded dismayed.

"No, they're clueless. Don't worry," Carrie assured them. Kit decided that was a directive she was going to ignore completely. She had every right and reason to worry, and she refused to give it up.

Kit came to a snap decision. Whatever Carrie was, whatever she wasn't, Kit was not going to move a step farther without some explanations. She planted her feet solidly and crossed her arms.

"Hmm. Not good enough?" Carrie sized Kit up as if she was thinking about bodily carting her off. Considering how she'd carried Avin, there was a real possibility she could pull it off, but Kit wasn't about to do the work for her. Not without some answers.

But instead, Carrie nodded to herself and smiled. "I'll need to take you somewhere before you truly understand. And I'm not dragging him along before his brain's fixed. I don't know what the realization would do to him if he woke up."

"Merdith, you stay here with Avin." Kit avoided meeting Merdith's eyes as she slung the bag of supplies down behind the counter. She silenced her teammate's immediate protests with a sharp jerk of her head. They needed answers, but she wasn't about to risk Avin's mind to get them. Or Merdith's safety, for that matter. If one of them was going to go traipsing off into the unknown with a relative stranger who had returned from the dead, it was going to be Kit. Still, as she walked out of the building with Carrie, she couldn't help but feel she was abandoning her friends.

Kit expected Carrie to lead her back the way they had come, perhaps towards the Blue complex where Stev and Mercy were being held. Instead, Carrie stopped at the foot of the stairs and spouted off an unintelligible string of gibberish. A blue portal materialized before her, much like the one that had taken Kit to the Red prison.

"After you," Carrie said.

She had come this far. There was no point in turning back now.

The room on the other side was swathed in mysterious darkness, but as soon as her feet were firmly on the floor, light blossomed around her. She stood in the center of a round, spacious room with a white tiled floor and walls of wooden slats. Her eyes flickered from one end of the room to the other, but nothing moved or looked the least bit suspicious.

The portal blinked shut behind her. Carrie had not come through. Kit's heart began to race. She shifted her weight into a defensive stance and nearly lost her balance.

The floor, which had been hard, solid tile just moments before, had transmuted into loose, white sand. She could still see the tiles at the edge of the room, rapidly disintegrating. The wooden boards of the walls narrowed and separated, becoming the trunks of tall, narrow trees, each of which sprouted broad, fanning leaves from their apex. The dim, theater lighting brightened into sunshine like liquid gold that gleamed blindingly off the sand. A light breeze wafted over Kit, bringing an unfamiliar mineral tang to her nose. The air was warm and full of moisture.

Before Kit had even begun to process the shift, the sand was clumping together and darkening into mossy earth. The narrow trunks were fusing together, some into giant trees that soared up into the sky so far that she couldn't make out their tops, and others into squat log buildings, smoke rising lazily from within. The light faded to the deep green shade of an old forest. The tang was gone from the air, replaced by the earthy richness of soil.

Almost before the trees had finished growing, they were melting into huge metal blocks. With a start, Kit realized they were becoming the huge mirror-tiled buildings she had come to expect in the area around the Extension. The light darkened into nighttime, and the buildings sparkled with brilliant artificial lights and colors, making the stars look faded in comparison. Distant music and laughter drifted through the streets.

The city melted into a single circular room again. This time, the walls were covered by heavy, red velvet drapes and the floor was cushioned by a thick carpet. Beneath her feet, there was a circle of lustrous wooden flooring in the exact center of the room.

The curtains directly across from her drew themselves open to reveal a large screen. Words scrawled themselves across it, as if drawn by an invisible giant.

Anywhere you can imagine, we can create, they read. *Try our game or vacation demos today!* Underneath, a logo flashed the name "Augrean Virtual." The circle of wooden flooring sprouted spokes, radiating out to five points around the room. Wherever it touched the wall, the curtains drew themselves aside to expose a door.

The room seemed to be done transforming for now. Kit took a cautious step, and the floor felt solid enough at the moment. Carrie still was nowhere to be seen. She had promised explanations, but Kit only felt more confused. When everything stayed stable for another few seconds, she paced cautiously towards one of the doors. It had a plaque beside it that claimed it led to "Demo 5: Beachside Villa Vacation." The door itself had a little window inset, covered by a curtain with a pull-cord. Kit tugged on the cord and gasped.

Beyond was the first scene the room had shown her, complete with white sand, sunlight, and fronded trees. She grasped the door handle and pulled it open. The breeze, which she now realized must carry the scent of the ocean, whipped into the room, setting all the curtains to blowing. But when she stuck her head through the door, she found herself in a doorway from nowhere. The room she was in simply didn't exist from the other side. She withdrew her head and carefully closed the door.

The next door revealed the dark forest with its little log huts. When Kit opened the door and stuck her head through, the man squatting next to the campfire turned to wave at her. She slammed the door again, breathing hard.

She expected to find the darkened city streets behind the third door, but instead rolling green hills stretched as far as the eye could see. When she glanced at the plaque for an explanation, she discovered that this one was much more informative:

Demo 3: Bountiful Fields

Build your own farm from the ground up! Grow crops, sell them at market, and improve your property. All produce is grown from real seeds and matured with our patented TimeWarp technology. All goods sold at market will be donated to charity!

Kit was beginning to get a glimmering of what was going on here. She moved to the next door. Here was her cityscape, and the plaque confirmed all of her suspicions.

Demo 2: Mirror Heights

Join the brave Blue Team or the rebellious Red Team in a thrilling battle for control of the city! Fight with friends or with the newest, most realistic bot AI available. Custom matches with up to ten players per side. Guaranteed completely safe, so shoot, rocket boost, and pilot a variety of vehicles with full confidence!

Those Red and Blue soldiers hadn't been real people at all, just a computer program running a pretty convincing AI. The General hadn't been any more real than the hologram that had taught them how to use those weapons. Battles had been scheduled because they weren't real. Defeated soldiers had vanished because they weren't real. Her capture by the Reds took on a whole new meaning. She'd been put in the corner like a child because she'd tried to use a real weapon rather than whatever harmless toys she'd been given by the Blues. She suspected that if she had tried to use that knife on a real person rather than the AI, the consequences would have been more severe.

Kit turned to stare at the door to Demo 1 with utter loathing. She could easily guess where that would lead. All of that terror and disgust and uncertainty—it had been set up for *fun*. She approached with heavy, hesitant steps.

Demo 1: Greyridge Laboratories

Based upon the very laboratory where this game was developed, now overrun with undead horrors! How long can you and your friends survive in this gruesome zombie wasteland? If you get bitten (don't worry, it won't hurt!), you can join the hordes of the undead to stalk your friends! Bonus points are awarded for uncovering the tragic story of Greyridge Labs.

"Not many of your teams show any interest in rescuing people anymore." Carrie's voice caused Kit to spin, ready to attack. She hadn't heard anything to indicate that another person had entered the room. Self-consciously, she relaxed her posture.

"I wanted to get to know you better, so I replaced the standard character in the scenario," Carrie continued, seeming not to notice Kit's confusion. "And you took me in, as apparently helpless as I was, and kept me safe to the best of your ability. Not unanimously or without protest, perhaps, but that was more than I expected. Being given a weapon and told to fend for myself, being dropped with the evacuees—that's the usual response. Most teams don't even look for survivors."

"So that was all a test? Was watching you die part of it? What are you?" To her intense embarrassment, Kit felt the prickling of tears in her eyes again.

Carrie shook her head. "That's the way the scenario plays out. I'm bound by my scripting as much as you are bound by your biological needs."

"Then why come back now?"

"I need your help."

"Our own people shoved us in here to get rid of us. You can pop around like a wizard, create any landscape you want, and rise from the dead. What could you possibly need from us?" Kit's voice sounded shrill in her own ears, but she couldn't maintain her usual iron control. She wasn't sure it mattered now anyway.

"Let me show you." There was an unexpected gentleness in her tone. She led Kit back to the central screen. The picture changed at her gesture, becoming a new type of cityscape, full of blinking electronics and whirring fans. "This is the true infrastructure of our world. We were supposed to be the next big breakthrough in entertainment." Carrie's smile became wry. "As it turns out, our creators' timing was poor. The war broke out just as the first big demo for the project was nearly completed."

"So this place isn't even finished?" Kit asked. Then the other part of the statement caught up with her. "Wait, the war broke out. There hasn't been a real war since the one that ended with the Great Establishment..."

"This whole space was created hundreds of your years ago, before there was such a thing as the Congress or the ORG," Carrie confirmed.

"And it's been running all that time?" Awe was eroding Kit's anger. This place had existed before the Congress, had been created by people who never lived under their laws.

"It may not run for much longer. It was never intended to hold so many people for so long. It was never intended to be a place where people came to die."

Kit pounced on that. "The lab, the city—those locations seem danger- ous. Merdith said that teams show up missing members. What happens to them?"

"They are sent to the Lobby, until they choose their next game." Carrie gestured, and a spacious hall emerged on the screen. "But they don't know that there's a next game to choose, so they just stay there, for the most part."

"You haven't told them?" Kit was aghast, her anger rekindled.

"The damage to the systems of this place is great enough when people stay quietly in the Lobby," Carrie said with a frown. "If they went gallivant- ing off throughout the levels, the system resources would be strained to the breaking point much more quickly. If the system crashed, I wouldn't be able to guarantee their safety anymore."

And just as quickly, Kit's anger went cold again. "What's wrong with the system. Can it be fixed?"

"That's where I need your help. The demo system was never completed. There were bugs that were never fixed, situations that were never foreseen. When a person entered the demo, the central processing nexus allocated system resources, memory, to that person's welfare. When they exited, those resources would be returned to the nexus. This system was never intended to deal with permanent tenants, with death from illness or old age. It wasn't programmed to release the resources in those situations. It has been several centuries since the nexus began to run out of resources. Keeping people alive must be our first priority, so resources have been pulled from other areas. But people keep coming in, and I don't know how long we can keep operational."

"Well...then...let everyone out." If the problem was the people inside the system, then the solution seemed simple to Kit.

"I would love to, but the script needed for autonomous exit was never finished. When our creators disappeared, they only had an exit script that could be executed manually from the development console. We lowly AIs are banned from using scripts that aren't specifically assigned to us, and we certainly weren't given the power to write new ones. We can't even approach the development console. That requires a human."

"Then why haven't you sent someone before?"

"Valid question." Carrie grimaced. "I didn't realize that any of you would have the knowledge to complete and execute the script. Then you found that scrap of code when you were sorting through the papers in the lab—a bug, by the way, which is why it messed with your vision—and managed to execute it merely by reading it. That was when I realized that your little brain computers ran on the same language as our base system."

Kit's brow furrowed in thought. "One of the first operatives to be sent here...he helped create the MDUs to win the war. If this place was in development just before the same war, then the technology should be similar."

"True," Carrie agreed. "It never occurred to me that outside technology would have stagnated so much that it still worked the same on a basic level. It is illogical."

"The Congress doesn't like things to change," Kit said wryly. "If things are still the same, then they're still in power."

Carrie huffed. "Humans are very strange." Kit couldn't disagree.

"So. You need someone to go to this console and run this script to get everyone out of here. It sounds like you need Mercy...so why not go get Mercy yourself?"

Carrie's head tipped to the side quizzically, as if she didn't quite understand the question. "Humans come in groups. The groups should be preserved when possible. You function better in your self-assigned groups, like a code library, where each script serves a function to enhance the whole."

Kit raised her brows.

"We have few enough resources to work with. Why should I try to use the minimum requirements? You stand a better chance of repairing the system with your team functioning properly."

"I haven't said I'll do it," Kit reminded her.

"You will. You don't want this place to crash any more than I do."

"It's not just my decision to make. Let's get Mercy and Stev away from the Blues and Avin back on his feet. Then we can make a decision." It was probably true, Kit thought grimly. If they didn't want this artificial world to come tumbling down around them, they would do what Carrie asked. There wasn't a compelling reason not to, but Carrie's certainty rubbed her the wrong way. She and her team would make their own choices.

"Let's get going, then. The sooner, the better." Carrie led the way to the door marked Mirror Heights. Kit followed close on her heels, and they stepped through the aperture into the courtyard that Kit had first seen after her release from the Reds' prison. There was the little table of brochures, the matching red and blue portals, and hidden by the foliage, the entrance to the Extension. Carrie paid no attention to the surroundings, making a beeline for the blue portal. Kit didn't want to hang around an entrance to the

Extension anyway. She didn't know what they'd do to her if they got their hands on her, and she didn't want to find out. Before they stepped through, Carrie pulled a blue armband out of a pocket and handed it to Kit. Kit eyed it with distaste, but put it on, watching it slither disconcertingly around her bicep.

"Follow my lead, and we'll be out in no time. This isn't going to be nearly as difficult or dangerous as you're expecting." Carrie smiled at Kit's skeptical expression and led on.

The blue portal dumped them directly inside the gate of the Blues' complex. At one point, not too long ago, Kit would have considered that supremely careless on the part of their security. It made more sense now that she knew this was all intended to be a game. This was the entrance for new players after they had selected their team.

Carrie strolled along the main path without any sign of nervousness, so Kit tried to emulate her lack of concern. She couldn't help shooting suspicious glances at the Blues moving purposefully around them.

"Are any of these real people?" she asked, eyeing the bustling forms around them.

"By your definition, probably not. Here we are!" Carrie had brought them, not to the Congressional Seat replica where the unit had originally been housed, but to the barracks building. "Your friends have been moved in here, due to their promotions."

"Promotions?" Kit asked faintly.

"They've both climbed the ranks quite quickly," Carrie confirmed with a smile. "This game was never designed for fully-trained military professionals, and the difficulty is still set on easy." She led Kit through the spacious lobby, still empty, to the elevator in its crystalline shaft. The robotic attendant pushed the call button and ushered them through the sliding doors. Kit looked at it askance. She was perfectly capable of pushing an elevator button for herself, thank you. What kind of players had they expected to come here?

They rode the elevator up to the third floor, labeled "Sergeant" on the directory, and stepped off into a long, blue carpeted hallway. It was dark and silent, and all the doors along its length were closed. Carrie approached the door directly across from the elevator, fiddled with the knob for a second, then knocked. She then repeated this performance with the next door.

The first door opened, revealing Mercy's sleepy face, full of suspicion, through a crack. When she caught sight of Kit, she flung the door open, and an instant later Kit found herself wrapped in an exuberant hug.

"I thought you were dead," Mercy squealed. She pulled away and grabbed Kit's shoulders. "Don't scare me like that. Stev and I aren't smart enough to figure this place out without you and Avin. Avin made it too, right? Where is—" That was when she noticed Carrie, and the flow of words stuttered to a halt.

At that moment, Stev's door flew open. Unlike Mercy, who had decided to take a cautious peek and identify the nighttime visitors outside her door, Stev, as usual, came out guns blazing—or would have, if he'd had guns. He jumped into the hall, fists raised, then instantly deflated when he found three women there, eyeing him with various levels of disapproval. His eyes flickered over the assemblage, Mercy, Kit, Carrie—flickered away from Carrie, then back—then he deliberately turned away from her. He didn't know how to deal with her, so he simply wouldn't.

"Operative. Report."

Kit felt like laughing. Here she was, facing her commanding officer in his pajamas (for he and Mercy were wearing much the same outfit as she'd been given at the Extension) in the middle of the night, and she was expected to report? All the same, she straightened her spine and filled him in as best she could on the capture by the Reds, the discovery of the Extension, meeting up with Merdith, and the subsequent rescue mission. She glossed over a few key points, namely, that the retrieval mission was not sanctioned by the Extension and that Avin was waiting unconscious in an abandoned building. She didn't even consider touching on the true nature of their surroundings or Carrie. Save that for a less precarious place where Stev's bellowing wouldn't disturb anyone.

There was a tense pause after Kit had finished. Then Mercy, who had spent the entire time staring at Carrie, asked, "Are you Carrie's sister? Maybe a twin?"

Kit was startled. Now there was a reasonable explanation, one that hadn't even occurred to Kit. She'd found it easier to believe a woman had come back from the dead than that she might have a similarly featured sibling.

"If it makes it easier for you, I can be."

"I don't understand," Mercy said.

"That's fine."

"We can figure out what's going on with...that...once we're out of here," Stev barked. "For now, let's get moving." A moment later, he and Mercy had changed into their uniforms, and the entire group was back on the elevator.

Once outside, Carrie headed confidently for the armory. Kit thought that surely this would trigger some sort of alert, but still no one stopped them. A touch and a jiggle later, all of their weapons were restored. Kit took charge of Avin's things, shoving his jumble of gadgets into her pockets at random. She offered Avin's pistol to Carrie. After all, Kit didn't need a third pistol on top of her original and the one she'd brought from the Extension. But Carrie refused it with an enigmatic smile. Despite her ORG uniform, she carried no overt weapons. Kit had an uncomfortable hunch that it was because she didn't need them.

In a blink, they were outside again, standing before the main gate.

"What are you doing?" Mercy hissed at their guide. "They're not going to just let us stroll on out."

"You're welcome to return to your apartment, Sergeant."

Mercy made a face that was somewhere between a laugh and a grimace. A sideways glance at Stev showed a frown, but he made no protest. Kit was relieved. If he dug his heels in now, they might never get out of the complex. Please, she thought silently. Just go along with it. Think that all this was your idea, and you're still in control.

Carrie spouted her string of gibberish again, and the blue portal sprang into being. Kit glanced over at her teammates to see how they were taking this new development. Stev seemed to have passed his threshold for surprise. At this point, he was beyond caring about the how or why as long as it got results. Mercy, however, was staring at Carrie with saucer-wide eyes. Something in that gabble had made sense to her.

"Soon," Carrie said to Mercy with a smile, and she led them through the portal. To Kit's intense relief, Mercy followed without hesitation, and Stev was close behind. Kit brought up the rear, and the portal snapped closed in her wake.

Chapter Sixteen

The portal dropped them on the steps of the library. Carrie had already started up the steps, but Mercy dashed after her and grabbed her arm.

"It's a simulation? That was computer code you used to open the portal. It must be a simulation, nothing else makes sense."

"It's—" Carrie started, but Mercy talked right over her, babbling in excitement.

"Not just a simple simulation though, to get the breadth and scope of the space in here, there would have to be some major spatial distortion—not to mention some solid components for us to interact with—not virtual reality, but augmented reality? And then if everyone we've met has been some sort of advanced AI, that would explain—you're not Carrie's twin at all, are you?"

"I—no, I'm not." Carrie looked thoroughly discomfited, and Kit couldn't help enjoying it. She savored the speechlessness of the omniscient AI for a moment, then stepped in.

"Let's go inside, and I'll explain everything I know. Merdith is waiting with Avin, and she'll want to hear this too."

"Why didn't they come along?" Mercy asked as they climbed the steps.

"Avin is...ah...out of commission for the time being," Kit said delicately.

"Is he hurt?" Mercy's brows drew together in concern.

"No," Kit hurried to assure her. "Just—it's complicated."

Merdith came hurtling towards them as they walked in the door. "You made it! I was so worried!" She hugged Kit and Stev, and even, after a moment's hesitation, Mercy as well. Mercy didn't seem to mind, even though they had never met before. But as Merdith drew back, Kit noticed a large purplish bruise swelling on her jaw.

"Has everything been okay here?" she asked.

Merdith grimaced. "Fine, mostly. His Highness over there tried to fool me into thinking he was still passed out, but I managed to tag him with another tranq before he got more than a few steps toward the door. He's too fast for his own good—and mine."

Kit could see the questions looming, and leaped to intercept them. "Avin is trying to return to the Extension," she told Stev and Mercy, and quickly filled them in on Avin's condition and the internal politics that had led them to flee the Extension. Mercy's face grew bleak and hard, but she didn't seem surprised. It was Stev, however, who Kit was most worried about. She didn't know whether he would believe her.

His face became more and more red as she went on until Kit half expected steam to start coming out of his ears. She couldn't tell whether he was mad at her or the situation. She finished explaining that the ORG had disposed of inconvenient operatives for centuries by sending them here, and then trailed off into silence.

"Those bastards," Stev growled. "How dare they treat me and my team like that? We were solid. We got the job done. And what they did to Avin—best damn fighter I've ever seen. Those bastards!" He looked around helplessly, fists balled. Kit knew that look. He was desperately looking for something safe to punch. When he didn't find anything, he turned to Kit, forcibly unclenching his hands.

"What do we do now? We can't leave him like that, tranqed out of his mind. You've got to have found something."

"I think so. In my reading I found out that inducement is performed through modification of the MDU. I thought maybe Mercy..." She trailed off. Mercy's pale skin had gone visibly paler, and there were red spots on her cheeks.

"I can't—I mean, I don't—I don't know what to do," she mumbled, her eyes flickering from one face to another.

"I know it must be an intimidating idea, but you've worked with the MDUs before. You must have learned something that would give us an idea of where to start." Kit had never seen Mercy look so scared, not even before their first mission together.

"It's not that," Mercy said in a tiny voice. She spun to look at Carrie. "Are we ever getting out of here? Is there a way?"

"The plan is to get all of you out of here and back to your reality, yes."

"What if one of us wanted to stay? Could I claim sanctuary here?"

Carrie looked startled. "You would have to leave for the reboot, but yes, if you wanted to return after that you would be welcome. This place was created for the enjoyment of humans." Mercy nodded jerkily and addressed the rest of the team.

"If I help him, you all have to promise that you'll keep me safe."

Kit looked at Stev and Merdith in confusion, but their faces showed no more knowledge or insight. Nor did they seem eager to respond.

"I don't know why you think your safety would be any more at risk by helping him," Kit said. "But I think we can promise to protect you if you need it. That's what we'd do anyway. You're one of the team."

"One of the team," Mercy repeated bitterly. "You may not want me anymore after I come clean. And you've got a replacement all lined up. But you're good people, and I know you'll keep your word. I want to help, I really do. Just promise."

"I promise," Kit said, still confused. Stev and Merdith followed her lead, with no less bewilderment.

Mercy steeled herself, taking a huge gulping breath, and said, "I know exactly how to help him. I have a cleaner app on my memory chip." She flinched as if one or all of them were about to strike her, but no one moved.

"I don't understand," Merdith said slowly. "How would you have such a thing? No one of our rank even knows that inducement is connected to the MDUs—and somehow you have a cleaner for it?"

"No one knows...in the ORG," Kit pointed out sharply. Mercy flinched. Bits of information zipped together like pieces of a puzzle inside Kit's head.

She remembered Mercy stalking along the streets of the Limits as if she owned the place, her unusual affection for other people...her skill at soothing frightened children...

"It was you I saw from the wall. Getting the kids out."

Hope flared in Mercy's eyes. "I didn't think you'd seen us."

"I saw...something. But the kids...I couldn't sound the alarm."

Stev looked like he'd been punched. Two of his operatives had just admitted to treason, and the other one was passed out on the floor, a victim of government-mandated brainwashing for an equally heinous crime. His face flushed, his fists clenched—and then he seemed to deflate. All the bluster went out of him, and he began to chuckle weakly.

"Well that explains how a screw-up like me got promoted to lead. Always thought you were all too good to be under the command of the likes of me."

Kit gaped. This was almost more of a shock than Mercy. Stev, the cocky, swaggering show-off, always doing his best to assert his authority even when it wasn't called for, strutting and barking orders—well, maybe it shouldn't be that much of a surprise. She had never looked closely enough to see the seething nest of personal inadequacy that lurked behind the facade. She had never bothered to do anything except sidestep orders she didn't like or tear him down when she thought he'd gotten too arrogant. Even his rampant womanizing fit the pattern, and she hadn't put the pieces together.

Kit looked at the faces around her and was filled with an unexpected wave of deep affection. Before they had been dumped here, she had been numbed by the constant assault of daily routine and imposed disinterest. She had thought herself loyal to her teammates, but it had been an empty loyalty to an idea rather than a real attachment to real people—deeply flawed, but still wonderful, unpredictable, unique people.

"We're a team," Kit said firmly. "We are all good enough, and we're going to find a place for ourselves." Three sets of wide eyes met hers, but there was no dissent. Standing quietly in the background, Carrie smiled.

"So what do we do next?" Stev asked, meeting her eye steadily. The message was clear. The mantle of leadership settled heavily on her shoulders.

For a second, her mind reeled. A little voice in the back of her mind began to babble frantically. She didn't want responsibility. She didn't know what to do. She couldn't possibly make the right decisions. Then she took that little voice, clamped a hand around its throat, and thrust it away. She did know what needed to be done.

Kit turned to the youngest member of the unit. "Mercy. I have questions."

The girl blanched, the whiteness of her face standing out in stark contrast to her black hair. But she launched into an explanation without further prompting.

"I grew up with the group you call the Swampies. I know people in the city think we're just a group of gross savages, but...well, I suppose half of it's true by City standards, and half is a front to keep us from looking too dangerous. We regularly send our people into the city for intel, and to help any like-minded City-dwellers find their way to our settlements. My mom and dad were escaped City-dwellers, and I got a pretty thorough education in City customs and mannerisms. It made sense that when I got old enough, I'd get sent in. It was a five year assignment, long enough to really work my way into the ORG, but not so long that I'd run the risk of getting retired. We always figured that was a straight death-sentence." Mercy sent a glance at Merdith and flushed. "Turns out that's not the case, but we weren't willing to risk it to find out. It was supposed to be only intel, but when we took in those kids...I couldn't leave them to be tortured and brainwashed, I just couldn't. They were so little. I have a brother that age back home."

"So when we went into the Limits..."

Mercy hung her head. "It was a stop-over point for the kids. I warned them we were coming. I don't think the ORG knew it was me, or they would have just arrested me, interrogated me, and then dumped the body, I'm sure. But they knew it had to be one of us at that point, so they ditched the lot of us. I'm sorry."

There was a long silence, then Merdith broke it with a laugh. "I'm not. I'd be all on my own if you hadn't gotten everyone in trouble." Mercy flashed her a grateful smile.

As strange as it was, Kit couldn't feel sorry either. Everything that had happened to them was wild and confusing and terrifying, but she felt somehow lighter.

"And the Swampies taught you how to fix MDUs?" Stev's skepticism was obvious.

"Believe it or not, we're not some backwards degenerates who wear weeds for hats and dance around bonfires to call the rain," Mercy replied. Her pained smile was equal parts amusement and frustration. "The people who are most likely to join us are also the ones most likely to have been put through inducement. We've been working on a solution for generations." She pulled a storage chip out of her MDU. "It's still not perfect. There are a lot of safeguards in place to make sure that no one can reverse-engineer the exact process of inducement. We've been able to work out some of it and do a roll-back to the original code, but for other bits all we can do is sort of...cancel out the symptoms by triggering other hormones or bodily processes. That means if someone fights a particular trigger too much or too often, they can end up a bit of a mess, so it still takes some special management, but no more than a particularly annoying disease, really." She shrugged and looked nervous, as if she was the bearer of bad news. At that moment, Kit could have kissed her.

"That's more than I ever thought to hope for," she told Mercy instead.

"You're not angry I got us dumped here?" Mercy reminded Kit of a very small child in that moment.

"Maybe I would have been at one point. But not now," Kit said thoughtfully.

"We all made mistakes," Stev said gruffly, staring at his boots.

"I would have been here no matter what," Merdith said cheerfully.

Mercy glanced at Avin's slumped, unconscious form. "He's going to be the most grateful of all," Kit assured her. "What do you need to do to run the cleaner?"

Mercy moved to Avin and straightened his limbs. "Lay all the packs around him and cushion his head. He might convulse."

They removed any hard objects from the packs and used them to cushion Avin's body as well as they could. Two blankets were folded and placed beneath his head to make the floor as forgiving as possible. Then Mercy knelt on one side of Avin, and Kit took a place on the other.

"This isn't going to be easy." Mercy's warning was unnecessary. Kit hadn't expected anything about this process to be easy. She watched stoically as Mercy plugged one side of a networking cable into Avin's MDU and the other into her own.

"Have you actually done this before?"

Mercy sucked in a deep breath. "Nope." She pushed her chip into the slot on Avin's MDU and closed her eyes. "Here we go."

Avin stiffened immediately. He didn't flail or thrash as Kit had feared, but every muscle on his body stood out in cords, tensing to the point where he began to tremble violently. His breath came faster, until he was sucking in great gasps of air, and his hands clenched and flexed spasmodically. Kit found that her own hands had clenched into tight fists on her knees. Her fingernails were digging into her palms. She forced herself to relax her hands and stared at the little red crescents etched in her skin rather than the furrow in Mercy's brow or Avin's tightly clenched jaw.

She hadn't asked the risks of this little procedure. She didn't really want to know. If Avin's mind came out of this damaged in some way, would he thank her? He had adjusted to living within the constraints of the inducement. He'd never seemed too miserable. But if it worked—he would be his own man again. She hoped it was worth the risks, that she had made the right call. That he would forgive her if she hadn't.

Sweat beaded on Avin's forehead and dripped down his face with each shivering spasm. Kit leaned forward and mopped it up with her sleeve, pushing his dark, wet hair back from his brow. The shivers quieted. In a moment, Mercy's eyes popped open.

"Done," she said, popping out the chip and unplugging the cord that had connected them.

"That's it?" Merdith said, coming forward. It seemed like quite enough to Kit.

"I sent a shock of adrenaline through his system to burn off the last of the tranq. He should wake up any—" Mercy jumped back and almost lost her balance as Avin jerked upright violently. He stared around wildly, eyes wide and pupils dilated, until he focused in on Kit. His hand shot out and grabbed her wrist with bone-grinding intensity.

"I have to—we have to go back! Why did you—we have to..." He trailed off, looking confused. "I—don't have to...?" He released Kit's wrist to stare at his own hands, as if they belonged to someone else. "You left—disobeyed orders—you knocked me out—and I don't have to...?" He turned his gaze to Kit. "What did you do?"

"We fixed it." Kit spoke haltingly, unsure of how much to tell him right away.

He shook his head. "It's not possible."

"Merdith and I are deserters, Mercy is a spy, and Stev—" Kit hesitated.

"At this point, I'm a traitor, or enough of one for the ORG's standards," Stev said gruffly.

"We're all traitors, then. What are you going to do about it?"

Avin looked around him, studying each face as they looked down at him in concern. "I..." A smile crept across his features, lighting them up like a slowly rising sun. "I'm not going to do anything. I don't have to do any-thing!" He began to laugh, quietly at first, then with greater abandon. He laughed until he choked, and the heaves of laughter turned into dry, heaving sobs, the sobs of a man who has endured too much for too long.

Tentatively, Kit leaned forward and put her arms around him. He col-lapsed against her, any self-consciousness lost in the tumult of emotion. She tightened her arms and laid her cheek against his damp hair. A sense of relief so profound it was nearly transcendent gripped her. She had done the right thing.

Gradually the sobs quieted. She hurriedly released him when he started to pull away. He wiped his face, ran his fingers through his hair, composed his features—and suddenly, he was the same old Avin. Except not quite. There were deeper lines in his face and a sparkle in his eye that no amount of composure could hide. Kit smiled, and pushed herself to her feet. She had lost track of how long she had been kneeling there. Her legs felt cramped and her knees ached. She offered Avin a hand up, and he grasped it firmly.

"I feel like I've just been kicked all over by someone very large and angry," Avin declared, straightening his cuffs. "And I would really like to know what's been going on, both inside my head and out."

It took a while to get him up to date and fill in the bits that the others hadn't heard yet. Mercy handed him a ration bar out of the supply duffel, and he munched quietly as everyone spoke their piece. He seemed unsurprised—or at least unworried—by much of it.

"You have no idea how hard it was to not notice odd things about you," he remarked to Mercy.

Her face fell. "Was I that obvious?"

"Not at all, but I used to work in the division of the ORG dedicated to unearthing moles."

That explained a lot.

The revelation that they were trapped inside an ancient gaming system was greeted with general consternation, but the rest of the team took it in better spirits than Kit had expected. Stev was angry about being fooled, but Mercy shrugged it off now that she knew Carrie was not only alive, but also unable to be killed. Avin seemed to find the whole situation ridiculous and kept chuckling under his breath, perhaps because he was so relieved to be able to express himself again.

But the whole group sobered quickly when Kit spelled out the reality of the situation at the Extension.

"So we really have been tossed away," Stev said. All of the growl had been taken out of his voice. He sounded wistful.

"Best thing that could have happened to us," Avin said. They all fell quiet for a moment, pondering the severance of their allegiance.

"What do we do now?" Stev asked, honest bewilderment on his face. "All my life, I've followed orders. Now what do we do? We can't go home even if we get out of here. And if we stay here, what do we do with ourselves?"

Kit shook her head. She had no idea what to do in the long term. "First we have to focus on surviving, and that means making sure this...place, this world survives. Then we can figure out a new purpose for ourselves."

"If—if we did get out, my people would take you." Mercy looked nervous at even suggesting the idea, as if they might jump on her. Kit thought of her own sleepless nights after the raid on the orphanage, and found nothing but understanding for Mercy's supposed betrayal. Perhaps joining the Swampies wouldn't be that bad. She looked around and saw that the others wore similarly thoughtful expressions. Mercy looked heartened.

"It's where I intended to go before I got...scrambled." Avin tapped the side of his head.

"First, you need to fix the scripts." Carrie's voice startled Kit. She realized that the AI had been absent for the majority of their discussion. She hadn't noticed either her departure or her return.

Kit stood up to face her. Carrie was still dressed in an ORG uniform, looking like the sixth member of an unusually large unit, though she was now without an MDU. That made sense. A computer wouldn't need to wear another computer.

"First, we need to let the other people in here know what's going on."

Carrie frowned. "I'm not sure that's wise."

"It doesn't matter if it's wise. They deserve to know what's going on. And if we're going to drop them outside, they *need* to know what's going on. A panicked mob is the last thing we want, especially when the people in the mob are potentially unstable and have military training."

Carrie cocked her head. "Perhaps you have a point," she said mildly. "There are two main centers of human habitation: the Extension and the Lobby. There are a few scattered settlers in Demo 3, but they can be brought to the Lobby easily. I should point out, not everyone in the Lobby is an operative. There are many non-military personnel who are brought in, as well—scientists, government officials, and the like. Without military train-ing, they all end up in the Lobby one way or another."

Kits brows rose. That would complicate things.

"I'm going to need as much time as possible to get a handle on the script-ing of this place," Mercy said. "If things are really degrading as quickly as you say, then I need to get started."

"I'll help," Merdith offered. "I don't know as much of the scripting lan-guage as you do, but I've got plenty of hacking experience." Mercy shot her a grateful look. She looked especially young right now, twisting her hands nervously in her lap, her shoulders slightly hunched.

Kit turned to Carrie. "Is there a way we can communicate if we split up?"

"I can set up a private chat room for the group."

"I don't know what that means."

"It means yes."

"Then I think we should divide our forces. Stev, you feel up to bossing around some civvies for me?"

Stev straightened, and his eyes took on a more alert gleam. "I'd like noth-ing better." Kit smiled thinly. It wasn't going to be easy breaking the news, but Stev wouldn't put up with any nonsense. And she knew that giving up command must have been hard for him. She would not discount his experience.

"The Lobbyists know me," Carrie said. "I'll go with him." Kit nodded curtly.

"Where does that leave us?" Avin asked. There was a wary note in his voice, as if he already knew the answer and didn't like it.

Kit took a deep breath. "We're going back to the Extension." Avin's eyes went flat and his lips thinned. Kit could tell he was fighting for control of his reactions, but she suspected it was harder now, in his freshly unbalanced state. She hoped that she was making the right choice in bringing him back into the sphere of the ORG.

Kit put a steadying hand on Avin's shoulder. "You know ORG politics better than any of us. I'm no good at reading people. And if it comes to a fight, I need you at my back." He swallowed hard, but met her eyes solidly and nodded. She gave his shoulder a squeeze and turned back to the others.

"Let's get moving."

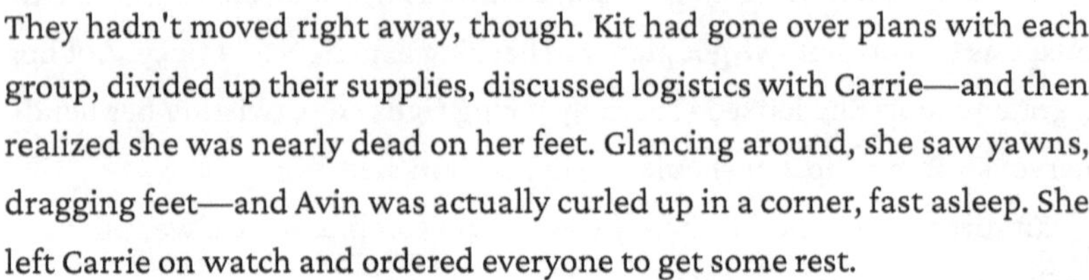

They hadn't moved right away, though. Kit had gone over plans with each group, divided up their supplies, discussed logistics with Carrie—and then realized she was nearly dead on her feet. Glancing around, she saw yawns, dragging feet—and Avin was actually curled up in a corner, fast asleep. She left Carrie on watch and ordered everyone to get some rest.

When she woke, she found that Avin had moved. He was now sleeping curled on his side with his back facing hers, not close enough to disturb her, but near enough that he would be aware if anything had threatened. Kit smiled, touched.

It was late afternoon by the time they all felt rested and ready to depart. Kit wondered if everyone was as jittery about the plan as she was, or if that was one of the joys of leadership.

The chat room turned out to be a little floating screen that followed Kit around like a particularly inquisitive recruit. When she raised her hands, floating keys displaying letters, numbers, and symbols appeared and allowed her to type out a message. For someone who was used to having mental control of her computing, this was painfully slow and unwieldy, but it was better than nothing. The range of MDU pings would not suffice to keep them in touch, and she really needed more precise reports anyway.

Now they had all gone their separate ways. Carrie had created a portal for Mercy and Merdith. The door to the command console had given them no issues, according to the text in the chat room. Despite Carrie's assurances that only AIs would have trouble entering, Kit was relieved. Without that console, there was no escape for any of them. Mercy was hard at work deciphering the code and locating the relevant scripts. Merdith was assisting, and keeping the rest of the team updated with regular messages.

Carrie and Stev had departed through a different portal, and they had yet to check in. Kit wasn't worried yet. She hoped that Stev didn't lose his temper during the explanation part of the assignment. Carrie could probably keep him in line. If nothing else, she could conjure up one of those armbands and use it on his mouth.

As she and Avin approached the tunnel mouth, she turned her attention away from the chat log. It had been a strange walk, now that she knew the reality of the situation. She could see the growing realism of the setting as they trudged towards the Extension, as if more layers of color were being added to a painting until a picture emerged.

Before the operative standing guard at the tunnel mouth caught sight of them, Avin ghosted away. The dark gray uniform, so suited for urban warfare, was just as good camouflage in the hazy gray light of evening. He blended into the shadows perfectly.

Kit, however, approached the guard openly, her empty hands raised to show that she was unarmed.

"I need to speak to Jak," she called, hoping she didn't sound as nervous as she felt. With any luck, the guard would be part of his rebellion and would assume she was coming back from a mission for him.

Luck wasn't with her. The operative who ducked out of the blind was eyeing her with suspicion bordering on hostility, and his gun was trained unwaveringly on her chest.

"Who are you? What are you doing outside the Extension?" he barked.

"I have very important intelligence to report to Jak. I'm a member of his unit. It is quite literally a matter of life or death for everyone inside the Extension." Technically, she didn't know if those who didn't evacuate would die, but it seemed a safe bet that they wouldn't enjoy the experience of having time and space collapse around them.

The guard huffed in disbelief. "Right, like I'm going to believe that one." He reached slowly for the alarm cord without taking his eye—or his weapon—off of Kit.

Before he could pull the alarm, a bullet whizzed over Kit's shoulder. The man stared at her in shock, clutching his abdomen, then vanished.

Avin appeared silently at her side. "He'll be Stev's problem now." The lights on the Blue gun twinkled sinisterly, and he frowned in disapproval. "Too flashy," he grumbled.

"Better than actually killing people with our weapons."

She strode into the tunnel, trying to project confidence and a sense of belonging. Avin followed a step or two behind, the most dangerous of shadows. A brief pause before stepping out of the passage. No one was nearby. They stepped out with assurance and headed briskly for the archive. They hadn't been gone long enough to be truly missed by their comrades yet, and Kit thought it unlikely that the story of their desertion would be widely circulated. The Commander wouldn't want the embarrassment publicized.

When she paused before the archive, she kept her tone casual. "Is Jak in?" And the guard nodded, gave the door a quick tap, and went back to staring straight ahead with barely concealed boredom.

Now was the crucial moment. Jak could sound the alarm the moment he saw them. He could refuse to hear them out.

The door opened, revealing Jak's heavily lined face. His jaw tightened, his eyes narrowed, his brow puckered. His face couldn't decide whether to express disbelief or rage.

"We have absolutely vital intelligence to deliver, on behalf of the entire Extension," Kit said, quiet urgency suffusing her voice.

Jak stared at her for a long moment, a muscle in his scarred cheek twitching spasmodically. But he finally stepped back and allowed her to enter the archive. He twitched again as she entered, as if he would like to slam the door in Avin's face, but Avin was too quick for that, and far too determined to stay by Kit's side. Once they were both inside, he didn't quite slam the door, but there was a bit of unnecessary force in its closing.

"What could possibly have possessed you to come back here?" he asked, turning to face the pair and glaring as if they were disobedient children. Kit suppressed the urge to shuffle her feet guiltily. She was, evidently, a lead now, and a commander of any rank didn't scuff her feet and avoid eye contact. No matter how much she wanted to. Instead, she took a deep breath and recited the message that she and Avin had prepared.

"We have ascertained the true nature of this place, and acquired knowledge that there is a clear and present danger to all inhabitants of the Extension. We have returned in good faith to help organize a response." She hoped that sounded official and practical. She feared that it just sounded pompous.

"Clear and present danger? There's always a clear and present danger. We're squatting in the middle of a war zone!"

"You're not—"

"Maybe you don't understand the situation here, but we are balancing on a knife's edge, and your little mutiny could have unbalanced the whole thing. And now you come back? It's not like I can just say you were taking a break!"

"But—"

"And how you convinced the whole unit to go with you in this lunacy is beyond me. You've dragged Merdith down with you, and if you ever get out of here alive, that stiff-necked bootlicker," he jerked his chin toward Avin, "will slit both your throats in your sleep one day, mark my words—"

"Shut up!" Kit's patience, currently in short supply, had run its course. "If anyone doesn't understand the situation here, it's you. We are living inside a computer that's about to crash! We need to get these people out, and we need to do it now, regardless of what you think of me and my team."

Jak's tirade finally came to a halt. He stared at her, jaw slack, then shook his head in disbelief. "A computer? What...?"

"Experimental technology created before the Congress even took their seats," Kit explained succinctly. "You were right, they don't know we've survived here—or care, as long as we don't return." She filled in the details as best she could, but Jak was still shaking his head in confusion when she finished. Well, it was a lot to digest.

"Then what's the deal with the time difference? Why even do that?" Jak sounded outraged, and considering how long he had been surviving here without explanation, Kit felt it was justified. For her, only a few months had passed, but he had now outlived everyone he had known by centuries.

"The—person—we spoke to believes that it was done to aid in construction. This place was still in development when it was abandoned, and speeding up the interior time may have helped them locate glitches in the system. Eventually, the time distortion was meant be reversed, to give players more time in the game so they could play for an hour and have only five minutes pass in reality."

"A game..." Jak shook his head in absolute disgust. "Tera's going to be livid—if she believes any of this at all."

"I'm surprised that you believe us," Avin said, breaking his silence for the first time.

Jak looked at him askance. "I can't imagine you two risked coming here to play a practical joke on me. And if you wanted to expose my little—project—there are far easier ways to go about it. Still, it's pretty farfetched."

Kit reclaimed the thread of the conversation. "We've got a team working on the code for this place right now. They should be able to open an exit for everyone and then restart the system."

"And what then? We start a new life outside?" Jak asked mockingly. "I'm sure the ORG and Congress would welcome us with open arms."

"If you're not comfortable with your options on the outside, we've been told that anyone who wants to return after the restart is welcome." Kit kept her voice neutral. If he wanted to hide inside this simulation, that was his choice.

Jak sighed and rubbed his temples. "I assume you're not planning to tell the Commander about this yourself."

Now it was Kit's turn to look at him like he was insane. That would be suicide. The only reason she'd felt even slightly confident about waltzing in here to talk to Jak was because she had something on him. He grimaced.

"Do you have anything approaching proof? Give me something to work with."

Kit shrugged. "I can ask the—person—in the Lobby to open a portal. That's where the exit will open, and we'll need to transport everyone within the Extension over there."

"Why not open the exit here?" Jak frowned.

"The Lobby is where the exit was originally set to manifest, and there's a significant population, ORG and civilian both, living there," Kit admitted. "Anyone who gets shot by Red or Blue weapons or who doesn't make it past the lab monsters gets sent there, rather than actually dying."

Jack visibly paled. "Are you sure?"

"That's what we were told. It was supposed to be a game. No one was ever supposed to be hurt."

Before she had finished speaking, he was striding for the door. "That's all we need. Let's go."

Kit wondered if she should protest. There was every possibility that she and Avin would be arrested the second the Commander laid eyes on them—but it seemed they had convinced Jak, and she didn't want him to start questioning them again.

She glanced to the side. There were several new messages on her floating board.

Merdith: We found relevant script for manual exit. Currently works for only one person at a time. Modifying.

Stev: Made contact with Lobby. Not hard to convince. Weird place.

Kit typed up a quick response as she strode after Jak. *Arrived. Working on it.* She probably looked like a lunatic, waggling her fingers in the air in front of her, but she needed to check in as regularly as the others did.

Jak didn't even bother to knock on the Commander's door. It was a good thing it wasn't locked, or he might have knocked it off its hinges.

The Commander shot to her feet, radiating outrage. Jak cut her off before her remonstrations could even begin to find voice.

"Kris and Asa," he blurted. "They're still alive."

The Commander fell into her chair with a thump. "Have you finally gone and lost your mind?" she asked weakly. "We saw them die, Jak. It's been three decades."

"Tell her," Jak said excitedly, waggling a finger in Kit's face. The Commander's formidable attention turned on Kit, who quailed beneath the fresh wave of anger that swept across her features.

"What is going on here?" The Commander's growl told Kit that if she didn't spit out her explanation quickly, she wouldn't ever get the chance. Never mind that she had never intended to be the one to talk to the Commander. That was why she had approached Jak.

Kit babbled out her message as quickly and precisely as she could. Almost as an afterthought, she added, "—and any operatives killed in the lab or by the Reds and Blues are actually sent to the Lobby." That bit of information seemed to have been what set Jak off.

A pleading tone entered Jak's voice. "Tera, they've been waiting for us all these years, them and who knows how many other operatives. We owe it to them to at least investigate, don't we?"

Tera shook her head slowly, but it wasn't clear if she was actually disagreeing. Then she was on her feet again. Her fist slammed down on the table.

"The ORG wouldn't just throw us away. We were their best! The Elite!"

"We weren't!" Jak shouted back. "As much as I loved them, Kris was a drunk and Asa was dead lazy. I had no ambition. And you had too much of it!" He paused and composed himself. "No one here is the best the ORG has to offer, and you well know it." His eyes flickered to Kit. "No offense."

"None taken," she replied steadily. "Three out of the four members of my unit were guilty of treason. And we didn't even collaborate."

Tera stared at her, shocked, then her head drooped. Jak leaned forward and put his hand on her shoulder across the desk. "You're not induced, Tera. You don't have to keep doing this. Let's go find our teammates."

She shrugged his hand off her shoulder, sat down in her chair, and twitched her shoulders to straighten her uniform. Folded her hands tightly before her. Stared at them with piercing eyes.

"Jak. Take a unit. Scout it out."

Jak's eyes blazed with victory.

When Jak wanted to get something done, he didn't waste any time. Half an hour later, he and three other operatives had assembled, geared up and fully briefed, to assess the situation at the Lobby. Kit stood with Jak at their head. Avin stood just behind her left shoulder. He said little, but stuck with her like a very protective burr. At one point, Jak asked if she was ready and absentmindedly patted her back when she answered in the affirmative. She could hear Avin's breath hiss between his teeth and sent him a warning glance. Not only did she not need an incident right now, but she was well able to take care of herself. He looked sheepish.

Kit turned to her chat window. *Carrie. Portal to Lobby from current coordinates.* Then she jumped back, cursing, when the portal opened right in front of her nose. That had been slightly too literal in following orders. Apparently that was what happened when you were working with an AI, even one as advanced as Carrie. Jak let out a guffaw, then motioned to her to lead the way. He believed her, but not enough to take point going blind through a mysterious portal. She couldn't blame him.

Carrie was waiting for them on the other side, attended by Stev and a man Kit didn't recognize. She'd thought Stev was large and muscular, but he was dwarfed beside his companion. The man stood a full head taller than Stev, his broad shoulders knotted with muscle and his legs like the trunks of small trees. But the face that surmounted that mountainous body had a genial smile and guileless blue eyes that crinkled engagingly at the corners.

The space that they stood in was so large that it actually made the mountain man appear to be the correct size, while everyone else was too small.

The walls yawned wide around them, enclosing a space that looked as big as a full city block. Snowy white columns marched in rows around the edge, supporting a balcony that circled the outline of the room, and through the center, she could see an intricately embossed ceiling far above them.

The space itself was quite elegant, but it was filled to bursting with makeshift tents, cook fires, and wash lines. Shabby, harrowed people bustled everywhere on a hundred different errands. Little children with tangled hair dodged around the adults' feet, caught up in their own games. In the distance, a baby's wail cut through the general babble.

The huge man stepped forward. "Jak? Glad to meet you." He enveloped the other man's hand in his and shook his whole arm without any sign of self-consciousness.

"This is Breck," Stev said, his face a mix of apology and exasperation. "He commands the ORG operatives who made it this far, and also sits on the governing council."

"Not ORG anymore, no offense," Breck said gruffly. "We've made our home here, and our allegiance is to these people."

Jak's face stiffened. "Understood." Kit wondered if he had intended to come in here and take over. If so, he was going to be disappointed. He'd probably be broken like a twig in Breck's giant hands if he tried.

"We have no problem working with you on the evacuation," Breck said, brow furrowing in concern. He evidently wanted this meeting to go well, but he wasn't going to compromise on behalf of his people. "You have your ways and we have ours, and that's fine."

When Jak didn't respond to this, Kit rolled her eyes. "We can figure out all the chains of command and who answers to whom after the restart. This is not the time."

Both men turned to her, and she suddenly wished that she hadn't spoken up. She felt strangely small.

Whatever. I can still take them if I have to, no matter how big they are. Go for the knees—or possibly the ankles, depending. She drew her lips together in a thin line and lifted her chin.

The men didn't exactly quail before her, but Jak lowered his gaze and Breck shifted his bulk uncomfortably from one foot to the other.

"Are you both convinced of what's going on here, and what needs to be done?" Kit asked. Breck nodded agreeably.

"Made solid sense, once the lady explained it all," he said, bobbing his head at Carrie with respect. "Wish she'd explained it sooner, but that's the way of it." Kit was impressed by his good-natured acceptance of the situation.

"I'll be convinced if I can find my teammates." Jak was not so easy to win over, but he had been living in a warzone rather than a fancy hall. This place was at least peaceful, if unsuited to its current purpose.

"What are their names?"

"Kris and Asa."

Breck's face lit up. "Oh hey, I know them. C'mon." He led them on a meandering path through the tents. Some were propped-up field blankets, but many were made of fabric that matched the abstract pattern of deep green, burgundy, and gold that carpeted the floor. Kit suspected drapes. Luckily, there was no weather to shelter from here, and the tents merely provided a bit of privacy.

They entered a section of the camp where the tents were arranged with more precision around a communal fire pit. The carpet had been cut back in a circle to leave a space of bare concrete around the flickering blaze. A woman was poking at it carefully, and she addressed the group without looking up.

"If you're looking for food, dinner's not for half an hour and you well know it."

"Asa—" Jak sounded as if he was choking on the name. His eyes were very bright. The woman jerked upright. Her handsome face lit up with pleasure and disbelief.

"Jak, you rogue! Never thought we'd see you again!" She dropped her stick and wrapped him in an enthusiastic hug.

"Asa I'm—I'm so sorry—"

"For what?" She pulled away and held him at arm's length. "Kris and I are fine, and I wouldn't trade the life I've had here for a hundred ORG commendations." Jak shook his head, unable to speak.

The flap on the tent behind Asa opened, and a teenaged boy emerged. He sized the group up, then turned to Asa. "I'm going to pick up the dinner ration, Mom. I'll be back soon." She nodded and thanked him with a smile. Jak's eyes followed the boy as he walked away.

"He looks exactly like Kris," he murmured.

"We've had a good life here," Asa repeated firmly. "Kris is on duty right now, but he'll be so glad to see you! You have to tell me everything that's happened..." She firmly drew him away from the group. Stev made as if to protest, but Kit shook her head.

"There's been no word from Mercy and Merdith yet. Give him a minute at least."

As she expected, Jak wasn't gone long anyway. His sense of duty was too strong for that. He jumped into the conversation that Breck and Carrie were having about the best way to organize everyone for the evacuation as if he'd never been gone. But there was a new relaxation about him that was hard to miss.

It didn't take long before Jak was on his way back to the Extension, thanks to Carrie's portal-making script. Though she couldn't write or create scripts, the ones she had the ability to run were extremely useful. After Jak was gone, Kit turned to Breck.

"We, um, may have shot a guard at the Extension before I explained things to Jak. Is he...?"

Breck chuckled. "Yeah, don't worry, we've got him. He's a little disoriented, but aren't we all, to start?" He smiled and ambled off to report to the other council members.

Interesting that these people had formed such a cooperative form of government. Representatives for the fighters, scientists, and crafters met regularly and ran the whole little settlement in a strangely gentle and equitable way. Kit thought she liked it.

Perhaps this had been what Zo and her unit had envisioned when they fought to put the Congress in power.

Before this experience, Kit would have looked at this with a jaded eye. People couldn't live this way without tearing themselves apart, she would have thought. They need discipline from above, or their innate selfishness will overtake them. Those were the words of her superiors, drilled into her head from the time she was a little girl. Those words which had once inspired confidence in her mission now turned her stomach.

Kit turned to her chat window. *Update?* she typed.

Merdith: Mercy is finishing up the exit script. I'm working on the reboot. Their documentation is terrible. And there isn't a safe testing area set up because everything here is supposed to be the test area.

Kit grimaced. *Do your best. How long?*

Merdith: Tomorrow at the earliest. Carrie says we still have time.

Carrie: Some. But it's impossible to tell which entry to the system could be the one that crashes everything.

Merdith: We'll hurry. Work all night if we have to.

A more technical discussion started then, about what some of the variable names might mean and whether it would be safe to test them. Kit turned away. It made her head hurt, and even if she had something to add, she couldn't keep up with either Merdith or Carrie's typing. By the time she had pecked her words in, they would be on a new topic.

When Kit finally bedded down for the night, she was more than ready to sleep. The Extension operatives were pouring through a portal in a steady, organized stream, filling the space that had been emptied for their occupancy. When morning rolled around, they would be ready for whatever scripts Mercy and Merdith had prepared. As she drifted off in her borrowed tent, Kit thought sleepily that it seemed as if things were finally going smoothly.

CHAPTER SEVENTEEN

Screams woke her in the dead of night. She dove out of her tent, pistol in hand, to find absolute chaos. Men and women were fighting desperately all around, and Kit couldn't even tell who was from the Extension and who was from the Lobby. Everyone seemed to have ORG uniforms on!

Not all of those uniforms were from the Extension, she realized. Operatives wearing dusty, faded, patched uniforms and older MDUs were fighting others in shiny new uniforms, with MDUs that made hers look bulky and outdated.

Her first thought was that the ORG had found out that they were still alive here and sent a force to wipe them out. Then she glanced at the chat log, still floating innocently on the edge of her vision.

Mercy: I've got the exit script worked out. I'm going to test it.

That was the last message.

What happened? Kit typed out as quickly as she could. The letters printed out slowly and haltingly on the screen. When she tapped the key to send her message, nothing happened.

Avin appeared at her shoulder, and Stev blundered through a knot of fighters, punching indiscriminately until he reached her side.

"Where's Carrie?" she yelled over the din.

"She was by the portal before—"

"Let's go," Kit cut Stev off.

They cut a swathe through the attackers on their way to the portal. The newcomers weren't well organized, Kit realized. There were small knots of fighting everywhere because each unit of attackers seemed to keep to itself. In fact, the units of newcomers were fighting each other in some areas. As if they were just attacking anyone who wasn't in their particular group.

The portal was still up, still pouring a steady stream of very surprised Extension operatives into the fray. Jak was standing near the portal, rallying them into organized ranks as they came through. Asa and her son had gathered as many noncombatants together as they could and were setting up a perimeter using both Lobby guards and Extension operatives. An older man who must be Kris, judging by his resemblance to his son, was putting together a group to venture farther into the Lobby and retrieve anyone who couldn't fight.

As Kit reached this area of relative calm, she realized that the attackers were pouring into the room from lines of doors that opened from every wall in the Lobby. No wonder they were fortifying this central area rather than trying to get a wall at their backs. No wall was safe. Kit ground her teeth. What had Mercy done? There was still nothing on her screen. Her message hadn't even sent, let alone gotten a reply.

Avin pinged to get her attention, then pointed to a still figure beside the portal. She hadn't even noticed Carrie standing there, still as a statue, not even blinking. Not even breathing.

Kit ran to Carrie, dodging incoming operatives who were tossing their packs in a pile and dashing to join the defense. Carrie stared right through her as Kit grabbed her shoulders and shook her. It was like shaking a board.

"I need to get to the console!" Kit shouted, frustrated. How could she get there without one of Carrie's portals? She didn't know the way. For all she knew, there might not be a way to physically navigate there at all!

Was that a flicker of Carrie's eyes? Slowly, with painful effort, they focused on Kit's face. After what seemed like an eternity, a glimmer emerged beside her. It grew into a glowing orb, then stretched slowly, agonizingly into a flat plate, then its edges crawled outward until it finally became a portal.

"Let's give it a minute," Stev suggested, looking a bit nauseous. Kit didn't blame him. What would happen if they went through a portal that hadn't fully formed?

"I'll give it a minute," she assured him. "You go help Jak with organizing the defense." Stev nodded and jogged off without an argument. Avin wouldn't be so easy.

"I'm going with you," he said as soon as she turned to him.

"You're not. I can take care of myself," she said flatly. Then she softened a bit. "We need every operative here, making sure the civilians are kept out of this. It's not their fight." He didn't say anything, but she could sense he was wavering. "Go help Breck protect these people."

Avin's eyes flickered wildly about, taking in the chaos of the Lobby, then locked with hers. His expression firmed, and he stepped in close, laying a gentle hand along her cheek. She froze, eyes wide. She had no idea what the gesture meant—and at the same time, it meant everything. He let his fingers trail along her cheek, the line of her jaw, as he dropped his hand. She caught his hand in hers as it fell, squeezed it once, hard, and then bounded for the portal. He stood still, watching until she was gone.

Each time before, the step through the portal had been like stepping from one room to the other, seamlessly. This time, Kit found herself falling through a gut-wrenching infinity. She couldn't feel, couldn't see, couldn't move, was barely even aware that she possessed a body. Her mind spun dizzily, trying to find something, anything to hold on to as reality. Then, as suddenly as she had entered, she found herself on the other side, stumbling to her knees and retching.

"Kit!" Mercy cried, rushing out of the console room to support her. "What's going on out there? Everything just stopped working!"

"People started pouring into the Lobby, attacking everyone. Carrie's slowed down to a crawl and the portals are barely working. What did you do? We need to reverse it, now!"

"I can't!" Mercy said frantically, rushing back towards the console. Merdith was still bent over a screen, pushing keys repeatedly, as if that would make them work.

A flash at the edge of her vision caught her eye. Her message had finally gone through. Below it, a line of text winked into existence.

Carrie: Time variable slowed. First level player limit exceeded. Overflow to Lobby. Revert ASAP. Crash imminent.

Mercy began to curse herself, the console, the long-dead designers, and everything else in her line of sight as she mashed on the console's controls. "I thought that variable was a timer for how long the exit would stay open! It didn't say! You can't leave a variable that important unlabeled. What were they thinking?"

"Slow down!" Merdith told her, grabbing her wrist. "All the available memory has been used up, and it's lagging. You're just going to make it worse if you enter the command ten times in a row!"

"First level player limit exceeded, what does that mean?" Kit asked, trying to make sense of the message.

"It means I really, really messed up!" Mercy said. "I accidentally changed the time distortion level, so time in here compressed even more. Years have passed on the outside and everyone the ORG dumped appeared in here within seconds of each other. The lab couldn't hold all of them, so it bumped them out, straight into the Lobby!"

And those grim-faced operatives with their sleek MDUs and brand new uniforms—they were still following the last orders they were given. Secure the lab, or what they thought was the lab.

Mercy stared at the screen, practically dancing in place with impatience, jabbing at buttons every so often as if the harder she pressed, the faster they would work. Kit stood by helplessly, wondering if she should have stayed in the Lobby, where her skill set would be of more use.

"Got it!" Mercy cried triumphantly. Nothing happened, as far as Kit could tell, and Mercy's triumph was short-lived. "It didn't speed the system up at all. We need to start getting people out of here now."

"Can you open the exit?" Kit asked.

"Yes, it should work now. But there's a problem." Mercy and Merdith exchanged a glance that Kit didn't like.

"I finished the script that will start the reboot," Merdith said.

"But?"

"We didn't get a chance to link the two together. The reboot script will have to be run after everyone is out. From here."

Kit felt as if she'd been doused in ice water. "What happens to the person in here?"

Mercy shrugged uncomfortably. "Whatever happens to everyone if they don't get outside before this place shuts down."

"There might be a brief window of time before the shutdown is complete, especially considering how the system is lagging," Merdith said. "Whoever is here might be able to make a run for it."

The three women stared at each other for a long moment, each waiting for the others to say something. But really, Kit knew there was no choice at all.

"Can you show me how to run the script?"

Mercy paled. "Are you sure?"

"I'm the fastest. I have the best chance of getting out."

"But—"

Kit cut off both of their protests with a sharp gesture. "We don't have time for this. No one argued when I took command, now I need you both to follow my orders. Show me what needs to be done, and then get back to the Lobby. Get everyone out."

With a grim face, Mercy showed her what buttons to press and the screens that should hopefully begin to show what was going on in the Lobby, once the evacuation began.

"Start the reboot as soon as you can. This place could go down at any minute." Mercy closed her eyes. "This is all my fault."

Kit chuckled, and Mercy's eyes flew open in surprise. "That's what I thought at first, too," Kit told her. "We can discuss whose fault it really is over a drink once I make it out, okay?" She held out her hand. Mercy shook it, her eyes full of unshed tears, then pulled Kit into a rough hug. Merdith threw her arms around both of them.

"See you on the outside," Kit said thickly when they'd released her. "Now get going."

They went without a word. None of them said goodbye.

Kit found herself alone before the console. It was a thick table covered with buttons that resembled the virtual keys she had used to type in the now-defunct chat window. Around the buttons were rows of indicator lights, all glowing a stable red, and above were several screens, their video feeds now static as the nexus resources were redirected to more vital functions.

For a long moment, nothing happened. Then it was like the entire world heaved a great sigh of relief. Though nothing had actually moved, Kit stumbled against the console. Some nameless pressure had abated, leaving her off-balance, as if a heavy wind had suddenly stopped blowing. The lights on the console began to blink slowly, heavily, and the screens crept into motion. Kit leaned forward eagerly, focused on the screen that displayed the Lobby.

It was chaos in slow motion. The screen updated every few seconds with a new still frame. She couldn't make out much in the sea of bodies that filled the Lobby, but she could see that a massive set of doors had materialized at the far end of the room. Frame by frame, she saw the Extension and Lobby guards pushing back the intruders, opening a safe corridor through the room, ushering the survivors along the pathway to the real world. The floor of the hall was littered with the bodies of the dead and dying. The green and gold of the carpet were now obscured by splashes of rusty red. Kit hoped that none of it belonged to people she knew, people she had left behind. She strained to pick out Stev or Avin in the heaving throng.

The defenders reached the massive doors and heaved them open. The video began to speed up, frames popping up in more rapid succession, and Kit realized that what she was watching had already happened. People must have already exited the simulation, or the lag wouldn't have alleviated even this much. The video scrolled forward more and more smoothly, showing the rush of people out the doors, the desperate fight to protect them from the operatives, who were, in their minds, only doing their duty. Confused, crazed killing machines, and she couldn't help but understand them. The doors by which they had entered the Lobby had disappeared. Now they fought not only for duty, but in desperation, against not only the Extension but each other, against anyone who crossed their paths. It was every unit for themselves.

It was pitiable, really, but no less deadly for all of that. She saw Jak take a bullet in the shoulder, saw Stev pull him behind the lines and take over, yelling orders that she couldn't hear. Mercy and Merdith were by his side, a seamless unit helping to hold the line as the last of the noncombatants rushed out the door, burdened by the wounded. Now the combined forces of the Extension and the Lobby began to retreat, leading the intruders towards the door, disengaging one painfully slow step at a time.

Kit's eyes raced over every face, every body visible on the screen. There were Stev, Mercy, and Merdith, all together, fighting as one. Why wasn't Avin with them? He couldn't have been wounded, or worse—no, it wasn't possible.

"Your screen's slow."

Kit whirled. "You idiot! You were supposed to get out with the others!"

"Did you really think I was going to leave you behind?" Avin's face was splattered with blood, his eyes wild with battle fury.

"Yes, dammit, you were supposed to be safe!"

He crossed the distance between them and closed his arms around her, crushing her to him with bruising force. Then he released her, almost shoving her away. "Your screen's slow. Everyone's out. Start the reboot, and let's get out of here."

With a last accusing look, she spun back to the console and followed Mercy's instructions. Drag this thing, here. Push that button. Type these letters. Enter.

"Run!" she yelled, and he grabbed her hand, dragging her after him. The portal went more smoothly than last time, but she still felt her stomach drop sickeningly as they hurtled through.

Then it dropped again. The floor of the lobby wasn't where it was supposed to be.

They dropped an extra three or four feet and hit the floor hard. The carpet was gone, and so was the concrete underneath, leaving the matte gray surface that Kit had seen as they walked through the unfinished section of the mirrored city. It continued to sink, breaking into chunks as it went. Bits of column and balcony floated by, and the bodies of the slain drifted amongst the wreckage weightlessly, as if the entire world had become a wrecked ship, broken upon the ocean floor.

Kit dropped Avin's hand and took a running leap for the nearest, highest piece of wreckage. He followed confidently, leaping the gap as if he too had the security of climbers. She looked ahead and saw the gaps widening. She took the next leap, activating her climbers as she ran, then spun to catch Avin's hand as he leaped, pulling him forward as he teetered on the edge.

"Just go!" he told her. "Don't slow down for me."

"No chance!"

They leaped between bits of rubble until they were nearly to the door. It was floating only a couple more hops away, but the chunks of floor and column were getting smaller and more perilous. Kit jumped to a rounded fragment of column, gripping with her climbers and wobbling wildly, then launched herself at a larger piece of floor. Her gloves grabbed on, and she was able to haul herself atop it. One more hop, and she could reach the door—but as she looked behind, she saw that there was no way that Avin could follow her. Her jump had pushed the tiny stepping stone too far for him to reach, even if he could manage to balance on it unassisted.

"Go on!" he shouted to her again, and she shook her head stubbornly, looking around for a solution. She was within reach of the door, but she refused to leave without Avin.

The door. She looked again. Even as every other bit of wreckage was floating freely, it stood firm and steady. The chunk of floor that it sprung from was unmoving. If she leaned out just a bit, she could reach it—not to climb up, but to push away. She locked her gloves onto the solid chunk of flooring, its carpet still clinging to it in strangely jagged shards, hauled herself slightly closer so she could really get some muscle into it, and shoved.

If she hadn't had her boots locked on, she would have stumbled backwards into the void. As it was, she windmilled her arms wildly to catch her balance as she and her perch floated backwards towards Avin. Catching her balance, she spun around, only to find that his piece of floor had sunk. She flopped down onto her stomach and stretched her arm towards him, holding to the ground with every bit of strength her climbers could muster. He leaped upward, his hand closing around her forearm, and she hauled with all her might. She could feel herself slipping towards the edge, her climbers giving out under the strain of supporting two full-grown adults...

And then he was laying beside her, panting with effort. He stared up into the endless void above them for a long moment, then staggered to his feet.

"Come on, we're almost there," he gasped. He offered her his hand, and she allowed him to heave her to her feet.

The last jump was a long one, now that she had pushed away from the door. Avin gave her hand a squeeze before he released it, then backed to the edge of their hunk of floor. He took a running start, and vaulted over the yawning gap. His momentum smacked him into the door frame, but he stayed within the simulation, waiting for her.

She followed his example, backing up to the edge—but the world was done supporting her. The block she was standing on started to crumble beneath her feet. She staggered forward, then launched herself into a run as she realized that the entire thing was disintegrating into gravel. She flung herself into the air, reaching desperately for Avin's outstretched hand, but the distance was too far. The empty maw of space gaped beneath her, ready to swallow her whole.

The tips of her fingers grazed the rough bottom edge of the floating island. Her climbers locked on, and she instinctively swung around, locking her knees and toes onto the underside of the hunk of floor. Carefully, she crawled around the corner, hauling herself one limb at a time around the bend and onto the top of solid ground. Avin grasped under her arms and heaved her up as she released the toes of her climbers.

"Now—we're even..." she wheezed as she labored to catch her breath. Avin's only reply was a strangled laugh that might also have been a sob. She struggled to her feet, every muscle exhausted, and he ducked under her arm to support her. He was staggering as much as she, but between the two of them, they managed to stumble against the great doors, bear them open with their weight, and fall out into the harsh light of the sun.

It was bright—too bright after the endless darkness of the dissolving virtual world. Kit shaded her eyes and peered around, still leaning on Avin's shoulder.

The fighting was over. Those wearing old uniforms and new both milled vaguely around the area outside the door. The wounded had been laid out nearby, and their moans filled the air as the survivors tended them as best they could with the supplies that had been salvaged. Underneath their cries, a confused murmur buzzed.

The outside of the lab was recognizable, and yet utterly different. The walls were covered with a thick layer of vines, and the barricade surrounding the compound was partially collapsed. There was no guard at the gate—or even a gate. It had fallen in and nearly rusted away. The road outside was cracked and pitted, with vegetation creeping from every crevice. As Kit's eyes roamed farther, she saw that this building was not unique.

The city was abandoned. The buildings were hollow shells, covered in green. Trees had sprouted in the upper stories, growing through caved-in roofs to better reach the sun. Beyond the sounds of the wounded and confused was a deep, heady silence, broken only by a distant twittering song.

As Kit struggled to take in their surroundings, she was nearly knocked off her already unsteady feet when Mercy hurtled into her, throwing her arms around both her and Avin. Merdith and Stev were not far behind, and she found herself surrounded by cheers and hysterical laughter. Then she was laughing herself, hugging everyone around her, crying for joy that all her friends were alive and safe.

Finally, their celebration ran its course, and they all stood in a circle, beaming at each other. Kit took a deep breath of fresh, clear air.

"I may have made us into time travelers," Mercy said sheepishly. "Welcome to the future."

"What do we do now?" Stev asked.

"Everything seems awfully ruined," Merdith put in doubtfully. "How will we survive here by ourselves?"

But Avin looked around at the quiet, still city, slumbering under a blanket of green. "If this is the future—maybe it's not so bad."

Kit gazed around and thought—no Congress, no ORG, no rules. An empty city. A clean slate. No, not so bad at all.

Hannah Harless is an author, editor, and gigantic nerd who loves science fiction, fantasy, gaming, and the written word. She studied video game design and multimedia before going on to become a full-time magazine editor. Throughout it all, her dream has always been to publish her own novels, and after a decade of re-writes, edits, and mental health struggles, she released her debut novel, *Yesterday's Soldiers*. She currently lives in Florida with her husband, child, and three cats, though she's still slightly perplexed as to how she got there.

Visit hannahharless.com for behind-the-scenes news and updates!

www.ingramcontent.com/pod-product-compliance
Lightning Source LLC
Chambersburg PA
CBHW061239310726
48971CB00007B/2143